CRULUS

LLRÂC NÔDBÉ

Published by The Voices Made Me Do It
https://www.thevoicesmademedoit.com
Paperback ISBN: 978-1-917966-00-9
Hardback ISBN: 978-1-917966-01-6
eBook ISBN: 978-1-917966-02-3

Cover design by Saber: www.sabercore23art.com
Manuscript assessment by Russel McLean, Jericho Writers
Proofreading by Leah Fox

AUTHOR NOTE:

Please note that, as a British author, I use UK English spelling and grammar throughout my writing. Therefore, US readers may notice less Z's than they are used to. These are not typos, it is simply just UK English. There are also Welsh words and colloquialisms used within the dialogue and text, such as 'Butt" and 'Mun,' which are explained in further detail at the back of this book. Again, these are not typos.

Dedicated to my father, Barrie,
Who will be loved always and never forgotten.
Rest in peace, Dad.

And to Trevor Allsopp,
Who had so much confidence in me, when I didn't.
But he never got to read my book.
Rest in peace.

If I feel so lost
How can I find you, again?
To get to where you are
To the place I fear the most
I'm so scared
So much anger
Darkness taking hold
Voices in my head
Give me a sign, Dad
Help me
I love you
I miss you
Dad?

A dawn would follow the long and weary night,
    but no light would come to his wretched heart;
    His soul must wander for ever in darkness,
    for ever in darkness, for ever.

— W. SOMERSET MAUGHAM, 1900

O my soul, do not aspire to immortal life,
    but exhaust the limits of the possible.

— PINDAR

The writer must be playful and serious at the same time.

— W. SOMERSET MAUGHAM, 1933

CHAPTER I

IN THE AIR TONIGHT

Sunday 6th September, 1981
Trugaredd Hospital, Newport, South Wales

The walk through the hospital made Dylan Wolfendale nauseous; the smell of disinfectant and surgical cleaning products stung his sinuses. He gripped his mother, Chrissy, tighter by the hand when they followed his brother, Kaelum, into the lift.

Six lives were extinguished before the lift had reached level four and Dylan could feel their confused souls wandering the hospital corridors; he was terrified he might see them.

The lift lurched to a stop and the doors *dinged* open onto the lobby for respiratory medicine.

Chrissy stepped forward, paused to scan the signs, then tugged Dylan through a set of double doors causing his legs to buckle when his feet tried to keep up. Overhead fluorescent lights produced a blurred, almost horrific, reflection of them on the corridor's shiny floor. Trollies littered with medical paraphernalia made Dylan light-headed and his hand began to sweat inside his mother's grip. Sensing his concern, Chrissy smiled and wiggled his arm when they turned into the ward.

The atmosphere changed instantly; the chatter of nurses replaced by the *schtup schtup* of oxygen machines forcing concertinaed air into struggling lungs. Behind each bed, huge machines spewed out wires and tubes—their life-saving tentacles stretched over headboards, slid over bedsheets, and wormed their way into patients wrists, arms, and noses.

The small room housed six beds separated by grubby, green, plastic curtains. Dylan's father, Gwynfor, was in the first bed on the left. The oxygen machine chugging away behind the bed pumped its produce into a mask on his face. Large black straps stretched above and below his ears and forced his short, silver-grey hair into wild clumps resembling iron fillings squashed between opposing magnets.

While Dylan stood by a chair and watched his mother remove the mask, Kaelum crept up behind him and shoved him forward into the bed.

'That's my seat,' moaned Dylan, his eyes pleading with his mother.

Kaelum smirked. 'Prick.'

'Oi!' Chrissy hissed, clipping Kaelum across the head. 'Find another chair, Dylan.'

'But I was there first.'

Chrissy scowled.

At thirteen, Kaelum was two years older than Dylan and could do no wrong. Sulking, Dylan crossed his arms.

Gwynfor nodded toward an empty cubicle by the window. 'It's okay, son ... j-just *huh* get another *huh* chair,' he said, puffing.

Dylan glanced at Tom Morris—known as 'Tom the Coal' around Draigwen Town—in the neighbouring bed. Despite only being in hospital a few days, everybody knew him, as he entertained everyone with corny jokes and stories, daily. Today,

Dylan saw a different man entirely: pale, withered and frighteningly brittle. He averted his eyes when Tom's family caught him staring.

Head bowed, Dylan collected the spare chair and raised it aloft ensuring the chair didn't snag on anything, but his feet had other ideas. He trod on his own lace and fell forward, face planting the floor and sending the chair hurtling across the ward. Whispered conversations were silenced while everyone turned toward the source of the deafening intrusion. Dylan's cheeks reddened in response to the glare of condemning eyes, including the beautiful green ones peering at him through ugly, black, NHS spectacles belonging to a pony-tailed girl on Tom's right.

She smiled and Dylan returned the gesture, or at least he hoped he had. His brain was telling him he was smiling, but he wasn't sure his face knew what to do. He felt her eyes follow him when he shuffled back to his father's bed.

'You're such a pleb,' said Kaelum, his hands clapping in silent applause.

'Leave your brother alone,' Gwynfor admonished, although his glare alone would have been enough.

Chrissy nodded toward Tom before whispering, 'How's he doing?'

Gwynfor breathed deeply from his mask and replied, 'Not good.'

'Poor dab.'

'Yeah. I think they know ... you know? Like they can feel it coming.'

Chrissy looked skyward and crossed herself. 'Mmm, something in the air. So sad.'

Dylan ignored Kaelum's attempts to goad him into another argument and stared at the floor. He sunk into the hard plastic chair and a long sigh escaped over his quivering lips like a failed party balloon. His foot caught the edge of one of the bed's wheels, which juddered its defiance. He stamped again and again, mesmerised by the jerky rotations, each spin diminishing the world around him.

As soon as he heard the voice, he knew he was dead. But now was not the time to engage in conversation. Dylan had had imaginary friends for as long as he could remember, but it wasn't until both his grandparents had died that he realised that they weren't exactly imaginary at all; they were dead. When it came into his head, the dead's chatter was surrounded by low hissing, reminiscent of badly tuned TV channels. His grandad, Lazarus, said his tinnitus sounded like a fuzzy TV, but he never mentioned hearing voices.

The voice's volume increased sharply and Dylan glanced around. The ward, and all the people within it, had changed. He was now staring at a sepia-toned world. A vintage photograph of a modern time. The edges of objects blurred, as though he were looking at them through a 3D ViewMaster in fading light, but the edges of the people shimmered brightly, like sunlight reflecting on slow moving, clear blue water.

The plastic curtains were now drawn around Tom's bed and he watched while nurses and doctors dashed to his aid. At least, it *looked* like they were dashing; their movement almost imperceptible, so it was easy to mistake them for shop mannequins.

Seconds crawled like squirming maggots.

Almost, but not quite, outside of time.

Tom's distressed, confused voice was starkly juxtaposed against the silent, frozen melee, and he stumbled from behind the curtain, hands outstretched.

Dylan screamed. He knew he was dead; he could feel his soul. With his eyes clamped shut, Dylan turned away, breathless and trembling.

Please go away. Please go away.

Images of rotting undead filled his head and it took several, terrified seconds before he opened his eyes.

Tom just looked like Tom; the only scary thing about him was how his hospital gown rose dangerously high when he placed his hands on his confused head.

Dylan relaxed.

This sepia world was familiar, but when Dylan tried to grasp the memory, it faded away. Shadows moved out of time and some of the shadows were sourceless. Wispy, black and grey shadows began to form dark figures, which quickly dissolved when Dylan looked at them.

He peered through the curtain at Tom's bed. Tom's bed, with Tom still in it, and his family sobbing by his bedside, their every move impossibly slow. Dylan's throat emitted a noise like rising phlegm when he tried to speak. He froze. Seeing Tom's lifeless body confirmed what he already knew in his heart.

'I'm sorry you're dead,' he blurted, and instantly regretted it.

'What? No, that's not possible ... I-I-I can't ... I ... can't b—'

Dylan stepped aside, gesturing to Tom's bed.

Tom watched his family grieving as though he were viewing a Betamax home movie in slow motion, with him as the star.

'But ... How is this happening?'

Dylan shrugged. 'I've spoken to the dead, but I've never seen one.'

'Do you realise how crazy you sound?'

He did, only too well, which was why he'd kept his gift a secret. He didn't intend giving the bullies more ammunition.

Was it even a gift? He didn't think so; he felt cursed. It was getting stronger.

To Dylan's right, between the empty bed and the window,

the sepia wall began to shift and dirty fog billowed from behind bright, constantly changing, sparkles, like a migraine aura floating in the air. Silver fish and lightning without the kaleidoscope of pain.

'Umm, Tom?' Dylan said, nodding towards the shifting lights, which had now formed two shimmering doors. But as the visual aura settled and his eyes focused through the fog, he could make out many more, less prominent, doors, like he was in a corridor or lobby. 'I think it's time.'

Tom sunk to his knees, frantically waving his arms and muttering that it wasn't fair. 'If I'm dead, how can you see me?'

Dylan mumbled a response while his heart felt ready to implode with anxiety, but he couldn't feel a beat. Not a single beat. He felt sweat running down his brow, but his forehead was dry to the touch. He didn't know what to think and, strangely, the voices had gone quiet. Hearing the teeming dead was one thing, chatting to them as they walked around in skimpy hospital robes was another thing entirely, and he wasn't so sure he liked it. Could the dead hurt him?

Shadows, which had no reason to move, slithered everywhere and dark whispers teased Dylan's ear drums. He glanced at his family for support but they were almost on pause, too. Fuzzy lines and the slow, monotonous whirr of the tape in the video recorder were the only things missing.

Then he saw his own, slumped, body.

Am I dead, too? Is that why there are two doors?

The thoughts washed through his brain on a river of adrenaline and he ran trembling hands over his body.

It felt solid.

Drawn towards the shimmering lights, Tom began to panic. Instinctively, Dylan touched Tom's shoulder and felt his hand tingle as something flowed between them.

Now calm, Tom looked lovingly at his granddaughter, Emily. 'Promise me you'll look after my little butterfly.'

Dylan followed his gaze to the pony-tailed girl. 'I promise.'

Tom studied his family's faces and closed his eyes, as though developing a final Polaroid of them in his soul. His body began to dissolve into shimmering dust, causing an image of an eraser to pop into Dylan's head—one of those two-tone ones that legend had it could erase ballpoint ink—wielded by an unseen hand until Tom was almost erased from existence.

'Wait!' yelled Tom, grabbing for Dylan, but his hand and forearm disintegrated before it reached him. 'The money.'

'Money?'

Tom's undulating voice faded, and Dylan strained to hear his final, disjointed words. Something about money and Grandfather clocks.

'I will!' shouted Dylan, hoping he'd heard it right.

'You will, what?' asked Chrissy.

Dylan's eyes snapped into focus and he sat bolt upright in the uncomfortable plastic chair opposite a grinning Kaelum.

'That's weird, Mam. I'm sure he's said that before. By here,' observed Kaelum.

'That's déjà vu,' explained Gwynfor. 'You okay, Dylan? You look confused.'

His eyes rattled in his befuddled skull when he shook his head. 'I'm fine, I just ... Umm—' He looked around, but there was no sign of Tom. The curtain around his bed remained drawn. 'I was just daydreaming.'

'Well, pay more attention to the real world,' advised Chrissy. She raised a finger to her lips, before gesturing to Tom's closed curtain.

CHAPTER 2

HOLD ON TIGHT

16 Valley View, Cerrig Brig Estate, Draigwen

Dylan lay on his bed too afraid to close his eyes. He picked up his copy of *The Whizzkids Handbook* and read about making concrete conkers, but his mind kept drifting off like the fog that had swirled into the hospital ward, and his eyes struggled to focus. Eventually, sleep engulfed him and he gave in to his dreamscape ...

He is walking through Markham common with bats dancing overhead. Ahead of him is an old man walking his dog. He stops when the dog emits a deep, evil growl and begins scraping and clawing at the undergrowth. Something white, draped in red cloth with polka dots, protrudes from the hole he is digging. When he moves closer, Dylan sees a woman's face obscured with foliage, her lower leg bending unnaturally as it brakes the surface. Moonlight glints off a blood-spattered silver chain around her neck; a sapphire stone embedded in an ancient arrowhead. The dog stops digging as it senses Dylan's approach. His scarlet eyes glowing in the fading light while it watches the boy move closer.

Now, the old man turns towards him; Dylan cannot avoid his eyes. He raises a withered arm, pointing a bony finger at him. It reminds Dylan of a dream he has had many times before.

His dreamscape blurs and takes him there.

Now, he is standing in Larkmead graveyard. The old man is there once more, his disfigured lips curling into a knowing smile. A man, or at least what is left of him, lays in an awkward heap amongst the gravestones. The white shirt and grey tie being the only masculine features left. Large lacerations resembling fleshy blinds open up his face and throat.

Dylan feels sick as he looks upon his remains.

The old man's bony finger seeks him out once more. 'You know the truth, Kordialis,' he croaks.

Monday 7th September, 1981

Dylan's arm shot out from underneath his blanket in search of the alarm clock. It found his Ten-Four walkie-talkie instead and sent it crashing to the floor. Alarm silenced, he slid under the blanket, but the persistent hiss from the fallen walkie ruined any snooze attempt. He peered out and his sleepy eyes spotted Kaelum's worn, hand-me-down, school uniform hung over his wardrobe door. He muffled a scream with his pillow.

His first day at Draigwen Town Comprehensive School had arrived. It was seven-thirty.

After using the bathroom, Dylan put on Kaelum's old uniform and stared at the mirror. His collar looked wide enough to fit another head through it and he couldn't see his hands. He rolled back the sleeves until he could and tucked several inches of unneeded shirt tail into his trousers. His belt, one of his father's old ones, was on the last hole, yet he still had to pull up his trousers every few strides.

He jumped when his walkie squawked into life and Mark Jones' statically charged tones blared out of the tiny speaker.

'One-four, one-four, for a copy. Bubblegummer Sparky here. You awake, Dylan? It's Comp' day. Whoop whoop! Over.'

Why was he so jovial? If only Dylan possessed an ounce of his confidence. Dylan's reply was positive but curt, even if it was a fib. It wasn't school he feared, it was the classmates. He broke transmission, and checked on his mother.

Several drawers were hanging open with clothes scattered over the floor. His foot connected with an empty bottle of vodka, which hurtled across the carpet and thudded into the wardrobe.

Chrissy didn't stir.

Dylan picked her handbag off the bedside table and dug around inside. He pulled out a small, plastic case, flipped it open and held it over her face. After a few nervous seconds, her breath condensed on the mirror, and Dylan sighed. He returned the mirror and pulled the pink candlewick bedspread over her. He placed her discarded clothes neatly on her chair and crept downstairs.

Kaelum was nowhere to be seen and, as usual, he'd left a trail of destruction in his wake. When Dylan finished clearing up, he took two paracetamol and a glass of water up to his mother, setting them down on her bedside table next to the dusty, unused, Goblin Teasmade.

When Chrissy finally surfaced, she made Dylan twirl around in his uniform, inspecting him. 'Bad dreams, again, Dylan?'

Embarrassed, he leant on the kitchen countertop to prevent another rotation and also to avoid the fag clinging precariously to her bottom lip. 'How'd you know?'

'Heard you talking in your sleep. Sounded like proper Welsh, too, which is amazing seeing as none of us can speak it. Well, Nan used to, but that was years ago, see. Auntie Louisa was learning it until she—' Her eyes glazed over, tears welling in the corners, and she sucked in a breath. 'You were born the day she left us. My little miracle child.'

Dylan leant back as Chrissy's fingers reached for his cheek. 'I know, Mam. You keep saying.'

'*So*, it's true.'

Dylan pinched his lips. He never really understood why she kept referring to him as a miracle. His birth brought his mother comfort at a sad time, but was that the only reason? Did she know about his gift? Doubtful, but he was too afraid to ask. He'd never even seen a photo of his auntie; apparently, the grief was too much for Chrissy to bear.

'We're visiting Dad, tonight,' she reminded, dragging Dylan back to the present. 'Hopefully, he'll be home soon.' She stubbed her fag in the overflowing ashtray, which made the dining table resemble a Pompeii diorama, and immediately lit another one. Through the smoke haze he saw her wipe tears from her eyes.

Adults always lie, he thought, but the dead can't.

He filled a bowl with cereal and sat down opposite his mother, who had begun wrapping fag coupons in elastic bands like bundles of drugs money. After a tiny trickle of milk drizzled from the bottle over his cereal, he spotted Kaelum's discarded bowl—half full of cereal and milk—and poured Kaelum's leftover milk into his own bowl.

Chrissy took another long drag and disappeared behind a cloud of smoke once more. 'Same dream as always?'

'Sort of. I saw a close up of the woman's body this time,' he said, excitement causing him to lean forward on his elbows. 'She had a lush necklace. An arrowhead with a heart-shaped blue crystal in the middle.'

Chrissy yelped mid-drag, coughing and spluttering, and scattering the remains of Pompeii everywhere. Dylan tried to slap her back, but she shoved him aside.

'I'm okay,' she wheezed. 'Must 'ave gone down the wrong way.' She took a swig from a small pop bottle which, Dylan noted, never left her side. Although, she needn't have bothered trying to hide it. He wasn't stupid enough to think that there was actually lemonade inside, as the label suggested. 'I'm going back to bed. Mark, Gwendolyn's boy, should be here soon to walk you to school, so stop worrying.'

'I do know who Sparky's mother is; we've been friends for years.'

'Cut the sarcasm. It's Mark, not Sparky. He has a perfectly good name, so use it.'

Yes, and you have a perfectly good name, too, Christiana, he thought, but didn't dare say.

She kissed his head and stumbled away, leaving a trail of ash breadcrumbs along the plastic carpet runner.

It was quarter past eight and Dylan had a twenty minute walk to school. Registration for new starters was at half eight but he was in no rush, yet his bowels were. He had been dreading this day throughout the summer holidays.

Between mouthfuls of cold Ready Brek interlaced with cornflakes—he liked the contrast between the oaty mess and the crunchy flakes—his eyes wandered around the room.

The antique Welsh dresser to his right was littered with photo-frames displaying family snapshots of happier, sunnier times and his eyes paused at a studio photograph of his mother's parents; he never knew his father's parents. He spent more time at their house than his own when they were both alive. It had been less than a year since they lost his grandad and it made him think of how Emily and her family must be feeling the morning after their loss. He needed to pass on

Tom's broken message; hopefully it would make sense to them.

His mind replayed the moment he saw Tom's soul; he was so relieved that he looked normal. Talking to the dead for so long had meant that he knew, sooner or later, he would meet them. It terrified him. What if they weren't all nice, like Tom? What if something happened to his body when he wasn't in it? Would he be dead, too? And why were there two shimmering doors? Maybe one led to Heaven and the other to Hell, so there wasn't one for him. That made more sense, and he preferred that explanation.

The door knocked three times in quick succession and he jumped, spilling gloopy cereal into his lap.

'Shit. Just a minute!'

He opened the door to a short, scruffy-haired boy wearing a huge smile. His school tie was as short as it was wide and his white shirt was spilling out from under his blazer.

'Hiya butt'. How's it hanging?' Mark spotted Dylan's soiled trousers, flung his head back and laughed. 'You're such a tit, Dylan.'

Dylan frowned. 'You can talk. You look like Wurzel Gummidge and Mrs McCluskey's love child.'

Mark ran the fingers of one hand through his dark hair and grinned. 'I know. It's hard being this handsome, mun.'

'Yeah, I bet.'

Mark wrestled with the multi-coloured door tapes. 'What *is* the point in these?'

'Dunno, keep the flys out?'

'Do they work?'

'Nuh.'

'You alone?'

Dylan's eyes looked toward the ceiling and he paused. 'Erm, yeah, why?' he finally answered.

Mark half-heartedly shuffled his feet on the door mat before wandering past Dylan.

The house decor consisted of wood panelled walls and polystyrene ceiling tiles. Seventies beige, green, orange and brown dominated the interior design and matched the colour scheme of the worn, paisley-design carpet, which they couldn't afford to replace.

Mark jabbed a finger in Dylan's back. 'You saw a ghost,' he declared, causing Dylan to choke and splutter.

'W-What?'

Mark circled a finger in his face. 'You're white as a sheet. Did you see *Zombie Flesh Eaters*?' he asked, excitedly. 'There was this zombie, right, with loads of worms coming out—'

Dylan laughed. 'You didn't see it. It's banned.'

Mark clenched his jaw. 'You calling me a liar?'

'No,' mumbled Dylan, averting his eyes. 'I'm lucky if they let me watch *Condorman*!'

~

When Dylan finished putting on his shoes, he discovered Mark in the living room, his nose almost touching the photo frames.

'Is that your mam?'

Dylan grabbed Mark's arm and pulled him toward the dining room. 'Get out. My mam'll go nuts if she hears you in here. And you've got your shoes on!' he snapped.

'So do you! I wiped my feet. Anyway, I thought you said you were alone?'

Dylan looked away. 'I am.'

Mark nudged a photo. 'Is that your mam when she was younger?'

'Yeah.'

'Weird.'

'Why?' asked Dylan, straightening the frames.

'There's family photos out there,' said Mark, pointing towards the dining room. 'But in here, it's just old photos of your mam.'

Dylan scratched his chin. 'Never really thought of it.' He had, he just never understood it.

Mark leant forward and picked up a frame. 'Wow! Tidy necklace.'

Dylan snatched the frame and glowered. 'Don't touch!' he hissed, under his breath, before returning the photo. 'She'll kill me if they break.'

In the black and white photograph, Chrissy was sat on a large rock amongst a field of bluebells wearing a frilly, spotted dress. Sunlight glinted off her necklace drawing Dylan's eyes toward it. He gasped and flung a hand to his mouth. 'Oh shit! That necklace and dress was in my dream.'

'What? The dead people dream you always have?'

'Yeah.'

Their eyes met.

'Oh ...' Mark's face dropped. 'It's probably just a coincidence. It doesn't mean—'

'Wha'? That my mam's gonna die?' snapped Dylan, pushing Mark towards the archway between the rooms.

'It can't be a premonition,' insisted Mark. 'Your mam's really young in these photos, like the woman in your dream.'

'Good. Now go!'

'All right, touchy.'

'Whatever.' Worry curled the edges of Dylan's lip and he glanced up at the living room ceiling just as his mother's bed creaked. What if it *was* a premonition? Could he use his gift to stop it? If he could help Tom passover, could he also stop someone dying? After all, isn't that what miracles are for?

Dylan ditched the remains of his breakfast in the sink and described his recent dream. When he finished, Mark lovingly stroked the school badge on his blazer pocket. 'Do you know what DTCS stands for?'

'Draigwen Town Comprehensive School, *obviously*.'

'Nope. Dylan Talks Crap Sometimes.'

'Whatever.'

The smirk faded from Mark's face. 'Seriously though, there are loads of different death omens in Wales. You can't ignore this.'

Dylan's jaw sagged. 'How'd you know?'

'Library. You should visit sometime,' he replied, sarcastically. 'They've got some awesome occult books.'

Dylan shook his head, amazed. 'Really?'

'Yeah. Beats being at home.' He tapped a finger on his shattered calculator watch. 'Chop chop, we're gonna be late.'

A smile crept across Dylan's face when he said, 'Oh, I forgot to say. My mam asked me to deliver a condolence card to Tom the coal's granddaughter, Emily.'

Mark picked up Dylan's bag. 'Tidy. We'll probably see her in school. C'mon.'

CHAPTER 3
BAGGY TROUSERS

Draigwen Town Comprehensive School

The school was nestled between Draigwen Town to the north, Colledig Wood and the local mining village of Bryncoed to the west, and Pontyfechan to the south of the Sirhowy River.

The yard off Ddraig Road was empty when they slipped into the school, but their late entrance hadn't gone unnoticed. The main assembly hall was brimming with kids on small plastic chairs laid out in rows and dissected by two aisles, which ended in double doors, one of which still creaked from their less than stealthy entrance. Two male teachers moved up and down the aisles like prison wardens, their eyes scanning up and down the rows.

Mark squeezed a finger between his shirt collar and neck. 'Why do we have to wear these stupid ties, mun?'

'Because it's the rules. Now, shut up!' growled a stocky teacher, with hair and beard straight from the Grisly Adams beauty salon. 'Lateness will *not* be tolerated,' he snarled, smacking Mark across the head.

Speeches from the heads of departments droned on until, finally, the Headmistress began her conclusion. Considering she was a thin, petite woman, Mrs Diane Griffiths knew how to use her lungs. No microphone was needed in her case. After roughly an hour, by which time Dylan could no longer feel his arse checks, each class were allocated a form teacher.

Dylan tapped his feet against a step while he waited for his name to be called. Several years of abuse by Kaelum had already left the leather on the toecaps crumbling away, exposing the light-grey inner layers. He couldn't see Emily anywhere, and when Mr Harwood announced his class, both Mark and Dylan were called forward.

Framed pictures of past teachers and prize winning ex-pupils wearing cheesy grins adorned the walls of 'A' block, the only part of the original grammar technical school building that hadn't been modernised.

Mark pointed to a black and white photograph dated 1948, which showed a smiling boy with an old-fashioned wooden leg, and whispered, 'He's stumpy.'

Dylan tried not to laugh as he stuck close to Mark, ready to jump behind the desk next to him. When Mr Harwood opened the classroom door and stepped aside, the pupils surged forward, noisily, and a thickset lump of a lad shoved Dylan's head into the doorframe.

'Pack it in. There's no need to rush,' bellowed Mr Harwood.

The boy, a skinhead with a neck as wide as his head, nodded and smiled. 'Sorry, Sir. I slipped on the floor. New boots, see.'

'Really?' Mr Harwood smiled sardonically. 'What's your name?'

'Dean, Sir. Dean Johnson.'

'Mmm, noted. Take a seat.'

While Mr Harwood was chalking his name in bold letters

on the blackboard, Dean slapped Dylan hard across the side of his face sending him reeling backwards into a desk. Dean raised a finger to his pursed lips, smirked, and headed for the back row. Three other boys barged past Dylan, flicking his ears and punching his arms, before following Dean.

Mark and Dylan never intended sitting in the front row, but it seemed the safest option.

Dylan wiped his eyes and whispered, 'Who was that?'

'The skinhead was Scrapper Johnson from Pontyfechan juniors, and you know the others, don't you?'

'Not really,' he lied, even though David Price had bullied him all through infants *and* junior school.

'Ian Pritchard, or Pritch, Kevin Franklyn and David Price, Scrapper's cousin. Bunch of tossers the lot of them. You okay?'

Dylan's bottom lip quivered and he lowered his head. His watery eyes became drawn to the pen scribbles and compass scratches on his desk. Years of abuse from pupils etched into the surface.

I know how you feel, he thought, running his fingertips slowly across the scarred wood.

Mr Harwood opened the register. 'Right then, Class 1c, settle down. If you weren't paying attention or can't read, I'm Mr Harwood, and I won't tolerate insubordination. As well as your form teacher, I also teach religious education. Aren't you lucky?'

Silence.

'That's my intro' over. Your turn. Name, junior school, and background, but no life stories.' He took a fag from a pack and balanced it, unlit, on his bottom lip before grabbing a pistol from his desk and strutting up and down the aisle, revelling in the fear in their faces as he waved it around. He stopped behind Mark and lifted the gun up to his head.

Sensing he was there, Mark swivelled his head around just

as the trigger clicked and a flame illuminated the fear in his face. Mr Harwood chuckled, tucked the fag behind his ear, and wandered back to his desk. Relief drew Mark's shoulders downwards.

'What's your name, boy?' snapped Mr Harwood, thrusting papers at Dylan.

'Dylan, S-S-Sir.'

'Dylan, *what*?'

'Umm, Wolfendale, Sir.'

'Hand these timetables out, then we'll start the intro's. You can go first,' he said, smirking.

Fear went through Dylan faster than a dose of Andrews Liver Salts and he launched his hand in the air.

'Yes?' snapped Mr Harwood.

'I need the toilet, Sir.'

'You should have gone earlier!'

He had, three times, before he had even left the house.

'Sorry, Sir,' mumbled Dylan, crossing his legs.

Mr Harwood waved him off as though swatting a fly. 'Make it quick.' He handed the papers to Mark. 'Looks like you're the man for the job, now.'

~

Dylan clenched his arse cheeks and waddled down the corridor. 'A' Block was a total maze, with more corridors and doors everywhere he turned, and he was certain he'd passed the same classrooms more than once.

The boys toilet was huge. The tiled floor sloped towards the middle of the room where two small, metal drain covers waited for shower water that would no longer come; the shower cubicles long gone.

On the left-hand wall were three hand-wash basins and

one long urinal which, despite a generous splattering of yellow fragrance blocks, stunk of piss, causing Dylan's nose to wrinkle. To his right, two rows of three toilet cubicles faced each other. Their grubby, graffiti covered chipboard walls reached just a mere inch or two below the height of the toilet seat, and below the first cubicle's walls were a pair of boots that moved at the sound of a flush.

Dylan froze when the toilet door creaked open and a boy stepped out.

'Did you get lost?' asked Pritch, grinning.

The index finger buried deep in his left nostril contorted his face and Dylan wondered whether he was searching for his brain. Prize retrieved, he rolled it several times before flicking it at Dylan, who was slowly edging towards the cubicles.

When Dylan reached for the toilet door, Pritch swung his leg out and slammed his Dr. Martens boot into Dylan's thigh. Dylan's knee and sphincter gave way simultaneously, and he face planted the floor, yelping.

Pritch stomped his boot onto Dylan's back. 'Stay down, numb nuts, and quit blubbering or I'll kill you!'

Whistling out-of-tune, Pritch strolled over to the sinks and began admiring himself in the mirror.

Dylan glanced at the cubicles. Could he lock himself in before Pritch caught him? He rose slowly, then froze when he saw that Pritch had two shadows: one trailed in his wake and the other clung to his back. Dylan watched in awe as it swirled and climbed, human-like, up his body. As it reached Pritch's neck, it began to solidify. A face materialised in its whirling blackness and dark lips appeared to whisper in Pritch's ear.

Thoughts of fleeing evaporated from Dylan's brain. He was petrified.

Pritch raised a boot up to the porcelain sink and slid a flick-knife from his sock. He twisted round to meet Dylan's gaze, and flicked it open. The nightmare shadow smiled: its mouth opening impossibly wide to reveal decaying, twisted teeth like the gravestones in Larkmead cemetery.

Dylan began hyperventilating.

Pritch dug chunks of mud out of the grooves in his soles before scooping the mud out of the sink and splattering it across the tiles. With one sweeping motion, he grabbed Dylan's hair and slammed his head into the mud.

Dylan felt blood leaking from his nose, but he could still smell Pritch's rancid breath.

'Eat it!'

Dylan shook his head and tried to push back, but Pritch was stronger. Dylan snapped his mouth shut but was unable to breathe through his damaged nose and he gasped, tasting mud.

The light above the cubicles flickered and extinguished, plunging the area in darkness.

Pritch scrunched his face and recoiled backwards, releasing his grip. 'What's that smell?'

Dylan spat bloodied mud onto the grimy floor and slid further away.

'You dirty bastard! That friggin' stin—'

'What's going on here?' bellowed Harwood, impatiently tapping a four-tailed leather tawse in his palm. 'Well?'

Pritch's demeanour changed instantly: his shoulders slumped and he raised his hands and eyes to the heavens. 'Oh, thank goodness,' he announced, like a thespian. 'He fell, Sir. I-I tried picking him up, but ... I ... I think he's shit himself,' he explained, gesturing to Dylan's rump.

Harwood's brow furrowed. 'Oh ... I see.'

Dylan stood, his face awash with both relieved and terrified tears, but he quickly wiped them from existence with his sleeve, biting his lip hard until he tasted metal.

'Right, Wolfendale, stop that blubbering or I'll give you something to cry about.' He pointed to the cubicles. 'Get cleaned up!'

Dylan gulped breaths like a steam train. 'Y-Yes ... S-S-Sir.'

Harwood turned toward Pritch. 'Name?'

'Ian Pritchard, Sir.'

'Show me your hands.'

Pritch grinned and flicked his palms up with a magician's slight of hand.

Harwood looked him up and down inquisitively. 'Sooo, you just *happened* to find him like that?'

'Yes, Sir. I thought he was dead.'

Harwood rolled his eyes and with a *whoosh* brought the leather tawse down hard, causing instant, painful welts that looked as though Pritch's hands had been burnt by a hot Kit-Kat.

Dylan cleaned himself up, whilst crying the whole time.

Coward! Why can't you be strong, like Mark?

He listened intently and, hearing nothing, he crept out of the cubicle. The room was empty, but he couldn't recall hearing the door.

Once his soiled Y-fronts were disposed of in the bin, he covered them with several sheets of medicated 'tracing paper' toilet roll, and washed his hands. Glancing at the mirror, a horrific boy stared back at him through puffy, red eyes. His face was bruised, bloodied and scratched; his mouth gaped, due to the clots in his nose; his hair stood up in wild clumps; his shirt was muddy, and he still had a dead leg. He wiped his eyes and gulped air through his open, sagging mouth.

He was officially a mouth-breather.

Hobbling forward, Dylan struggled to open the door, but then the gas strut relaxed, and it swung wide. Something thudded behind him and he caught a glimpse of Pritch staggering from a cubicle before someone, or something, yanked him back into the dark.

CHAPTER 4

ANOTHER BRICK IN THE WALL, PART 2

In the afternoon, Dylan found his mind drifting in several classes and, whilst in religious education, he couldn't help thinking about the dead woman's identity. His mind was full of images of the woman's eviscerated body and her unusual necklace. And he couldn't understand why his mother freaked out when he mentioned it.

The annoying *tick tick tick* of the wall clock and Mr Harwood's words droned on until they became one long, confusing, drawl. But, before the next tick came, the lights changed, dousing the classroom in a rich, brown, pigment.

Dylan strode over to Dean 'Scrapper' Johnson, his face frozen mid-laugh or possibly a burp; he couldn't tell which. But, whatever it was, it made him resemble a bulldog chewing a wasp. Dylan wanted to punch him but he was still afraid, even in this hidden, suspended world. He clenched his fist and raised it above Dean's twisted face, the temptation to strike him overwhelming, but he stopped. Dean's soul fluttered below his skin's surface, rufescent and wild, like a sparkly eel. Somehow, Dylan knew that, if he reached out and tugged, it would leave his body.

What is this place? he thought. One of the doors had taken Tom, but to where? Heaven? Hell?

This sepia world resembled an entrance; an old fashioned hotel lobby, full of doors. A prelude to something sinister and sombre, and Dylan could feel the boundary between worlds, thin and fragile, like aged paper.

Dylan's eyes trailed over the dark, eerie shadows that slithered across the classroom floor.

He was stood on one.

He arched his foot away from its iciness and gooseflesh crept up his leg, enveloping his body in frozen clingfilm. Dark souls scurried, ratlike. Swarming and burrowing into corners, their surface sleek and shiny, and their bellies bloated from the nocturnal nourishment of the evil they had made the living perform.

Slithering over his classmates, the misty darkness congregated around Dean and his mates, revelling in the boy's willingness to listen. Even Harwood had a faceless shadow that clung to his back like a squirming, black rucksack of hate.

Chittering drew Dylan's eyes upwards and his lungs gulped on vacant air when he saw the monstrous, evil souls in the ceiling-less void. Dense stalactitic pylons of hate hung in the air with teeth chattering within their faceless heads. Heads which constantly morphed from mobile, blurred masses to static, defined horrors. It reminded Dylan of his optician's Phoropter and its interchangeable lenses gradually bringing indistinguishable, black blobs into perfect focus, only to be smudged once more by another lens clicking into place.

'Better or worse?' the optician would ask, as he clicked another lens in place.

Worse. This was definitely worse.

THWACK!

The wooden ruler slammed into his desk with such

ferocity, that if he hadn't already emptied his bowels he would be sat in a steamy pile of shit.

Harwood was glaring like a rabid dog. Spittle, white and frothy, clung to the corners of his lips and he stunk of Hai Karate aftershave.

'Boring you am I, boyo?'

'N-N-No, S-Sir,' stammered Dylan. He furtively scanned the room for dark, ominous shadows but, thankfully, there were none.

'Well, pay attention boy, or one of my little friends will remind you to stay awake!'

Edward Harwood, nickname 'hardwood,' had a wonderful array of weaponry to *educate* his pupils: a wooden ruler for the back of your hand or knuckles; a gavel for crushing your fingers; a four-tailed leather tawse, which left painful welts and, if you were dull enough to annoy him after that, he would reach into his cupboard for the dreaded hockey stick, which he lovingly called Gertrude. He would lovingly apply fresh layers of insulation tape to the stick every new term to hide the previous year's damage.

Harwood stood in front of Dylan's desk and slapped his ruler repeatedly into his open left palm. The backs of his hands were thick with dark, black hair, which travelled up his arms and protruded in clumps atop his shirt collar like an old, busted sofa. It was so thick that Dylan thought he was King Kong's love child. The only place lacking in hair was the top of his head, although a dark band of it did run from ear to ear at the back of his shiny, sweaty, head.

When he eventually walked back to the front of the class, he snatched a box of Liquorice Imps from the boy in front of Dylan.

'No. Food. Allowed. In. The. Classroom!' he bellowed, before stuffing a handful into his slimy, fat, gob.

Harwood would never get his gross hairy mitts on Dylan's

sweets because he hated them. Disgusting, slimy, sticky blobs, akin to eating fruit flavoured slugs.

Dylan shivered in his seat as Harwood's lips parted to reveal a blackened tongue and Dylan was suddenly conscious of being watched.

In the same row, four desks to his right, a pretty girl was leaning forward and staring their way. When their eyes met, she smiled, but Dylan just rubbed the back of his neck, looked away, and fiddled with his Munch Bunch pencil topper.

'Do you know her?' whispered Dylan, nodding over his right shoulder.

Mark leant forward, glanced at the girl, and grinned, but before he could answer, Harwood's board rubber slammed into the side of his head.

'Owww!' yelled Mark, rubbing his scalp, which was already forming a lump.

'Do I need to separate you two?'

'No, Sir,' answered Mark, quickly. He put his head down and began scribbling.

'Tough. There's an empty desk at the front 'cause Emily Morris has had a family bereavement, so get your arse down here.'

'What's a breathment, Sir?' asked a rotund boy.

'It's 'bi-reev-muhnt,' and it means someone died. Now, get on with your work or you'll be dead, too!'

Mark stood, picked up his satchel, and began gathering his things. 'Isn't Emily the girl you wanted to find?' he whispered, but, judging by the disappointment he saw dragging Dylan's lip downwards, he already knew the answer.

CHAPTER 5

I DON'T LIKE MONDAYS

Monday 14th September, 1981
Draigwen Town Comprehensive School

The teacher's staff room resembled a second-hand furniture store room. A small kitchenette, with odd cupboard doors in various stages of neglect, dominated the far end. One cupboard, void of a door, was littered with stained coffee mugs and lonely teacups; their matching saucers long gone. The faded vinyl floor was doted with several canteen tables and chairs with teachers reading newspapers or frantically marking homework. In the middle of the lounge area was a low, square table surrounded by a mismatch of settees, armchairs and benches.

Sarah Lewis, an Art teacher fresh from graduation, was sat preparing for the trip. She double checked coach pick-up times, support telephone numbers and the chapel site-contact details. She was all too aware that the outcome of today's trip would be scrutinised and she prayed it went without incident. Every time the rotary wall-phone rang she bolted upright like a meerkat, hoping for a cancellation that never came.

Her allocated buddy teacher for the day was the Craft, Design and Technology teacher, Dafydd Williams. They had rarely spoken, but he seemed nice enough and, more importantly, he knew how to handle the kids. Over a coffee intended to calm her nerves rather than wake her, she divided the class into two manageable groups.

'Me and thee today, then?' Dafydd was beaming down at her, his bushy eyebrows bouncing up and down.

'Someone's happy.'

'Good to get out, see. Have I got time for a quick one?' he asked, waving a packet of Woodbines.

'Yes. I'm just checking my notes. We don't need to round 'em up for another—' She glanced at her wristwatch. 'Fifteen minutes or so?'

'Plenty of time, then.' He lit a fag and marched across the room, nodding and greeting teachers on route to make a coffee.

When he returned, his fag was almost down to the filter. He reached into his packet, took out a fresh one, and lit it using what remained of the first. 'Sorry, forgot to ask,' he said, waving away the smoke and holding out the packet.

She shook her head. 'No thanks, I don't—'

'Don't blame you. Filthy habit. Doc keeps telling me to pack it in.' He pointed towards his chest. 'Dicky heart, see, but I just can't seem to quit. Anyway, who we got today? Ed's lot, isn't it?'

'Yes, and there's a few to watch out for,' she said, handing him a slip of paper. 'Although, there's one less than we thought. Ian Pritchard's A.W.O.L., apparently.'

Dafydd took another drag and held it for longer than Sarah thought was possible before exhaling smoke from each nostril like a baby dragon void of flame. Sarah's face went green and she leant back.

'Sorry, love,' he said, taking one last drag before wafting the smoke and pointing to a name on her sheet. 'Dylan Wolfendale. Unusual surname and definitely not Welsh. What's his story?'

'I don't know. Edward said he's a dreamer. Zero attention span.'

'Well, we don't want him wandering off and getting flattened by a car, do we?'

'Oh, God, no. Not on my first trip.' She put her hands together, looked up, and whispered a prayer.

Dafydd laughed. 'Not on *any* trip!' he corrected.

'Of course. Sorry, I'm a bit frazzled. First trip nerves.'

Dafydd stood and dusted ash from his lap. 'You'll be fine. It's young Johnson and his mates we need to keep an eye on, so I'll take his group while you watch over dream boy.'

~

Sarah collected the class from Mr Harwood and escorted them to the front yard. Laughter and excited voices were replaced with groans and sighs when Dafydd appeared and announced he would be taking half the class.

Sarah checked her watch when a coach came down the road at speed. 'Blimey, he's early,' she noted.

'That's not our coach; that's a Cardiff bus,' advised Dafydd. 'What the hell's it doing this far up the valley?'

The brakes screeched, and they watched in horror as the bus crashed head on into a lamp post, shattering the windscreen, and sending the driver crashing to the pavement below.

'Shitty death! I'll phone for an ambulance. You check he's okay,' bellowed Dafydd over the children's screams. 'Calm down, kids! Stay where you are and do NOT go out the gate.'

He bounced his way back and forth through the children, knocking them this way and that, like a pinball en route to the main building.

When Dafydd barged past, Mark couldn't contain his excitement. 'Whoa! Did you see that, Dylan?' he asked, but Dylan was nowhere to be seen.

Sarah ran towards the bus and watched the driver roll onto his back, coughing up blood. The name 'Howard Cobley' was written on a blood spattered tag clipped to his chest pocket. His face was torn open in several places and a deep gash in his neck was bleeding profusely.

Sarah bent over him. 'Howard, an ambulance will be here, soon. You need to put pressure on that or—'

Howard's head tilted to reveal a compound fracture of his left collar bone, which he swiftly crunched back into place.

Sarah screamed. 'Sir, you really shouldn't do that. Medics are on their way.' She froze when his head swivelled towards her, his rufescent eyes forcing a dark sensation up her spine and she desperately tried to listen to the voice in her head that was screaming at her to run. When he slowly rose up, she backed away, but her shaky legs betrayed her and she tripped on the kerb, slamming onto her back on the path.

Her eyes never left his.

She watched his body and limbs contort, and winced at the loud, cracking sounds when bones snapped back into place.

'Is ... Is everything okay?' she mumbled.

Howard didn't answer.

He spat out a tooth and smiled at her, displaying teeth and gums smeared with blood. He looked down at his hands, wiggled his fingers, then patted himself all over. He stepped up onto the kerb and leant over Sarah. His eyes burned and she instinctively shut hers, pulling herself into a foetal position, clutching her folders tightly to her chest whilst praying.

Nothing happened.

When she finally opened her eyes, Howard was yards away, ambling backwards away from her. His eyes remained fixed on her while he moved down the path towards the school.

Towards the children.

When he finally turned his back on her, Sarah ditched her folders, ducked through a side gate into the school yard, and took off her heels. She hurtled towards the pupils that were howling and screaming by the main entrance, hoping to get to them before he did.

Howard stopped right in front of the huddled, gawping kids, their wide mouths resembling House Martin chicks waiting to be fed. He closed his eyes and sniffed hard. When they snapped back open, he slowly rotated his head from side to side, then tilted it to listen, like an inquisitive hound. Satisfied with what he discovered, he turned and crossed over the road.

When Sarah reached the main gate and edged her way through the throng, Howard Cobley had disappeared.

Dylan forced his way to the front. 'What's happened?' he asked, grabbing hold of Mark's shoulder.

'Where've you been?'

'Erm, nervous poo,' he whispered, in Mark's ear.

'Step aside! Step aside!' repeated Dafydd, over and over, as he stumbled through the kids until he reached Sarah. 'Where the hell's he gone?' he asked, clutching his chest.

'No idea. Did you see his eyes?'

'No, why?' he wheezed.

'They were menacing, and ... and red,' she explained, causing the kids to giggle.

Dafydd bent forward, hands on his knees, and took several deep breaths.

'You've been running, haven't you?' she asked, touching his shoulder. 'What about your dodgy ticker?'

'I-I'll be fine. The police will be here, soon. Not sure the ambulance will be needed, though.'

'Oh, I'm not so sure, looking at you. Are you okay to do this trip, Dafydd?'

'Yeah, I'm fine, but it won't be today, though. The fuzz will want to speak to you. Did you say *red*?'

CHAPTER 6
BRIGHT EYES

Draigwen Police Station

Woman police constable Fiona Brasking left the restroom and walked painfully slowly towards the offices as if she were carrying a suspect package that ticked and stunk of marzipan, rather than a large floppy tin-tray laden with mugs of tea and coffee.

Providing refreshments to every department took her three rounds and by the time she had finished the boiler was empty. She emptied the coffee granules from her mug, sighed, and slid it back into the cupboard. She jumped when a mug was slammed onto the counter beside her.

'Oh, Fi', you forgot my sugar!' It was the front desk Sergeant, Tony Thomas. 'Thought you would have known mine by now?'

'Sorry Sarge, not with it today. Two sugars coming right up,' she said, smiling.

Tony smiled back and gently tapped her shoulder. 'That's okay, Fi', I can see you had a lot to do.'

Fiona gestured to the nearly empty cupboard. 'Sixteen mugs worth. Wasn't even enough water for—' She paused, stirred his coffee and slid it towards him. 'Never mind. There you go, Sarge.'

He took it, winked, and walked away. 'You'll go far, Fi'. Just keep up the good work.'

Fiona's shoulders slumped. 'Can't see me going anywhere at this rate,' she mumbled, seriously doubting ever making it to the dizzy heights of detective, which she longed for.

Leaning back against the counter, she stared through the perspex partition into the offices and watched the staff milling about. Woman detective constable Kerry Edwards whizzed past with an overenthusiastic wave, whilst Tracy the cleaner, was busy creating her own work by dropping fag ash onto the desks she was dusting. The only voices came from the station enquiry officers, Linda and Suzy, who were dealing with an agitated resident moaning about, "*...bloody kids and their air rifles.*" As Kerry was a WDC, it meant Fiona was one of only two women in uniform and *boy* did she know it. Nansi Dooley, the other WPC, had an amazing knack of making herself scarce, especially before the morning coffee run.

No sooner was she back at her desk wading through other people's paperwork, the front desk window slid open and Tony's bum chin poked through. For an older man, he was rather striking and Fiona quite liked the dimple in his chin although, if he had too much stubble, the dimple went dark and looked as though one of the day shift had stubbed a fag out on his chin.

'*Pssst.* Brasking,' whispered Tony.

Fiona released the spoilt page from her typewriter, scrunched it up, launched it into the waste bin and made her way across the office. 'Yes, Sarge?'

Tony's bushy eyebrows wiggled up and down as he whispered with a smile, 'Fancy some fresh air?'

She sighed. 'Not washing panda cars, again?'

'Nope. You're gonna like this one. It'll keep you on your toes.'

'What is it?'

He handed her a telephone incident slip upon which he had scribbled, '*Hit and run. Draigwen comp.*'

Fiona's face lit up and her jaw dropped.

'See, told you you'd like it. There's no panda cars available, and the new jam sandwich has already been commandeered by Grumpy, so get those stumpy little legs going!' He laughed, walking two fingers across the counter.

'Cheeky bugger! Thanks, Sarge.'

Draigwen Town Comprehensive School

Dafydd Williams looked old for his forty-six years. Overweight *and* unfit, judging by the sweaty, furrowed brow and his constant deep breaths, as if the room's air was lumpy. Fiona scribbled notes while Dafydd described what he had seen, which didn't amount to much; after ringing 999 his attention had been on corralling the kids.

'Are you feeling okay?' enquired Fiona.

Dafydd puffed his chest out peacock style. 'Yes, I'm fine. It's just warm, that's all.' He raised the sash-window a couple of inches sending a cool breeze into the office, which ruffled the papers in the school secretary's in-tray. 'Anyone else hot?'

Fiona shook her head and looked at Sarah, who seemed very concerned about her colleague and begged him to sit and relax.

'Mr Williams has a heart condition, and he really should get it checked,' Sarah said to Fiona. 'Like most men, he's stubborn.'

Dafydd tutted and sat down. 'Why do women always have

to fuss, huh? I'm fine. Sorry, I couldn't be more helpful, WPC?'

'Brasking, but please call me Fiona. Thanks, Mr Williams, it all helps. After Dafydd left, what happened next, Sarah?'

Sarah had thought about nothing else. Usually adept, this morning's incident had her flummoxed. All she could think about was Howard. Howard *bloody* Cobley and those eyes. Yet, it wasn't just the eyes, it was his whole being; it didn't seem normal.

When he crashed through that window, got up, brushed himself down and walked away it reminded her of Clark Kent catching bullets. It wasn't human. But that was just silly and she should know better than to consider such idiotic ideas. There were no aliens *or* people with superpowers, despite what Hollywood would lead us to believe. He was either very strong or intoxicated. Yes, Howard Cobley was drunk and had not realised he was badly hurt. He was probably in a hedge somewhere, stiff as a board. She neglected to mention the eyes when she recounted the morning's events.

Fiona closed her notebook and slipped it back into her pocket. 'Thanks, you've been very helpful and the description you've given has matched that already provided by Howard's wife and—'

'Wife?' interrupted Sarah.

'Er, yes. Two children, too. Why do you ask?'

'Oh, no reason.'

'But you seem shocked.'

'Oh, no, it's just ... Well, he didn't seem a nice man, so I assumed he'd be single.'

'What made you think that he wasn't nice? I thought he didn't speak?'

Sarah shifted uncomfortably. 'He just ... Oh, I don't know. I'm just being silly. Don't mind me.' Sarah stood up fast, shoving her chair back, and pushing her dark, curly fringe out of her face. 'Was that all?'

Fiona retrieved her notebook and pen, as she sensed Sarah was holding back. 'Is there *anything* else?'

Sarah bowed her head and fidgeted with her skirt pleats.

'The eyes,' Dafydd pitched in.

'Eyes?'

Sarah's head spun around and she glared at Dafydd, pleading for silence.

Instead, Dafydd leant forward, closer to Fiona, conspiratorially whispering, 'Bright. Red. Eyes.'

'But I thought you said you didn't see him?'

'I didn't.'

Fiona placed a hand on top of Sarah's fidgeting fingers and gently squeezed. 'Is this true?'

Sarah lifted her head. Tears pooled underneath her terrified eyes and Fiona gestured for her to sit once more. 'It's okay, Sarah, just tell me what you saw. Did he hurt you?'

Sarah wiped her eyes with one of the secretary's tissues, but she couldn't hide how flushed her cheeks had become. 'His eyes were red. Not just bloodshot, *literally* red. They even seemed to—' She paused, glancing at Dafydd.

'Just tell her.'

'They glowed, and … and there was something else, too, but I can't quite put my finger on it.'

'You're doing great, Sarah. Just describe it as best you can.'

Sarah stared at her hands in her lap, rolled the scrunched up tissue between her fingers and breathed out hard. 'Well, it was his presence. I suppose you could say it was his aura, as though his body radiated badness.' She lifted her head and met Fiona's stare. 'I've never been so terrified in all my life, so how could someone like that have a loving family? It just doesn't make sense.'

Fiona wasn't sure what to make of it. 'I can't comment on

how you felt at the time, but his family are missing him terribly. Perhaps, he was in shock.' Fiona put her notebook away for what she hoped was the last time and stood up. 'If you think of anything else, no matter how trivial, please ring the station and ask for me.' She donned her hat, and raised her hand when Dafydd rose. 'It's okay, I'll find my own way out. Thank you.'

Out on the street, the mangled wreck of the Cardiff bus had been towed away and two council workmen were making a pig's ear of cleaning up the glass and debris.

Fiona needed to find Howard—dead or alive—and headed in the direction he had taken. She unclipped her Burndept radio and jabbed at the button.

'WPC234 to control, over.'

The radio crackled into life with Tony's dulcet tones. 'Control to WPC234, go ahead, over.'

'WPC234 to control. Interviews at school completed. I'm heading door-to-door to see if I can find any witnesses to Howard's whereabouts, over.'

'Control to WPC234, have fun, over.'

Door-to-door interviews were something that all uniformed officers loathed, but if just one viable witness could be found, it was worth it. She briefly closed her eyes, mentally preparing herself for the onslaught of diverse weirdos, lonely old biddies and unemployed layabouts, then stepped off the kerb in the direction of Brynglas Avenue.

Back at the station, the air was thick with smoke and the sound of Ian Dury begging people to hit him with a rhythmic stick. Fiona hadn't hit anyone with her truncheon, but she would gladly give Mr Dury what he wanted just to shut him up. She was in a bad mood. Her feet felt as though they had been punched for fifteen straight rounds by Muhammad Ali and her bra strap had made new roads through the skin on her shoulders. The three hours of pounding the streets had inevitably led to nothing, unless of course you count the twenty six 'crimes' reported to her, which were just neighbourly disputes, and the nine sightings of Howard Cobley, that she had discounted as incredible before they had finished their imaginative descriptions. Sometimes she could just sense when people were lonely, or simply wanted to be a part of something big to get their name in the paper or their ugly mug on *Wales Today*.

Tony was helping Suzy with another obnoxious customer at the front desk, so Fiona returned her radio, threw her hat onto a neighbouring desk, and took out a blank incident report form. Everyone was too busy on their desk phones or *clickety clacking* away at their typewriters to notice her return, so she quickly slipped into the restroom to make herself, *just herself*, a cuppa. She would have got away with it, too, if it wasn't for the lady killer, PC Brian Jukes.

'Oh, go on then. Coffee, white, no sugar.' He winked. 'I'm sweet enough, see.' He stretched his arm out and dumped his mug on the counter, his hand lingering far too long on the side of her chest.

Fiona put two fingers in her mouth and pretended to retch causing him to waggle a finger at her.

'Less of that, Fi' or I'll tell everyone you're making a round.'

Fiona threw the spoon across the counter and grabbed her mug. 'Piss off, Jukesy. I've been doing door-to-door all afternoon and my feet are killing me. I don't need this crap!' she barked.

Juksey picked up his mug, turned the handle towards her and shoved it in her face. 'That's why we're called the plod. Coffee, white, no sugar,' he demanded.

Fiona reluctantly took the mug and reached for the discarded spoon.

'See, that wasn't too hard, was it, eh?' His tone softened and he relaxed against the counter, arms crossed. 'Listen Fi' if you want to get along, you've got to play the game, see. I can help you, if you like. How about we have a chat over dinner one night?' he suggested. His eyes lowered towards her chest. 'You never know you might like it.'

'Yeah, maybe. I'll check my filofax and let you know,' she said, passing him his mug.

Jukesy smiled and almost skipped out of the room.

'In your dreams,' she whispered.

~

When she returned to the office, Tony was sat on her desk reading the late afternoon edition of the *Gwent Argus* newspaper.

The headline emblazoned on the front page above a grainy photograph of Howard Cobley read:

'CARDIFF BUS CRASHES INTO LOCAL SCHOOL.'

Fiona shook her head. 'They just love to exaggerate don't they?'

Tony lowered the paper, his forehead and nose scrunching up. 'Who?'

'Them!' Fiona pointed to the headline. 'It's not entirely accurate, is it?' She put her coffee down and dug out her notebook.

'What's wrong with it?'

'Well, no school was harmed during that crash.'

'Nope, just a bus driver that was reported missing yesterday.'

'Yesterday?'

'Yeah. South Wales Constabulary confirmed it earlier. Howard's family reported him missing around 3pm. SWC would like to speak to him when we find him, too. Apparently a man's body was found near to where Howard was last seen.'

'Weird.'

'Yes, it always is. Did you get any leads on his whereabouts?'

'Not a lot to go on I'm afraid, Sarge. The credible witnesses confirmed Howard's description but didn't really give us anything new, although the one teacher, Sarah, did say that his eyes—'

Tony held up his hand, silencing her. 'In that case, it's done. There's nothing more for us.'

'What do you mean?'

Tony rolled up the paper and walked around the desk. 'No crime committed. He didn't steal the bus; he worked for Cardiff Council. The worst that could happen to him now, *if* he's still alive, is disciplinary action for driving off-route. He'll probably lose his job. We can't prove he was drunk or off his face on drugs 'cause we weren't able to examine him at the scene and, even if he walked through those doors right now, it'd probably be out of his system. We'd just whisk him off to SWC for—'

'Yeah, but what about his injuries?' Fiona cut in.

'What about them? Jukesy checked the hospitals. No patients admitted in the last twenty four hours with cuts or injuries consistent with flying through a sodding bus window! So, to be honest, Fi', all we have here is another missing person. File it and move on.'

'A Misper? That's it?' she asked, raising her palms skyward.

'I'm afraid so.'

Fiona couldn't hold back her sarcasm. 'Hello. Dead man at Howard's last sighting.' She cupped her palms, mimicking a set of scales, raising and lowering her hands with each word. 'Howard. Murderer. Howard. Murderer.'

Tony simply shrugged. 'Talking of murder, a boy's body was found in the school's woodwork skip after you left. Judging by the decomposition, the poor sod had been stuffed in there for days, covered in wood, rubbish, and soiled underpants of all things.'

CHAPTER 7

THERE'S NO ONE QUITE LIKE GRANDMA

Tuesday 15th September, 1981
Larkmead Chapel, South Wales

When the Evan's Transport coach traversed the Sirhowy Valley and dropped down into the Rhymney Valley the early morning sun hung high over the west ridge, striping the hillside with hundreds of elongated shadows of trees and sheep. Gossip was rife about Pritch's death and the potential killer, although if they had been old enough to bet, most money would have been on Dean Johnson. Apart from a police cordon around the woodwork workshop, you wouldn't know a child had been murdered and dumped in the bin. The school should have been closed for mourning but, in Mrs Griffiths' absence, the Deputy Head, Mr Meredith, was too spineless to make a decision, at least that's what the kangaroo court at the back of the coach had decided.

Several windows along the coach were open to inject fresh, warm air. Yet, when they pulled up outside Larkmead chapel's wrought-iron gates, dark clouds swarmed overhead covering the hallowed grounds and graveyard in an eerie, cold, blackness.

Dafydd shivered when the pneumatic doors hissed open, and he stifled a laugh when the pupils, most of them in P.E. shorts, filtered off the coach.

'I'm not going out there, it's flipping freezing, mun!' moaned a gangly boy who matched Dafydd's height.

Dafydd smiled; he quite enjoyed seeing them squirm. 'Stop being a girl, it'll toughen you up. Now, move it!' he spat, shoving the boy off the coach.

~

The chapel caretaker, who was in the process of removing bat faeces off the window cusps, wore a shabby, brown wax-jacket over black trousers and wellington boots. Long, curly, brown hair stuck to his sweaty forehead below a dirty herringbone patterned Dai cap, and Sarah thought he resembled a farmer rather than a caretaker.

'Excuse me. Arwel Davies?' she called, timidly, but the caretaker didn't acknowledge her. 'Hi, Mr Davies?' she asked again, when she was certain he was within earshot.

The caretaker turned, looked her up and down but didn't reply; he just stared at her with a face like a slapped arse.

'I'm sorry, have you been waiting long?' asked Sarah.

Arwel turned towards the large wooden doors and huffed. 'Keep a tight rein on that lot,' he grumbled, nodding toward the two groups gathered on the gravel driveway. 'I don' wan' anymore damage caused by those hooligans.'

'Oh, no need to worry. They're not that bad.'

Arwel shook his head. 'Kids are a bane. Always vandalising something. There's only one good un amongst 'em.'

'Really? Who's that?' she asked.

Arwel pointed straight at Dylan. 'Him there. Comes to visit the graves regular, see. Thinks I don' see him sneakin' in, but I does. He don' cause any trouble, though. Quiet as a mouse.'

'I wasn't aware. Thanks for telling me. I'm sure we'll—'

Arwel abandoned his bucket, slipped into the chapel and slammed the wooden door behind him.

'Charming. Nice to meet you, too.'

Sarah returned to the pupils gathered on the recently mowed grass and sat down. 'Right then, I'm going to give you some background on this lovely place before we draw, okay?' She opened her folder and thumbed through a few pages before clearing her throat. 'Quiet, please!' she shouted, before reading, 'Larkmead chapel is a Welsh Congregational Church, but quite small in comparison to most churches. The parishioners are of the United Reformed Church, which is part of the Christian Presbyterian Church of Wales. It was originally built in—'

'Miss! Why d'ya call it a chapel, if it's a church?' one boy asked.

'Name?'

'David Thomas, Miss.'

'Very good question, David. Unfortunately, I don't know the answer, but I'll ask the Reverend. So, as I was saying, it was built in 1829, rebuilt in 1855, and extended in 1876 due to a population growth when the mining industry developed.'

'I thought this was Art, Miss?' someone shouted, causing a ripple of giggles.

'Of course. I'm just providing background on the architecture.' She took a beat, sighed, and continued reading, 'The 1876 rebuild was designed by architect Thomas Thomas of Landore and built in the classical style: gable-entry plan, two storeys and a large arch in this south facing façade. The arch you can see in the pediment above the entrance is said to be Thomas' finest and most sophisticated glorification arch in all the buildings that he ever designed before his death in 1888. Now, isn't that interesting?'

The class stared back in silence.

Mental note, stick to Art in future.

Dafydd clapped his hands. 'Right then, Group A. Grab a pencil, drawing board and two sheets of A4 and follow me,' he ordered. 'Leave your bags on the grass; I don't want you disrespecting the dead by eating on their graves!'

When Dafydd's group headed to the boundary wall to get a wider view of the chapel and graveyard, Sarah instructed her group to collect a small roll of tape, two sheets of A3 and a stick of charcoal. At a nearby grave, she demonstrated the correct rubbing technique, before letting them loose. 'Don't forget, have respect. No noise and NO sitting on the stones!'

Mark followed Dylan down a windy, grassed path between the graves, taking care not to step directly onto the graves themselves. They were so relieved that Dean was in the other group and almost skipped along. Dylan stopped in front of a tall gravestone. This one wasn't weathered by years of freeze-thaw and tinged with lichen like the others. It was youthful in appearance; ready to withstand a hundred years of weather. The stone was cold to his touch, but it gave him a feeling of peace; a feeling of home.

Dylan ran his fingers over the lettering, brushing away loose dirt and taped his sheet to the front of the stone. Mark stepped over to the adjacent grave and did the same. When he'd finished rubbing, Dylan sat back and admired his work.

The inscription in the charcoal read:

Here Lies
Keziah Louisa Hawker
Loving Wife, Mother and Nan
Died 3 May 1977

Lazarus William Hawker
Beloved Husband, Father and Grancha
Died 21 November 1980
Together Once More With God

'What did your Nan used to call you?' asked Mark. 'Action Man, wasn't it?'

A woman's voice burst into Dylan's head. *'My little Action Man, is that you?'*

Dylan jumped and fell backwards, hitting his head on the grave's low concrete surround. He cried out, more from shock than pain. When he sat up, Sarah's head appeared over the gravestone.

'I thought it might be you, Dylan. What did I tell you about being quiet?'

'Sorry, Miss, I—'

'I don't want excuses. Take this as a warning. Anymore fooling and you'll be in detention. Understand?'

He sighed. 'Yes, Miss.'

'Back to work,' she demanded, before disappearing out of sight.

'Dylan? Is that you?' asked the voice, croaky and distant, like low radio static.

'Not now, Nan,' whispered Dylan.

Mark lobbed a stone at him. 'Sorry, butt'. Did you say something?'

Dylan shook his head and dusted himself down. 'No.'

Mark laughed. 'If it's not bullies picking on you, it's teachers.'

'Tell me about it,' mumbled Dylan.

He stood in silence, staring at his grandparents' grave, zoning out until Mark pinched his arm, wrenching him from his daze. With a face like a scolded puppy, he whined, '*Oww*! Wha'd you do that for?'

'Just checking you were still with us ... and keep your noise down,' advised Mark, before continuing his rubbing.

'Stop pinching me, then!'

'Well, I had to. You're always away with the fairies. Sometimes, I wonder whether you're in the same world as us.'

'Huh, very funny.' He couldn't believe how close Mark was to the truth.

Are those occult books giving Mark powers?

Nah, they couldn't be. Dylan was the one interacting with the dead and he didn't understand everything, so how could Mark learn it from a book? Was the foggy realm part of their world, or somewhere in-between?

Dylan flicked loose charcoal off the inscription.

'Are you still there, Dylan?'

'Yes,' he whispered, hoping Mark wouldn't hear.

'I knew it! Didn't I say, Laz'? I'd recognise his voice anywhere.'

Just then, a deeper voice reverberated in Dylan's head. *'Who else would it be? Nobody else talks to us!'*

'Of course it's me,' replied Dylan.

Mark was leaning against a grave, staring and smirking.

Dylan turned away, placing his hands on his grandparents' gravestone. 'Quiet,' he whispered, lowering his head.

Pain shot through his skull when his head slammed hard onto the gravestone and he slumped into a heap at its base. Through blurred eyes he watched his paper slide off the stone and get rolled up by a figure to his left.

'Thanks, knob,' whispered the blurry assailant.

Dylan sprung up to snatch it back, but he wobbled on Bambi legs and stumbled through the graves trying to reach for a gravestone to steady himself, but his foot crashed through a crypt entrance. Fractured stone sliced into his calf and he leant forward to try and free himself, then stopped abruptly.

Something was oozing out between the stone slabs.

A stream of shadow poured up out of the grave, over his trapped foot, and rose up in front of him, forming a mound of darkness that moved like fluid. It seemed to lean towards him, as though it were studying him, then it shrank down and slid through the graveyard before disappearing out of sight behind a distant gravestone.

Dylan screamed.

CHAPTER 8

HELLS BELLS

Mark pushed on the stone slab, moving it sufficiently so Dylan could slide his leg out without ripping the wound further.

Dean, with a face resembling a demented clown, was already strolling away, waving Dylan's work about like a light-sabre.

After a few minutes, the adrenalin coursing through Dylan's blood began to disperse, lowering his pulse. His nerve endings woke from their own drug-induced daydream and stung. Blood trickled from a small cut above his hairline and his ripped trouser leg revealed a nasty gash. Small droplets of blood oozed from the exposed skin gathering size and momentum, before sliding down his leg. He felt sick and winced when Mark grabbed his shoulder. He buried his face in his hands and sobbed.

An awkward silence ensued until Mark placed his hand gently on Dylan's shoulder and waved a handkerchief in his face. 'It's okay, there's no bogies on it.'

Dylan tried to stifle a guffaw, but it sounded like a Whoopee Cushion being sat on. 'Thanks.' He glanced down at his shoe, but there was no evidence that the black spectre had touched it and he wondered if Mark had seen it, too. 'Did you notice anything strange about that crypt?'

'No, why?'

'Nothing ... Erm ... Weird?'

'Like what?'

Dylan shook his head. 'Doesn't matter.'

Mark picked up Dylan's torn and crumpled spare sheet, scrunched it into a ball, and stuffed it in his back pocket. He collected his own, unused, spare sheet, taped it onto a nearby gravestone and rubbed his piece of charcoal gently over the lettering. When he finished, he pulled it off and handed it to Dylan.

'Blimey, that was quick!'

'I picked an easy one, that's why. Take a look.'

Dylan read the chalk inscription:

Daniel Hawker
6 February 1943 ~ 28 February 1970
UNFORGIVEN

'That's harsh. Wonder what Daniel did?' mumbled Dylan, before scribbling his name on the back and rolling it up.

'Do you miss them?' asked Mark, pointing to Dylan's grandparent's gravestone.

The question came like a punch to Dylan's chest, which suddenly felt tight, and his lip quivered like a tuning fork.

'Always. I visit most nights. I sit and talk to them, you know, as if they were still here.'

Mark's eyes crossed and his tongue fell out. He staggered forward dragging a leg behind him, arms outstretched like one of the undead.

Dylan punched him in the arm. 'Thanks for understanding.'

'No problem, weirdo!' He laughed. 'Seriously though, you need to stick up for yourself or Scrapper and those dicks will just keep doing it.'

'I-I can't, though.'

'Why?'

'I'm scared.'

'Summon up an army of zombies to chew their faces off, then.'

Dylan stared wide-eyed at his friend.

Does he know?

Dylan nodded towards the grave and snickered. 'Don't be daft, they're just bones.'

'Oh, I heard that, Dylan!' snapped his grandmother.

Dylan was certain her withered arms crossed in protest. 'Sorry, Nan. I was only joking.'

Mark shook his head. '*See*, I said you were weird.'

Rather than ignore it, Dylan harrumphed and quickly changed the subject. 'Everyone's stopping for dinner. Come on.'

The majority of pupils were gathered on the grass or had followed the teachers into the chapel, but a couple of loners were sat on the wall near the entrance, their legs dangling over the edge while they stuffed their faces. They were well out of earshot and only just visible to the teachers, so the boys headed over.

Dylan was too shy to ask if they could sit with them, but Mark had no qualms. He jumped up next to a thin, gangly boy and together they hoisted Dylan up. The tall boy, Steven Evans, introduced himself as Slinky and his friend, who was engrossed in a small, black, plastic toy—that beeped when his thumbs jabbed repeatedly at yellow buttons—was called Benny 'Half-Lug' Lewis.

Dylan was about to ask why he was called Half-Lug, when he spotted the horrific scar on the left side of his face; half of his ear was missing. Dylan nudged his arm and gestured to the game. 'What's that?'

'Space Invader,' replied Benny, unmoving.

'It's new, and he's already worn the buttons. He's a spoilt git. Aren't you, Benny?' Steven asked, but Benny remained engrossed. 'He can't hear me; he's deaf in that ear. His parents spoil him rotten since the accident, even though it was his fault.'

'How come?' asked Mark.

'He was burning rubbish with some Pontyfechan morons. One of them threw a lit match into the jerrycan, but nothing happened, so Kevin Franklyn told Benny to stick his ear to it and listen for flames. He did. The can exploded and half of Benny's ear flew off.

Dylan and Mark compared gaping mouths.

'Well, you're obviously a Sparky, but what's his nickname?' asked Steven, pointing to Dylan.

'Hasn't got one,' explained Mark.

Steven stuffed a handful of chips in his mouth. 'Well, as his surname's Wolfendale, I'll call him Wolfy,' he said, spitting chewed up potato at Dylan. 'Sorry, Wolfy.'

'That's okay,' replied Dylan, nonchalantly picking squashed potato off his sleeve with a nail.

'Where'd you get them chips?' asked Mark, dribbling.

'School food van. Got 'em when he was setting up. They're cold, but still taste lush.' Steven held them out.

Dylan took a single chip off the top of the pile to be polite, but Mark grabbed a handful.

'Thanks.'

'What've you got?' Steven asked, when Dylan cracked open his Tupperware box.

Dylan smiled and tilted it so they could see the contents: one cheese sandwich (no crusts) cut into small squares, and four custard creams.

'I made it myself,' he said proudly, causing them all to laugh.

When the laughter died, Steven became mesmerised by a group of first year girls from Pontyfechan juniors who were sat cross-legged, eating dinner off their skirts.

'Which one do you fancy?' asked Dylan, stirring Steven from his stupor.

'Sian Hawkins. The one in the middle with long, blonde hair. She's stonking. I'd love to go out with her.'

'She's in our R.E. class,' noted Mark.

'You're lucky. She could be a catwalk model, better than Christie Brinkley,' mused Steven. 'Do you reckon I'd stand a chance?'

Dylan couldn't imagine the two of them ever going out. Popular girls simply had no interest in misfits. 'Yeah, of course,' he lied, although, having never had a girlfriend, he wasn't best placed to give advice on courting girls. 'Why do they call you Slinky?' he asked, changing the subject. 'Is it 'cause you're tall and thin or—'

'Nuh, it's 'cause he's a useless piece of shit, but great fun when pushed down the stairs!' interrupted Dean.

Kevin was with him. He smiled and waved at Sian, but she curled her lip in disgust and looked up at Steven, smiling. Kevin saw and scowled.

Dean's cousin, David Price, stood next to Kevin with hair that appeared to be soaked in engine oil and combed back with a garden rake.

Fear twisted Dylan's stomach and he began to shake.

Steven swayed like a drunk Humpty Dumpty, rubbing his

stomach as he mocked, 'Ha ha ha, you're soooooo funny, Scrapper.'

'Watch it, lanky.'

'No, *really*, you're hilari-arse!'

Dean lunged at Steven's long legs, reaching them with ease. Before he had time to react, Steven was tugged forward, slamming hard onto the ground. His hand flew to the back of his head and he struggled to catch his breath. Within seconds, his hand was drenched in blood.

Dean leant forward, whispering into his ear, 'Sian's mine. Back off, or you're dead.'

Terrified, Dylan lowered himself onto shaky legs. Kneeling beside Steven, voice breaking, he croaked, 'Leave Slinky alone.'

Unseen by the others, Kevin's shadow split into two. The abnormal one swirled and shifted before evolving into a small boy wearing a scruffy school blazer and knee length black shorts. The school badge on his blazer had the letters 'DTGTS' on it, rather than 'DTCS,' and his right leg was missing from just below the knee. In its place was a weathered and chipped, wooden leg. The stump was jammed into a black leather cup atop the wood and held in place by a single leather strap. He was Long John Silver minus the eye patch and parrot, and Dylan recognised him from the old school photos in 'A' block. The peg-leg boy leant close to Kevin and sharp, needle teeth chattered as he whispered in Kevin's ear.

Spurred on, Kevin kicked Dylan onto his side, straddled him, and squeezed his neck. Teeth dripping with spittle, a breath worse than Pritch's and veins bulging across his temples like a fisherman's bait box, Kevin growled, 'Shaddup, pussy, or you'll be next.'

'No, he won't!' snapped Mark, fists clenched.

Kevin released his grip. 'Oh yeah, and who's gonna stop us?' he asked, spinning around.

Mark raised his palms skywards and looked around in mock search. 'Us? What us?'

Dean and David were nowhere to be seen.

The boy's eyed each other for a moment and Dylan saw something pass between them. Did Kevin give a slight, knowing nod? No, he was just seeing things, like schoolboys materialising out of shadows. He really was losing the plot.

A grin crept over Mark's face when Kevin snapped, 'Watch your back, gay boy!'

'Nothing wrong with being gay, is there, Kev?'

Once Kevin scuttled away, Steven, holding a bloodied handkerchief to the back of his head, blew out hard. 'Wow, you've got big balls for a short arse.'

'I was shitting myself,' admitted Mark, shaking.

Steven wobbled to his feet and wrapped his arms around both boys, forming a mini scrum. 'Thanks, guys.'

Back up on the wall, Steven nudged Benny and added sarcastically, 'Thank's for your help, Half-Lug.'

'Anytime,' came Benny's curt reply, between beeps.

Steven wiped fresh blood on his trousers. 'Suppose I'd better go and see the nurse, later. Is she stonking or wh—'

Mark clamped a hand over Steven's mouth. '*Shhh!* Look, it's the bus driver!'

The boys followed his gaze to the wrought-iron gates, where a dishevelled man stared into the chapel grounds. Their vantage point afforded them a wider view of his approach and even from this distance they could see his clothes were drenched in dried blood from the gaping wound in his neck. His movements, when he stepped forward and reached for the gate, were stiff, robotic. Bones crunched and popped with every move when he swung one of the gates open.

Something flickered in Dylan's peripheral vision: shadows moving at speed from every corner of the graveyard before merging into a single black mass, which slithered between the graves until it reached the gate.

It was the dog from his dream.

Lowering its hind quarters, it leapt forward blocking Howard's way and tearing at his flesh. Howard tried to advance, but the black spectre resisted his every move. Howard screamed his defiance, eyes blazing with anger.

Instinct told Dylan that only he could see the spectral dog, while the others simply saw an enraged driver thumping and screaming at thin air. But they all saw his eyeshine, bright like a nocturnal creature.

Despite his injury, Steven jumped off the wall and hurtled into the chapel, screaming; quickly followed by the rest of the pupils like herded sheep, totally unaware of what they were running from.

Dylan followed a few seconds later, but a voice halted his departure.

'Kordialissss. Come to me!'

He glanced over his shoulder. The sight before him causing a strangled yelp to surge past his lips bringing with it stringy bile, which draped from mouth to shoulder like a dew covered cobweb.

Benny Half-Lug was dangling from Howard's fist, which was tugging Benny's collar skyward. Unable to breathe, Benny's body jerked violently, as though controlled by a puppet master with Parkinson's.

'Ten seconds, Kordialis!' bellowed Howard.

As the seconds passed, nobody came out of the chapel and Dylan had no idea how to save his friend. He turned towards the chapel and screamed, 'Help! ... Help him!' But no one came.

Howard shrugged, uncurled his index finger from Benny's collar, and gently touched Benny's neck. Now limp and motionless, Benny was tossed aside like a discarded coat.

Beep. Beep. Beeeep.

Dylan's eyes followed the high-pitched sound to Benny's discarded game on top of the wall and he jumped when Howard yelled for Kordialis once more.

Howard thundered forward, but the spectre remained impenetrable.

Seizing his chance, Dylan bounded for the chapel doors and almost collided with Dafydd, who had left Sarah in the chapel with the distraught kids and one very miserable caretaker to go and look for Howard.

The wind whipped up loose leaves and a whiff of mouldering, rotting meat, but there was no sign of him. Just Benny's crumpled, lifeless body.

CHAPTER 9

STAND AND DELIVER

Wednesday 16th September, 1981

Mark's semi-detached house in the Cerrig Brig estate was built onto the side of a hill, which sat lower than the road and footpath. When Dylan reached the front gate, he was at eye-level with the upstairs bedrooms, which were hidden behind dark, un-patterned, grubby curtains. He lifted the rusty catch and swung the gate inwards. The path curved down from the gate, terminating in several steep concrete steps by the front door. To the left of the gate, a large hole had been knocked through the boundary wall and a rickety wooden structure was strung across the gap, precariously fastened by two large, leaning, wooden posts. The whole thing looked as though it had been put up years ago by a blind, one-handed carpenter. An unfinished driveway behind the wall was piled high with rubble and old car parts, and partially covered by a blue, threadbare tarpaulin. The right-hand side of the footpath was lawned, but the grass had been left to grow wild. Large sods, uprooted plants, and bushes had been dumped there like a pile of dead Wookiees.

The breeze-blocks removed from the wall were stacked by the front door making it inaccessible, so Dylan walked down the side of the house and knocked on that door, which seemed to give way as he hit it.

He was brushing flakes of blue paint off his knuckles when Mark opened the door. Dylan smiled, stepped into the kitchen, and was immediately shoved back outside.

'She ... Umm ... Er ... S-She doesn't like mess in the house,' stuttered Mark, refusing to make eye contact. 'I'll be there, now. In a minute.' He slammed the door.

Dylan looked back at the garden bomb site.

She's right, all the mess is out here.

~

Light-headed and tight chested, Dylan slowed his pace as they entered the Broadmead housing estate and he became nauseous when they turned into Ebdon Road, Emily's street. Two doors down, a man blundered into their path, pointing to a shadow and muttering. Clearly agitated, he argued angrily with the shadow, the other half of the conversation unheard, before barging between the two boys muttering, 'The little bastards! Don't listen to them, boys.'

Dylan rubbed his shoulder as if he'd been hit by a train. 'What's wrong with him?'

'That's Victor, the local nutcase.'

As they continued down the street, Mark told him more about Victor Gaunt, a twenty-something mechanic who saw shadow creatures and was clearly a cornflake short of a packet.

Dylan thought about Peg-leg's appearance from the shadows. Was it the same thing? 'You sure it's creatures he sees?'

'Yeah, Calgonites, or some shit. They whisper and tell him

to do things.' He laughed, but Dylan was ashen faced. 'What's up?'

Dylan sat on the kerb and lowered his head between his knees. 'Just nerves.' Sweat had turned his fringe into dark, rat's tails.

'Shall I take the card? You look like shit, mun. It wasn't your fault Benny fell and died.'

'Don't keep on!' snapped Dylan. 'Just give me a minute. And anyway, he *didn't* fall!'

Mark held his hands up in mock surrender. Stepping on and off the kerb, fumbling with his collar, Mark asked, 'Do you fancy Emily, then?'

Dylan sneered, swatted the air with one hand, and walked away.

Mark sat on the kerb outside number six, while Dylan hesitated at Emily's gate. When he finally disappeared behind the Morris' tall privet hedge, Mark gathered small stones from the side of the kerb and began launching them across the road, aiming for a small black drain. His aim was abysmal with only one stone coming close to its target; a Storm Trooper would have done better.

Quickly out of ammunition, he squeezed his waist into one of the crenels of the garden wall and, with feet waggling in mid-air in an effort to balance himself, he stretched down until his fingertips dug around in the soil under the hedge.

Satisfied with his haul of stones, he pulled his shirt from his trousers, formed a kangaroo pouch, and stuffed the stones inside. He gingerly sat down, careful not to spill any, and was suddenly aware of someone approaching.

Howard Cobley glided slowly down the path and stopped by the opposite lamppost. He was closer than when they saw him at the chapel and Mark could now see how disheveled and torn his uniform was, as though he'd been thrown through several windscreens, not one. His hair was matted into clumps and his skin was filthy, but Mark knew it was blood, not mud, that covered his skin.

Howard appeared to be scanning the street, stopping every few seconds to sniff the air like a dog.

Instinct was telling him to run, but Mark nodded a nervous hello instead, which Howard didn't acknowledge. Unsure how to react, Mark launched another stone at the drain, which bounced off its target and landed at the driver's feet. Howard's head swivelled sideways, his pupils morphing from black, to carmine, to iridescent red.

Visceral fear froze Mark to the spot and, without taking his eyes off Howard, he screamed, 'DYLAN!'

Dylan shuffled his feet with one hand poised over the door knocker ready to knock, again. Mark screamed his name but, before he could reply, the door creaked open to reveal a bearded man with shoulders as wide as the door. The skin on his forehead squidged into neat lines when his eyes scanned Dylan.

'Yes? What do you want?' Dai demanded.

Dylan's legs shook. 'Erm ... Er ... I-I ... Umm—'

'Spit it out, mun. I haven't got all day!'

'S-S-S-Sorry, is Emily in?'

'Yeah, but she's not coming out. Who're you?'

'Dylan Wolfendale.' He handed Dai the condolence card and added, 'I've come about the money, too.'

Dai's eyes narrowed. 'We're not sponsoring anyone.' He slammed the door, causing Dylan's fringe to flick like a windscreen wiper across his forehead.

This was not the plan. He turned to leave, but Tom's words filtered into his head.

'You promised, Dylan.'

He leant forward, resting his forehead and palms against the door, while he pleaded for Mr Morris to return.

There was no response.

'I promised Tom I'd look after his butterfly. You need to know about the money ... Hello? ... Mr Morris?' He hovered his fist above the door, but the fear rumbling through his intestines threatened to buckle his knees.

You're such a loser, he thought, when his wobbly legs carried him back down the path.

'Where'd you hear that name?' asked a soft-spoken voice, stopping Dylan in his tracks.

Emily was leaning out of an upstairs window.

'Your grancha told me.'

'When?'

Dylan knew she wouldn't believe him, so he ignored the question and mumbled, 'The Grandfather clock. Tom said it's in there.'

Like a tortoise emerging from its shell, Emily's head edged past the sill. 'What is?'

'His money.'

Emily shook her head. 'He didn't have any.' Red faced, she pounded a fist on the window frame. 'Go away, you stupid boy!'

She slammed the window shut.

Dylan was devastated; upsetting Emily was the last thing he wanted. His body sagged, blood drained from his head, and bile burnt his throat. Dejected, he steadied himself, before walking toward the gate, which was slowly disappearing under an eerie, unnatural mist.

Someone called his name, but it couldn't have been Mark: the voice was behind him.

He turned, expecting to see Dai with fists clenched ready to thump him for upsetting Emily, but a much younger man stood several metres away. He wore a tatty Led Zeppelin T-shirt, faded denim jacket, and jeans that were slashed at the knees.

Dylan felt strange, woozy, and turned toward Mark for

support, but he was nowhere to be seen. When he turned back, the man was inches from his face, startling him.

'It's okay, don't be afraid, Dylan,' said the man. His voice was mellow, like a faint breeze through the trees. He extended a hand, but Dylan declined the offer. Something was weird about him, but Dylan couldn't grasp what it was.

'Hi. I'm Emily's brother, Gareth.'

'Oh, sorry,' replied Dylan, his face suddenly warm. 'I didn't know she had a brother.'

Gareth stepped closer and pulled a plastic bag from under his arm. 'Listen, this might seem strange, but I know what you can do and I can help.'

Dylan tucked his hands into his armpits, dug his elbows in tight and stared at the path.

Surely, he can't mean my dead friends? No, he must mean something else. But what?

Instinct was telling him to trust Gareth, but doubt lingered like the mist at his feet. 'I don't know what you mean,' he replied, slightly defensive.

Gareth smiled. 'Yeah, you do. That's how you knew about Tom's hidden cash. You spoke to him after he died.'

Dylan's jaw dropped and he swallowed hard, rubbing the nape of his neck.

'It's all right, I know everything, and you will too, once you read this.' Gareth held out the plastic bag. 'Take this book. It will show you everything you need to know.'

Dylan hesitated, but Gareth stepped closer. 'Here, take it.'

Dylan grabbed the bag, but Gareth's grip held firm.

'If there's anything you don't understand, the book will help, but it will only show you when you *need* to know, and not before. If you need me, I'll be there. This is just between us, okay?' He released his grip on the bag.

Dylan stood in silence for several seconds, his eyes flitting between the bag and Gareth.

'Umm, yeah, okay,' he finally said. He bent and struggled to close the gate latch. When he looked up again, Gareth was gone.

Mark's shoulder crashed into Dylan with such force that it sent him sideways into the gatepost, winding him.

'RUN!'

He grabbed Dylan by the arm and dragged him down the street causing Dylan to lose his grip on the bag, which slid across the path and into the gutter.

'Wait, the book!' Dylan wrestled with Mark, but his grip held strong.

'WE. GOTTA. RUN!'

'No,' snapped Dylan. He slowly prised one of Mark's fingers back until he screamed and let go.

'Fine!' spat Mark, looking behind Dylan with eyes wide with terror.

Over his shoulder, Dylan saw Howard bounding toward them. In one swift motion, Dylan dived into the gutter, retrieved the bag, and sped after Mark who had, inexplicably, stopped dead in the road.

'What're you doing?' bellowed Dylan, dumbfounded by his pre-occupied friend.

Mark rummaged in his pockets, pulled out a small firework then fumbled with a box of England's Glory matches. His hands trembled as he struck several along the side of the box, their heads snapping or crumbling away.

Howard was less than twenty metres away and closing fast.

'Come on!' Dylan yelled, as the fourth match finally ignited.

Mark lit the purple paper on the firework's tip, waited for the burst of sparks, then launched it at Howard, but he saw it coming and raised his hand to block it.

The banger exploded causing the windows of a nearby house to rattle.

Howard didn't flinch; he simply wiggled his little finger, which was hanging by a sliver of bloodied and burnt skin. Shock, or possibly anger, filled his face but dissolved instantly, as if blown by the wind, and a hideous smile filled the void. They watched in horror as Howard bit off the explosion ravaged finger, clenching the remains in his teeth like a bloodied cigar.

The boys bolted down the street, into alleyways, over walls and fences, through hedges and woods. They ran from street to street, eventually slumping, breathless, against the Larkmead Chapel wall, positive that they had lost him. Sweat was trickling down Dylan's spine and he leant forward, resting his hands on his knees.

'What the hell did you do?' Dylan asked, between greedy mouthfuls of air.

'I didn't do anything. He's nuts; he ate his own friggin' finger, mun!'

Dylan tutted. 'You must've done something.'

'I didn't,' he pleaded. 'One minute he was standing over the road, then the next he was roaring his head off and running at us full pelt. Weirdo.'

Dylan wiped sweat off his forehead. 'That was the bus driver.'

'Yeah, Howard Cobley, and his eyes were freaky, like a cat.'

'Freaky?'

'Yeah, you know. All shiny and shit, when you point a torch at 'em.' He panted. 'Anyway, lover boy, did you tell 'em?'

'Sort of.' He sounded sad; resigned. 'They didn't believe me.'

'Least you tried. Promise kept.' Mark pointed to the bag tucked under his arm. 'What's that?'

'Not sure. Some book. Weird though.'

'How come?'

'Dunno. Emily's brother gave it to me. He said he knew I'd spoken to Tom, after he—'

'After he what?'

Dylan shook his head. 'Doesn't matter.'

'Giz a look.' Mark lunged for the book, but Dylan snatched it out of reach.

'Nuh. I'm going home. I've gotta sort out our clothes for the funeral.'

'Won't your mam do that?'

'Yeah, course,' he corrected, looking down at the floor. 'I gotta help her, though. I'll see you tomorrow.'

Their heads spun in unison when a branch snapped behind them, but there was no tree and no branches to be seen; just Howard Cobley's bones cracking, as he climbed up over the wall behind them.

CHAPTER 10

OOPS UP SIDE YOUR HEAD

The sun was dipping behind the trees in Colledig Wood by the time Dylan safely arrived home. He paused outside the kitchen door and shivered, certain that Howard was behind him, but even in the low light he could see the garden was deserted.

The buzzing of the street lamps illuminating startled him and he cursed himself for being so jumpy.

Surprisingly, Kaelum was busy cooking tea and Dylan struggled not to laugh when he saw the bright yellow pinafore he was wearing, so he slipped into the passageway without saying a word, pulled the plastic bag from under his coat, and bounded up the stairs two at a time.

His bedroom was the box bedroom, which was another way of saying the smallest bedroom in the world. It was L-shaped due to the large cupboard built above the stairs, which left just enough room for a single wardrobe and bed. The cupboard was filled with everyone else's junk, so if his toys didn't fit under the bed or on top of the wardrobe they were sold at the next Jumble Sale because he *obviously* had far too much.

He dragged his bed against the door, and sat down. Slipping a hand inside the bag, his fingers touched something slimy and he jerked them back out. Pulling the handles slowly apart, he peered inside; the cover looked fleshy. Shock and revulsion caused a combined yelp and retch, while the bag flew through the air, bounced on the mattress, and sent the book sliding sideways onto his bedspread.

His door opened an inch and thudded into his headboard.

'Oi, dickhead! Mam's napping,' snarled Kaelum, through gritted teeth.

'Sorry, I stubbed my toe.'

When Kaelum disappeared, Dylan dropped to his knees and stared at the book. Dark metal hinges stretched the length of the book, while a menacing, crude clasp held the tome closed.

Why such a hefty lock? Was it hiding someone's precious diary or trapping something evil inside?

The book was covered in withered, rotten, dried flesh. Skin stretched toward the books spine and was sewn on with thick twine, which disappeared beneath the hinges; they, and the clasp, seemed to have been forged from old, rusty nails.

Pausing to psych himself up, Dylan stretched out a shaky hand and prodded the book. Satisfied that it wasn't going to grow limbs and articulate itself, he tried to open the clasp. Clamping the makeshift bolt between thumb and forefinger, he wiggled it. With each half-turn came a sharp metallic squeak until it finally sprung open, releasing the compressed pages with a dusty sigh. He flipped the cover to reveal worn and crinkly parchment pages with edges that looked chewed by rats and, if the cover was anything to go by, that didn't surprise him one bit; the pages were definitely human skin.

Someone had invited a colony of ants to a party on the page then slammed the book shut: none of the lettering made sense.

What ancient language is that? Why bother giving it to me if I can't read it?

The rest of the book was blank.

He gently pinched a page and his arm tingled, as though he'd touched a Van de Graaff generator, and then a strange voice filled his mind.

This knowledge will enter your mind at speed.

Don't fight it.

Breathe, or die!

A kineograph of images flashed into his mind, reforming his brain, and he felt a rush similar to downing a gallon of Slush Puppie with a brain freeze to match. When he released the page the veil of memories lifted.

He cradled his head in his hands until the pain rescinded, and gasped. Blood trickled off the end of his nose and he wiped it on the back of his hand before it reached the carpet.

He shook his head, whispering, 'Whoa! That was awesome.'

Each of the memories, clearly adult in nature, were now lodged deep into the fabric of his juvenile brain. Out of place and out of time, as though he were living them through another's eyes.

A man's, not a boy's.

He sat back against the bedroom wall, closed his eyes and tried to recall some of what he had seen.

~

He, or at least the man now in his head, stood in an endless, off-white fog that swirled around his whole being. His footsteps made no sound and there was no discernible ground beneath his feet. All around him black shadows appeared to pulse as their intensity changed. When they were close, they shifted and merged, smoke-like, into figures and faces—wispy and faint, then dark and solid. There one second, then wafted away by some unseen wind the next. Hundreds, maybe thousands, of faces flickered past his eyes in the merest of moments. He saw each one with perfect clarity, and they saw him, too.

The souls greeted his presence with love, a smile, a nod or a simple touch, and then they were gone.

But not all.

Many were unsettled.

Why me? Why now? What is going to happen to my kids, my parents, my wife, my husband, my brother, my sister … to me?

Their voices a cacophony of pain in Dylan's head. But, one caress, one consoling unspoken moment, or a winsome smile from the man behind the eyes, and they were at peace.

But not all.

Some of them felt threatened by the man's presence and reassuring touch. They didn't want to transition. They had unfinished business, or it just wasn't their time. When they saw the man with his open arms and pacifying touch they faded back into the vastness of the fog, only to reappear at another point. Those souls bounced around like black pinballs gathering anger and frustration until they forgot the reason for their restlessness—becoming all consumed with hatred for this man and the living.

Time seemed infinite in this place yet, far too often, some of the darkness found its way out through doors in the fog.

Doors that led back to the living.

Dylan felt their blackness coursing through him, as though he were actually there with them, and his eyes snapped open.

He remained on the floor staring at the book for what seemed like hours. Although he knew he should be terrified with what had happened, he wasn't. Talking to the dead for all these years made it seem normal. They were his friends, at least, that is what he hoped, anyway.

He stared up at Eddie brandishing his bloody axe on the Iron Maiden *Killers* poster on his wall.

'Let's hope they don't look like you in real life,' he whispered.

He was prone to inattentiveness and daydreaming, but this was something different; something real. In dreams, he had left his body numerous times, but since Tom's departure he wondered whether they *were* dreams.

It's the same sepia world.

'Oh, twerp. Food's ready!' Kaelum's voice boomed through the floorboards, wrenching him from his thoughts.

'Okay!' He stuffed the book into the wardrobe then made a sign of the horns hand gesture. 'Bye, Eddie.'

~

Dinner consisted of burnt baked beans, charred fish fingers, and lumpy mash. Nice one Kaelum.

Dylan moved the darkened blobs around his plate and wondered how he'd managed to burn them.

'Stop playing with your food,' Chrissy ordered, placing a hand on Kaelum's shoulder. 'He's worked hard on this tea. Haven't you, love?'

Kaelum smirked. 'Anything to help, Mam.'

Dylan lowered his head, stirred some food and offered a forkful to his mouth. It was vile, but he knew if he didn't eat it he would be the bad one. Chrissy beamed as if it were one of Fanny Cradock's finest dishes, which didn't surprise Dylan. Since Gwynfor was hospitalised, she smoked more than a pit chimney and drank gallons of 'pop,' so he doubted her tastebuds worked.

'How's school, Dylan? Making new friends?'

Kaelum laughed. 'Nope. First year kids are dropping like flys. Two dead, already. There'll be none left, soon!'

Chrissy raised her arm, sending a glare travelling along her gloopy fork. 'That's mean.'

'True, though.'

'Ignore him, Dylan. You have to mingle. You can't be shy all your life.'

Dylan's shoulders and head sagged towards his plate. 'I'm not shy. I've plenty of friends.'

'Real ones,' Kaelum snorted. 'Not imaginary ones.'

'Shut it, gormless.'

'Twat!' Kaelum leant across the table and swung at Dylan's head, barely missing his target.

Chrissy slammed her knife down. 'STOP IT! I've enough to worry about with your dad. I don't need this.' Her head dropped into her hands. Sniffing away tears, she reached for her bottle and swigged. 'Finish your food and get ready to go.'

Kaelum and Dylan exchanged confused glances.

'Hospital?' asked Kaelum, the despondency all too clear in his voice. 'I'm going out. Paul has got some tyres for my Grifter.'

Chrissy pushed her plate away and lit a fag, blowing a cloud of smoke toward Kaelum. 'Well, seeing as you cooked, you can skip tonight's visit.' She pointed a finger at him. 'But you're damn well coming next time!'

Kaelum kissed her forehead. 'Thanks Mam,' he said, before gathering the plates.

The smile on his face was too much for Dylan to bear. 'Aaaw Mam, that's not fair!' His bottom lip curled involuntarily over the top one and he sat, arms crossed, staring daggers at Kaelum, who was clearly loving every second of it as he gyrated his hips and whistled *We Are the Champions*.

Chrissy stood, took a long drag, and stubbed her fag into her remaining beans. 'I'm gonna have another lie-down. Help

Kaelum wash up and *no* arguing.' She ruffled Dylan's fluffy, blonde hair, kissed him on the cheek, and whispered, 'I love you,' in his ear, before disappearing into the passageway.

By the time Dylan had gathered his plate and cutlery, Kaelum was already half-way out the door, coat flapping off one shoulder like a cape.

~

Just after five, Dylan's uncle, John Hawker (Chrissy's cousin to be precise) honked the horn of his 1968 Volkswagen Beetle to announce his arrival and Chrissy finally emerged from the living room. She'd sat there, in the dark, for well over an hour, but Dylan knew better than to go in there uninvited. He never understood the atmosphere between Chrissy and John. They never argued. In fact, Uncle John always dropped everything to help her, but she just didn't seem to like him, which Dylan found strange. In fact, he found most human behaviour strange.

He was awkward around people, so everyone assumed he was shy, but he wasn't, not really. He preferred solitude to crowds and hated the spotlight with a vengeance; even standing at the front of class in junior school to recite his times-tables made him physically ill.

Chrissy grabbed her purse, stuffed it into her handbag and checked her hair in the passageway mirror. 'You ready, then?'

'Yeah'

'Good, 'cause you know how irritable John is.'

Actually, he didn't.

With Gwynfor in hospital, Uncle John seemed more talkative. Something was clearly bothering him, yet he would clam up when Chrissy appeared.

Adults were just too complicated unless, of course, they were dead; they were much better dead.

CHAPTER 11

UNDER PRESSURE

Trugaredd Hospital, Newport, South Wales

Gwynfor seemed chirpier tonight and Dylan noticed that he didn't take oxygen so often. With Kaelum absent, Dylan was able to speak to him uninterrupted. Also, as nobody appeared to be dying or about to die on the ward, hopefully, he wouldn't be chatting to more souls.

'You done any school sports, yet?' Gwynfor asked.

Dylan shifted uncomfortably on his plastic chair. 'A bit, not much, though.'

'Play rugby, Son. Toughen you up, see. One day you might be playing for Wales, huh?'

'Yeah,' he lied, without making eye contact.

Sport just wasn't his thing. He liked playing it amongst friends, but as soon as it became competitive he'd rather watch from the sidelines. He always worried about getting hurt, too; he was a huge cry-baby.

Gwynfor took a deep breath from his mask and sat up, so Chrissy could adjust his pillows.

'Do you remember that rugby player, Andrew something, who broke his neck playing for Draigwen?' whispered Gwynfor.

'Vaguely. Has he died, then?' asked Chrissy.

'No. He's still kicking. Well, actually, he's not … He's paralysed,' he explained, through struggled breaths. 'He's here, somewhere. I … I heard a nurse talk about him. Sad.' He sucked on the mask, while Chrissy shook her head. 'Bloody good player … Definitely on track to play … for Wales.' He coughed into his mask.

'Take it easy, Gwyn',' warned Chrissy.

'I … I'm okay,' he panted.

Dylan was gobsmacked. 'Play rugby? I don't wanna be paralysed!'

'Daft bugger. He was just … very … unlucky.' Gwynfor's oxygen levels were dropping fast and he fumbled for his mask, gulping greedily.

Chrissy stretched the straps over Gwynfor's head then reached into her purse and handed Dylan a pound note. 'Get your dad some squash and you can have 10p. We need to talk.'

'Where's the shop?'

Chrissy looked at Gwynfor.

'First … F-Floor,' came the croaked reply.

~

Andrew Thomas was just a head. He had been just a head for nearly two months. Two months since the rugby scrum collapsed, breaking his neck in two places and severing his spinal cord. Paralysed from the neck down, Andrew had nowhere to run and nowhere to hide, apart from his own mind. Propped up on several pillows, Andrew stared emotionless through the open door into the corridor.

A small boy with a horrendous basin cut hairstyle, polar-neck jumper, and green corduroy trousers, stood with his back to the room. His head flicked left and right, as though he were about to cross a busy road.

'You lost?' shouted Andrew.

Dylan turned and peered into the room. In the bed, swamped in tubes and wires, lay a man. On the wall above him a sign read, 'Andrew Thomas - Nil by mouth,' in large black writing.

'Just looking for the shop,' answered Dylan.

Andrew twitched his nose. His lip curling upward to blow air over it. 'Scratch my nose, will you?'

Dylan crept nervously into the room, taking care not to trip over any equipment, and stretched out his arm. Withdrawing his hand inside his jumper, he rubbed his cuff on Andrew's twitching nose.

'Oh, that's nice. Thanks—'

Dylan stared blankly at him for several moments before responding. 'Oh, sorry. Dylan.'

'Thanks Dylan. Don't let me stop you,' he snorted.

Dylan shook his head, breaking eye contact. He hadn't realised he was staring, open-mouthed. He paused by the door, considered something, then looked over his shoulder. 'Are you that rugby player with the broken neck?'

'Yep. Famous for cocking up. Good, huh? I'd shake your hand, but I can't be bothered,' he said, with a wry smile.

Dylan's mouth opened but, unsure how to reply, he simply half-waved and stepped into the corridor.

'Hey, Dylan! Do me another favour?'

'Wha'?'

Andrew nodded into the corner. 'See that machine, over by there?'

'Yeah.'

'Turn it off, will you. It's too noisy. I can't sleep.'

Dylan strolled up to the machine and stared at its vast

array of knobs, switches and lights. On the same trolley was a large, green screen, similar to the science lab oscilloscopes. A small bright dot drew squiggles in time with the rugby player's heartbeat.

'Just follow the black cable on the side and switch it off.'

Dylan leant forward, traced the cable, and paused. 'Wait, isn't this keeping you alive?'

Andrew rolled his eyes. 'Oh, don't worry 'bout a little thing like that. Just knock it off, mun.'

Dylan shook his head. Although the dead seemed to have a propensity to talk to him, he didn't want to add another to their numbers. 'I can't. That's murder.'

A tear welled in the corner of Andrew's eye before sliding down his cheek. His face reddened and he croaked, 'Oh well, worth a try.'

'I can sit with you for a bit, if you like?' suggested Dylan.

'Maybe next time, eh?'

'Okay.' Dylan smiled. 'I'm here most nights visiting my dad.'

Andrew turned away without replying and Dylan stood in silence for several seconds before carefully retreating back out of the room.

'Ta-ta,' he said softly, sadly.

'Oh, butt'!' hollered Andrew. 'Shop's on the first floor, past the lifts. If you reach the toilets, you've gone too far.'

Dylan smiled and threw a thumb up.

~

Dylan hated hospitals.

Before he had returned to his father's bedside with a bottle of apple and blackcurrant squash, he had escorted Ethel Warburton, aged seventy-four, with COPD, and car crash victim Charlie Brace, aged just fifty-two, to the other side.

Ethel departed wearing the pyjamas she had died in, but Charlie was naked apart from blood drenched underpants, resulting from the gaping hole in his chest. He tried to thank Dylan but, as his lower jaw was missing, he just gurgled and nodded. Although horrific, Dylan was more terrified by the shadows multiplying in the lobby. Something was coming; he could feel it.

A plethora of pillows held Gwynfor upright and he nodded when Dylan approached. He croaked a thank you. His mask now permanently fixed to his face, squidging the skin on his cheeks and forehead into puffy red mounds.

Dylan passed the bottle and change over the bed to his mother's waiting hands and sat down. He told them that the paralysed rugby player, Andrew, had asked to die, but they didn't believe him. When they eventually stopped laughing, Dylan was no longer in the mood to talk and he sulked in his chair, arms crossed, looking like he had just smelt a turd.

'Oh, stop sulking. We were laughing with you, not *at* you,' explained Chrissy, trying to pacify him. She held out her arms beckoning him toward her. 'Come and give me a cwtch.'

Her arms enveloped him, forcing his head into her warm bosom, which would have been comforting if the Anais Anais perfume had diminished the stench of stale smoke.

'Carry on, Dylan,' breathed the Sith Lord.

Dylan sat on the edge of his father's bed and composed himself.

'Okay, he didn't *ask* to be killed, but he wanted me to switch off his machine. That's the same thing, isn't it?'

Gwynfor nodded, and rubbed a spade-sized hand across Dylan's shoulder.

'Well, I said no, and left. He seemed really sad. I'm sure he was crying.'

'I'm not surprised, Son, b-being ... paralysed must ... ruin a man and—' Gwynfor coughed violently and Chrissy put a finger to her mouth.

'Shush. That's enough talking. Time to rest.' She gently lifted up his mask and kissed him goodnight.

Uncle John weaved the Beetle like a demented clown through Wattsville on their way back to the Cerrig Brig estate, sending Dylan's arse sliding from side-to-side over the vinyl seat. The car was Kaelum's age and apart from a bit of rust around the wheel arches and the lack of number 53 stickers and stripes, it looked just like Herbie.

John stretched across Chrissy's lap, flipped the glove compartment open and flicked through a pile of 8-track cassettes before selecting one and sliding it into the player. The dulcet tones of Nana Mouskouri's voice crackled out of the speakers either side of Dylan's seat but even she couldn't compete with his exaggerated coughing when Chrissy's lungs filled the car with plumes of smoke. She slid an ashtray from the centre console, but before she could flick her ash, John stopped her with his hand.

The tray was full of loose change.

'Out the window,' he commanded.

She dutifully wound it down. The tip of her fag glowed red in the wind before flying back towards Dylan.

John tutted. 'You ought to pack that shit in. It's not good for you, or them,' he said, jabbing his thumb backwards.

She launched the remainder of her fag out of the window and reached deep into her handbag, pulling out a shiny, silver hip flask, which Dylan instantly recognised as his father's.

John shook his head. 'Really? That as well? Isn't it time you accepted what happened to Louisa?'

Chrissy's head snapped around and she bared tobacco

stained teeth when her nostrils flared. 'Don't you dare mention that!' she scolded.

Dylan popped his head between the front seats. 'How *did* Auntie Louisa die?'

Chrissy dug in her bag, lit another fag and stared out of her window without replying. Only Nana's voice filled the car until it finally turned into their estate.

'Will Gwynfor be discharged, soon?' asked John, breaking the silence, but Chrissy remained silent. 'Is it bad, then?'

Chrissy took a long gulp from the flask, coughed, and sprayed drink over the dashboard. She wiped her mouth and put the flask away. 'Just watch the road,' she snapped.

Dylan had no idea how ill his father was, either, because his mother wouldn't tell him. "*You're too young*," or "*You wouldn't understand*," was all she ever said. Although, his all time favourite had to be, "*Not now, Dylan!*" as that one seemed to cover every situation. But had his parents lied about Louisa's death?

How did Louisa dying make me a miracle child?

During the last few silent miles his thoughts wandered back to Dean, who scared him more than ghosts; they were just dead, so they couldn't hurt him. Could they?

When the Beetle swung into their estate, Dylan lifted his cheek off the car window, wiped the breath mist away with his sleeve, and watched a blurred Howard Cobley whizz past his vision.

CHAPTER 12
GOING UNDERGROUND

It was just shy of nine P.M. when Dylan snuck out of the house leaving his mother to her Embassy cigarettes and cheap Leo's supermarket vodka. Kaelum was the scarlet pimpernel again, so it wouldn't take his mother long to drink herself to sleep uninterrupted.

The sun was low in the sky and he estimated he had less than an hour of useable light. Over his shoulder was a small, brown bag covered in pin badges; inside was his homework, pen, walkie, penknife, Pac-a-Mac, torch, and Bazooka bubble gum (more for the Bazooka Joe comic rather than the gum itself).

He straddled his silver Raleigh Strika but rode stood up—force of habit, after slipping off the saddle of Kaelum's Grifter and jamming his testicles between the mudguard and knobbly tyre, which hammered his nuts faster than a midget on a speedball. The Strika was too small for him, but Kaelum refused to pass on his Grifter, despite having two bikes.

Mid-way down Valley View, he swung a hard left through a broken chain-link fence into Colledig Wood and followed a dirt track, which wound its way from the Cerrig Brig estate towards the Broadmead estate. After several minutes, he left the track and cut through a tall fern field, with only his head in view, before breaking out the other side into a small clearing beside dense woods. Dominating the skyline was a huge weeping willow surrounded by hawthorn bushes and stinging nettles. The boys camp.

Half a mile further, the woods thinned and the rear drystone wall of Larkmead chapel rose up before him on the east bank of the Rhymney valley. Dylan made his way down the left-hand side where he ditched his Strika, climbed the wall, and dropped down behind a yew tree. He knew Arwel had seen him in the graveyard many times, but he still preferred not to announce his arrival.

Even in the low light, the graveyard was alive with colour. The long meadow grass at the back of the grounds was dotted with oxeye daisies, yellow rattle and the occasional poppy. The lichen's greys, greens, and yellows gave the gravestones a feeling of warmth despite the eerie shadows that they had begun to create. When he crept through the graves, several bats danced overhead causing him to think of black-and-white horror films, and his shoulders jerked from an icy shiver. He loved watching them swoop through the graveyard picking off midges mid-flight before flying back up under the chapel's roof gable, so he was annoyed with himself for being scared.

He held his breath, motionless, listening to the faint fluttering of their wings and wished he could hear their high-pitched calls, too. They were busier this time of year, preparing for winter hibernation.

He dumped his bag by the side of his grandparents' grave and hoisted himself up, swinging his legs over the front of the cold stone. Silent, he listened to the roosting bats and the distant *tu-whit tu-whoo* of a pair of tawny owls.

When he was certain there was nobody around, he whispered, 'Nan? Grancha?'

There was no reply.

Seconds seemed like minutes and he felt his heart rate rising. He blew out hard and wiped his sweaty palms on his thighs.

The dead don't sleep; had he lost his ability?

'My Action Man!' Where've you been?'

The voice startled him. It popped into his head with such clarity that he spun around looking for the source, positive that there was someone there.

It was his grandmother, Keziah. After an ear bashing for not coming sooner, Dylan shook their headstone with excited kicks as he regaled them with the details of Tom's revenant, the crashed bus, and its weird driver. They listened intently; what else could they do? Then, as always, they argued, and Dylan quickly lost interest until his grandmother mentioned that she had always known he had the gift of sight.

'Sight? But I can't see you,' he said, and instantly felt stupid for looking around.

There were no bones walking towards him, or zombie granny sat beside him.

'Doesn't mean you couldn't if you really wanted to. Have you seen Transmogoria, yet?' she asked.

'Transma—'

'Transmogoria. It's where the souls go after death to transport.'

His grandad's voice rose up through the soil and filled his head as though he were sat beside him.

'Transition, not transport, you twp!' Lazarus corrected.

Dylan stifled a laugh. 'Not sure, Nan. Everything goes brown. There's strange shadows and blurry doors, like Tom went through.'

'Tom the bins, or Tom the coal?' asked his grandmother.

'I thought you'd know, Nan. Isn't he with you lot, now?'

His insincerity cut Keziah deep.

'Us lot? Do you know everyone living *in Draigwen? No! So how'd you expect us to know every dead one?'*

Dylan pictured his grandmother sitting by the coal fire, the *clickety clacking* of her knitting needles stopping abruptly and her stern, admonishing eyes burning into the back of his skull.

'Sorry, Nan. It was Tom the coal.'

'Sad. Your Grancha knew him.'

The cold night air started to creep through his clothes and he wiped his nose on his sleeve. 'Did you know him well, Granch'?'

'Yes, lovely man. Brilliant gardener, too. How's his family?'

'Upset. Tom made me promise to tell them about some hidden money. I thought I'd dreamt it, but now—'

'A promise is a promise. Don't you go upsetting the dead.'

Dylan shivered. 'I wouldn't,' he replied, adamant. 'I told them, but they didn't believe me. Nobody ever believes me.'

He was sure he felt his grandmother stamp her feet below him.

'Be confident and stop putting yourself down. You'll never get anywhere if you don't push ...'

The sound of his grandmother's voice drifted to a low murmur, as if someone had lowered the volume on the radio inside his head and his mind drifted.

After a few minutes of ignoring her waffling, he remembered something Uncle John had said.

'Nan, how did Louisa die?'

BOOM! The radio hit full volume.

'OH. MY. LORD!'

Her voice was so loud in his head that he fell backwards off the gravestone and landed with a thud in the long grass.

'Laz', you'll have to tell him. I can't. I just can't!' she wailed.

'What's wrong?' asked Dylan, clambering back onto their gravestone.

'Long story, but you deserve to know. Where do I begin? ... Right. It started with Daniel Hawker, my nephew. It happened the day you were born and it destroyed our—'

A low guttural voice interrupted his grandad's story which, not for the first time tonight, sent Dylan sprawling backwards onto the floor.

'Dylaaaannnnn! ... Dylaaaannnnn!' droned the voice.

Dylan shuffled his bum across the grass until his back was against the gravestone. He clamped his hands to his mouth, silencing his groans, and desperately tried to calm his breathing. He stole a glance over the top of the stone and saw an angel statue, roughly six metres away, which towered above the other gravestones, its wings casting long, curved, shadows. A dark hooded figure emerged from those shadows and moved slowly towards him.

'Dylaaaannnnn!'

Dylan belted towards the front gates, but his ankle twisted on the uneven ground and he fell forward into a gravel pit in front of a wonky ancient crypt, its large wooden doors obscured by cracked stone blocks. As the dark hooded figure loomed over him, Dylan quickly swung his torch beam upwards to reveal Mark laughing like a drunken monk.

'Dickhead!' spat Dylan, rubbing his painful ankle.

'Language, Dylan!'

Dylan apologised to his grandmother, then realised what he'd done. He avoided Mark's gaze.

'It's okay. I heard you talking to them, earlier. Hiya, Nana and Grancha Wolfendale.'

Dylan shook his head. 'It's Hawker, not Wolfendale,' he corrected. 'They're my mam's parents, and they can't hear you.'

Mark tilted his head and frowned. 'How do you know?' he asked, smiling. 'Maybe I'm a weirdo, too.' He plonked himself down, cross-legged on the path, and began tugging at the long strands of grass sprouting out of a nearby grave surround.

'Nan, Granch', Mark says hello.'

'Gwendolyn's boy?' asked his grandmother.

'Yes.'

'Oh, he's lovely. Say hello. How is Gwendolyn? Is she and Paul back together, yet? Such a shame, she—'

Dylan shook his head and tried to block her out. 'My nan said hi.'

'Tidy. Sorry about you ankle.'

'That's okay. How long have you known?'

'Ages. You're always talking to someone; I just couldn't hear the replies. I read about it in the occult books; It's called necro' something or other. So, how's this happening to you, then?'

Dylan shrugged. 'Wish I knew. It's only since they died that I realised my ...' He held up his fingers to make inverted commas in the air. '... *friends* were dead and not imaginary.'

'That's awesome. Is it scary?'

'Not really.'

'Are you gonna tell Emily? She might go out with you, then. Girl's love superheroes.'

Dylan stood, brushed himself down and limped forward to retrieve his bag. 'I'd better go. It's getting dark.'

'Oi! You didn't answer me,' reminded Mark, slapping him too hard on the back causing Dylan's ankle to give away.

Mark watched in horror as the weathered crypt doors cracked and splintered under the strain of Dylan's weight against the stone blocks, and Dylan was devoured by the crypt's darkness, engulfing Mark in a cloud of dust.

Mark coughed violently. 'You okay, Dylan?'

Seconds passed like minutes, then muffled scraping and short, strained, coughs echoed from below. 'I'm okay,' spluttered Dylan, searching for his torch.

He brushed loose stone and chunks of wood aside and ran his hands over the floor until he felt something long and round. An electric pulse shot up his arm, which tugged at his whole body drawing him closer, but it wasn't his torch. He used the stick to move rubble and, after a while, he felt the smooth plastic of his torch and flicked the switch.

Nothing happened.

He sat up and banged it with the stick until the torch finally flickered to life, illuminating the damp crypt. Swinging the beam, he took in his surroundings expecting to see a coffin or the disintegrated remains of one. There was no coffin; just a floor littered with bones, just like the one in his other hand.

He screamed and threw it.

'Shit, what's up?' shouted Mark.

'Bones ... Just bones.'

Dylan scrambled to his feet, but pain shot up his leg and he felt woozy. He cradled his head and felt dampness in his hair. He rubbed the gritty, sticky, blood and dirt mixture between finger and thumb before a wave of nausea struck. He sat back down, mumbling, 'I don't feel well.'

Sudden movement caused him to glance upwards. His torch beam guided his focus, but blinded Mark's.

'Not in my eyes, you tit!'

Dylan lowered the torch and watched Mark clamber over broken planks and rubble. He dragged a flat stone across the floor next to Dylan, sat down, dug his balled fists into his sides and looked straight at him.

'Well, here's another nice mess you've gotten me into.'

They both burst into laughter.

~

When the dust settled, Mark surveyed the devastation and nodded towards the scattered bones. 'Gross.'

Dylan dabbed at the cut on his head with his sleeve and winced. 'Yeah. He must have been poor. He's got no coffin.'

'Why's he got a massive crypt, then?' asked Mark, scratching his chin. 'It doesn't make sense.'

'There's animal bones, too,' noted Dylan, pointing to a jaw with long, sharp, canines. 'C'mon lets get out of here before Arwel shows up.'

'Who's Arwel?' asked Mark, helping Dylan to his feet.

'The caretaker. That old guy opposite the chapel, with the Robin Reliant.'

'Oh, him. How do you know his name?'

'Miss Lewis mentioned him on the art trip. He's caught me in here loads of times, but he doesn't complain.'

Mark pointed up at the busted doors. 'Well, if he sees this mess, you're done for.'

A breeze swayed the remains of the doors, which squeaked on rusty hinges, their planks so darkened with age that they actually looked burnt.

Could they bodge them shut and get the hell out of there?

Dylan wasn't so sure. His torch beam snagged on something on the back of the doors causing eerie shadows, which piqued his interest. He crawled forward, his fingers tracing the unnatural vertical grooves, and he shivered uncontrollably.

'What is it?' Mark asked, joining him by the entrance. 'Are they knots?'

Dylan shook his head. 'No, not knots. Nail marks.'

'Hammered in?'

'No. Nails,' he said, waving his fingers at him. 'That guy must have done it.'

They both turned and stared at the scattered bones. The dead man's skull peeking out from under a plank of wood; its dark, empty, eye sockets staring up at them.

'Buried alive,' they said in unison.

Dylan gripped Mark's shoulders, lifted his sprained ankle, and hopped out of the crypt.

Pulling the remains of the doors together as best he could, Mark tied them with a piece of lace cut from his scruffy basketball boots, then stepped back to admire his work.

'Not bad, eh?'

Dylan shone the beam over the entrance and there, carved into the damaged lintel, were the letters, 'P KING.'

'Very good. Mr King would be proud.'

'Huh?'

Dylan pointed to the lintel.

'P King? He must have been a duck!' laughed Mark.

Dylan waggled his finger and tutted. 'Never speak ill of the dead.'

'I'm not. He'd be happy with that, mun.'

Dylan shook his head causing Mark's eyes to widen, despite the torchlight glistening off them.

'Why not?'

'What about the shattered stone blocks that are supposed to cover the doors? You can't tie them.'

'Oh.'

Dylan closed Mark's gaping mouth and hobbled towards the gate; climbing the wall to retrieve his bike wasn't an option.

Two pairs of eyes watched them go: One pair of eyes glowed like distant car brake lights while the other pair, belonging to a young boy, stared in disbelief as the unnatural red eyes glided through the graveyard.

When Mr Red Eyes passed the boy's hiding place, the boy slowly turned his head and watched him fade into the distance. When he disappeared out of sight near the main gate, the boy bolted out from behind a headstone, dropped the bag he was carrying, and ran through the graves, down the driveway, to the main gate.

When he clocked the thick, rusty chain draped around the gates like an old brown scarf, he scaled the wall, instead. His head slowly peered over the top; eyes furtively searching for signs of movement.

Arwel's beloved three-wheeled Robin Reliant was parked on the street outside his house and, for once, it hadn't been vandalised by the skinheads from Pontyfechan.

They must be Paki' bashing, thought the boy.

Only last week, they had overturned Arwel's car and slid it into the main road. Some paintwork and fibreglass was ruined but, other than that, it was fine. Arwel refused to speak out, but he had no problem finding his voice tonight; his speech was loud and frantic.

The boy couldn't see past Arwel's car, so he shifted along the wall until he could. Illuminated by the street lamp, Arwel was arguing with a man in dark uniform. Mr Red Eyes.

He grabbed hold of Arwel's arm and, although Arwel didn't retaliate, the boy watched in awe as Mr Red Eyes instantly collapsed at Arwel's feet, without a single punch being thrown. The man was motionless.

Somehow, Arwel murdered him.

A wry smile split the boy's face. He wouldn't get into trouble for being in the graveyard, now. Arwel would have to overlook it: he needed a good witness to backup his self-defence story.

Glowing with confidence, the boy leapt off the wall and landed on the pavement with a thud, alerting Arwel to his presence. When the boy looked across the road, Arwel stared back at him with glowing, red eyes.

The boy ran.

CHAPTER 13
VIENNA

Thursday 17th September, 1981

Fiona arrived at the station at five A.M., two hours earlier than normal at the Inspector's request, so she could help clear up the mess in the police club after the previous night's shenanigans.

Officers from every police division in Gwent had competed in a snooker tournament throughout the summer, and last night was the big final. Jukesy invited her, but when she shunned his advances he happily told the Inspector that she would *love* to come in early, without claiming overtime, just to do her 'bit' to help.

While she cleared the tables and emptied dregs into a bowl, the stench of fags and stale beer made her gag, and her mind conjured up revenge against the slimy twat. The more she thought, the more painful the revenge became and, after finding her police photo full of holes on the dartboard, she decided to think of something else before she ended up planning Jukesy's funeral.

She finished just before six-thirty, which gave her just over thirty minutes before shift started; plenty of time to make herself a coffee before the hangover crowd bimbled through the door.

After she left the club, she stuck her head into the Custody Unit to see how many 'guests' had stayed over.

The duty custody sergeant, Bill Parkes, from Tredegar, nodded and pointed to the cells. 'Any of that lot yours? There's one burglar and four drunk and disorderlies, and three of them are coppers!'

Fiona laughed. 'Really? No taxis available, then?' She slid a metal catch to the side and lowered the viewing hatch of the nearest cell and peered inside. Green and magnolia walls, wooden bench with no mattress, and one snoring plod. 'Is that Simon Davies?'

Bill flicked through the custody logs. 'Erm, could be. He mumbled "Simon" then tried to kiss me, so I bundled him in straight away. Is he on shift today, then?'

Fiona smirked. 'Yep, in about thirty minutes. Somehow, I don't think he'll make it!'

'I beg to differ. The buckets are ready,' he said, pointing at the front of the custody suite desk.

Fiona peered over the top, dipped her hand in, and whipped it back out sharpish. 'That's bloody freezing!'

'Yep. Perfect alarm clock. Whether they are mustered, in uniform, and *compos mentis* by seven is down to them.'

Fiona would have loved to have stayed to watch, but caffeine was calling.

~

Tony was as cheerful as ever, and she wondered what he did, or didn't do, in his spare time to make him so happy at work.

Whatever it was, he was good to have around, especially when she was on one of her off-days. She made him a cuppa and sat with him in the enquiry office.

Station chatter was rife about Ian Pritchard's death, but the autopsy had revealed nothing; it was as if his soul had just upped and left. Fiona suspected a heart attack, but why hide his body in the woodwork class bin? His classmates were the last to see him alive and, according to Mr Harwood, after Ian had gone to the toilet, nobody saw him again.

Tony had already taken a few calls and had the *perfect* job for Fiona. Anyone else and she would have suspected sarcasm, but not Tony; he hadn't shat on her; not yet, anyway.

Two calls had come in within fifteen minutes of each other from the same concerned gentleman, a Reverend Alfred Foster, of Larkmead Chapel.

The first call concerned the vandalisation of an ancient burial crypt, which he was very upset about as, apparently, that crypt contained the first person to be laid to rest at Larkmead, back in the early nineteenth century. The second call, which was much more bizarre, related to the grisly discovery of a bag of animal remains on one of the graves.

Satanic rituals and zombies were popping into Fiona's head and she was eager to get there. It must have shown because Tony's eyes went wide and the deep lines on his forehead pushed his bushy eyebrows together like kissing caterpillars.

'Whoa! Calm down, missy!' he said, patting down the air in front of him with both hands. 'I know this one sounds exciting, but you can't just go charging in there like a bull in a cattle market, you'll need to—'

'China shop,' corrected Fiona, and instantly regretted it.

'Sorry?'

'Doesn't matter. Sorry, Sarge. You were saying?'

Tony slurped on his coffee and gave her a thumbs up.

'Mmmm, nice. Where was I? Oh, yeah. Softly, softly with this one. There's a funeral, today, so don't make the force, or me, regret sending you in. Okay?'

Fiona grabbed her coffee mug with two hands and took a big sip. 'Calm as can be, Sarge.'

'Good. Make your way there anytime, but don't expect the reverend to be available until after the service. His caretaker's AWOL, which is out of character for him, but he can't have gone far.'

'All right, no problem. I'll finish my paperwork and take a gander before the service starts. I can catch up with the reverend, later. Do we have a working camera?'

'Don't know,' he shrugged. 'Check the V&A cabinet. The combination code is the bottom two buttons together and then the top one.'

Fiona's jaw dropped.

He had entrusted her with the code to the 'valuable and attractive' equipment locker. Usually, only sergeants and above had access, so she felt privileged.

Inside the locker, she found a couple of Kodak Disc cameras and three fixed-lens 35mm Nikon cameras with slings. Despite only having fifteen exposures per disc, she opted for the Disc camera due to its compact size and grabbed a box of film. She signed them all out, inserted a fresh disc into the camera and pocketed the rest.

'Find one?' asked Tony.

'Yes,' she replied, holding it aloft.

'Good. How come you didn't go to the club last night? Boyfriend wouldn't let you out?'

'I don't have one,' she said, blushing. 'I just didn't fancy it.'

The front desk window slid open with a squeak and two feverish looking officers squeezed their heads through the opening.

'Well, if it isn't Bodie and Doyle,' chuckled Tony, while Jukesy and Simon stared at him.

'*Sssh*, not so loud, Sarge,' whispered Simon. 'Jukesy's gotta bad head.'

'Oh, and you're perfectly fine?' asked Fiona.

'Nothing wrong with me, Doris. I'm cracking,' he said, smirking. 'Any chance of a cuppa, love?'

Fiona hated female coppers being referred to as 'Doris' and snarled, 'Make your own!'

'Ooooh, touchy. Did someone grow some balls last night?' sneered Jukesy.

Tony stepped forward and grabbed the handle of the sliding window. 'Leave Brasking alone, at least she's doing some police work. Now, piss off before I put you both on report for being late!' He slid the window shut with a clank and nearly took their faces off in the process. Turning to Fiona he said, 'Don't let them bully you. They were in your shoes not so long ago.'

Fiona shrugged. 'I know, its just, you know ... Different being a woman.'

'You're a woman?' Tony asked, his mouth dropping in an exaggerated gape.

She picked up their empty cups. 'Yeah, I'm about to wash the dishes, so I must be,' she said, with a wink.

~

Dark clouds appeared as Fiona stepped through the small gate in the rear wall of Larkmead Chapel's graveyard and she emerged between two, huge yew trees that dominated the grounds and swathed a vast area in eerie shadow. When she left the tree's canopy, the cold, empty silence was dissected by the light patter of rain on her hat, and the swish and flick of her skirt through the tall, cocksfoot grass.

While she wondered why the caretaker hadn't cut the grass, the patter of raindrops increased and a cold breeze funnelled through the graveyard.

She shivered, but not from the breeze.

A strange, dark, foreboding flooded her senses, which felt like her entire soul was being crushed in a vice. Sharp pain stung behind her right ear, as though some unseen person had stubbed a fag on her scalp. She took her hat off, ran her fingertips behind her ear, and felt the rough edges of her childhood scar.

It felt hot.

A figure slid past the gate, startling her.

Was that the caretaker?

When the figure disappeared from view, the dark feeling she experienced drifted away like the rain clouds. She closed her eyes, looked skywards, and felt the late morning sun warm her skin. A rainbow had formed and its end, complete with its pot of gold, dipped out of reach behind the trees.

The reverend was adamant that the grisly discovery was cleared away before the funeral procession arrived and Environmental Health Services were already on their way, so Fiona knew she had to take photographs quickly before the remains were disposed of.

She stepped out of the long grass, brushed seeds from her skirt hem, and walked gingerly down the narrow, uneven, path between the graves. Here, the grass was short and shiny like a lawn but as her eyes followed the path, dark patches began appearing. Glistening globules of blood stuck to the blades of grass much like the revolting smell that was now stuck to the back of her throat.

She didn't need to check the inscription on the headstone to know this was the grave Reverend Foster had mentioned; the blood spatters on the aged stonework's lettering was a big hint. A Carrefour plastic carrier bag at the base of the gravestone had spilt part of its contents over the surrounding area and Fiona retched as she stretched her fingers into rubber gloves and cursed herself for forgetting a mask.

Before her was a gruesome collection of decapitated animal heads and corpses. Mice, rats, rabbits, birds and even a cat's head with its pink, bloodied tongue poking out between its front teeth. The floor was littered with giblets, feathers, and torn limbs and, on closer inspection, she could see that some of the bones had saw marks.

They weren't killed; they were butchered.

She knelt down and, while covering her mouth and nose with one hand, she peeked inside the bag.

On top of what remained of the cat was the beautiful chest and feathers of a Kestrel, her favourite bird of prey, and she could make out a small, circular wound to the centre of the bird's chest, possibly from an air rifle pellet. The last time she had seen a Kestrel was at the Welsh Hawking Centre in Barry, as a child, and she couldn't help but weep.

'Sick bastards,' she mumbled, before her sleeve became an unwilling tissue for her runny nose, and she tried to compose herself before taking pictures.

She laid out the grisly array of animal carcasses and snapped her way through several discs before carefully returning each body part to the bag, including the spilt items that were scattered across the graves. Confident that she had enough evidence, she picked up the bag and carried it out through the back gate and leant it against the outside wall. There was still no sign of the caretaker.

She turned the bloodied gloves inside out and dropped them into the bag, unclipped her radio and contacted the station.

Tony said he would ring Mr Davies' house and let him know she needed his assistance at the rear of the grounds. The funeral procession was already arriving, so all she could do was wait until Arwel, or EHS, turned up.

Standing by a gravestone, she bowed her head in respect and watched a shadow slide over her foot. She spun around searching for the source and was confronted by more shadows, sliding up and over gravestones, rolling over flowers and wreaths, before combining into a single mass.

CHAPTER 14

THE MAN WITH THE CHILD IN HIS EYES

Corroded wrought-iron letters spelt out the words 'Larkmead Chapel' in the archway overhead as the cavalcade passed through the gates and wound its way up the gravel driveway.

The shiny, black Ford Granadas crunched to a halt outside the chapel doors and Dylan watched Emily's family disembark. Dai tugged his suit jacket down at the sides and straightened his tie. He paused to look at Tom's coffin draped with a Welsh flag.

A high-pitched wailing to the rear of the grounds, far from the mourners, turned Dylan's head that way. The shrieking grew louder and closer, but he couldn't see the source. The chapel grounds, towards the east wall, were empty except for an area of long grass leading to several proud yew trees casting unnatural opposing shadows. Dylan watched in astonishment as the shadows started moving, like spilt blobs of black mercury, before converging in one spot amongst the long grass and rising slowly upwards, forming a dark figure.

It was a man; his wizened flesh struggled to coat his skeletal frame. Sinews like taut elastic bands bulged from beneath the merest of skin when his hands appeared below the maculate sleeves of his suit jacket. His head swivelled in Dylan's direction like some demonic, possessed doll. The face was disfigured, like a burns victim void of skin grafts. Unkempt black hair poured down the sides of his face, spilling onto his jacket. Dylan was lost in his rufescent eyes; they burnt through his retinas and stung his mind.

Towards the back of the graveyard, beside a lone policewoman, shadows morphed into a dog. Sitting back on its hind legs, the dog raised a paw and stared up at her, but her eyes were fixated on the old man who had dropped to his knees.

Looking skyward, his mouth opened abnormally wide, revealing long, blackened teeth within his fragile skull while he wailed.

Something touched Dylan's shoulder causing him to scream and fling his hands out to protect himself.

'Whoa! Calm down,' said Mark. 'It's only me.'

'Shit! You scared me.'

'I'm not surprised. You were in a world of your own, *again*.'

'*Phew*, glad it's you. That screaming old bloke freaked me out.'

'Which one?' quizzed Mark, looking at the mourners lining the drive.

Dylan grabbed Mark's shoulder and spun him around. 'No, not them, that guy over there.' He pointed at the overgrown grass below the trees. But the old guy, and the shadows that had brought him there, were gone.

'That's not an old man. That's a woman, and she's a copper!'

Fiona searched in-between rows of graves just a few metres from where the shadow man had been. After a few moments, she paused to look at the mourners.

'Bollocks! The crypt. They know it's us,' whispered Dylan.

'No, they don't. How would they? Nobody saw us.'

'Maybe Arwel told them?'

With Tom's coffin and family entering the chapel, Chrissy tugged on Dylan's arm. 'C'mon, you two. Stop yakking and behave yourselves,' she ordered, leading them inside.

Mark turned to Dylan and mouthed the words, 'Say nothing.'

Dylan spent most of the service glancing nervously at the door expecting the police to storm in. The reverend stated it was a celebration of Tom's life, yet no-one was happy. Dylan assumed that would come later, when the sad thoughts were drowned in alcohol back at Draigwen's rugby club.

Both Dai and the reverend gave powerful eulogies, which caused a flood of emotion that Dylan didn't know how to react to and when he saw Emily crying it made him angry.

They sang two songs, *Calon Lân* and *Amazing Grace*. The latter was his grandmother's favourite song and Dylan could hear her singing along in his head during the service.

Later, when Tom was wheeled out, Dylan tried really hard to make himself cry, but he just couldn't do it. When Emily and her family walked past, he simply looked away. He had helped Tom transition, as his grandad had put it, so he didn't feel sad.

Handfuls of soil thumped the top of Tom's coffin, tears flowed, and Dylan kept his dry eyes, and his thumping head, lowered. Sunlight sparkled off the brass plaque bearing Tom's name and he glanced towards the crumpled crypt and shivered.

At least you weren't buried alive, he thought.

'No, I'm at peace, thanks to you.'

Tom's voice startled him and he slipped on the freshly dug soil around the grave. He stopped himself from falling in but not before sending a ton of soil crashing down onto the coffin. Before apologetic words could grace his lips, Chrissy's nails dug deep into his arm and she yanked him backwards.

'Careful!' she hissed, before mouthing an apology to everyone.

'You're hurting me,' whined Dylan, trying to pull free, but she held firm.

'Tough.'

Dragged to the back of the mourners, Dylan could no longer see their glaring, accusing faces, so he was happy to stay put. From his new vantage point he could see the policewoman across the graveyard, arms crossed and head bowed in silent respect, and he wondered how much more trouble he was going to be in before he got home, *if* he ever did.

He nudged Mark. 'Do you think she knows?' he whispered, his reddened cheeks replaced with bleached, fearful skin.

Mark shrugged and ducked back behind his father, Paul, who, once again, had materialised unannounced this morning with another guilt gift for Mark.

He and Gwendolyn had divorced when Mark was only four and his father never really conversed with him. Mark didn't hate his father; he just didn't know him. He'd much prefer it if he stayed around long enough to *actually* help his mother, rather than just turning up all 'teeth and grins' and stinking of Brut whenever it suited him with another cheap, knock-off, present under his arm for Mark and his older brother, Darren. Although, in some ways, he did help in a convoluted sort of way because Mark always sold his father's guilt gifts and then snook the money into his mother's purse.

Once the funeral cortege had left for the wake, the rest of the mourners began filtering away in dribs and drabs. Chrissy was adamant she was going to walk home even though Mark's father offered to give them a lift in his Vauxhall Chevette.

She never liked him; he was slimy.

When Dylan clocked Fiona approaching, he begged to go in Paul's car, but Chrissy was distracted saying her goodbyes.

Fiona seized Dylan's arm, pulling him out of earshot from the other mourners. 'May I have a quick word?' she asked, staring into Dylan's terrified, watery eyes. 'You haven't done anything wrong.'

Dylan swallowed hard, grimaced, and held a fist to his temple. The voices in his head were manic. Usually, he could tune out all but the voices he wanted to converse with, or shut them off completely, but not today. Since he had read that book or, more precisely, since the book had read to him, the voices had become deafening, like standing in the middle of Cardiff Arms Park with Wales scoring a try against England.

'Are you all right?' asked Fiona, her face full of concern.

'I'm fine.'

Fiona knelt in front of him and briefly stroked his hand. 'Don't look so worried, I just want to ask you something. What's your name?'

'Dylan.'

He lowered his head and absentmindedly scuffed his shoes on the gravel.

'Hi. I'm WPC Brasking, but call me Fiona. Earlier, before you went into the chapel, did you see me in the grounds?' she asked, softly.

Dylan nodded.

'Good. Did you see anything else? Anything ... Well ... Different?'

Dylan tilted his head to the side like a curious puppy and stared at her. 'Why? Did you see it, too?' he whispered.

'Yes,' Fiona replied, excitedly. 'The man in the black suit that ... that came out of nowhere?'

Dylan's jaw went slack. 'You saw him? Face like a melted welly.'

Fiona couldn't hold back a giggle. 'That's not how I'd put it but, yeah, I did.'

'Wow. I can't believe you saw the man and dog from my dreams.'

Fiona shook her head. 'It wasn't a dream. I didn't see a dog, though. Just an old man. He came from—'

'The shadows,' finished Dylan.

'*Phew*, I thought I was going mad, and that scream wa—'

Fiona stopped talking when Chrissy trotted over looking rather flustered and yanked Dylan to her side, wrapping an arm around him.

'Something wrong, officer?' asked Chrissy.

Fiona stood and brushed her skirt. 'Everything's fine. I was asking Dylan whether he'd seen anything unusual. He's been very helpful, Mrs?'

'Wolfendale.'

'Hi, Mrs Wolfendale. I'm WPC Brasking, I'm investi—'

'Asking him about what? The funeral?' Chrissy cut in.

'No. I'm investigating a couple of things, actually: a bag of animal remains dumped on the graves and a vandalised crypt. I really needed to interview others but it's been awkward, you know, under the circumstances.'

Chrissy nodded, but still looked confused. 'I understand.'

'Nice meeting you,' Fiona said, as Dylan limped beside his mother.

At a safe distance from Fiona, Chrissy grabbed his collar, wrenching his head backwards. 'What did you do?' she snarled.

'Nothing,' he lied.

With each step, the bag of animal remains pulsed and squelched like a rancid water balloon, splashing blood and entrails up Fiona's wrist. She plopped the bag next to the caretaker's shed and wiped her hand on the grass.

Stupid girl. Why only bring one pair of gloves?

She rolled her eyes at nobody and went off in search of the damaged crypt, which she found just a few metres from the chapel.

Weathered and rotten wooden doors had collapsed inwards under the combined weight of the original stone and that of the perpetrator and had been crudely tied shut with a shoelace. Presumably, some relative of Mr King had leant too hard against the stone; age and neglect had done the rest. She scribbled 'no flowers?' and 'hospital admissions?' into her notebook and took photos of the crypt's exterior.

After the lace was freed, the hinges shrieked their defiance when the doors swung inwards but, thankfully, they didn't crumble entirely.

Like Fiona, the warm sun seemed reluctant to enter. The dark, creepy crypt smelt stale and damp when she clambered over the first of the shattered stones.

Something moved in her peripheral vision and a coldness slid up her spine.

Stop being so jumpy; there's nothing there.

Surprisingly, there were no steps leading down. The deceased wouldn't have needed any, but surely the grave diggers would have, after depositing the coffin? Yet, there was no coffin on the floor, not even the crumbling, rotten remains of one; just bones scattered amongst the debris. Small pools of rainwater had collected on the surface of the floor and this additional moisture sent fresh earthly smells up her nose.

Whilst trying to avoid the bones, she edged her way in. A

shadow moved and she froze, heart slamming against her chest.

It's just your imagination.

The shadow moved again. Spreading wider. Closer.

She reached for her truncheon, but the shadow was quicker. It launched at her face; clawing, scraping and slicing her skin and then, several frantic seconds later, it was gone. It's glistening, black wings flapping a huge arc as it squawked skywards.

Fiona continued to swing her truncheon wildly from side to side whilst she fumbled for her torch. Her eyes squinted at the sudden brightness, but she forced herself to look around.

She was alone.

She exhaled hard and tried to settle her nerves. Blood surged back into her knuckles when she finally relaxed the grip on her weapon. She wasn't sure who was more scared, her or the crow. Heart settled, she rolled her neck, slid the truncheon back into her belt and continued forward. Pieces of skeleton were scattered everywhere with no signs of graffiti, rubbish or fag butts, which ruled out kids messing about.

When she stepped down over the rubble, she gripped one of the doors to steady herself and her fingers slid into the vertical grooves.

What the hell ... Are those nail marks?

When she ran her fingers over the deep scratches in the burnt wood, a feeling of pain, suffering and loss overwhelmed her, followed by a vision of an old man and his dog.

Stepping backwards, she carefully avoided the deceased's bones before quickly photographing the crypt's interior and scrambling back up into the sunlight.

It just didn't feel right being in there.

CHAPTER 15
KNOCK ON WOOD

Fiona trod quietly through the chapel looking for Reverend Foster and eventually found him sat alone in an anteroom staring at a glossy magazine through small, half-moon glasses that were balanced precariously on the tip of his nose.

Embarrassed, she crept back out of the room, composed herself, and knocked the door.

'Just a minute!'

Frantic rustling and fumbling ended with a drawer being slammed shut.

'Enter.'

'Hi, Reverend Foster?'

'Yes, and you are?'

'I'm WPC Brasking. I've come about the animal remains and damaged—'

'Well, about time! he snapped. 'I was about to telephone your Inspector. I needed this sorted *before* today's internment, not after.'

'Actually, the bloodied remains *were* removed before the

procession arrived. We couldn't have mourners seeing such horrific remains, could we?' she said, softly.

'Oh ... Absolutely, my dear. My apologies. Thank you. Have the remains been disposed of?'

Fiona shook her head. 'No, I've put them by the caretaker's shed for collection by EHS. Is Mr Davies around? I'd like to speak to him.'

The reverend scraped his chair backwards, walked over to a small wooden table, and switched a kettle on.

'Forgive my manners, dear. Do take a seat, you've been on your feet for hours,' he said, gesturing to two leather chairs either side of a small fireplace. 'Shall I tend to your wounds?'

Fiona dabbed at her scratched cheek and smiled. 'I'm fine, thanks.'

'No problem at all, my dear.'

Fiona took off her hat, and cursed herself for not doing it sooner. She sat, breathing in the comforting aroma of Bees Wax and Duraglit that penetrated the smokiness.

The reverend placed two cups and saucers on the table and sat opposite her. His frail arms and the meagre skin between his knuckles reminded her of the man who had miraculously appeared in the graveyard. She stared into the coal-fire's flames and wondered if she was losing her marbles. The heat was intense, but he probably welcomed it seeing how thin he was.

'Right, where were we, dear?' he asked, between sips. 'Oh, good heavens. We can't have tea without biscuits.' He rose to his feet. 'I'm sure I have some.'

'That's okay, Reverend. I'm fine.'

'All right. If you're sure.' He sat once more.

'Have you seen Mr Davies, today?'

'Yes.'

Fiona leant closer. 'Today?'

'What? Sorry. No, not today. He'd better have a jolly good

excuse or there'll be hell to pay. Excuse the expression. I shall pop and see him, later.'

'What's the address? I need to speak to him, anyway.'

'One Larkmead Drive, opposite the main gate. He has a Robin Reliant.' He pursed his lips, loudly slurped tea, and shivered. 'Dangerous thing, but he loves it.'

'Yes. Very unstable around corners, not that I'm suggesting he speeds,' she said, jokingly, which finally cracked the reverend's crusty exterior.

He laughed. 'I very much doubt that.'

'That's good to hear. Married?'

'Widowed. My wife, Carys, departed many—' The skin over his prominent cheekbones reddened and something glinted in his eyes. He looked away.

Fiona reached across the table and gently brushed his sleeve. 'Sorry for your loss, but I was enquiring about Mr Davies.'

The reverend cleared his throat and dipped his chin.

Well done, Fi', compassionate as ever.

'Sorry, how silly of me. Of course you meant Arwel. But married? Oh, dear Lord, no.'

'Why not?'

'He lacks the temperament for wooing ladies. Upstanding gentleman nonetheless, and, ex-Army, too,' he added.

Fiona placed her cup down and smiled. 'Tea was lovely.'

In a blur, moving faster than Fiona thought possible, the reverend jumped up, both knees cracking in unison, and grabbed the teapot. 'Another cup? They are rather small and I—'

Fiona showed him her palms. 'No, thanks, but I could use your loo.'

'Of course, my dear. The lavatory is near the main entrance.'

Fiona stood, adjusted her uniform and said, 'Oh, nearly forgot. I took pictures of the crypt. No sign of vandalism or meddling kids.'

'I agree, and Dylan wouldn't have done it.'

Fiona froze. 'Dylan?'

'Yes, Master Wolfendale. He visits his grandparents' grave most nights. He thinks we don't see him but Arwel and I both do. Lovely boy. Very strange.'

'Oh, okay. I'll eliminate him, then. I didn't see any flowers, but it's possible a visiting relative fell in there. Do you know the occupant's family or keep any burial records that could identify them?'

The reverend stared into the fire. Mesmerised. His eyes aglow with red flame, as sweat trickled down Fiona's back. 'Yes, we do have parish records,' he said, finally. 'But not for that burial, especially under the circumstances.'

Fiona was torn between opening her bladder or her notebook. She chose the latter. 'You must have some record of the name, surely?' She briskly thumbed the pages. 'Ah, here it is. The name above the crypt entrance was P Ki—'

'No,' the reverend cut in harshly. 'Not when it involved a sacrifice.'

Fiona slumped back down.

'More tea, dear? You look ghastly.'

Fiona listened intently for over half an hour as Reverend Foster explained the history of the chapel and the shocking, centuries old rituals that the Welsh Methodists and early parishioners practiced. He was in his element and she suspected that he hadn't had anyone *truly* interested in his opinion for a very long time. He explained how early

Christians called the followers of unfamiliar religions Pagans, as they believed they worshipped false gods. These Pagans, heathens, and such like, were also known to worship nature. Life was precious and always would be, but death was incredible: fascinating, foreboding and fearful.

Fiona cricked her aching back and stared at her notebook. She had only written one word.

Ritual.

'I think I understand, Reverend Foster but, if life's precious, why would they sacrifice someone on consecrated ground?'

'Please, call me Fred.'

Fiona smiled. 'Call me, Fiona.'

'Lovely name. It suits you.' He pointed at her notebook. 'I wouldn't bother, dear. You're a bit late finding this killer and I doubt it was murder.'

'No?'

'No. In the late eighteenth and early nineteenth centuries, Welsh villagers believed the deceased's soul could be at risk from evil. Protection was needed through the realm between the living and the dead. Beyond the veil of the living lies Transmogoria; the transitional realm, which is vulnerable to ... let's just say, uncooperative spirits.'

'Transmogoria? That sounds more like a planet,' she suggested, scratching her chin.

'In some ways, you could say it is. Have you heard of astral planes?'

'Vaguely.'

'Well, think of it like a cake, umm ... a Victoria sponge, with several layers of yumminess. If you think of the living being the layer of cream, it's surrounded by other layers. Now, if your mother makes them like mine did, that cream would be completely surrounded, above and below, by juicy jam.'

The pain in her bladder had made her forget how hungry

she was and she regretted turning down the offer of a biscuit. 'Sounds lush.'

'Oh, it was, my dear. You would have loved it. Now, the jam would be the realm of the dead or the spirit wor—'

'Wait, if the jam's all the way round, does that mean the dead are, too?'

'Yes, undoubtedly. In this scenario, the top and bottom sponges would be Heaven and Hell. Do you understand?'

'Yes.' She didn't, but she wasn't going to admit it. Her bladder needed him to get to the end, if there was one.

'Our ancestors believed that souls unwilling to cross-over would find a way out of Transmogoria and back to the living.'

'Unwilling?'

'Yes. Nobody wants to die, Fiona. It's a simple fact. Some souls feel that it's not their time. They become envious of the living, hateful and, well, just evil.' He shrugged. 'Many people believed these dark souls could jump into someone, push their soul out, and steal the body. They would be reborn, so to speak.'

'What, like a zombie?'

'*Ha ha*. No, not quite. They would be alive once more, like you and I.'

Fiona coughed, spraying tea. 'Sorry, went down the wrong way,' she spluttered, and dabbed at her chin with the back of her hand. 'Alive, you say?'

'Oh, yes, very much so. There have been many documented cases of people whose personalities have suddenly changed from one day to the next. After waking from a coma, for example. It's believed that, although it was the same physical body, the soul was new and unknown.'

'Bodysnatchers!'

'Yes, that's one way of putting it but not quite like the film. These aren't aliens; they are our own departed.'

Fiona finished her tea and returned the cup to the saucer

with a clink. 'Creepy, though.' She thought of the man she had seen amongst the graves. Was he on the hunt for a new body? Selfishly, she hoped he would find one soon—just not hers, she was quite attached to it.

'Yes, very scary, which is why there were so many rituals and talismans used to protect the dead and the living *from* the dead: coffin nails hammered into door frames; lines of salt on thresholds; arrowhead necklaces to defend after death; sapphires to ward off the malevolent glare of the dark soul's evil eye, and graveyard dirt to repel the dead. Oh, and not forgetting of course, the Bible and holy water, although, they only work if you *truly* believe in God. The list is endless, but you get the idea.'

'I must admit, this is fascinating, but where does the body in the crypt fit into all this?'

The reverend paused before dismissing her question with a wave of his hand. 'It's all in the past, and nothing you need to be concerned with.'

'But you mentioned a sacrifice.'

'Ramblings of an old man. More tea, dear?'

Fiona scrunched her lips together and rocked her head gently from side to side. His demeanour had changed and she knew he was withholding information, but the pain in her bladder was preventing cognitive thinking.

'Can you ask Arwel to come and see me when you've finished with him?' asked Fred. 'We've got builders due soon to sort out the drains.'

'Of course.' She raised a hand and smiled. 'Don't get up, I'll see myself out. Thanks for the tea.'

~

The putrid smell hit her before she had even reached Arwel's beloved Robin Reliant and her stomach retched, but she couldn't see the smell's source. She sidled up to the car and aside from a dented and badly scratched roof it appeared intact; no broken windows or signs of damage to the locks.

She bent down, cupped her hands against the glass, and peered through the passenger window. The car was empty, but from this lower viewpoint she could now see straight through the driver-side window to Arwel's front garden and the source of the smell.

She ran.

She wasn't quite sure why she ran *towards* the body. The vile smell should have made her realise that this person couldn't be saved and, less than two metres from the body, she emptied the contents of her stomach onto Arwel's lawn—tea, bile, and some stomach lining resembling diced carrots.

When the involuntary retching ceased, Fiona stood, composed herself, and surveyed the scene. Judging by the decomposition of the body, there wouldn't be a murderer lurking in a nearby hedge, but she took out her truncheon just in case. She covered her mouth and nose with a handkerchief and cautiously approached.

Blood containing foam leaked from the man's open mouth and his body was so bloated that normal visual identification would have been impossible, even for close family members, but for the name-tag on his chest that read, 'Howard Cobley.'

Howard's bloated body stretched his uniform to its limit.

His fat neck bulged against the shirt collar and the button behind his tie strained on its last thread. A foul stench emanated from every orifice, yet there wasn't a single maggot in sight. The long gash in his neck matched Sarah Lewis' description of the bus driver's wound, resulting from the crash three days earlier. The ripple effect of bulging skin against tight clothes made Howard resemble a marbled, green, Michelin man.

It was the most horrific thing she had ever seen.

Howard's head was tilted towards his left side and she knelt to inspect the back of his head for wounds.

Behind his right ear, Fiona spotted a mark identical to her own, childhood, scar.

CHAPTER 16
THIS OLE HOUSE

Friday 18th September, 1981

Dylan, Steven, and Mark jogged noisily down the front steps of Mostyn 'Mossy' Lloyd's semi-detached house, rounded the corner, and scattered like bowling pins when a figure exploded from underneath the bushes near the coal shed, as though the bush had given birth.

The figure rolled onto the path and rose up in front of them. It wore a camouflage jacket and trousers, leather boots and gloves. A black, SAS style, balaclava covered the head and face.

Steven was already back on his skateboard and heading for the garden gate when Dylan yelped and jumped behind Mark.

'Mark!' shouted the figure, before rolling the balaclava up over his face, forming a bobble hat minus the bobble.

'Mossy, you knob! Can't you use the gate like normal people? I nearly shat myself,' moaned Mark.

Mostyn brushed foliage off his jacket and stepped back into the bushes to retrieve his rucksack. 'Well, I've told you before; be prepared. You never know when the enemy will strike. Gates are overrated. Who's this 'en?' he asked, prodding Dylan in the shoulder.

'That's Dylan.'

'Hi,' said Dylan, timidly holding out his hand to welcome the bush baby.

Mostyn's huge, vice-like hand squeezed.

Blood evacuated, bones crunched, and a cry was stifled.

'Hiya, butt'. You brainy like Mark, then?'

'Not really,' replied Dylan, nursing his hand.

'You must be. I'm in D block with the rest of the mongos 'cause I'm a twp. But my brother, Alan, said you don't need to do well in school to be in the Army. My brother's infantry, Welsh Guards. I'm joining, too. Or maybe the Royal Marines. I've met them, see,' he boasted, proudly pointing to one of the badges on his jacket. 'There's nothing round here, mun ... Unless you wanna go down the mines, or be a Thatcher YOPper for twenty-three pound fifty a week.'

'What's a YOPper?' asked Dylan.

'Young Obnoxious Prick,' answered Mark. 'You'd fit right in, Mossy.' He punched Mostyn's arm and instantly regretted it.

'Youth Opportunities Programme,' corrected Mostyn. 'A full day's work for shit all pay. Nah, not for me. I'm gonna see the world.' Mostyn opened the kitchen door. 'Come in.' He glanced up at Steven peering over the garden wall. 'And you, ya lanky whippet!'

Pungent smells violated their sinuses and the grubby, vinyl, kitchen flooring was littered with dead flies, bugs and dried animal faeces. Cat litter crunched underfoot and balls of dusty cat hair rolled away like tumbleweed. Dark patches of damp and mould crept up the wood-chip covered walls and across the ceiling tiles, reminding Dylan of the graveyard shadows.

Broken furniture and heaped clutter occupied every conceivable space. Round chocolate tins, broken Tupperware, plastic bags and boxes were piled high, crammed with all manner of items: cardboard and used packaging, bottles, brittle and yellowed newspapers and ephemera, toilet rolls, Christmas trimmings, toys, clothes and blankets, balls of wool, and hundreds of jam jars full of buttons, rusted nails and screws, bottle tops, and multi-coloured marbles.

The boys walked slowly, arms clamped to their sides like plastic soldiers, to circumnavigate the clutter and crap. Although to Mostyn's mother, Ethel, this was not crap; this was her life.

Nothing was thrown out.

While the family ate dinner at a rickety camping table in the kitchen, the boys squeezed onto a busted two-seater settee in the adjacent dining room. Ethel offered the boys a portion but, after seeing the state of the house, they all declined, so Ethel shoved a huge plate of home-made Welsh cakes in front of them.

Dylan hated anything containing sultanas and currants or, as he preferred to call them, "spider bodies and rabbit poo," so there was no chance in hell that he would eat any, but Ethel insisted and Dylan reluctantly took one.

Steven and Mark had no such gripes and they lunged at the plate, grabbing several cakes each and stuffing them into their eagerly waiting gobs. Seconds later, after Ethel returned to the kitchen, their faces screwed up in disgust.

'Oh, my God, their gross,' whispered Steven, with a half-chewed lump of cake stuck to his outstretched tongue. 'It's like chewing an Arab's flip-flop.'

Mark nodded in agreement, rubbing his fingers together. 'And that's not sugar.'

'What're we gonna do?' asked Dylan, pretending to nibble a cake when Ethel glanced over.

'Dunno, but I can't eat this shit,' mumbled Mark, leaning forward to return an un-bitten cake to the plate, but Ethel saw him.

'That's it, love. Help yourself,' she said, smiling. 'There's plenty more.'

By the time the family had finished their meal, the boys had launched eight cakes under the settee, and despite the boys blowing out hard and rubbing their 'full' bellies, Ethel wrapped more cakes in clingfilm and handed them to Mostyn.

Walking into Mostyn's bedroom was like stepping into the vastness of Doctor Who's Tardis compared to the claustrophobic clutter of the rest of the house. Camouflage netting, rather than curtains, were draped over the window and the sunlight that filtered through peppered the room in strange blurry dots.

Sunlight and sound engulfed the dark and dingy room when Mostyn flung back the netting and dropped the arm of a small, wood framed, record player onto a seven-inch single. After some crackling, Marc Bolan's voice filled the room telling everyone how he loved to boogie. Dylan remained standing, unsure how to interact, while Steven grabbed a Commando comic and plonked himself on the bed.

Mark couldn't resist nosing; the room was full of wicked stuff. Drawn to a long, sharp wire with a ring on each end, Mark uncoiled it and ran his finger along its length, drawing blood. Wincing, he sucked his finger.

What the hell is it? he thought.

As if hearing his thoughts, Mostyn said, 'It's a wire saw. I ordered it from a magazine after forging one of my brother's bank cheques. Since joining the Army, Alan's loaded, so he doesn't notice a few quid missing.'

Dylan was mortified, although he suspected Mostyn was exaggerating. He spotted two electronic games on Mostyn's shelf, Astro Wars and one other.

'Benny had one of these,' noted Dylan, holding up Space Invader.

'That *was* Benny's,' replied Mostyn.

Dylan frowned. 'How come you've got it?'

'Well, he won't be playing it anymore, will he?'

Stunned, Dylan flicked a button on Astro Wars and his envious eyes lit up when it started beeping, and invaders from space filled the display, causing him to zone out. When Mostyn turned away, Dylan slipped Benny's game into his coat pocket.

'Alan loves the army,' continued Mostyn. 'He's hoping to get posted overseas or to a war zone.'

Mark was flabbergasted. 'What if he gets killed?'

'He joined up to see some action. Kill some terrorist prick with a double tap to the head. Pew pew!' he yelled, pointing a gun hand to Steven's head, causing Steven to throw himself theatrically off the bed with a groan, his tongue lolling out of the side of his mouth.

Mostyn laughed. 'That was terrible!'

'Shut your face!' snapped Steven, before lying back on Mostyn's bed, fingers interlinked behind his head.

'What the hell's a double tap?' asked Mark.

'You're thick as shit.'

Mark stood nose-to-nose with Mostyn, fists clenched and knuckles white. 'Piss off. I'm not stupid.'

'I don't know what double sink is either,' mumbled Dylan, who was still jabbing buttons on the game and losing badly.

'It's tap, not sink!' said Mostyn, shaking his head in

disbelief. 'Oh, it doesn't matter. Look butt', I was only screwing with you, okay?'

Mark visibly relaxed. '*So*, what is it then?' he asked, again.

'It's what the SAS do, see. They shoot 'em twice in the head, through the mouth.' Mostyn illustrated his point by shoving two fingers towards Mark's mouth. 'The bullets take out the central nervous system and it stops them pulling their trigger.'

Mark slapped his hand aside. 'Yeah ... I get it. You don't need to show me,' he snapped, slumping back onto the bed. When Mostyn strolled toward the door, Mark quickly slipped the wire saw into his pocket, unseen.

'I'm going for a shit,' announced Mostyn, grabbing that afternoon's *Gwent Argus* newspaper. 'Break anything and you're dead!'

The newspaper's front page had a huge photo of the finger-eating bus driver, Howard Cobley, below the heading, '*Cardiff bus driver's decomposed body found. Police baffled.*'

Mark jumped up and snatched the paper from Mostyn's hands despite Mostyn's attempts to retrieve it. It wasn't Howard's death that shocked him, he kind of expected that, but the coroner's estimated time or, more importantly, the *date* of his death did.

Mark repetitively jabbed a finger at Howard's photo before repeating, 'Look at it! ... Look at it!'

Mostyn shrugged. 'So what? He's dead.'

'Yeah, but he wasn't Wednesday night when we saw him eat his own friggin' finger!'

When Mostyn's laughter died down, Steven swung his long legs over Mark's head and sat up next to him on the edge of the bed.

'Okay, but he's dead now. So what's your point?' he asked.

'Duh! ... He *was* alive on Wednesday night, but it says here that, "*...early indications suggest he had been dead for several days.*" But they only found him yesterday!'

'You know what this means?' asked Mostyn.

Before they could answer, Mostyn strode across the room, reached into the dark recess beside his wardrobe and pulled out a long, padded, green case. He unzipped it and slid out an air rifle. 'We need to go zombie hunting!' He jammed the rifle's wooden butt into his hip, gripped the barrel, and pulled it downwards, breaking it open. He inserted a .22 pellet into the barrel and snapped it shut. Then he rummaged in his pocket, unwrapped his mother's Welsh cakes, and launched them out of the window before leaning against the frame. 'Watch this.'

In a huddle, the boys stared out over the long back-garden, which stretched down towards a huge, open field.

After a few minutes, a crow landed on top of the shed and strutted, chest out, towards the discarded cakes.

'If you miss, the cakes'll kill him,' joked Steven, feeling brave.

Crack!

Mostyn's pellet hit the bird and sent the carcass flying backwards over the shed and into the field beyond.

Dylan was appalled and looked away in disgust.

'What a shot!' yelled Steven. 'Can I have a go?'

'Nuh. I've just bought it,' he said, glancing at Mark. 'I don't want it broken. Anyway, how come you're seeing zombies, Sparky? You got some second sight or something?' He smirked.

'No, but Dylan can talk to them,' blurted Mark.

Dylan's head spun around and he glared at Mark. He didn't want anyone to know about his dead friends, least of all Mostyn.

'We're all friends. Just tell them,' pleaded Mark.

Dylan refused to answer and got up to leave, but Mark grabbed his arm.

'Oh, don't be like that. Tell them. It's awesome what you can do. It's like a super power.'

'He's right,' agreed Steven. 'It's wicked, if you can. I wish I could do something like that.'

Mostyn slid his rifle back into its case and began sniffing the air. 'What's that smell? Oh, wait, I know ... Bullshit!'

'Shut up, Mossy. You're jealous,' said Mark, his tone shifting. He sounded angry.

'You actually believe this crap? You lot are off your heads.'

'Honest, it's true. I've seen him do it.'

Mostyn couldn't stop laughing. 'Seen it? What? Dylan talking to himself? You guys are killing me!'

'Prick!' snapped Mark, before grabbing Dylan's arm. 'C'mon, lets go.'

Mostyn held up his hands, surrendering. 'Okay, okay, I'm sorry, butt'. We'll just have to disagree 'cause I don't believe in all that shit, but stranger things have happened.' He held out his chunky hand to Dylan. 'Friends?'

Dylan hesitated, thoughts of crushed bones filling his mind. Gingerly, he slipped his hand into Mostyn's.

'Friends,' agreed Dylan.

'Anyway, the police have probably got it all wrong,' suggested Mostyn.

'Or the press, they're always full of crap,' added Steven. 'So are we still looking for pop bottles, then?' he asked, his head clunking into Mostyn's ceiling light.

'Yeah, I need 50p more to get a new Pocketeer,' replied Dylan.

Mostyn shook his head, mumbling, 'Sad git.'

Embarrassed, Dylan lied, 'I don't play with them. I collect them.'

'Yeah, *whatever*,' replied Mostyn. 'You're in Comp', not

play-school.' He put on his cherry red Dr. Martens boots, donned his camouflage jacket, and slung his rifle bag over one shoulder. 'C'mon, let's go.'

'I thought you needed a shit?' wondered Steven.

'Nah, I've lost the feeling.'

Dylan hung back and whispered to Mark, 'Does he sleep in that coat?'

'Probably,' said Mark, waving his fingers under his nose and grimacing, before following Mostyn and Steven out of the room. 'Oh, don't forget, even though it might be fun, you can't push Slinky down the stairs.'

'I heard that!' shouted Steven.

~

Dylan dragged his heels, keeping a gap between him and the others. When they passed the lane which led to the field behind Mostyn's house, he whistled and indicated his need to piss. When he was half-way down the lane, he checked it was clear and relieved himself.

Once he'd zipped up his fly, Gareth appeared, startling him.

'Go and get the crow,' he suggested.

Dylan was annoyed. 'Are you spying on me?' he asked, but Gareth simply pointed to the field. Dylan followed his finger and shook his head. 'It's dead.'

'Not quite.' He turned his back on Dylan and headed for the street whilst adding, 'I'm glad you're using the book.'

He is spying on me.

In truth, he longed to find the crow alive, but his gut feeling said otherwise. Although, to his surprise, a crow hopped up from inside an abandoned car tyre. Its black feathers glistened around the pellet hole in its chest while it hopped around, cawing.

Dylan slowly knelt and reached out a hand to stroke the crow's back expecting him to peck him or attempt to fly away, but he did neither. The crow wasn't wary of him; he leant close, pushing back into Dylan's hand, relishing the attention like an old friend.

Dylan slid his bag from off his shoulder and gently scooped up the bird. Sensing his good nature, the crow nustled its black beak in and out of his fingers, before it emitted a plangent caw and settled down inside his cupped hands. Taking care not to aggravate the bird's injury, he lowered it gently into the bag. With a rolled up test paper preventing the bag from zipping fully, he hoisted the strap over his head.

He jumped when several crows engaged in venery flew low over his head and landed in the tyre's centre before scolding something within. More crows flew down, increasing the raucous gathering until a macabre mob surrounded the tyre's contents.

CHAPTER 17
MESSAGE IN A BOTTLE

Garrett's Newsagents

The bell dangling above the shop door chimed when Mostyn walked inside and he breathed deeply savouring the smell of bread, sugary sweets, cinnamon, chocolate and lemon. A stack of baskets in front of the magazine racks were brimming with fresh cakes and bread from Brace's Bakery, and his eyes lingered over a custard slice. The door chimes faded and were replaced by the low hum of the Slush Puppie machine's blades, swirling blue and red ice.

The shop owner, Mr Garrett, was busy selling three fags to a ginger kid from form five and he nodded when Mostyn put four empty Corona pop bottles on the counter.

'I'll be there, now. In a minute,' he said to Mostyn, before holding out three Embassy's to the boy. 'Thirty pence, please, butt'. And you didn't buy 'em from here, okay?'

While the kid was fumbling nervous hands through his pockets looking for change, the chimes rang once more and Mostyn glanced back to see the other three boys walking in.

Pointing at Mark, he whispered, 'I told you to stay outside.'

'It's all right. I don't mind waiting here.'

Mostyn shoved him backwards. 'Just go!' he hissed, through gritted teeth.

Mark was confused. Why was he singled out? What did he do wrong? He shrugged his shoulders, turned on his heels, and left.

Dylan thought about leaving, too, but Mostyn's face told him it would be a bad idea. He shimmied on top of the Wall's ice cream freezer, legs dangling, and let his mind, and bottom, chill.

'How many we got then, boys? Four is it. You haven't nicked any 'ave you?' teased Mr Garrett.

'Nope,' Mostyn said, staring him straight in the eyes, so he wouldn't know he was lying through his teeth.

'Well, that's all right, then.' He pushed a lever and the till drawer opened. 'Here you go, 40p, and don't spend it all at once,' he said, before adding with a chuckle, 'But, if you do, make sure you spend it in here.'

Abruptly, everything stilled and the room went brown. Doors between the living and Transmogoria materialised around Dylan. The silence was tangible and his soul stepped forward, surveying the scene. His body remained seated on the freezer, static, but the other boy's and Mr Garrett's were moving, albeit extremely slowly, as he had come to expect in this place. Their souls fluttered underneath their skin; luminous and blue.

Something moved quickly, out of sync, and Dylan watched as his bag shuffled and wobbled, and then the crow hopped out onto the freezer's surface.

It walked forward, unfazed, in realtime. How was that possible?

Dylan rounded the counter and hovered a hand above Mr

Garrett's arm; the blue luminosity rose to meet his touch. He raised and lowered his hand to within millimetres of his skin, teasing Mr Garrett's soul to the surface and back again.

As if in warning, the crow emitted a hoarse, rattle caw.

Dylan should have flinched, pulled back, but curiosity killed the cat and he touched Mr Garrett's arm, instead.

Mr Garrett's soul leapt out of his body, lost and befuddled, before an unseen force sucked it away. In the same instant, Dylan's soul was drawn into Mr Garrett's body, and he opened his eyes, Ernie Garrett's eyes, and stared straight at Mostyn. He felt itchy and uncomfortable in this body, as though he were draped in a thick wool blanket.

It didn't belong.

He didn't belong.

Dylan surveyed the scene once more, but this time from Mr Garrett's perspective. The crow was back in his bag and the boys were patiently waiting. When he saw his daydreaming body still sat on the ice cream freezer, he almost screamed.

Mostyn stared at Mr Garrett, who was studying his own wrinkly hands, as if seeing them for the first time. Saliva slid out of his gaping mouth and, weirdly, he began to cry.

This guy is losing the plot, thought Mostyn.

'Everything okay, Mr Garrett?'

Dylan stared at his empty body. Was he dead? Blood froze in veins that were not his. He started to hyperventilate.

This is so wrong, he thought, as panic took hold.

'Mr Garrett?' Mostyn said, raising his voice.

Dylan looked at Mostyn, then back at his own body, frozen like the ice lollies it sat on.

'Mr Garrett!' yelled Mostyn, clanking two bottles together.

Finally, he realised where he was or, more importantly, *who* he now was. 'Sorry, Mostyn,' he croaked, as smokers phlegm jiggled in the back of Mr Garrett's throat. 'I-I don't ... What do you want?'

Mostyn couldn't recall telling Mr Garrett his name, but he gestured to the bottles. 'We brought them in,' he reminded.

'Oh, yeah,' Dylan said, before absentmindedly shoving a hand in the till drawer, pulling out a pound note, and handing it to a shocked Mostyn.

'Thanks,' said Mostyn, incredulously. He shoved the note into his pocket before Mr Garrett could change his mind, and turned to the boys. 'C'mon, let's go.'

Steven was prodding Dylan in the arm, trying to rouse him from his daydream but, instead of jerking back to reality, his body slid off the freezer and came to an abrupt stop when his head thumped the concrete floor.

Dead still.

'Dylan. You okay?' asked Steven, concern etched across his face.

The shop doorbell jingled when Mostyn held it open, trying to hurry them up.

Steven shook him, again.

Nothing.

'Stop messing about, Wolfy. It's not funny.'

Mostyn let the door close and stomped back down the aisle. He knelt, causing the butt of his rifle to clunk on the floor. He slid the strap off his shoulder, laid the rifle down gently, then slapped Dylan across the face.

Still dead.

I'm not going to move, thought Dylan. I'm not there; I'm *here*. What if I can't get back to my body? A nervous laugh escaped him.

The boys glared at Mr Garrett. Shouted at him. Screamed at him. They dragged their friend across the floor and Steven covered his mouth with his.

Why is he kissing me? thought Dylan.

Mostyn screamed a number in Mr Garrett's face. Nine something, maybe another nine? Dylan wasn't sure. He didn't feel well. He wanted to sit, but Mostyn was tugging his arm and pointing at his friend.

His friend.

His dead friend.

Dylan.

Terror shot through Dylan and Mr Garrett's body shook in response. He felt as though he were standing on a precipice, with the edge crumbling away.

He closed his eyes, steeled himself, and steadied his breathing. He felt his soul tighten under vice-like pressure, and he tried to fight it, but he was going nowhere fast. Instead, he relaxed, and felt his soul slip sideways.

There was no sun, moon, or night, but there was darkness, damp and earthy, like a wet night in autumn.

Dark shapes, wispy and fluid, hurtled all around him.

Transmogoria.

He concentrated on Mr Garrett's soul, before calling out his name. His confused soul appearing almost instantly, a trail of light snaking behind him like a burning wire.

Dylan mumbled an apology before thrusting him back through his door ...

~

Mr Garrett withdrew his hand from the till.

'Here you go, 40p, and don't spend it all at once,' he said. 'But, if you do, make sure you spend it in here.' He laughed, but his face showed no humour. He shook his head, dazed.

Mostyn couldn't quite believe it when the money dropped into his hand.

'Wait, you've already said all that.' He failed to mention the one pound note that Mr Garrett had already given him.

'Never-mind the bloody deposit, Dylan needs an ambulance!'

Mr Garrett scrunched up his face, confused.

'Déjà vu,' mumbled Dylan, scratching his arms. He wanted to crawl out of his skin. He had defiled that man's body, and he vowed, there and then, that he would *never* enter another person's body, for as long as he lived. The way he had effortlessly exorcised Mr Garrett's soul terrified him.

Steven's gangly arms wrapped around him and almost squeezed his soul out, again.

'What're you doing?' asked Dylan, trying not to sound callous while he wriggled free.

'I thought you were dead, mun!'

Dylan stood, brushed himself down and said, with a shrug, 'I fell asleep.'

'Asleep? You were dead to the world ... Literally.'

'You really are a weirdo,' added Mostyn. He was talking about Dylan, but his eyes were fixed on Mr Garrett who looked confused and distracted. He mumbled something under his breath then expertly grabbed the bottle necks between his fingers and sauntered through his multi-coloured door tapes into the back of the shop, mumbling the whole way.

~

There was no sign of Mark out front, but the boys found him sat on a low wall around the corner, swinging his legs and sulking. Mostyn quickly explained his reason for sending him out; they were going to get paid for returning the same bottles.

They watched Mr Garrett come out of the shop's back entrance and slip into the yard. His hands were full of the Corona pop bottles they'd just handed in. He randomly dropped them into plastic crates, lit a fag and drew on it, hard.

He exhaled a plume of smoke, then studied the sky as if searching for some forgotten task. He shook his head, clearing away the muddled thoughts, and went back inside.

After a minute or two, Mostyn scaled the fence, dropped down inside the yard and passed four bottles under the fence to Mark, which he nervously returned to Mr Garrett.

Fifteen minutes after originally leaving the shop, they now had one pound eighty and Mr Garrett had no idea he had been fleeced.

'Right, forty-five pence each. Here's five pence of my share to make yours up to fifty pence,' Mostyn said, as he divided out the money and held a fifty pence piece out for Dylan.

Dylan stared at him, lost and disorientated. He was still scratching at his skin.

'That's how Mr Garrett looked, just now,' noted Mostyn. 'Here, take it,' he added, shoving the coin in Dylan's hand.

'How come?'

'Well, now you can get that Pocketeer.'

Dylan's head was a swirl of thoughts and he mumbled a thank you, turned on his heels, and bimbled away.

While Dylan anxiously headed back into Garrett's shop, the other boys sat on the low wall out front, which gave Mostyn more opportunity to ridicule Dylan's hidden talent. No matter how much Mark tried to convince him, Mostyn was having none of it. Mark eventually gave up and conversation returned to the 'zombie' bus driver who's picture was plastered over the metal *Gwent Argus* newspaper advertisement sign placed outside the entrance to the newsagent.

'He ran at us like a mad man,' said Mark.

'Why?' asked Mostyn. 'What did you do to annoy him?'

'Nothing. Why does everyone think that?' asked Mark, sulking. 'I was only chucking stones across the road. One minute he was staring with colour changing eyes, and the next he was running at us, full pelt.'

'Colour changing eyes?' asked a soft voice, startling them.

Fiona was stood behind them.

Mark swallowed hard before mumbling, 'Erm ... Yeah, why?'

'Can you describe him?'

Mark lifted his arm and pointed at the newspaper sign, forcing Fiona's eyes wide.

'Really? When was this?'

'Wednesday night, about six, six-thirty, in Broadmead.'

'Thanks. What's your name?'

He stared at her with a 'rabbit in a headlight' look. 'Mark ...' He swallowed hard. 'Jones.'

'Well, Mark, would you like to accompany me down the station and give a quick statement on what you saw? You'll be doing us a favour.'

Her bewitching smile made him blush and he turned to Mostyn for moral support, but he was nowhere to be seen and Steven simply stared back at him with a 'don't ask me' look.

'Yeah, I suppose so,' Mark finally replied.

~

'What took you so long?' quizzed Steven, when Dylan sat beside him. 'Did he have you for nicking those bottles?'

The crow fluttered in Dylan's bag and he coughed a loud 'no' to hide the noise, but he needn't have worried because Steven was busy typing '5318008' into his calculator watch and giggling.

Dylan held out his new Pocketeer.

'Tidy,' said Steven, without looking up. 'Which one will you get, next?'

'Dunno, maybe Rally,' mumbled Dylan, distant. He glanced at the receding sun. 'Bloody hell, what time is it?'

Steven sighed and cleared the screen. 'Five past six, why? ... Wait, don't tell me. You gotta be home before the street lights come on,' he said, without attempting to hide his sarcasm.

'I've gotta see my dad in hospital,' he explained, before sitting bolt upright like a meerkat. 'Where's Mark?'

'Arrested!' sniped Mostyn, causing both boys to jump.

'Don't listen to him,' said Steven, shaking his head. 'He scarpered when that copper appeared.'

'Oh shit, the crypt!' gasped Dylan.

'What crypt?' mused Steven, scratching his chin.

'Oh, it's nothing,' replied Dylan, unconvincingly.

'She overheard Mark talking about seeing Howard, so she took him to the station.'

Mostyn held his hands out in front of his chest. 'Miss Piggy had massive knockers, too. Much bigger than Linda Lusardi's. I would have gone anywhere with her,' he mused.

Steven towered over Mostyn. 'You're always talking about girls, but I've never seen you with one.'

'Yeah ... Well ... I-I fingered a girl from Pontyfechan!' he exclaimed with pride, while his face wrinkled with disgust. 'Anyway, I'm gonna buy some bangers and blow shit up,' he blurted, absentmindedly kicking a can across the path. 'See you later.'

When Mostyn was out of earshot, Steven whispered, 'Oooh, I think I've found the chink in his armour.' But he was talking to himself; Dylan was already several metres away, cradling his bag like he was holding a baby.

Steven skated after him.

'Can you really talk to the dead?'

'Erm ... Yeah,' replied Dylan, hesitantly.

'Wow, that's wicked!' admitted Steven. 'What crypt were you on about? Is Mark in trouble?'

Dylan put a hand to his chest and felt his heart. *His* heart. 'God, I hope not.'

CHAPTER 18

ONE DAY I'LL FLY AWAY

In his garden shed, Dylan constructed a makeshift shelter from a cardboard box lined with paper and sawdust. From his father's wood pile he found a small log with a branch still intact, which he placed in the box for a perch. While Dylan busied himself, the crow shuffled back and forth across Dylan's penny skateboard, head and eyes twitching, and wings stretched wider than Dylan expected. Strangely, there was no blood around the hole in his chest.

Dylan giggled when the crow began pecking at frogspawn in a jam jar.

He radioed Mark on his walkie: thankfully, he wasn't incarcerated and Fiona knew nothing about their involvement in the crypt.

At the mention of the crypt, the crow cawed and nuzzled into him.

'I'm okay, birdie,' he whispered.

His mind was a whirl of thoughts, mostly scary ones, and he tried to shake off the memory of Mr Garrett's soul. It had been so easy to take it away and the thought made him shiver. The crow's beak seesawed between his fingers, tickling him.

He stared at it and wondered why he had seen it in the sepia realm, with its corridor of doors to Transmogoria. Had he imagined it there? His memory was blurred, tainted.

The crow nudged him from his reverie.

'What shall I call you, then?'

The low light shone through the shed's small window making his obsidian feathers glisten, like an amphibian.

'Newt!'

'*Caw*,' replied the crow, as if in agreement.

A car's horn sounded and Newt hopped onto his perch.

Dylan ignored the beeping and stroked the bird's feathers while he clicked his tongue. When it blared several times in quick succession, he bid Newt farewell and quietly closed the shed door.

Due to the bloodthirsty killer stalking the valley, Uncle John insisted that he escort them to the ward, much to Chrissy's annoyance. Dylan saw straight through Kaelum's pathetic homework excuse, but Chrissy fell for it. Even murder by Kaelum's hands would go unpunished. Dylan's homework was piled higher than his ironing and another red mark was on the cards, but he chose not to mention that little nugget.

When they exited the lift, Chrissy popped to the toilet and Dylan seized the opportunity to speak to his uncle. He was itching to know more about Louisa's death and Daniel Hawker's involvement. The sheer mention of her death had made Chrissy and his grandmother go berserk, but John was also reluctant to discuss it, despite Dylan's pestering.

Resigned to failure, Dylan turned on his heels, which squeaked with each footfall, and sulked towards his father's ward.

Suddenly, John grabbed his arm, spun him around, and

blurted, 'The police reckon my brother, Daniel, killed Louisa. They're wrong.'

Dylan was gobsmacked. His uncle looked angry, and he took a step back.

'It was so out of character for him, almost as though he were a different person entirely. That's why your mam doesn't like me very much. Don't tell her I told you, though!'

'Why has no one told me? Does Kaelum know?'

John shrugged. 'No idea, and you can't ask your mam; she'll know I've blabbed.'

No matter what had happened to Auntie Louisa, there were only two people who *would* tell him the truth.

The dead don't lie.

Gwynfor's health had deteriorated considerably since their last visit and his muffled Darth Vader voice scarcely uttered a word while Dylan sat staring at the oxygen machine droning on and on with each hypnotising *schtup schtup.* It didn't take long before Chrissy gave Dylan ten pence and sent him off to the shop, but he chose to visit Andrew, instead.

Before he reached the lift, an A&E crash team hurtled through the corridors, parting visitors like a scalpel through flesh. In the confusion, Dylan became disorientated, and he backed into a curtain to avoid the patients—miners with coal blackened faces and hands—that were being wheeled past, their souls rising out of their bodies, screaming and clawing at nothing, before slipping back beneath the skin's surface.

Behind him, a nurse's voice asked, 'How big was this tree? You must have hit every branch.'

Curiosity drew Dylan's eyes over his shoulder.

A young boy, naked apart from a flimsy gown, was covered in dark, angry, bruises. The nurse was dressing deep cuts in his back. Before Dylan could avert his gaze, the boy's head swivelled around.

It was Kevin Franklyn.

Dylan shuffled backwards, stumbled into a passing nurse, and ran.

He didn't stop running until he burst into Andrew's room.

Despite Dylan's flustered state, Andrew was happy to see him. Conversation flowed at first but when it waned Andrew nagged Dylan to switch off his machine. Dylan's brain whirred away, desperately trying to think of a subject that wouldn't upset him or make him miss being able bodied.

It was impossible.

Anything and everything that anybody ever did involved more than just being a head, so Dylan chose to tell him the unbelievable, far-fetched story of his ability to speak to the dead and it seemed to work. Andrew listened attentively while Dylan described his conversations with the dead, the souls he'd helped to passover, and the weird book with its wrinkled, dried skin. He chose not to mention invading Mr Garrett's body.

'Nice story, Jackanory,' Andrew said, smirking. 'I'd clap, but I can't be bothered.'

Dylan smiled through pinched lips, unsure if Andrew was being genuine; he hoped with every last tittle of his soul that he was. Although, as with all adults, he suspected Andrew wasn't being entirely truthful.

'These people you helped to die—'

'Passover,' Dylan corrected.

'Sorry. These people you helped to *passover*. Did you know them?'

Dylan shook his head. 'No, but my parents knew Tom.'

'So, why you?'

Dylan shrugged. 'Dunno.'

'Aren't you curious?'

Dylan had thought about nothing else, apart from Emily, since that day, but he'd given up on answering the 'why me?' questions years ago. 'Yeah, but—'

'But what? Life's too short to bimble with your head in the clouds. Look at me. I took everything for granted. Now, I'm nothing. I'm trapped. Life isn't a VHS movie; I can't rewind.'

Dylan lowered his head and mumbled, 'Sorry.'

'For what? You didn't collapse that scrum. Stop worrying what others think.'

Dylan shifted in his plastic seat and stared into space. 'I'll try.'

'Good. Promise me one thing though, if you—'

'I'm not going to kill you,' Dylan cut in.

Andrew sighed and scrunched up his nose. 'If you feel the need to *passover* somebody, then keep me in mind. I can't live like this.'

Dylan could feel the sadness coming off him in waves and he fought to hold back tears. He didn't know what Andrew's predicament was like, but he could certainly imagine. Back in junior school, he had been playing 'Cowboys and Indians' in the woods when Cowboy 'Crazy Sparks' Mark had tied him to a tree and was about to burn Indian Chief 'Tufty Wolf' Dylan when he disappeared in search of wood to place around the Chief's feet. As a cub scout, Mark had done an amazing job of tying Dylan's torso, arms, and legs to the tree, so all that Dylan could do was move his head.

After what seemed like an hour, with the remnants of daylight flickering between the tree branches, brave old Tufty Wolf began to scream at the top of his lungs. It was almost pitch black when Mark finally returned. His torch lit up circular patches of undergrowth like Jamie and the Magic Torch minus his dog, Wordsworth.

Dylan endured nearly two hours as just a head; Andrew had the rest of his life.

Dylan grabbed a tissue from the bedside cabinet and wiped the tears from Andrew's cheeks and the two lines of snot from under his nose.

Andrew mouthed a thank you and stared up at the ceiling. 'So there's definitely an afterlife, then?' he asked.

'Seems that way.'

'Good.'

After a long awkward silence, Dylan asked Andrew if there was anything he needed from the shop. Andrew declined his offer, which was good because his ten pence wouldn't have gone far.

'Don't forget the book,' Andrew reminded, when Dylan edged toward the door. 'Maybe Gareth's right and all the answers are in there.'

Dylan paused in the doorway.

'Maybe.'

'What you really should be asking is, how come this Gareth knows so much? Where did *he* get the book?'

Dylan shrugged, took a step forward, and paused. 'Please don't ask me to kill you, again. I won't do it,' he said, resolutely.

Andrew mumbled, 'I'll *never* mention it, again,' before staring at the ceiling.

Dylan wondered how many times boredom had caused him to count the ceiling tiles, when it suddenly dawned on him that there was no television in the room. Andrew couldn't even hold a book to read.

What did he do to pass the time?

Dylan felt his bottom lip quiver, so he quickly waved goodbye. He paused on the threshold, making Andrew wonder if he had forgotten his bearings, before traipsing towards the lifts.

The journey home was more awkward than usual as neither John or his mother spoke. He suspected John was feeling anxious about speaking out, but he was glad John had trusted him enough to speak the truth, rather than hiding it from him like everyone else. It made Dylan feel slightly more adult, if only for a short time.

While Nana Mouskouri's dulcet tones and Chrissy's fag smoke filled the Beetle's interior, Dylan's thoughts drifted back to Emily. Apart from helping her and her family find the money, which allowed them to give Tom a good send off, he had done nothing but embarrass himself in front of her: he ignored her when she walked out of the chapel; almost threw himself on Tom's coffin, and got interrogated by a policewoman—although he hoped Emily's funeral cars were out of sight by that point. He longed to be her friend, but he was terrified that she now hated him for being such an inconsiderate, clumsy, dick.

He pushed the thought aside.

It was time for the dead to reveal their secrets.

CHAPTER 19
EVERYBODY'S GOT TO LEARN SOMETIME

Dylan shifted uncomfortably, feeling the cold, damp gravestone through his corduroy trousers. He wondered whether his grandparents were also restless after he'd enquired about Louisa's death. It must be bad. Why else would they hide it from him?

He shook his head, focused, and listened intently to his grandad ...

'Louisa and your mam were identical twins. They were inseparable, which is common for—'

Dylan's brain was whirring faster than a cassette tape on rewind. Twins! Why would you hide the fact that your dead sister was a twin? Surely, you would keep your sister's life alive in stories and photographs.

Photographs.

The truth had been in plain sight all along.

It wasn't Chrissy in the living room photographs; it was Auntie Louisa. Chrissy wasn't a narcissist; she was keeping her alive; even if she was keeping her all to herself, which meant the dead girl in his dreams, wearing the sapphire, arrowhead necklace, was *actually* Louisa.

Lazarus was still talking, but Dylan hadn't registered anything after the twin bombshell had hit.

'Twins?'

'What? Yes, Dylan, twins, and they seemed more linked than any twins we'd ever heard of. When they were little, your nan had to dress them the same, otherwise they would scream the place down.

'They wore matching dresses on the day Louisa died, too. They were both pregnant, you see. It was like they did everything in tune with each other. Within minutes of your mam telling us she was pregnant, Louisa waltzed in and announced the same thing. They were like that their whole lives, and that's why Christiana was hit so hard when Louisa was murdered. Her personality totally changed, like she was a different person entirely, she just —'

'Murdered!' Dylan cut in.

'Sadly, yes,' answered Lazarus.

'Who killed her, Granch'?'

'Patience, Dylan.'

'Sorry.'

'Where was I? Oh, yes, their twin link. Even if they went shopping separately, they still bought the same dresses nine times out of ten. The link was uncanny. It was there the day Louisa died. Your mam had a heart attack and collapsed at the exact time that the police believe Louisa was killed. Luckily for us, though, your mam was rushed into hospital and they restarted her heart, so we didn't lose both daughters on the same day. You died, too.'

Dylan gripped the gravestone. 'I died?'

'Yes, they couldn't resuscitate with you in her belly, so they performed an emergency caesarean, but you were stillborn. They re-started your heart, although, yours took a few minutes longer. They never explained why. Faulty machine, I reckon. We never got to meet your cousin; he died with Louisa.'

The wind blew through the graveyard with a high-pitched hiss, but the tree branches and their leaves refused to sway. It was if the trees themselves were listening to his grandad's story. Dylan's breath condensed and pain shot down his arms when the fear inside him froze.

Lazurus sensed it, too. *'You okay, Dylan?'*

His eyes, now accustomed to the dark, scanned the moonlit graveyard. He felt unseen eyes bearing down on him from the shadows and wondered if Mark was hiding again, waiting to pounce. The graveyard was empty; even the bats had deserted it.

'I'm fine, Granch'. He shivered uncontrollably. 'P-Please go on.'

'Okay, if you're sure. Well, Louisa was out that day. She'd been invited by her cousin—my brother's son, Daniel Hawker—to a stroll over Markham Common. My brother, Rhys, had a 1950's Land Rover on his farm. It was in really good nick, too, considering it was nearly eighteen years old. Anyway, Daniel would often take the girls for a drive, but Christiana was busy with housework and declined. We are so thankful that she did. Neither Daniel or Louisa returned from the common that day and it destroyed our family. Strangely, Daniel's body was found miles away.'

'Did someone attack them and steal the Land Rover, then?' asked Dylan, his curiosity piqued. He felt his grandad shift position. Was he sitting, too? Dylan used to imagine him lying in his coffin, but now he knew better.

'Nobody attacked them. Daniel killed Louisa and then killed himself, possibly out of guilt. There were two bodies found on the common that day.'

'I thought you said Daniel's body was found somewhere else?'

'That's right. The two bodies on the common were Louisa's and a strange man's. He was slumped on a park bench,

decomposed. The police never did find out who he was, but he'd been dead a long, long, time before Daniel and Louisa had arrived, possibly several weeks. A tramp probably. Horrific scene. No one will know the truth.'

Dylan raised his palms to the moonlit sky, tutted, and said, 'Don't the dead talk to each other? Just ask Louisa and Daniel what happened.'

'We, the dead, as you so eloquently put it, only speak to those that we knew amongst the living. We can't reach Louisa, it's like her soul is lost, and we refuse to acknowledge Daniel, despite his pleas of innocence. Maybe you can find out why he did it.'

A ferocious whisper rose up from the myriad dead, overwhelming Dylan's soul before sending a surge of radio static into his brain.

'RUNNNNNNNNNN!' screamed the dead.

The deep, *thud thud thud,* of approaching footfalls caused him to jump to his feet. The caretaker, Arwel Davies, was hurtling down the small path between the graves.

Dylan sighed and his shoulders relaxed. 'It's okay. It's just the caretaker.' He stepped forward and waved. 'Hi, Mr Davies. It's Dylan!' he shouted, but Arwel's pace increased. When Arwel rounded the corner into the row of graves where Dylan now stood, Dylan saw his eyes.

His shiny, red eyes.

Dylan turned on his heels and ran, but his short legs were no match for Arwel's bounding strides and he closed on Dylan within seconds. Dylan darted from left to right, and back again, over and over, like a squirrel running from danger, undecided on his escape route.

When Arwel's hand brushed Dylan's shoulder, Dylan ducked and spun round. Gravel shot up in the air like a wave and he quickly doubled back. He darted back and forth between the gravestones, his mind desperate to source an exit.

He glanced over his shoulder to see red eyes bearing down on him.

While his lungs struggled to take on oxygen, a faint taste of iron crawled into his dry throat and his heart slammed in time with his feet. When he dashed into the next row, his wide eyes scanned left and right and spotted something in the shadows.

In the middle distance, a winged cherub statue stood over a child's grave and from the shadows behind it rose the scarred, emaciated, old man who had appeared during Tom's funeral.

Dylan was trapped.

While Arwel's feet pounded closer, the old man raised a withered arm and pointed a bony finger, not at Dylan, but at a cluster of blackberry bushes in front of the rear wall.

Behind the bushes urged the old man's finger.

Dylan didn't stop to argue. His feet pelted over gravel and uneven grass verges, ankles threatening to give way any second. He whizzed past the suited man toward the bushes and slid beneath them like an American baseball player sliding for home base. His face and arms slashed open as he slid deeper into the dense brambles. Ignoring the pain, he scrambled to his feet at the back of the bushes and his shoe clanked against something metal in the darkness. Blindly, hands searched and found a rusty gate, while slivers of rusted metal sliced into his skin. His fingers quickly located and wiggled frantically at the bolt that barred his freedom.

An abrupt, high-pitched wailing pierced the silence, slicing into his brain and freezing his body.

'Come on!' he screamed, willing the bolt to loosen.

After a final, defiant squeak, the bolt clanked free, but the gate failed to budge; years of corrosion held it stiff. Frantic, Dylan screamed, and violently shook the gate. It moved an inch.

Hope.

He raised his right leg and repeatedly kicked the bolt. Each kick moving it a painstaking inch until he was finally able to squeeze his scrawny frame through the gap and into the woods. He didn't stop running until his damp feet slid across the linoleum of his kitchen floor.

He slammed the kitchen door shut, locked it, and slumped against it. The only sounds he could hear were his hungry lungs and his pounding heart.

What the hell was going on? First Howard, and now Arwel.

Heartbeats and breaths settled, he tiptoed upstairs, stood on the landing and listened. The house was silent apart from the grunts and guttural snores emanating from his mother's bedroom. He lightly rapped his knuckles on Kaelum's bedroom door before braving a peek inside; he was out.

Dylan checked on his mother, who smelt of coconuts and sugar. He emptied her ashtray, removed a glass and an empty bottle of Malibu, and silently prayed his father would get better before she drunk herself to death.

In the living room, he viewed the vast array of photographs of Auntie Louisa, but what he really wanted to see was not on display, and never had been. He searched the kitchen, dining room and, finally, the living room. Searching through his parents private things made him nervous and ashamed in equal measures. What would he say if he was caught? He was a terrible liar. He always looked away and never maintained eye contact, which was an obvious tell-tale sign of a storyteller, at least, that is what his junior school form teacher had told him when he lied about stealing a bottle of milk during his stint as milk monitor.

What did he learn from it? Well, the cane bloody hurt, and

not doing the crime in the first place meant there was no need to lie. Perhaps his parents weren't aware of the tell-tale signs of deception and that was something that only teachers, and the military interrogators that Mostyn spoke of, were trained to spot.

With a chest full of worry, he continued his search.

It was ten P.M. when he found a tatty biscuit tin, which creaked and clanked as he prised the lid off. Inside were handfuls of loose black and white photographs. The images, their edges crinkled and torn, were faded and speckled with brown patches. He selected a handful and shuffled through them like a pack of cards, before he finally found what he was looking for: a picture of twin girls, Christiana and Louisa.

Proof that the dead don't lie.

~

Dylan sat with his back against his headboard and the grizzly book laid across his knees.

It really was a thing of nightmares.

Terrified that the brain freeze and nose bleeds would result in a tumour, Dylan chose to handle it with gloves. If nothing happened, he would revert to touching it, letting it re-write his brain once more.

For several minutes, he pondered what to ask it. Despite being alone—apart from Eddie who stared at him from the poster above—he still felt stupid speaking aloud.

He opened it, expecting blank pages, but new words in the same ancient language were already scribbled there.

Dylan could now understand them. It read:

You are a Psychopomp destined to escort souls to Transmogoria.

You possess the power of Nekrôspiél. The ability to decipher the dead's babble and incessant chatter, allowing you to communicate with an individual soul amongst the myriad dead.

"You are a Psychopomp" made him sound like a superhero. His teeth bit into his bottom lip and he gripped the book tightly as a wave of childish excitement flowed through him. His head was a swirl of thoughts but the important one was, why did Daniel kill Louisa?

As if reading his mind, new words scrawled across the page, written by an unseen hand ...

He didn't kill Louisa. She was dispatched by a Cythraul—a death-dealer.

His jaw dropped and it took him several head shakes before his brain fog cleared. His grandparents had to forgive Daniel, now. More questions poured into his skull and he remembered what Andrew had said to him earlier, '... *Where did he get the book?*' Andrew was onto something there, but maybe it wasn't *where* Gareth got the book but rather who was *in* the book? Who was answering Dylan's questions? Could he, or she, be trusted? Unfortunately, Dylan couldn't monitor his or her eyes for tell-tale signs of lying, so he just had to go with his gut.

'Who are you?' he asked.

We are Kordialis, Dylan.

Dylan stifled a scream. How did this thing, whoever or *whatever* it was, know his name, and why did Kordialis sound so familiar? Had he dreamt it or had it been implanted with those new memories? He was stupefied, but he needed the truth.

'*So*, who killed Louisa?' he asked.

Nothing.

He sat in silence, repeating the question over and over, but the book failed to respond. He flexed his fingers, knuckles white. Why wouldn't the stupid book tell him?

Gareth's words floated into his head, "... *it will only show you when you need to know and not before."* Dylan remembered a memory that the book had given him about restless souls, so he decided to change tack.

'Are all souls good?' he enquired.

Good and bad are two sides of the same coin. Which side shows uppermost depends on the soul. There are three archetypal evil souls.

'What are they?' asked Dylan.

Bogies — restless, tempting, spirits desperate to commit the acts they did whilst alive. They are the voices in your head, the footsteps behind you as you walk, and the silence when you turn around.

The words faded when Dylan blinked and new letters bled onto the page, quickly forming sentences.

Coblynau — evil spirits that haunt the corridors of Transmogoria searching for weakened souls to wrench from the living, so they can live again in that poor souls body.

'Weakened? How?'

Unconscious. Heart attack. Coma. Resuscitated bodies do not always contain the original soul.

The Coblyn is limited only by the flesh of its human vessel.

'I wouldn't want to meet them in the dark,' murmured Dylan.

They are the dark.

But there is darker.

Dylan watched the word 'darker' fade until there was nothing. He waited for more words to appear but none came. He got off his bed and began pacing up and down. Minutes later, the page remained blank.

Dylan crossed his arms over his chest. 'What about this death-dealer?'

Cythraul are demons that take life at will, jumping from body to body to remain amongst the living. They are the purest of evil, and one is here.

CHAPTER 20
KILLER ON THE LOOSE

Monday 21st September, 1981
Draigwen Police Station

The chatter in the briefing room instantly fell silent when Detective Constable Kerry Edwards read out Howard Cobley's autopsy results. The pathologist's report, which Kerry had read several times in disbelief, revealed that the decomposition of Howard's body had been well into the putrefaction stage. This suggested that the time of death was at least four to five days *before* his body was discovered. The report also highlighted several inconsistencies and anomalies surrounding the state of the body.

Despite obvious stage three decomposition throughout, resulting from tissue and cell breakdown and the release of foul-smelling gases, there was minimal necrophagous insect activity on, or within, Howard's body. This suggested that his body may have been stored in a sterile environment that prevented insects from reaching it. The report also highlighted that the lacerations to his face, hands, arms and neck occurred post-mortem.

'So this guy who drove all the way from Cardiff to Draigwen, crashed his bus and ran off, was already dead?' interrupted a grinning Jukesy.

'Yes, that is what the report is suggesting,' Kerry retorted, her glare dissolving his smirk. 'However, WPC Brasking has interviewed a credible witness to the crash who's description of the driver matches the deceased's description, so we have to assume that the there are tenuous circumstances here. Fi' also took a statement from a young lad who claims he saw Howard alive on the Broadmead estate twenty-four hours before Fi' found the body.' She tapped a finger on the report and added, 'But, considering what we know from this, that statement is fantasy.'

Kerry turned to Fiona. 'We can disregard any comments of glowing red eyes, too. Don't you think, Fi?' Her exaggerated eye roll causing stifled chuckles.

'I'm not so sure,' Fiona said, defiantly. 'And we can't disregard Mark Jones' statement, either.'

Kerry tucked her hands into her armpits and tilted her head. 'Oh, and why is that?'

Her condescending tone and pinched expression hurt Fiona and she paused to retrieve her notebook to provide confirmation before answering, but Kerry had a stick up her arse.

'I don't have all day!'

Fiona found the page. 'Here it is. Wednesday sixteenth of September, six thirty-four P.M. Call from a Dai Morris at number six Ebdon Road on the Broadmead estate. A dishevelled bus driver was outside his garden, raging like a madman. Dai's a well built miner but when he attempted to confront him the guy ripped their gate clean off the hinges with one hand. Dai also stated that the man oozed evil and his eyes appeared to glow red. He was also chewing a finger—Dai's words, not mine—so he ran back into his house.

'Prior to all of this, another boy, Dylan Wolfendale, had asked to speak to Dai's daughter, Emily, while his friend waited by their gate, but Dai didn't know him,' explained Fiona.

'How old is Dai? Is he credible?' Kerry asked.

Fiona closed her notebook.

'Fifty-three and, yes, he is. His story corroborates Mark's,' assured Fiona.

'Okay, we'll pay them a visit. Right, we know pathology's time-of-death calculations aren't always exact, so we have to assume they're *way* out in this case—at least a day or two—and as for the crash injuries being post-mortem, well, God knows. They did find the remains of Howard's finger in his stomach, so that fits Dai's story.'

Jukesy laughed. 'Cannibal zombies!'

'There are no dead men walking!' snapped Kerry, glancing at the coppers sat beside Jukesy expecting retaliation, but they lowered their gazes to the floor.

Fiona gingerly raised her hand. When Kerry nodded, she asked, 'Does the lack of insects suggest Howard's body was moved to Arwel's house to frame him?'

'Good point. If Howard succumbed to his injuries elsewhere, why was he moved? Maybe the killer had something on their property they didn't want us to see.

'I want ears to the ground with any known informants, authorised or otherwise, and plod on door-to-door around the divisional area. There's been no sightings of Arwel. I don't think he's involved, but I'm not ruling it out. What *does* he know and why's he gone walkabout? Panicked? Scared? He's ex-Army, so possibly not.

'SGT Thomas will be co-ordinating all teams and PC Jukes has just volunteered himself for night shift, seeing as he likes all things dark.'

Kerry couldn't help smiling when the bravado slid from

Jukesy's face and the room erupted with the sound of laughter and 'friendly' slaps to Juksey's head.

Tony crept in amid the chaos, sidled up to Kerry, and whispered into her ear. She recoiled, mumbled a reply, then bellowed, 'QUIET!

'SGT Thomas has just informed me that a young girl's body has been found under a tarpaulin on the Cerrig Brig estate. Drag marks suggest she was killed elsewhere before being propped up like a Penny-for-the-Guy in a garden. She was strangled, but too early to tell if she was sexually abused. This is a brutal one, so I need everyone focused. DI Grundle is leading the investigation and he's cancelled all leave for the foreseeable,' explained Kerry, to groans around the room.

'Another dead child? Who is she?' asked Fiona.

'Unconfirmed,' explained Kerry. 'Arwel is still a priority, but we need to stop and search everyone in the area, suspicious or not, and get as many witness statements as possible. Be vigilant; killers like to watch and gloat. Forensics will also need a hand to secure the crime scene.

'Right! It's six-fourteen, so there's roughly forty minutes of usable light. SGT Parkes will co-ordinate the search teams on the ground, but expect radio directions from the DI forthwith.'

Kerry pulled Fiona to the side and probed her for further details on the animal remains and, more specifically, *how* they were killed.

Fiona duly obliged, causing a shiver to creep up her spine as she recalled images of severed limbs, stab wounds, burnt flesh, lacerations and sawn bones, and she subconsciously wiped the animal's blood from her hands. 'Do you think the same person killed both kids?' she asked.

Kerry shrugged. 'Dunno. Ian wasn't strangled, but whoever killed those animals could have been practicing for something bigger. So, yeah, it's possible.'

Fiona picked at a hangnail and asked, 'Do you believe in the supernatural?'

Kerry's eyes shot to the ceiling, as though the answer was written on the polystyrene ceiling tiles, and Fiona instantly regretted asking.

'Don't tell me you believe this red eyed, zombie shit? I thought you were better than that?'

Fiona waved it off and began walking to the door. 'Just curious.'

'Wild imagination, more like. Listen, I want you to be family liaison. You're good at it.'

'You mean Nansi's made herself scarce, again,' Fiona admitted with a grimace.

Kerry wilted. 'You're reliable. Good eyes. Quick thinker. You don't mess around like those cock-swinging wannabes,' she said, nodding towards the departing officers. 'Join the plod, but expect my call, okay?'

Compliments were nice, but Fiona still felt punished. She ached to be part of the murder investigation, rather than making cups of tea and handing out tissues to grieving relatives. Perhaps the FLO duties could be turned to her advantage and garner time to do her own investigating, so she could prove she had the potential to make detective.

'Of course. Thanks Kerry,' she finally answered.

Kerry raised a finger. 'Oh, one more thing. That boy's statement might be subterfuge.'

Fiona frowned. 'Mark's?'

'Yeah. Sian's body was found in *his* garden, so careful who you trust.'

Was I wrong about him? Her gut was saying no. 'Mark's a good kid. There's more to these murders than we can comprehend.'

Kerry turned on her heels and headed out. 'Get a grip, Fi'. There's no zombies; just bad evidence.'

Fiona hung back until the briefing room was empty. This would be her first FLO role during a murder investigation and the thought of telling this family that their beloved daughter was never coming home made her feel sick. She sat in silence and stared at her quivering hands.

Dead bus driver. Spectral geriatric. Dead miners. Murdered kids. What the hell is happening in Draigwen?

Most murders were committed by someone known to the victim, so she needed to keep her mind focused; family members couldn't be ruled out just because they appeared distraught.

Some were good actors.

Guilty until proven innocent, was the advice from Tony during her first FLO job, and that had stuck in her mind ever since, but there was something else lodged in her thoughts, the Reverend's words, "*They would be alive once more, like you and I.*"

CHAPTER 21

FADE TO GREY

Tuesday 22nd September, 1981
Trugaredd Hospital Morgue

Sian Hawkins' naked body was laid out on a cold, steel gurney while the pathologist prepared his tools for her post-mortem autopsy. An array of surgical scalpels of various shapes and sizes, forceps, tissue retractors and clamps, and long embalming tubes and extractors were arranged across a surgical trolley draped in blue paper. But it was the sight of the polished bone saws, chisels, and hammers that turned Fiona's stomach. She covered her mouth when an involuntary stomach spasm forced it wide.

A mortuary technician covered Sian's body with a sheet and wheeled it into a neighbouring viewing room. Fiona didn't want to see her cold, grey features for the first time in front of Sian's grieving parents, so she followed the technician and slowly pulled the sheet back from Sian's face.

'Can I have a moment alone, please?'

The technician nodded and left.

Fiona leant forward and studied her face, and was

pleasantly surprised at what a superb job the technician had done on applying Sian's makeup. Taupe eye shadow, a warm ivory foundation and a subtle natural sheen to her beautiful, full lips, which was just enough to distract attention from the fading blue-greyness that was covering the rest of her body. Sian's makeup wasn't perfect, but it was the best anyone could have applied to her dead, soulless skin.

Fiona had never been a girly-girl so her makeup skills were somewhat lacking, especially with regard to eye makeup, but as most men weren't looking at her eyes, she couldn't care less. A light dusting of powder was about all she did before leaving the house for work. Au naturel, as they say in France, rather than a face full of makeup layered on with a trowel. That last thought reminded Fiona of night patrol through Draigwen on a Friday night when some of the local girls, in their low tops and skimpy skirts, were scrambling for taxis and buses to get to the Double Diamond Club in Caerphilly for a night of fun and dancing.

Sian would never dance again and Fiona wondered what sort of sick bastard could bring such a beautiful young girl's life to such an abrupt, horrid end. What was their motive? What did Sian do to them that was so bad that they needed to do this to her? What worried Fiona the most was the lingering, nagging feeling that he had done this to her for no reason whatsoever other than for the macho, sexual superiority that it might have given him over her. Whoever the perpetrator was, they were undoubtedly a coward, as they attacked her from behind before they carried out their sick sexual desires on her dead or dying body. Being the FLO meant she was not actively part of the murder investigation, but that didn't stop her from using her, "*good eyes*," as Kerry had put it.

It had dawned on Fiona last night, when her brain woke her at two A.M. and refused to be quiet, that she had been roughly Sian's age when she had obtained her strange scar, which was shaped like a three-pronged circle.

It was late summer 1970; two weeks into her first year at Draigwen Town Grammar Technical School, which was what it was called before it became a comprehensive. She had been walking home from a girl-guide's meeting and had just said goodbye to her friend, Jackie, when she was attacked by a man.

Well, *sort of*, attacked.

There were only two things Fiona could remember about that night: a man approaching her rapidly from behind, and his red eyes when she spun around to see who it was. After that it was just blackness. She woke roughly ten minutes later with a tremendous headache, holey stockings, and scuffed knees. The only lasting effect from that strange encounter had been vivid dreams, which seemed like they were someone else's, and a strange scar under her curly brown hair just behind her right ear.

The same exact scar that Howard Cobley had.

Fiona stretched her hands into some surgical gloves and slowly tried to turn Sian's head to the side, but rigor mortis had stiffened her neck and it failed to budge under Fiona's gentle touch. After applying more pressure, Fiona heard a faint crack and quickly released her hands. There was no way to move her without the mortuary staff knowing.

She changed tack.

After brushing Sian's long hair away from her neck, she pushed back the velvet covered cushion, and gently pulled her right ear-lobe upwards. The base of her skull and neck had bluish-purple discolouration due to the blood draining, under gravity, to the lower parts of her body, but there was no scar. After checking her left side, she gently smoothed and brushed Sian's hair back into place.

'Goodnight sweet angel,' she whispered, before crossing herself and placing the sheet back over Sian's head.

Once Sian's parents had completed the formal identification, Fiona escorted them back to her panda car, leaving the pathologist to ruin the mortuary technician's lovingly applied makeup during the autopsy.

The thought of Sian's face being peeled away to extract her brain brought the gut wrenching feeling back and she tried to shake the horrific thoughts from her mind. The last thing Sian's parents needed was an overly-emotional copper driving them home; they needed support and focused distractions.

Whilst driving slow and steady, with traffic permitting, she posed mundane questions relating to Sian's likes, dislikes, hobbies, favourite subjects, friends and teachers.

Her mother, Jacquelyn, was inconsolable, but her father, Bill, seemed happy to answer. So, once he began to open up, Fiona asked whether Sian had mentioned any arguments or fights at school. He couldn't recall anything. Sian, it seems, was a popular kid, loved by her family and peers alike.

When asked if any family members or school friends had become *too* friendly towards Sian, Bill went ballistic. By the time his lengthy, foul mouthed rant was over, Fiona had reached their street. It was nearly ten in the morning when she slowed to a stop a few doors from their house; it was impossible to park any closer due to the huge collection of cards, flowers, teddies, trinkets and candles that now adorned the wall, path, and road outside their house.

While Jacquelyn sobbed on the settee, Bill stroked a photograph of Sian, each swipe wiping away fresh tears. They were oblivious to everything Fiona said and the pot of tea she had made was now cold. She wrote a note detailing her contact details and a promise to keep them informed with regular visits, what good it would do. Finding out Sian had been sexually assaulted had torn them apart. There was no solace. No peaceful death.

Her goodbyes unheard, Fiona slipped away.

It was ten-forty. Tony wasn't expecting her FLO duties to end for hours, then she was due at the school. She had promised Jacquelyn she would ask Sian's closest friends to attend a private memorial service at Sian's favourite park. Secrecy was paramount; she couldn't risk the press turning it into a publicity stunt.

Her hand hovered over the car's police radio.

If she checked in now, Tony would make her join the door-to-door or, worse still, share a car with Bodie and Doyle. Although, Fiona thought the pair were more dabblers than professionals, and would be lucky to get jobs as extras on *Juliet Bravo* never mind a top-level anti-crime unit.

She turned the key and the Ford Escort coughed and grumbled to life. She crunched it into gear and drove to the Broadmead housing estate.

Indicating to turn into Ebdon Road, she spotted Kerry and two MIT officers leaving the Morris' home, and quickly swerved back onto the main road, hopefully unseen. Grumpy would have a hissy fit if he knew she was meddling in his investigation.

Dai Morris was down Oakdale Colliery pit, working longer shifts due to the recent incident—four miners killed—so Zara reluctantly led Fiona to their living room.

It was a mess; much like her hair, which was wound tightly in hot rollers and covered with a scarf. Zara was working her way through the ironing pile as a respite from cleaning the house, although she wasn't quite sure which one she hated the most.

The paisley carpet was covered in Shake n' Vac powder, which made the room look like a Columbian drugs factory that smelt like a Spring flower bed. Yet, there was a stronger smell burrowing into Fiona's sinuses. 'What's that smell?' she asked, sheepishly.

'Oh, it's vinegar,' replied Zara, slightly embarrassed. 'My mam swears by it. Makes your hair shiny and keeps the grey hairs at bay, apparently. I'll make tea.'

The smell of vinegar made Fiona think of Rawlings Fish Bar on a Friday night after way too many drinks in the Working Men's Club in Pontyfechan. She licked her lips absentmindedly while she surveyed the room, thoughts of saveloy and chips with lashings of salt and vinegar popping into her head. Despite the clutter, this was a home; a proper home. Nothing like the tiny bedsit that Fiona went back to after each shift. It was obvious that the Morris family weren't well off, but they certainly appreciated and looked after what they had.

Fiona untangled herself from the rainbow coloured doorway beads and followed Zara into the kitchen. At least Zara's kitchen was full size and in a separate room. It made Fiona's kitchenette look like a kids play set.

Zara placed two mugs on the counter. 'Kettle's on.'

'Do the coal board know what killed those miners?' asked Fiona.

'Nope. Their souls just upped and left. It was Coblynau!'

'Really?'

Zara rolled her eyes. 'Don't laugh. Some saw a floating light before they found the dead; the Cannwyll Gorff.'

Mine Goblins. Corpse candles. Normally, Fiona would have laughed but, after what she had seen, she refused to ignore anything supernatural.

'And Gladys Pugh said Nigel Parsons isn't the same man that went down the pit Friday morning,' continued Zara. 'He doesn't know his wife, anymore.'

'Scary,' muttered Fiona, whilst thinking of bodysnatchers.

'Absolutely.' Zara shivered. 'Emily is terrified for her dad. We both are.'

'How is Emily? Is she coping, after what happened to Sian?'

'Is that why you're here? Your colleagues that just left asked about that bus driver. We saw his photo in the paper. Dai said it was definitely the guy who came here.'

'I discovered his body.'

'Oh, God. How awful for you.'

Fiona couldn't hide her emotions and Zara saw the stress etched in her face.

'Sounds like you could do with this tea,' she said, handing Fiona a mug.

'Thanks. Yes, it wasn't pretty. Did you see Howard, or was it just your husband?'

Zara shook her head. 'Just Dai and Emily.'

'Emily?'

'Yeah, she was looking out of the landing window.'

Fiona took out her notebook and scribbled some notes. 'Thanks for letting me know. Is it okay if I speak to Emily? I'll be at the school, later.'

'Yes. Happy to help. Any leads on Sian's killer? I saw the awful news on telly. Emily had already left for school; she doesn't know.'

'Sorry, I can't comment on the investigation. It'll be announced in school, later, and officers will be there to conduct interviews.'

'It's scary that there's a sicko about. That could've been Emily. Gives me the creeps.'

'Try not to worry, there'll be regular patrols in the area for a while, now.'

Just then, the side gate creaked and Zara jumped up, peaked inside the kettle, and flicked it back on. 'He's early, today,' she said, before turning the oven on.

Dai Morris dumped his NCB duffle coat, boots and helmet by the back door and began stripping off his blackened clothes. Fiona could see the shape of his pecs through his tight, dirty T-shirt and she watched while he slowly tugged it over his head revealing a chiselled stomach. She didn't realise she was licking her lips again, and instantly blushed.

'Whoa, hang-a-banger, love!' Zara admonished. 'Our visitor doesn't wanna see your white bits.'

Dai put his T-shirt back on. 'Sorry, love. Didn't see you there.' He kissed Zara and trotted through the kitchen. 'I'm off for a bath.'

Fiona grabbed his thick forearm as he went past. 'Actually, I need to ask you a few questions. It'll only take a sec'. I promise.'

'Is this about the murder? Is Emily safe, then?' asked Dai.

'We're advising parents to keep their children close at all times and, if possible, keep them in at night. Especially young girls. We'll do all we can to catch this killer, but we need parents to cooperate and isolate their children to ensure their safety. A curfew, so to speak.'

'I understand,' said Zara. 'Let's hope they catch the twat, soon.'

'So, what d'you want me for, then, love?' asked Dai.

Fiona asked Dai to confirm Howard's injuries and whether he'd seen a scar on the back of Howard's head, which he hadn't; he didn't get close because the guy was deranged. When asked if Emily and Sian were friends, they both shrugged. Emily had never mentioned her, although she had mentioned the school bullies—Dean and his friends—several times, so Fiona jotted down their names.

Zara giggled when Dai recalled slamming the door in Dylan's face when he mentioned money. She believed Dai had inadvertently shut the door on their future son-in-law; Emily hadn't stopped talking about him.

'Why?' asked Fiona, pen poised for action.

'He told us about the money, see.'

'Sponsorship money?'

'No, Dai was wrong about that. Tom's savings were hidden in the Grandfather clock. We'd never have paid for the funeral without it, and none of us knew it existed. Tom never said.'

'How did Dylan know?'

'It's a mystery. We've never met him. Emily saw him the night Tom died, but he didn't speak to Tom.'

'Could he have met Tom before?'

'It's possible. But why would he confide in an outsider? It doesn't make sense, unless he's—'

Dai sighed. 'Not that, again.'

'Unless he's what?' urged Fiona, bemused.

'Psychic,' continued Zara.

Dai rolled his eyes. 'He's not psychic. He's weird, and he's *not* dating my daughter! I'm having a bath. Nice to see you again, Fi'.'

Fiona watched his broad shoulders disappear down the hallway before she whispered, 'What makes you think he's psychic?'

'How else *would* he know? Some people have the gift, you know. Do you know Madame Zina on Snailcreep Road?'

Fiona shook her head.

'She's a Fortune Teller and Clairvoyant. She does private readings for one pound fifty per session. You should go. She's amazing. She probably knows who killed those people.'

Zara tilted the dregs in her tea-cup to one side and pointed at the scattering of tea leaves in the bottom. 'She can read your future in these, too. Amazing, I tell you.'

Fiona wouldn't normally believe such crap, but she was becoming more receptive. 'Thanks, I'll look her up.'

~

Fiona parked up outside Arwel's house, which was still surrounded by police tape, and walked across the road to the chapel. The gates were blocked by a large temporary warning sign and she could see an area fenced off near the caretaker's shed. One builder was busy at work on the drain while two others leant on spades, smoking.

Typical council job, she thought, as she tried to get their attention.

After a few moments, two of the builders squabbled to come to her aid until another burly builder came out of the chapel and shouted for them to get back to work. He stomped down the driveway towards the gate with one seriously huge, anvil-shaped, Desperate Dan type jaw leading the way and, judging by his enormous physique, he could probably devour several cow pies. He was dressed smarter and somewhat cleaner than the others, so Fiona guessed he must be the foreman.

'Can I help you, officer?' asked Desperate Dan.

'Is Reverend Foster about?'

'Sorry, you've just missed him. He's gone to sort out our money. Fixing the drains, see, love. He asked us to keep it all closed until he returned 'cause the caretaker's buggered off.'

'He's back. That's him, there,' Fiona replied, pointing a finger through the gate.

Arwel Davies was standing near to the spot where Fiona had cleaned up all those dead animals. Fiona watched as he sniffed the air and, weirdly, bent forward and sniffed a gravestone, too.

'Mr Davies!' shouted Fiona. 'Arwel! Can I have a word, please?'

Arwel Davies stood motionless, staring straight at her.

Fiona rattled the gate. 'Can you let me through. That man is wanted for questioning.'

Desperate Dan obliged and stood aside to let her pass.

Fiona stepped through and unclipped her radio. 'WPC234 to control, over.'

'Control to WPC234, go ahead, over,' replied Bill Parkes.

'WPC234 to control, I've eyes on Arwel Davies. He's at Larkmead Chapel, over.'

'Control to WPC234, wait for backup, do not approach him. I repeat, do *not* approach. DC Edwards and SGT Thomas are in your vicinity, so I'll divert them to you, over.'

'WPC234 to control, roger and out.'

When Fiona started up the driveway with the man-mountain Desperate Dan in tow, Arwel Davies was nowhere to be seen. The area near where she saw him was swathed in jet-black shadow, which moved like silk over the graves and poured into the ground.

Fiona and the builders thoroughly searched the chapel and grounds, but there was no sign of him. While Fiona waited for her colleagues to arrive, she couldn't shake off the feeling that she was being watched, or the niggling pain behind her right ear.

CHAPTER 22

Making Your Mind Up

'Sian's body was in my garden!' crackled Mark's voice over the walkie.

Six in the morning and Mark had verbal diarrhoea, whilst Dylan was barely able to focus; his mind in turmoil. The recently deceased were queuing for a ride to Transmogoria—three last night—and Dylan was starting to wonder how many had been killed by the Cythraul or Coblynau. He wasn't exhausted, though. Sometimes you just have to slow it down, so he slept in the lobby under the floating aura of his family's doors. Sleeping outside his body, close to the dead, was peaceful. Eight hours there was merely minutes here.

He replied *ten-five*, and maintained radio silence while Mark vented for nearly an hour.

He and his brother, Darren, had been interrogated for nearly eight hours, but their mother was too inebriated to stand, never mind speak coherently. Thankfully, as Darren was eighteen, Social Services wouldn't be taking Mark into care, but that was the least of his worries. Initially, both boys were accused of murdering Sian, which terrified the crap out of them, and their house was now a full-on crime scene complete with white tent and crime scene investigators in white overalls dotted around like marshmallow men.

'You've done nothing wrong. Skip school and go to bed. Over,' suggested Dylan, after Mark went quiet.

'I can't. I've been making cups of tea for everybody since they brought me home. Over.'

An image of Mark in an apron forced a smile across Dylan's stressed face before they finally said goodbye.

Dylan sat on the large stone steps leading to the school's tennis courts and stared at the red 'D' scribbled on the corner of his mathematics test. Despite no longer being sleep deprived, he still couldn't concentrate on schoolwork.

'I wouldn't worry about it, Wolfy,' Steven said, nudging Dylan from his thoughts. 'Mark will help you,' he reassured.

Dylan frowned. 'With what?'

'Maths.'

'Mark?' he said, incredulously. 'He's done worse than me!'

'Weird. He helped me get a B,' advised Steven, as Mark ambled towards them. 'Where were you? I thought we were going on our bikes, last night?'

Dylan glanced at Mark, who subtly shook his head. Although gossip in the town was rife, Mark didn't want people thinking he was a murderer, so Dylan had reluctantly agreed not to tell Steven about Sian.

Mark sat and rummaged in his pocket. 'You weren't in,' he grumbled.

'Huh? I never went out,' Steven said, exasperated.

While another ant popped and sizzled under the concentrated sunbeam of Mark's magnifying glass, a scream drew the boy's focus in that direction.

Dean and his gang were laughing at a boy clutching his crotch and rolling over the grass. As the duty teacher approached to see what all the fuss was about, the gang disappeared faster than the Bucks Fizz girl's skirts, leaving their victim to the mercy of gawping onlookers.

'What happened?' asked Dylan.

'He was posted,' answered Steven.

'What's that?'

'It's when three or four people grab you by the legs and arms, then they run you, legs open, into a post.'

'Or a tree,' added Mark.

Steven laughed. 'Yeah. It sends your bollocks back up. *If* they've dropped.'

Dylan cringed and crossed his legs. 'Owww, the poor bugger.'

'Yeah. He won't be pissing straight for a while and no fun with the ladies, either,' winked Steven. 'Talking of ladies, how's your girlfriend? You kissed her?'

Dylan felt his face burn and he shook his head.

'You asked her out?' Steven continued.

'Not spoken to her.'

'Well, now's your chance.' Steven said, as a girl with pigtails and thick, black glasses approached.

Dylan's mouth gaped and he went white. 'Oh shit, it's Emily. What do I say?' he croaked.

'Don't ask me, I haven't got a Scooby,' replied Mark. 'Just talk to her.'

Emily sat down on the steps beside Dylan, while Mark and Steven busied themselves doing nothing. She sat cross-legged; her plaid skirt ruffling in the cold breeze, and Dylan could see goosebumps appearing on the flesh above her knee-high white socks.

He offered her his dap bag. 'Sit on this. The floor's really cold.'

Emily smiled and slid it underneath her. She poked and prodded it for a long while, like a cat kneading its bed, before finally settling in one spot.

'Sorry, it's not very comfortable,' apologised Dylan.

'It's fine. Thank you for telling us about my grancha's money.'

'No probs.'

Dylan shifted uneasily. He knew where the conversation was heading.

'How did you know where it was?'

Dylan bit his lip; he didn't want to lie. While he debated how to answer, Steven did it for him.

'Tom's ghost told him,' he blurted, pulling a Commando comic from out of his satchel.

Dylan groaned and wilted.

Mark's jaw fell open.

Emily glared at the back of Steven's head, waiting for another response, but none came. 'Pleb!' She directed the outburst at Steven, before turning on Dylan. 'Well? How *did* you know?'

Dylan leant away from her clenched fists and mumbled, 'Slinky's right.'

In one swift motion, Emily stood and kicked Dylan's bag at his face. 'I thought you were different,' she said, sadly.

Mark rested his hand gently on her shoulder when she turned to leave, but he jumped backwards when she swung a fist at him. 'Whoa! Calm down, feisty,' he yelled, waving his palms at the floor. 'It's true. Dylan is ... Well ... Umm, just listen to him.'

Emily looked at each boy in turn and, one by one, they nodded in agreement. She sat back down and crossed her arms over her chest. 'You have two minutes.'

Dylan intertwined his fingers to stop his hands shaking, checked that there wasn't anyone within earshot, and explained as best as he could. Emily sat in silence and barely moved the whole time, so he had no idea what she was thinking. Despite his nerves, she made him feel at ease, and he opened up way more than he expected. When he mentioned his frequent visits to his grandparents' grave to chat with them, he began to well up but he sniffed it back and continued. When he recounted Tom's passing, she cut in.

'Was he in pain?' she asked, wiping her eyes on the back of her hand.

'No, not at all,' assured Dylan. 'Very relaxed, actually,' he lied. 'I promised him I'd look after you,' he added, with a smile.

Emily stared at the three boys for several seconds before slowly shaking her head. 'This is crazy. Do you believe all of this?'

Steven lifted his head from behind the Commando comic and met her stare. 'I didn't know about the out-of-body stuff. Is that why you were dead to the world in Garrett's?'

'I didn't know, either,' moaned Mark, looking dejected, and Dylan realised he'd said too much.

'Would you have believed me if I had?'

The boys shrugged.

'I knew about talking to the dead,' continued Steven. 'It's weird, but Wolfy's not a liar. Too much of a worrier for that, see.'

'Yeah, that's true,' agreed Mark. 'Where'd you get that comic?' he asked Steven, before trying to snatch it from his grasp.

'Piss off, mun! I nicked it off Mossy. He won't mind.'

Mark threw his head back and laughed. 'No, of course not. He'll just kick your head in. Giz a look,' he demanded, before diving on top of him.

'Gerroff me!' bellowed Steven.

As the two boys rolled around on the grass, Emily leant

closer and Dylan could smell a hint of coconut on her skin when she whispered, 'Can you talk to my grancha?' The warm breath on his ear sent a tingle throughout his body and the hairs on his neck stood up.

'Y-Y-Yeah,' he stuttered, fumbling with the strap of his bag. 'It's called Nekrôspiél.'

Falling silent, Emily fidgeted with the pleats of her skirt, while her toecaps tilted inwards, and several minutes passed before she finally asked, 'Could I talk to him, you know, through you?"

'Yeah. In the graveyard?' he offered, but Emily cringed. 'Oh, okay, umm ... We've got a camp in Colledig Wood, we could meet there one night after school?'

'What about the twentieth of October? Say, 5pm?'

Dylan felt his heart quiver and smiled. 'Tidy, but that's weeks away.'

'That's my birthday. I'm staying over my Uncle Clive's while they prepare our house for my party. He always falls asleep on the sofa, so it'll be easy to sneak out,' she explained.

Dylan gave her directions to his camp and promised to meet her, although, deep down, he was disappointed that he wasn't invited to the party but, then again, he hadn't exactly made a good impression with her father.

'I can't wait,' she said, her feet tapping with excitement. She smiled and brushed his hand. 'Thank you.'

Flustered and embarrassed, Dylan turned his head away and stared out across the tennis courts to the gymnasium, and she followed his gaze.

'Is that your gym teacher?' she asked, pointing.

Arwel Davies was stood by the gymnasium entrance, his head swivelling back and forth as though he were watching tennis, before it stopped abruptly and he looked their way.

DING-DING, DING-DING, DING-DING!

The sound of the school bell ringing startled Dylan and he jumped.

'Are you okay?' Emily asked, concern creeping across her face.

'Erm, yes,' he mumbled, his eyes scanning the middle distance when hordes of kids began running towards them.

She smiled. 'Good. See you later, then.'

The boys watched Emily catch up with her friends before pouncing on Dylan and chanting, 'Wolfy! Wolfy! Wolfy!' He tried to pull away, but they kept on cheering and prodding him.

'STOP IT!' he snapped. 'This isn't the time for pissing about, is it, *Mark*?'

Steven stared at Mark, who lowered his head in shame. 'Why, what's happened?' asked Steven, confused.

Dylan glanced at Mark, but his face was saying *shut it, bigmouth*. 'Umm, I just saw Arwel.'

'Which one?' asked Steven. 'The normal one or the mad bastard with red eyes?'

'Dunno, he wasn't that close.'

'Where to?' asked Mark, looking around.

'By the gym.'

'We've got P.E. next. Lets get him!' Mark proposed, full of bravado, before marching down the steps, chest puffed out and arms curved as though he were carrying a carpet under each one.

The duty teacher's voice crackled over her megaphone announcing that lessons were suspended, and that all pupils were to immediately attend the main hall.

'Saved by the bell, Wolfy,' joked Steven, slapping Dylan across the arse and running up the steps. 'Last one there's a girl!' he taunted.

Dylan nudged Mark's arm. 'We should've told him.'

The Headmistress, Mrs Diane Griffiths, broke the horrific news of Sian Hawkins' murder to gasps and screams from around the hall. One girl fainted and another was sick over the back of another's head, but the majority of the room were simply dumbstruck. Some of Sian's closest friends were inconsolable and it took the teachers several minutes to calm them so the Headmistress could continue speaking. Despite classes being suspended, there was no celebrations like on a snow day; the atmosphere was like walking through treacle.

Steven had buried his head between his long legs like an ostrich checking the warmth of its eggs. Both Mark and Dylan rubbed his back and asked if he was all right, but he simply grunted and mumbled something about his laces.

Mrs Griffiths continued by saying that, because there were no suspects in custody, all pupils, especially girls, should remain with a parent or guardian at all times and a night-time curfew was imminent.

'What's a curfew?' asked Mark.

'We're not allowed out at night,' grumbled Dylan.

'Will they arrest us if we do, then?'

Dylan shrugged.

The Headmistress continued by saying that officers would be interviewing everyone throughout the day, and the nurse would be available if anyone felt ill after this shocking news. Pupils who would normally return home for dinner were advised to remain in school and would be given a free meal in the canteen. Parents would be notified although, as not every family had a phone, this would not be possible for everyone.

The Headmistress was joined on stage by Fiona, Jukesy, Simon and two police staff in white coats. When the Headmistress finished her update, PC Jukes was called up to the lectern, which he approached with an air of arrogance.

'Hello, I'm PC Brian Jukes. I can clearly see how distressing this is, so I'll keep this short. We cannot reveal details of the investigation, so please don't ask. All I can say at this stage is that Sian's body was discovered in the front garden of a house on Bryncoed Road, Cerrig Brig Estate yesterday evening. The Jones family have been helping us with our enquiries. So, thanks for that, Mark, wherever you are.'

Heads turned in Mark's direction, like a Mexican wave, and he slid down in his seat.

'You knew,' snarled Steven, through gritted teeth.

'I said we should have told Slinky,' whispered Dylan, and regretted it when he saw the anger on Steven's face.

PC Jukes continued, 'I must add that Mark and his family were *not* involved. Now, we are doing everything in our power to catch this killer, but we need your help. PC Simon Davies and I will be interviewing everyone and fingerprints will be taken by the fingerprint analysts in the white coats. Once interviewed, pupils living locally will be sent home, whereas those who ride the bus will gather in the gymnasium to await their arrival.' He glanced at Mrs Griffiths, who confirmed with a nod. 'WPC Fiona Brasking is the Family Liaison Officer assigned to Sian's family. She's only here for a short while to speak to a few of Sian's closest friends, so please make yourself known to her.

'We want this killer behind bars ASAP, so I cannot stress how important it is for you all to be open and honest. It's imperative that you come forward with any info, no matter how insignificant you think it might be. We'd particularly like to speak to any boys who saw Sian after school yesterday. Thank you.'

'They must think a boy did it,' whispered Mark.

Steven's knuckles went white when he gripped the back of the chair in front of him and said, 'There's only one knob who would do such a thing and that's Scrapper.'

'Fiona will catch him. She's a really good cop,' reassured Mark.

Steven leant closer to Mark. 'We need to do our own investigation. We'll meet at Mossy's. He'll know what to do.'

Dylan made himself as tall as possible in his seat, scanned the room, and spotted Dean and his gang a few rows back. He was ashen faced, but as mean looking as ever. 'Do you think Scrapper did it?'

'Probably. He told me to stay away from her,' reminded Steven. 'Maybe he asked her out and she said no.'

'Only Sian can answer that, but she's dead,' said Mark.

Steven stared at Dylan.

After a few seconds, the penny dropped, and Dylan's heart raced in his chest. 'I can't,' he said, feebly.

Steven glared. 'Why not?' he asked, his voice risen with anger. 'You're the only one who can, unless of course you've been bullshitting?'

'Leave him alone,' warned Mark. 'He said he can't do it.'

Steven jabbed Dylan hard in the arm. 'Well, is it bullshit?'

'No.'

'Prove it, then.'

CHAPTER 23

BRINGIN' ON THE HEARTBREAK

The A block toilets weren't the nicest of places to hold a seance, but it was unoccupied and, hopefully, he wouldn't be stuffing soiled underpants in the bin this time. Although he could speak to his grandparents in his head, Dylan had no idea whether this would work with Sian.

He locked himself in a cubicle and composed his thoughts, trying to filter out the babbling voices.

Nekrôspiél.

He closed his eyes and tried to focus on Sian's soul.

In his mind he said, 'Sian Hawkins? Can you hear me, Sian?' And even though nobody could see or hear him, he still felt stupid.

As he waited on that grubby toilet for a reply, he read some of the graffiti that adorned the cubicle door and walls:

Plop, plop, ahh...
Hail Hitler!
Dazza woz ere
KF loves SH
Wot no paper

How to avoid roadworks, by Dai Version
Don't beam me up Scotty, I'm having a sh—
Draigwen Town sucks
...So does Scrapper!

The last one made him chuckle and he wondered if the boy who wrote it was now out of hospital. Dylan called Sian's name a few more times, but nothing happened. It was useless. His talent, if you could call it that, simply didn't extend past his own family.

He was just about to give up when a trembling voice popped into his head.

'Yes, I'm here. Who's this?'

'Oh, hi,' he replied, the shock in his voice all too evident. 'I'm Dylan Wolfendale. We're in the same school ... Er, I mean you were ... Well, you are, but you're not here anymore, 'cause, erm ... You're ... You know—'

'Dead.'

Dylan lowered his head in shame even though he suspected, and hoped, she couldn't see him.

'Huh-uh ... Yeah. Sorry. We're both in Harwood's RE class.'

'I don't remember you.'

'That's okay. I'm not popular,' he said, truthfully.

Trying not to be blunt or fumble his words, he asked if she wouldn't mind talking about the attack. She had no reason not to, and no inclination to lie or exaggerate like a living person might.

Sian had been making her way through the Cerrig Brig estate to meet friends when she was attacked. Something or someone, hit her in the back and she fell forward. When she described being strangled, struggling to breathe, and coughing up blood, Dylan felt sick. Thankfully, her ordeal didn't last long before everything went dark. Incorporeal, she saw her killer standing over her wearing a flimsy, plastic Frankenstein Halloween mask. Before the fog blurred her vision completely, she saw him retrieve his school tie, which she had ripped from his neck.

What piqued Dylan's interest was her description of what happened afterwards: a crow strutted into view, cawed, and walked towards a shimmering door. Its hopping gait amplified as it got closer and, somehow, Sian knew she had to follow it. It wasn't her sudden demise that terrified her, it was the strange shadow that tried, and failed, to enter her fallen body.

~

Dylan's shoes squeaked on the polished hallway floor when he ran back to class and he nearly slammed straight into Emily and Fiona, screeching to a halt just inches away. Visions of the inside of a cell flashed into his brain and he averted his eyes.

Rather than cuffing him, Fiona cooed while ruffling his fluffy hair. When Dylan and Emily exchanged diffident glances, she composed herself. She sensed a chemistry between them and didn't want to embarrass him further.

Fiona thanked Emily and sent her back to class. Dylan seemed on edge and she wasn't sure whether that was normal '*What have I done?*' nerves, or something more sinister. He denied seeing the dark suited man since the funeral, although judging by his body language, she suspected he was lying.

'Reverend Foster said you visit the cemetery most nights. Is that correct?'

Dylan opened his mouth but nothing came out.

'It's all right, Dylan. You're not in trouble,' she said, with a reassuring smile.

Dylan nodded.

'Were you there the night before Tom Morris' funeral?'

Dylan shifted his weight from foot to foot and nodded, again.

'Thanks for your honesty. Did you see anyone else? Was anyone with you? Perhaps, they saw something?'

Dylan's mind was a tornado of voices and thoughts, which made him feel more nauseous than earlier. He didn't want to drag Mark into this; a crime scene for a house was bad enough.

'I was alone. Someone scared me and I ran,' he finally blurted.

'Can you describe them?'

Dylan shook his head. 'Too dark. I ran through the graves but then I fell into ... Umm, I mean ... I-I hurt my ankle.'

Fiona's eyes bulged. '*You* fell into the crypt.'

Dylan held his hands up in front of him. 'It was an accident. I tried to tie the doors shut. Please don't arrest me, my mam will go nuts! I'm sorry, I really—'

Fiona cut him short when tears welled in his eyes. '*Shush*. Don't be silly. I'm not gonna arrest you.' She pulled him to her bosom. 'Don't cry. I'm not that scary, am I?'

Dylan laughed and rubbed his eyes in his sleeves. 'No, Miss.'

'Ahem?'

'Fiona,' he corrected, giggling.

'Good. No more silliness. I'm just trying to get the facts. There's some very nasty people about and we need to get them locked up.'

'Okay.'

'I won't mention this to the Reverend. It'll be our little secret, okay?' she said, ruffling his hair once more. Dylan visibly relaxed, and Fiona sensed he was warming to her, so she delved deeper. 'You saw him again, didn't you? The shadow man.'

Dylan nodded sheepishly. 'But it wasn't that night, though, it was last Friday. He helped me get away from him.'

'From who?'

'The caretaker.'

'Ah, I see. Was he annoyed that you were there?'

'No, it's not that. He's usually fine with it, but—'

'But what? Did he hurt you?'

'No, he ... He wasn't the same. It wasn't him.'

Fiona shook her head. 'Sorry, Dylan, I don't understand. You said it was the caretaker, Arwel Davies?'

'Yes, it was him, but not ... Erm—'

Patience straining, Fiona knelt in front of him and switched off her radio. 'Listen,' she said, softly. 'We've both seen and done some weird things, lately. Personally, I've seen that weird guy rising up out of the shadows; I've scooped up mutilated and shot animals, which was gross by the way; I've seen a man's rotten corpse, which was even more gross, *and* I've had people who saw the same guy before he died, running around with bright red eyes. So, whatever you've got to tell me isn't going to come as a shock, I can tell you!'

'Arwel had red eyes, too.'

Fiona's jaw dropped. 'Oh.'

~

'Where's Slinky?' asked Dylan, when Mark appeared by the main gate.

Mark pulled a face. 'Home, I think. Why?'

Dylan sauntered forward and scanned the street for signs of Arwel, before walking up the road. 'He won't like what I've got to say.'

Mark grabbed his shoulder, tugging him backwards. 'You've spoken to Sian. Did she see the boy?'

'How'd you know it was a boy?'

Mark scratched his face and dipped his chin to his chest. 'It's *gotta* be Scrapper, mun,' he urged.

Dylan sighed. 'We don't know that.'

Mark's expression softened. 'Of course. She definitely didn't see him, then?'

'No!' Dylan sniped back, 'Don't you believe me?'

For the second time today, Dylan fell into an awkward silence. He was hurt and frustrated in equal measures. Didn't Mark trust him?

They reached the lane beside the local park before Mark spoke again.

'Maybe Scrapper got one of his gang to do it,' he suggested, taking a sidewards glance at Dylan. 'Or they all did,' he added.

Despite Mark's eagerness for Dean's downfall, he was probably right. It was the obvious answer, but Dylan couldn't shift the irritating feeling that something really dark and evil was behind all of this.

But there is darker.

Mr Red Eyes.

Both Howard and Arwel had them. If the book was right, there was a Cythraul in Draigwen, and Dylan was the only one who knew about it.

The only one who could do something to stop him, it, or whatever *this* was.

He couldn't do this alone.

Dylan grabbed Mark's arm and whispered in his ear, 'I need to show you something.'

CHAPTER 24
ARE 'FRIENDS' ELECTRIC?

The house was empty, so Dylan led Mark straight to his bedroom, sat him on his bed, and made him promise not to tell. When Mark swore on his mother's life, Dylan fetched the book from the back of his wardrobe and warned him to keep quiet.

It didn't work; Mark was like a kid in a sweet shop.

Luckily, Dylan calmed him before Kaelum's footsteps thudded up the stairs. Seconds later, *Ghost Town* lyrics boomed through the door. The song was stopped before it had finished and another tape was inserted. Clicks and faint whirring sounds were heard as Kaelum tried to find the right song.

It infuriated Dylan. Why couldn't he listen to an album from start to finish?

When he heard *Friggin' in the Riggin'* being sung by the shipmates on the Venus, Dylan barricaded his bedroom door with his bed and sat down.

The book's rotting flesh glistened when Mark pointed at it, excited. 'Is *that* what Gareth gave you?'

Dylan nodded.

'Doesn't it freak you out?'

Dylan ran a finger over the cover and smiled. 'I thought you were into the occult?'

'I am. That book's gopping. I love it! How come it doesn't scare you, though? You're scared of everything.'

As usual, Mark was spot on. Dylan was a complete wimp when it came to everything involving the living. It made him wonder if he'd be better off with the dead permanently. He shook the thought from his head and explained everything to Mark over a ten pence bag of sweets, a box of Chocolate Cigarettes, a Milky Bar and two sachets of Space Dust.

The sweets and cigarettes were devoured before he had finished relaying what his grandparents and the book had taught him, and Mark hadn't reached for Dylan's unread copy of *Look In* once, so that was a good sign.

'So, Psychopomp, will *that* know how to stop Arwel?' Mark asked, pointing to the book.

Dylan cocked his head to the side and shrugged.

'What about those other things?' asked Mark.

'Oh, umm—' Dylan's eyes rolled back into his skull, as if searching for the answer on his brain. 'Coblynau,' he finally answered, with a click of his fingers. 'Why?'

Mark shook his head and groaned. 'You said they tempt people to do bad, right?'

'Yeah.'

'Maybe they told the killer to do it, but they don't even *know* that they killed her.'

'Shit. It could be anyone, then.'

Mark's head rocked. 'Nah, it's still Scrapper.'

Dylan undid the cuff on his right wrist, withdrew his hand inside his sleeve and opened the book, making sure he didn't touch the pages with his skin. The last thing he wanted, with Kaelum just across the landing, was Mark freaking out because he'd blacked out with a nosebleed.

The book creaked open to reveal a blank page midway through the book.

Mark leant forward. 'There's no writing,' he said, reaching for the page.

Dylan quickly grabbed Mark's wrist to stop him touching the book and a tingling sensation, like static electricity, shot up his arm, as if he had touched the book rather than Mark. But this time, instead of some random strangers memories re-writing his brain, he saw fragments of Mark's soul flash before his eyes in a split-second, like a VHS on fast-forward, with no fuzziness, jitter or annoying white lines.

Panic set in and a vision of Mr Garrett seared into Dylan's hippocampus like a red-hot poker. He refused to invade and defile his best friend's body in the same way, so he quickly released his arm.

Mark winced and clasped his hands to his temples.

'What's wrong?'

'Nothing,' whined Mark. 'Just a bad head.'

Dylan knew that he had caused the pain. Flushed with guilt, he looked away, but Mark nudged his arm and pointed at the book.

'Well, go on then. Ask it something.'

Dylan looked down at the page. 'Who is the red-eyed man?' he asked, embarrassed.

They leant forward, staring at the page.

After a few seconds, strange writing scrawled across the page and Mark's mouth dropped open, drizzling stringy saliva across his lap. 'Wow. What does it say?'

Dylan read out the words perfectly as they appeared on the page.

A Cythraul.

Dylan sighed. 'Okay, but who *is* he?'

Crulus.

'What does he want with Draigwen?'

Nothing.

'Oh ... So, why is he here?'

He does not know your likeness, but he senses you are near.

'Me? Why?'

To kill you.

Dylan started trembling and stared at his wall, unblinking. Tears dripped from his chin and two mucus snail trails adorned his top lip.

Mark rubbed his shoulder and stared at the same spot on the wall. 'Don't worry. We'll stop him,' he said, unconvincingly.

'How?'

Mark shrugged. 'I dunno. Ask the book.'

Dylan smeared snot and tears in his sleeve, and exhaled hard. He shook his arms and clicked his neck from side to side, like a boxer warming up before a bout. 'How do I kill Crulus?'

You can't.

'Shit.'

'What?' asked Mark.

'It said we can't.'

'Bollocks.'

'How do I stop him killing me?'

No response.

'Tell me.'

The page remained blank.

'*Pleeeease*!' pleaded Dylan. 'I don't want to die.'

While Dylan stared at the page willing it to answer, Mark sat in silence, unsure how to react. When he saw tears welling in Dylan's eyes once more, he put his arm around him, and the bed jerked backwards.

'Wha' you morons up to?' asked Kaelum, poking his head through the gap. 'Oh, why's he crying? Wha'd you do to him?' he growled, shoving his weight against the door.

'Nothing,' yelped Mark.

Kaelum's eyes lowered to the book in Dylan's lap. 'Whoa! What's that?'

Dylan quickly slid it under his pillow. 'Nothing.' He leant back, pushing his weight onto the bed as Kaelum tried to squeeze through.

'Let me in!' bellowed Kaelum. He shoved harder, but the boy's concerted effort forced him to retract his head before the door slammed shut. 'You can't stay in there forever. Pricks!'

Deflated, Dylan was about to hide the book when more writing materialised.

Prevent Crulus from taking more lives.

'How?'

When the time comes, you'll know. But remember ... To see, is to be seen.

'That's not an answer!' snapped Dylan. He slammed the book shut, slid it into the bag and launched it into the back of the wardrobe.

CHAPTER 25

UP UP FATTY

Monday 19th October, 1981

After several weeks of rain, a dry spell warmed its way through the Sirhowy Valley turning the fallen autumnal leaves crisp and brown, and they crunched under foot as the boys headed to Mostyn's house.

Sian Hawkins had been laid to rest beside her grandmother in Larkmead. Unlike Pritch's council arranged pauper's funeral, which was barely attended, hundreds lined the streets to give Sian a proper send off; even the school had closed. Steven kept it together for most of the morning, but when he saw her name in flowers beside the coffin, he had fallen apart.

Murder investigations were ongoing, although nobody had been charged. Despite the curfew, Dean and his gang of reprobates were seen out-and-about most evenings like nothing had happened and, in a live police press conference, DI Grundle stated that they were simply, "*... tying up loose ends before a suspect would be charged.*"

Although Dean wasn't named, rumours spread quickly. Dean's family, friends, most of the population of Pontyfechan, and even some of the teachers, reacted incredulously to the accusations; they simply could not believe that Dean Johnson could commit such an atrocity, with many no longer referring to him as Scrapper, as if he had suddenly grown angel wings. The community were in uproar and protests were even staged outside the police station, however, the boys were under no such qualms about Dean's guilt, so they began their own murder investigation.

~

On his bedside table, Mostyn unfolded a piece of wallpaper, on the reverse of which he had crudely drawn a map, and smoothed out the crinkles. Operation Fatty was scrawled across the top of the sheet and three houses were highlighted in red pen crosses: Dean's, Kevin Franklyn's and David Price's.

'So, all three suspects live in Pontyfechan?' asked Steven.

'Yeah,' replied Mostyn, pointing to his map like a proud General.

'No 'fechan way!' yelled Mark, punching Steven in the arm.

Mostyn groaned, tapped the map with an irritated finger, and laid out their plan of action.

David's house on Fenni Road was the nearest, so that was their first target. Dean and Kevin both lived on Snailcreep Road, so they would follow later. They were to survey each property and, if a suspect was seen, they were to observe and gather intel only; not that anyone *wanted* to willingly engage.

Mostyn stood with his rifle slung across his back and read out an inventory of items, and they all shouted 'check' as they pocketed each one: Ten-Four walkie, peg gun and bullets (made and supplied by Dylan), torch, penknife, gloves and snacks.

Steven's contribution to the operation was a handful of cat biscuits for each of them in case there were any dogs on guard; he was adamant that dogs would eat anything.

Mostyn also wore an army webbing belt with pouches containing a first-aid kit, lighter, a small pair of binoculars and, concealed inside his jacket, was an uncocked .177 Diana air pistol, pellets and darts.

~

Outside, the boys—wearing Mostyn's borrowed camouflaged jackets—removed the wooden pegs and playing cards from their spokes, and pulled their bicycle light dynamos away from the tyres; they needed stealth tonight. Mostyn also removed the battery from his yellow handlebar mounted horn in case an accidental button press caused a burst of ambulance, fire or police sirens blaring through the night.

Steven watched from the sidelines, his right foot sliding his skateboard back and forth in eagerness.

Around five-fifteen, they stopped two houses down from David's house. The curtains were open and they could see him huddled around the TV with the rest of his family. While the others kept watch, Mark entered via a side gate and searched the garden, outside lavatory and shed but didn't find any incriminating evidence.

After sixteen minutes, Mostyn gave the order to advance to site two: Dean's house. This was the one they were all nervous about, so they were all inwardly elated that there were no signs of life. It was Dylan and Steven's turn to stake this one out and they reluctantly crept up the lane beside Dean's house.

Huddled side by side in the darkness, Dylan began to tremble, but Steven roughly gripped his shoulder, urging silence.

Crouching against the garden fence, Steven slipped and put his hand down to stop himself falling backwards. Something moist and squidgy seemed to pop underneath the weight of his body and he shone his torch onto the floor. Protruding from beneath him was a dead rat, its entrails exploded in a mushy, bloody mess.

'Urgh, that's disgusting!' he groaned, with slimy guts dripping off his hand.

The dim circle of luminance from Dylan's torch revealed two putrid rats underneath Steven's bent knees and the stench finally wafted up his nostrils.

He vomited.

'You all right, Wolfy?'

Dylan wiped his sleeve across his mouth and nodded.

Chomp chomp chomp

'What's that noise?' asked Dylan, trying to remove stringy vomit from between his fingers.

'Huh? ... *Chomp* ... *Chomp* ... Dunno, I didn't hear anything,' replied Steven, his teeth tugging on a Curly Wurly.

Dylan watched as the caramel stretched about four centimetres before snapping. 'What're you doing?'

Steven shrugged and held up the chocolate bar.

'Seriously? I'm covered in sick and you're kneeling on rotten giblets with a gob full of chocolate!'

'I was hungry.'

Following a quick search of the garden, Steven spent over five minutes thumbing away at the combination lock on Dean's shed before the lock finally clicked open. After searching inside the shed, he climbed back over the fence and slowly lowered himself into the lane before running, crouched over, back to Dylan.

'Anything?' asked Dylan.

'Nah, but I'm not sure what we're supposed to be looking for.'

'Weird stuff, I suppose.'

'It looked normal. Messy, but normal. I don't think fatty's home.'

'And the shed?'

'Just garden tools, plant pots ... Oh, and an awesome sled with runners made from chrome car bumpers. There was something long rolled up in a sheet but it could've been anything. C'mon, I don't feel safe here.'

~

When Mark and Dylan crawled through long grass toward the back of Kevin's house, Dylan couldn't help wondering how he was going to get the grass stains out of his trousers before his mother saw them.

Mark's elbow nudged him from his thoughts. 'Don't army officers take the lead when troops attack?'

'Think so.'

'So, how come Mossy's been on rear guard at every house? He hasn't done a stake out, yet!' moaned Mark.

Dylan shrugged. 'Overwatch?'

The joint kitchen and dining room was ablaze with light and they could see Kevin's mother in the kitchen, but there was no sign of either Kevin or his dad.

Located in the bottom corner of the garden was a small brick lavatory with a shabby wooden door flaking with paint. From where they lay, the moonlight lit the building's exterior, and the corrugated roof looked to be clinging on for dear life.

When they crawled closer to the garden, the door's metal catch suddenly clanked upwards and a man exited, moonlight bouncing off his shiny, bald head.

'What's Harwood doing here?' whispered Dylan.

'That's Kevin's sick stepdad, you tit.'

'Really? I didn't know,' grumbled Dylan.

They watched as Harwood pulled his trousers up over his hairy, silverback arse and zipped himself up. He tightened his belt, turned, and barked at the door, 'The best part of you ran down your mother's leg. You piece of shit!'

He strutted down the garden and disappeared around the side of the house.

Seconds later, he waltzed into view through the kitchen window wearing a huge smile. Grabbing a can of beer from the fridge, he pulled the ring and took a long swig, before wrapping his hairy arms around Kevin's mother, Carol, who was busy washing dishes in the sink.

The boys cringed as he slobbered all over her, kissing and licking her neck and face, before disappearing out of sight.

'What a freak! Did you see his hairy ar—'

Mark smothered Dylan's words with his hand and nodded at the toilet door, which was slowly creaking open. A boy's head poked out through the small gap and his eyes, glistening with tears, scanned the garden and house. When he seemed satisfied with what he saw, he stepped out onto the grass.

It was Kevin Franklyn.

His T-shirt was yanked up under his armpits, revealing severely bruised ribs. He clung onto his trousers with one hand while he bent to retrieve his belt and Halloween mask, which had been discarded amongst the weeds.

Belt replaced, he stumbled down the garden and slipped out through a side gate.

Dylan dived behind a metal dustbin, but there was nowhere for Mark to hide, and Kevin saw him.

Mark fired his peg gun.

The projectile sliced Kevin's cheek, but instead of confronting Mark, Kevin simply nodded.

From the darkness below a privet hedge, Peg-leg materialised out of nowhere. He slithered up Kevin's back, leaving a trail of wispy shadows in his wake when Kevin walked down the alleyway.

CHAPTER 26

IS VIC THERE?

Dylan mounted his Strika and clipped his playing cards and dynamo back onto his wheel. Stealth mode revoked, the boys cycled back through Pontyfechan, over the Sirhowy River, and into lower Broadmead.

Mostyn shot sideways, dragging his leg out like a motocross racer, and disappeared down the lane to Dylan's left.

Bye, then.

Hills were a struggle for a skateboarder, but Steven was surprisingly close when Dylan glanced over his shoulder and spotted his gangly limbs, adorned with elbow and knee pads, stomping and flailing in his flared jeans like a handful of Twiglets.

As the incline increased and muscles burned, their pace slowed when they entered St Mary's Street.

Half way down, MIT had cordoned off an area believed to be the site of Sian's demise. Unable to brake in time, they broke through the police tape.

'Oops,' said Mark, glancing back to see Steven removing tape from his neck.

A woman's scream pierced the roar of their playing cards and they screeched to a halt beside a flickering street lamp, which forced dark shadows away with pulses of light.

'What the hell was that?' yelled Steven, as the monotonous *click click click* of his skateboard wheel-bearings slowed and he kicked his board up into his waiting hand.

When another scream was abruptly cut short and replaced with choking sounds, Mark swept his torch beam past several figures before quickly swinging it back, again.

It took the boys a few seconds to comprehend what they were seeing.

Fiona was being hoisted in the air by Arwel Davies; his vice-like grip crushing her windpipe. To his right, the local crazy, Victor Gaunt, was frantically trying to pull Arwel off.

Arwel laughed. A deep, throaty, laugh that vibrated the windows of the house in front of him. His head swivelled sideways and he studied Victor as though he were sizing up a new suit.

Mesmerised, Dylan watched Arwel's soul rise upwards, bubbling below the skin's surface like an egg on too high a heat. With his free hand, Arwel grabbed Victor's arm. Dark smoke billowed from Arwel's pores, combining, congealing and moulding into death itself. It curled around Victor, flowing over limbs and smothering flesh and bone.

Arwel crumpled to the floor, releasing Fiona, who fell onto her back, gasping greedily on the fetid air emanating from Arwel's rapidly decomposing body. She dragged her arse backwards, trying to distance herself from the stench, but her back slammed into a garden wall.

Before she could scramble to her feet, Victor grabbed her arm and hoisted her the rest of the way.

'Thank y—'

Victor's free hand slid around her throat and tightened. Fiona's eyes rolled back until white, her thrashing becoming laboured. Victor's head tilted to the side and he whispered, 'Why won't you die?'

Knowing Fiona had seconds to live, Dylan begged the boys to help her. Steven skated off towards a nearby phone box with a promise to call the police while Mark just gawped, slack-jawed, until Dylan shook him. 'We have to stop him,' he urged.

'H-How?'

Mostyn's rifle might have helped at this point, but he was long gone.

Dylan rummaged in his bag and pulled out a peg gun. 'We could shoot him with these.'

Mark pointed at the sorry looking chunk of wood. 'With that? You're having a laugh, mun.'

Mark was right, but what else could they do but try? If they dithered any longer, Fiona would be killed.

They mounted their bikes and cycled to either end of the street.

Gun primed, Dylan's voice crackled over Mark's walkie, 'You ready? Over.'

'If I must. Over.'

Like a medieval joust, the boys pedalled as fast as they could towards Victor with their peg guns resting on their handlebars. When the boy's bullets thudded into him, Victor lowered Fiona to the ground and pressed her against the wall.

'It's not working!' screamed Mark over the radio.

'Yes, it is. She can breathe, now. Keep doing it.'

Mark had the feeling Dylan was going to be the death of him, but he simply shook his head, sighed, and primed his gun.

They sped towards Victor, once more.

He seemed amused; turning his back on Fiona and leaning against the wall to watch the show.

Mark's bullet released too early and he fumbled with the gun whilst trying to keep the bike steady. Victor lunged for him and Mark slipped off the kerb into the path of a passing car, causing the driver to swerve. The car mounted the pavement and imbedded into the wall where Victor and Fiona had been standing.

Caw.

Newt appeared on the wall beside the wrecked car and Dylan knew he'd come for a soul, but who's?

Ditching their bikes, the boys ran over.

Victor was lying broken and bloodied on the road behind the car, but they couldn't see Fiona. Fearing she was crushed, Dylan began to cry, but a croaky voice stopped his sniffles.

Clambering out of the rubble, dazed and bleeding, Fiona stumbled forward. 'I'm okay, Dylan.'

Mark took a wide berth around the irate driver, who was busy ranting and raving over the damage to his beloved Morris Marina, and stepped behind the car.

'Is Victor there?' shouted Dylan.

Mark shook his head.

The road was empty, and the only body in their vicinity was Arwel's, which was rapidly leaking fluid from his liquified organs.

Fiona didn't need to be a forensic pathologist to realise that Arwel's body had undergone a month's worth of decomposition in under a minute. Whatever had caused this was now inside Victor. It was a crazy thought, but nothing else made sense. Something supernatural was killing people and switching bodies, and there was only one person who would believe her.

The boys sat beside the anteroom's fireplace and deconstructed slices of Battenberg cake. All Dylan could think about was the black, molten soul that had engulfed Victor. Mark, on the other hand, was thrilled by the whole experience and couldn't stop talking about Arwel's rotting corpse. Dylan was pretty sure that, if he'd had a camera, Mark would have gone through roll after roll of film.

While the boys ate and gossiped, the reverend put his teacup down, sat back, intertwined his fingers, and lowered them into his lap. Fiona sensed this was either going to be a long, drawn-out lie or a complex biblical explanation that would be way over her head. Fred had sat in silence without batting an eyelid while she and the boys had blurted out details of the evening's incident—even Arwel's death hadn't phased him.

Had he known something evil was here? Did he believe them?

Fred cleared his throat. 'Well, you've had a frightful evening, my dear. Your neck looks terribly swollen. Are you sure I can't tend to it?'

'I'm fine, thanks,' she lied. She'd stared death in the face, so she wasn't even close to fine, but she certainly wasn't going to cry in front of two boys and a reverend.

'Terrible news about Arwel, too,' added Fred. 'I had a soft spot for him. The boys seem well adjusted, though. Kids are so resilient, you see.'

Fiona sat back in her chair, her eyes flitting between Fred and the boys. It was as though she had told Fred that they had lost the boy's football rather than a man's life. Maybe he was senile. 'You do understand what we've just told you?'

'Absolutely.'

'It was *you* who told me about these ... bodysnatchers.' She resisted the urge to point a finger at him, but only just.

'The bodysnatcher's called Crulus. He's a Cythraul, and

Dylan's a Psychopomp,' spouted Mark, earning him a kick from Dylan.

Fred snorted. 'Poppycock. Where did you hear such terms?'

'I ... umm ... read about them in an occult library book,' lied Dylan. He didn't want to mention *the* book. Not yet, anyway.

Fiona was shocked how easily Fred dismissed the boys.

'Well, that must be a *very* interesting tome, Dylan. I thought you'd prefer comics to the occult. Besides, the shadowy figure you both saw isn't the killer; he's from the damaged crypt,' advised Fred, causing the boys to exchange worried glances.

'Really?' asked Fiona, stunned.

'Let me explain. Our ancestors believed that the last person to die in a parish each year would become the graveyard watcher—or 'Yr Angau' as it's known in Welsh—to protect the peace of the dead. However, when Larkmead chapel was opened in early 1829 the villagers feared their deceased loved ones would be vulnerable before the year end and, as such, the worshipers believed a death omen was needed immediately to ward off such evil. So, they created one.

'The first grave in the chapel grounds was dug by local miners and a poor soul was buried alive within it thus, they believed, creating a revenant guardian to protect their future departed souls. Local folklore has it that Yr Angau is a tall, haggard, old man, who still wears the suit he was buried in. Some even believe they've seen his dog, Brass, that refused to leave his master, and died with him.'

Dylan: 'I've seen both of them.'

Fiona felt the colour drain from her face. They were fully down the rabbit hole, now. She ignored Fred's smirk and asked, 'So this, man. This ... What did you call him?'

Fred's eyelids fluttered and his head shook, as though his brain had just rebooted. 'Erm ... Yr Angau. The watcher.'

'Right. So, this watcher would only appear at funerals?'

'Anytime, but sightings were just folklore.'

'And he was buried alive?'

'That's correct. An immurement.'

'But the doors looked burnt. Volunteering to be burnt alive is ... well ... unbelievable. He was murdered.'

'Not necessarily.' Fred stuck his index finger in the air and paused; his eyes lost in the flames. After a few moments, he lowered his hand and continued, 'Willing sacrifice or a victim? That I cannot answer. I did find some letters a few years back written by the chapel's first Reverend, a Tomos Llewellyn. He was a Welsh Methodist from Carmarthenshire but, sadly, some of the letters were destroyed in a fire. I do, however, recall reading that the honour of Yr Angau was bequeathed to a older gentleman, but his name escapes me. My memory is not good, anymore.'

'Seems okay to me.'

He chuckled. 'Thank you, but Carys would have disagreed if she were still with us. Cause of death is unknown. He had a young family, but no further details other than the family name above the crypt, which you saw.'

'Shame. Do you believe Yr Angau exists?'

He sighed long and hard, and sagged into his leather chair, as if the fate of mankind depended on his answer. 'What I believe is of no real consequence, my dear. What matters is whether *they* truly believed in that ritual.'

'Do you?'

He slid forward in his seat and gazed at her as if he were a Headmaster about to reprimand a child. 'If you believe hard enough, anything is possible.'

'Dad always said he'd win the pools, but that never happened,' she mumbled, causing giggles from the boys.

Fred tapped at his hearing aid. 'Sorry, dear, my batteries must be failing.'

Fiona waved it off. 'Never mind.'

'If the scriptures are true,' continued Fred, 'Yr Angau *protects* the dead, he doesn't create them. Your killer could be a Cythraul, after all.'

Dylan's ears pricked up when he returned his plate to the table. 'So, you've heard of it?'

'Hearing or *reading* about things doesn't make them true, Dylan, but if it *is* a Cythraul, then we are all in grave danger. Yr Angau may be able to protect the dead, but I doubt he can save the living, dog or no dog.'

~

Uncle John was revving his engine outside the front of their house when Dylan burst out of Colledig Wood, slipped into his back garden, and dumped his bike and peg gun by the side of the shed. He checked on Newt and, as he suspected, the crow was nowhere to be seen, despite the shed being locked.

Chrissy was waiting in the kitchen with a fag dangling off the edge of her lip like a female Andy Capp and massive, dark bags under her eyes. It looked like Dylan's three year old cousin had applied her make-up. Surely his father could see that she wasn't coping?

~

At the hospital, Dylan never got the chance to speak to him. Chrissy shoved twenty pence into his hand (a one hundred percent increase on the last bribe) and pushed him towards the ward's door.

After buying Emily a birthday card, Dylan took a slow meander up the stairs to visit Andrew who was, understandably, his usual suicidal self. While they chatted, Andrew asked him to switch him off sixteen times in forty-five minutes, which was probably the record so far.

Some of Andrew's family had visited earlier all *"full of hope and fluffiness"* as he'd put it, which just made him feel worse and probably explained why his death knell was ringing loudly in Dylan's ears.

His family were desperately trying to raise money to pay for a residential hospice, which prided itself on their award winning specialist care. This was a complete waste of time, money and effort as far as Andrew was concerned. Concerns, which he had explained to his family in very loud, colourful language according to the nurse who came in to check on him.

Despite Dylan's empathy for Andrew's predicament, he still refused to kill him. Although, by the time he left his room, Dylan would have quite happily wrung his neck just to shut him up.

Today had been a bad day, but tomorrow was going to be better.

It was Emily's birthday and he had a date in the woods.

CHAPTER 27

THE MOB RULES

Tuesday 20th October, 1981
Draigwen Town Comprehensive School

While Fiona was trying to explain last night's incident to DI Grundle and the Murder Investigation Team without mentioning anything remotely supernatural, Emily was heading down through 'A' block during morning break searching for Dylan.

She found him, and his friends, on top of the perimeter wall within proximity of the snack van, which was waiting patiently to extort money from the sugar addicted pupils.

When Dylan spotted her, he jumped down and came bounding over, so excited to see her that he nearly knocked her flying.

'Whoa, careful!' she warned, holding him back by his chest. 'Everyone's watching.'

'S-Sorry Emily, I er ... I fell. I mean tripped. I tripped,' he burbled, red-faced.

'Clumsy.'

She smiled, and the world evaporated. In that instant, nothing else mattered. Dylan's pent-up fear and anger subsided.

'What's up? Is something wrong?' Emily checked her glasses were straight and her pigtails were safely tucked into their bobbles, before covering her mouth to hide her braces. 'You're staring.'

Dylan snapped out of his trance. 'Sorry, I didn't mean to. It's just you're, umm ... really pretty.'

Emily blushed. 'Don't make fun.'

Dylan was shocked. How could she not know she was beautiful?

'I'm not. You are.'

She picked imaginary fluff off of her skirt, mumbling, 'Thanks.' Her hand brushed his arm and she held it there for the briefest moment, sending a tremor through his body. 'You're very sweet.'

He leant toward her and felt himself drawn to her lips, which curled back over her braces as she smiled. 'Here's your card,' he chirped in a loud, high-pitched voice, before shoving an envelope unceremoniously into her hand. 'Happy Birthday.'

'Thanks.' She walked away from the gawping crowd and gestured for him to follow. 'Sorry, Dylan, my dad said you can't come to my party. I don't know why. He's just grumpy.'

Unable to hide his disappointment, he smiled weakly. 'That's okay.'

'Can I still see you in your camp at five?'

'Yeah.'

'Great. See you tonight,' she said, stepping forward.

Ignoring the multitude of eyes that stared their way, she kissed his cheek and, with a swish of her pigtails, she disappeared into the throng.

Dylan raised a palm to his rosey cheek, which was soon to be vastly more crimson.

Due to teacher illness, Mr Harwood was drafted in to cover today's Physical Education lesson and he relished the chance to torture kids in plain sight without fear of reprimand.

P.E. was Kryptonite to Dylan and he looked like a walking jumble sale in his mis-matched, borrowed, gym kit. His mother couldn't afford the full kit, but she had managed to buy him a pair of black daps.

When the rugby teams were being picked, Dylan wrinkled his nose at the pungent sweat smell that emanated from the borrowed shirt, and he didn't want to think about what had been inside the shorts.

As anticipated, he was picked last, but that didn't stop him being embarrassed; even 'Wheezy' Williams was picked before him.

With no idea of the rules of rugby, he made half-hearted attempts to tackle the ball carrier, not knowing if they were on the opposition team or not. He never *actually* dived for anyone because thoughts of Andrew's broken neck occupied his mind, plus he didn't want to get dirty.

His avoidance of mud didn't last long, though, as a thick hand slammed between his shoulder blades sending him face down.

'Move it, Wolfendale, you idle wanker!' screamed Harwood, whistle in one hand, balled fist in the other. 'Get after that ball before I break your face.'

Dylan refused to cry. Instead he bit down hard on his quivering lip, drawing blood. He dragged himself up and staggered his way down the field.

While the majority of boys whizzed around the pitch on

studded rugby boots, he slipped and slid about the field, his daps no match for the muddy ground. He sauntered around trying to look interested, but his mind quickly wandered from the field. He could still feel the warmth of Emily's hand on his arm and he closed his eyes, trying to picture her perfect lips.

When he opened his eyes the ball was twirling majestically through the air towards him. He glanced left and right and realised too late that he was between the ball player and the winger. He flinched, then side-stepped to avoid him, but his daps failed to grip and one of his spindly legs launched forward, tripping the winger, David Price, who slammed hard into the ground, while the ball sailed over his head.

David jumped to his feet and bounded toward Dylan, fists clenched. 'Arsehole! You did that on purpose.'

Dylan opened his mouth to respond, but David tripped him and sat on his chest. His fat, sausage fingers wrapped around Dylan's neck and spittle sprayed his face when he spat, 'Spastic! You never learn. Me and you, in the park after school!' He slapped Dylan's face hard.

Dylan simply curled up, defeated.

A crowd had gathered to watch his demise, with a chanting chorus of *fight, fight, fight.*

Dylan yelled for the teacher and, after an age, Harwood finally strolled over.

'Right, enough of that, get back to the game. Wolfendale, see me in class, later. Gertrude wants a word with you.'

'But, Sir, I didn't do anything,' pleaded Dylan, which earned him another clip across the head.

~

News of the impending slaughter spread like a bush fire through the school. Dylan's arse still hurt from Gertrude's wallop and his bowels continuously convulsed. For once, he didn't gaze out the window: his focus was on the large clock above the blackboard. The hands moved painfully slow and he began to think it was going back in time. Four times he begged his mathematics teacher if he could be excused for a toilet break, and even though he stood cross-legged and squirmed with agony etched on his face, she still refused.

After the final bell rang, a baying mob jostled and almost carried Dylan to his fate. Nowhere to hide and no means of escape, he frantically searched the horde for Mark, but it was useless. He sank into the swell of bodies that bundled him onwards. Terrified, shaking faster than a builder on a pneumatic drill, he was blackballed.

Boys and girls alike, chanted endlessly as the mob hustled him onwards:

'He's a dead man.'

'You're going home in a flashing ambulance!'

'He don't stand a chance, mun.'

'Poofy fairy's gonna get his face smashed in.'

'Pricey'll destroy you.'

'Fight! fight! fight! fight!'

There was nothing quite like the merciless cruelty of children.

When they finally reached the park, the mob parted slightly and David slid into the swaying circle's centre. Surprisingly, he looked nervous, but his face soon hardened when Dean whispered instructions in his ear.

The threat of shit in Dylan's underpants was real, and he felt hot sweat beading on his scalp.

A short, sharp, punch to the gut buckled him and David straddled him once more, pounding fist after fist into his face and hands, while Dylan desperately tried to protect himself.

'Gerroff me!' he screamed. 'Help! ... Stop! ... Pleeeease!'

His pleas quickly turned to cries of pain as the punches rained down.

'Hit him, Pricey, you're punching like a girl. He's not even bleeding, yet,' shouted Dean, directing the action from the sidelines, like a ringside boxing coach. 'Smash that poncy face in!'

The embarrassment of continually being bullied was too much to bear, but Dylan did nothing. Battling to block the blows he closed his eyes, but he didn't pray.

He slipped out of his body, instead.

The vastness of the lobby, which now felt like his second home or, more accurately, his second bedroom, stretched out before him, and he finally relaxed.

David's right fist was on an extremely slow downward trajectory.

Destination: Dylan's now bloodied eye socket.

He couldn't let this happen but, then again, he couldn't banish David's soul to Transmogoria like Mr Garrett's. Plus, if David simply went back to his body, would he only suffer mild déjà vu? Would he remember the encounter?

What if I bring him here, to the lobby? thought Dylan. I spoke to Tom here, so why not David, too?

But there was one niggling thought that wouldn't leave his cerebrum: What if David fades into Transmogoria? Would that be murder?

He wanted to cry, but he knew that no tears would flow. The pent-up anger that wanted him to throttle Andrew now wanted him to beat this bully, even if it wasn't quite a fair fight.

Mind made up, Dylan grabbed David's arm but, instead of letting go, he held on until David was stood before him, confused and disoriented, like Tom had been.

David's befuddled soul couldn't understand why he was

no longer straddling Dylan. His face morphed into pure hatred and he lunged at Dylan, but he was slow and weak, and Dylan sidestepped with ease.

When David spun on his heels and attempted to come at him again, he saw himself straddling another Dylan.

He froze.

Dylan took a beat, then swiped David's legs away.

David felt the shock, but no pain. 'W-What's going on? Where am I?'

Dylan needed shock and awe at full volume if he was going to make this dullard understand.

'You're dead. That's your body, right there, and only *I* can bring you back.'

David started crying, then freaked out even more when he realised there were no tears.

'You can't cry. You're dead, remember?' Dylan was shocked at how much he was enjoying this revenge. He no longer just wanted to win this fight; he wanted to stop this bully forever. He needed to break his soul, crush it, like he had crushed his, day after day after day. 'You'll never see your family, again.'

David sunk to his knees and clasped his hands together in prayer. 'Pleeeease! I'm sorry. I'm really sorry. I swear I'll never hit you, again. I don't want to die.'

He was pathetic. He had spent years hiding behind Dean and something within Dylan, something dark and primal, wanted to end him there and then.

'You won't hit me ever again.'

'No, I won't. I swear.'

'It wasn't a question.' Dylan stepped closer until their faces were almost touching. 'You won't hit *anyone*, again!' He grabbed David and virtually threw him back into his body.

When Dylan opened his eyes, David screamed, jumped off

him, and ran for his life. Dylan stood and watched him running through the crowd dodging everyone as though they carried the plague.

'You little shit. What did you do to him?' bellowed Dean.

Dylan spun around to answer him, but the faces in the crowd blurred and everything went black.

CHAPTER 28

HAPPY BIRTHDAY

Dylan couldn't remember Mark walking him home. His eyelashes were still encrusted with blood and there wasn't one part of his body that didn't hurt. Mark was proud of him. He swore that he had won that fight, but Dylan seriously doubted it. He had only ever won arguments and fights in his head—with style of course, always with style—but he never imagined he would win a fight by torturing someone's soul. The fact that a skinny, wimpy kid, who couldn't punch his way out of a wet paper bag had fended off a known bully without throwing a single punch was going to be *big* news. This was bad news as far as Dylan was concerned; Dean's revenge would be far worse.

'Hiya, love. Cheese and potato pie for tea, okay?' he heard his mother say as he walked into the kitchen. The smell of baking wafted up his nostrils like a rat up a drain pipe. Mouth agape, he let his bag fall to the floor, then quickly covered his ears as the desert spoon she was holding clattered to the floor.

'Oh, God, your face!'

He tried not to wince when she grabbed his arms, pulled

him close, and inspected him like a monkey grooming its infant.

'There's blood everywhere. Who did this?'

'No one. I fell down the steps.'

'I wasn't born yesterday. Shoes off. I'll clean you up after tea. Dad's home,' she said, giddy with excitement.

Dylan took a step back, mumbling under his breath.

'He's in the living room.'

It took him a moment to process the news before he hurtled past her and, sure enough, his father was sat in his armchair.

'Dad!' He flung his arms around him and the pent-up tears flooded out. 'I've missed you.'

Gwynfor rubbed his back, kissed his hair, and pushed him away. 'Careful, watch the pipes,' he warned.

An oxygen pipe was clipped into his nostril and extended over his ears and down to a small black and white cylinder on the floor.

'Sorry.'

'That's okay, Son. It's temporary until I get a proper machine installed. Looks like you've done twelve rounds with Gordon Ferris instead of falling down some steps,' Gwynfor said, with an accusing tone, causing Dylan to blush. Gwynfor pursed his lips. 'Anything I should know?'

Dylan shook his head and lunged in for another cuddle.

Gwynfor pushed him away, holding him at arms length. 'You sure?'

'Yeah,' replied Dylan, averting his eyes.

Across the room, Kaelum mouthed the words '*Cry baby*' and rubbed his fists on his temples.

'Sod off!' snapped Dylan, suddenly feeling braver than he had ever been.

'Tea's on the table,' shouted Chrissy.

It had been well over a month since they had gathered together as a family. Chrissy was like a new woman with shiny, curled hair, and perfect makeup. Her 'pop' bottle had also vanished, although Dylan wondered for how long. Mr Harwood had mentioned alcohol's addictive properties in R.E. class, the Devil's work, so he guessed the bottle hadn't gone far.

With a stomach fit to burst, he finally retreated to the lounge, but not before staring at the pictures of his aunt. Crulus took her from him and ruined his mother's life, never mind poor Daniel's.

Shit.

He suddenly realised that he hadn't told his grandparents about Daniel's innocence although, as they weren't going anywhere, he supposed there was no rush.

He slid fifty pence into the TV's meter and assumed his usual viewing position: propped up on his elbows in front of the television, head in his hands, close enough to reach up to the buttons. There were five on their rental TV, but only three were live: BBC1, BBC2 and HTV.

The TV jingle for John Craven's Newsround stirred him from his thoughts. John was discussing the Ninth U.S. Circuit Court of Appeals ruling that some home videotaping of television programs violated copyright.

Apparently, Benny 'Half-Lug' Lewis' family had two video recorders, Betamax *and* VHS, and Dylan wondered if they would ever watch videos, again.

'Dylan, put HTV on,' said Gwynfor. 'Emmerdale's on soon.'

Dylan clicked button three. 'Isn't it too early?'

'Daydreaming again?' asked Chrissy. 'It's nearly quarter past five.'

Dylan jumped to his feet and looked at the wall clock. 'Shit! I gotta go,' he cried, running toward the door.

Chrissy caught his arm. 'Whoa! No, you're not. It's nearly dark, and your dad's only just come home.'

'But I promised her. Pleeeease!' begged Dylan, stamping his feet impetuously.

'Promised who?'

'Emily. I said I'd meet her at five.'

'Awww is ickle Dilly late for his first date?' sneered Kaelum.

'Piss off!' snapped Dylan. He felt his heart thumping out of rhythm and he knelt next his father. 'Please, can I go, Dad?'

Gwynfor took a deep breath and shook his head. 'Listen to your mother.'

'But I was meeting her in the woods. She's all alone.'

'You should have thought of that before you arranged it.'

'Yeah, but I didn't know you were coming home and then we—'

'Only a weak man blames others,' his father cut in. 'Now, sit and watch telly, or go to your room. I'm not in the mood for arguing.'

Dylan turned to his mother. 'Can you ring Emily's mother?'

She shook her head. 'I don't know her number. Do you?'

Dylan lowered his head and started to cry, causing Kaelum to laugh harder.

Gwynfor thrust a finger toward Kaelum who instantly fell silent.

For the briefest of moments, Dylan thought of sneaking out, but fear made his legs scuttle up to his room.

He slid out of his body and wandered through the lobby. As soon as he thought of Emily, he was stood by her door. He spread his fingers wide and reached out but quickly snapped them back; he couldn't put her through that.

Back in his body, he laid on his bed and cried himself into an early, disturbed sleep, but visions of a beautiful succubus calling to him haunted his dreams.

'Dylannnnnn.'

He awoke fully clothed and drenched in sweat, but the voice continued to call him.

'Dylannnnnn.'

It was Emily.

CHAPTER 29
WRATHCHILD

Wednesday 21st October, 1981
Draigwen Police Station

At two forty-three A.M. the smoky room fell silent when a short, stocky, overweight man with no neck entered with a fag dangling off his bottom lip, which was dangerously close to setting fire to his curly, ginger beard. His large, round head shone under the office lighting and, if it wasn't for the beard, you'd think he was Sontaran.

Detective Inspector Graham 'Grumpy' Grundle, head of MIT at Gwent Constabulary, transferred from Liverpool in mid-1977 after marrying a lady from Pontyfechan. Cancer took her less than three years later and he has hated the Welsh ever since, which begged the question: why didn't he bugger off back to Liverpool?

'Right then, Taffy twats. This is the second girl we've lost in a month! We're still no piggin' closer to catching this kid-killer. Ten hours gone, so I'm assuming she's dead, but some evidence to the contrary would be nice.' He stubbed his fag out on the desk and flicked the butt at the nearest Sergeant. 'You can start, Tony.'

Tony Thomas sighed, walked over to the county map pinned on the notice board and began updating the team.

'All wooded areas to the North and Northwest of Emily's house have been searched. No sightings. The parents were questioned straight away. No signs of interference or foul play. Her father and his brother-in-law, Clive Barker, are out searching, too. WPC Brasking is the assigned FLO. The last positive sighting was by one of Clive's neighbours at roughly sixteen thirty-five yesterday evening. Emily was at her uncle's house whilst her parents decorated her home for her twelfth birthday party, but she snook out to meet a schoolfriend, Dylan Wolfendale, and—'

'Has he been interviewed?' DI Grundle cut in.

'Umm.' Tony rifled through his file. 'Er, yes. They're in interview room two, and there are some strange murmurings coming back from uniform.'

'Such as?'

'Well, *apparently*, he's claiming Emily's dead and she's in the woods.'

'What's strange about that? Sounds plausible, especially if he's the killer. Did he kill both girls?' the DI asked, stroking his beard.

Tony couldn't help smirking.

'What's so bastard funny?'

'He reckons he's spoken to her. That's how he knows she's dead. He talks to the dead.'

The room erupted with laughter.

Grundle slammed the desk, silencing the room. 'Enough! ... Listen divvys, I haven't got time for bullshit. Tony, make sure the Psychologist evaluates him. Emily may have confided in him.'

'All in hand, Sir. Dr Francis is observing the inter—'

Grundle held up his hand, crossed his legs, and slowly stroked his beard, once more. After a long pause, he gestured for Tony to continue.

'The search teams have covered all wooded areas marked with a green pin. All woodland should be complete by midday tomorrow based on our current establishment, however, we are hoping to have assistance from SWC by nine A.M., which should speed things up. We'll probably need more torches, if this—'

'Get a bloody chit and buy some!' bellowed Grundle. 'It's not rocket science.' He clicked his fingers. 'Sit.' He searched the room until his eyes fixed on someone near the back and a cheesy grin spread across his face. 'Aha, my favourite Doris, WDC Edwards.'

A slim, bespectacled twenty something dressed in a pinstripe suit stood up to a chorus of low wolf whistles and gibes. Kerry Edwards was one of the youngest Detective Constables in the force and she hated people assuming she was sleeping her way to the top. Granted, she had had a few romantic interludes with colleagues, but no colluding. The only passion she had was for her job; she worked hard at it and it was paying off, albeit slowly. Females grappled for mutual respect in the force, and it was a struggle to get away from the usual dogsbody, tea making, paper shuffling jobs that a Doris usually had. She only had to look at Fiona to remind herself of where she used to be.

Despite her full respect for the DI's rank and superiority, he was a big, fat, pervert, with no respect for women—they were just meat to him—and his close proximity made her nervous, nauseous even. She refused to look at him, turning to the others instead and, after clearing her voice, spoke with perfect clarity.

'PNC and the Missing Person's Bureau have been updated and Emily's details have also been faxed to neighbouring forces and the British Transport Police. We have had one possible sighting of a girl fitting Emily's description leaving Newport train station, which BTP are looking into. We're expecting an update, soon.'

Grundle rose to his feet, coughing violently, before spitting phlegm into the bin behind him. He retrieved another fag from his jacket pocket and Kerry secretly hoped he would choke on it.

'Anything else? ... No? ... Right, we'll re-convene at five A.M..' He lit the fag and took a drag like it was his first one that month and disappeared behind a cloud of smoke. 'Radio chatter to a minimum,' he ordered. 'DC Edwards, stay behind.'

Kerry's shoulders sagged. 'Sir?'

'Get me the latest on that sighting, love.'

I wouldn't love you if you were the last fat, bald twat on earth, she thought, drawing her lips into a thin smile. 'No problem,' she replied, making a dash for the door, but he cut off her escape, stretching his stumpy arm across the doorway.

'Soooo, how's tricks? Still no fella, then?' His wink was so slow and laboured that he looked physically retarded. His breath stunk of smoke and she felt nauseous.

'Too busy, Sir.' She cocked a thumb over her shoulder. 'I arranged to speak to BTP, ten minutes ago.'

'Fine. Don't let me keep you.' He dropped his arm from the door, then swiftly brought it back around and slapped her arse. 'Go get 'em, girl!'

Kerry glared at him, but thought better of saying anything.

~

When Dr Floyd Francis, clinical psychologist, entered the

small observation room to finish up his notes, DI Grundle was staring through the glass at Dylan and his mother.

'Well?'

'It's not clear cut. If I had to put money on it, I'd say it was childhood schizophrenia. Strange thing is he's only displaying the positive symptoms, auditory hallucinations and delusions, but none of the negative symptoms are apparent in his behaviour, thus far,' explained Dr Francis.

'Never mind the psycho babble. Is he a fruitcake or what?'

His lack of compassion irritated Dr Francis. He lowered his gaze and muttered under his breath.

'What was that?' snapped Grundle.

'That's not what I'd call it but, yes, these active psychotic symptoms certainly suggest that he undergoes prompt consultation to ascertain the cause. I would need to run some tests. These stories and voices in his head could simply be the wild imagination of a young, attention seeking chap due, of course, to all the attention currently being focused solely on his missing girlfriend.'

Grundle liked the sound of the latter. 'Just another stupid kid then, eh?'

'What? No, he—'

Grundle elbowed him towards the door. 'Thanks for your time, Doc. We love to hear such eloquent words from a learned man such as yourself. It keeps us in our place.' He looked at his officer. 'PC Davies, escort Dr Francis out.'

'I haven't completed my consultation. That *is* why you dragged me out at this un-Godly hour, isn't it?' asked Dr Francis, returning the sarcasm, but Grundle ignored him and left.

Dr Francis gathered up his notes and hurled them into his briefcase. 'Is he always like this?'

'Always. He's a pretty good judge of character, though,'

PC Davies replied, while watching his DI enter the interview room. 'Not many coppers like him, see.'

'Maybe that's not such a bad thing.' Dr Francis got up quickly, flinging the chair out from behind him. 'Well, everyone's entitled to their opinion regardless how unfounded. Here's my card, please make sure that Dylan's mother gets it. Your DI knows the procedures. I *will* need to see Dylan as soon as possible.'

~

When Grundle entered the interview room, the PC sat in the corner leant over to switch the tape recorder back on.

'That won't be necessary, PC Jukes. The interview's over. Get on with the paperwork.'

Dylan's pasty pallor made Grundle wonder whether he was going to puke, if he hadn't already. He waited for Jukesy to leave before addressing Chrissy and Dylan.

'Just one more thing before you both leave.' He grabbed a plastic chair and sat opposite Dylan, who was yawning uncontrollably. 'Stop the bullshit!' he commanded, jabbing a fat, nicotine-stained finger in Dylan's face. 'A young girl is missing and I'm wasting my time with some stupid woolyback lad who makes up stories.'

Chrissy grabbed her handbag and debated whacking him over the head. 'Whoa, hang on. You haven't heard Dylan's story.'

'Don't go gerrin' in a tizzy, Mrs Wolfendale. I've heard every jarg word through there,' he said, pointing towards the mirrored wall. 'And it wasn't that convincing. Complete bollocks, if you ask me.'

'He's adamant he can hear her. I know it sounds stupid, but he's not a liar, he ... he's gifted,' Chrissy explained, unconvincingly.

'You really believe that a dead girl is talking to your son?'

Chrissy paused. She honestly had no idea. She believed in spirits and such like, but that wasn't the point. She wasn't going to sit there and let this obnoxious policeman put her son down.

'Yes, I do!' she professed.

Grundle's eyes widened and he shook his head. 'Bloody Welsh freaks!' He opened the door, gesturing with an outstretched arm for them to leave. 'Go on, bail out!'

'You can't talk to us like that,' Chrissy said, thumping her hand on the desk. 'Who do you think you are?'

'We're the bizzies. This is my station. I can say what I want. Now, sod off and stop wasting my time!'

Several inches taller than the DI, Chrissy had to bend in the doorway to match his lowly stature. Her head stretched forward, like a turtle, until her nose almost touched Grundle's.

'Find that girl,' she spat.

He watched them walk down the corridor and waited for them to open the door to reception.

'Oh, I nearly forgot,' he shouted. 'The shrink thinks your son's a schizo', so he'll need to see him, again. Our Family Liaison Officer, Fiona Brasking, will be in touch soon. Reception will have her details.'

Dylan tugged on his mother's sleeve and looked up at her with tearful eyes. 'Will they take me away?'

Chrissy hesitated. 'Not if your dad and I have anything to do with it.'

CHAPTER 30

WAITING FOR A GIRL LIKE YOU

At four A.M. Kerry took a call from the British Transport Police based at Reading railway station. A girl fitting Emily's description was discovered stowed away on the early London Paddington commuter train. The description of the detainee fitted Emily in every detail, even down to the clothes on her back and the pen marks on her tatty trainers, although her demeanour sounded way off.

Kerry rapped her knuckles on Grundle's door and went straight in. PC Jukes made no attempt to offer her his seat. She handed the DI the report sheet and stood, arms crossed, waiting for his response, which didn't take long.

'Offered him her services? Is this guy for real? She's only twelve! This can't be her.'

'I agree, although her physical description sounds spot on. I've asked them to fax a photo. The conductor swears blind that she was talking dirty, grabbing his crotch, and offering sex, so she could stay on the train.'

Grundle flung the report across his desk. 'Edwards, it's not her. File it and move on!' he snarled.

An hour later, Kerry sat in silence at her desk twirling her straight, blonde hair around one finger whilst staring at the fax from BTP.

There was no mistake.

The girl staring at her from that grainy picture was Emily.

Thames Valley Police agreed to escort her back to Gwent but, because Kerry didn't want anymore verbal bashings, she advised them to take the girl straight to Trugaredd Hospital to be examined. She radioed Fiona and told her to bring Zara to the hospital as soon as possible. It was better to meet them there, confirm her identity, and *then* inform Grundle.

She grabbed two Brufen and swilled them down with a strong, sweet coffee before heading out to the traffic yard. It had been over twenty four hours since she'd crawled out of bed, and her head was in a vice.

The twenty minute drive to the hospital gave her time to mull over that morning's chaos. She was chuffed that Emily was alive; she couldn't face anymore dead bodies.

Due to a criminal record as long as his arm, the conductor was no longer a credible witness, so his story would be discredited, which was why she deliberately neglected to tell Grundle that the girl was adamant that her name was Parthena Love.

There were no active Mispers for a girl with that name, or fitting that description, in fact, no record of any living person with that name existed in Wales or England according to the Public Record Office, so she searched old Police records to be certain and, sure enough, she found that name on microfiche. Problem was, it belonged to a Victorian prostitute born in Whitechapel, London in 1870. Parthena Love had been investigated during the Whitechapel murder of Frances Cole back in 1891.

This wasn't even remotely connected, so she saved herself from another embarrassing reprimand by withholding that information, too.

Back on the Cerrig Brig estate, Dylan had been sent to his room despite his protests. He had guessed from his father's tone that he didn't believe him and he wasn't sure his mother did, either. He wanted to talk about Emily, to search for her body, to discuss his ability, to do something, *anything,* rather than just sleep. Kaelum was dead to the world and, thankfully, it didn't take long before he heard a chorus of snores from his parent's room, too.

After getting dressed, Dylan crept downstairs and slipped on his Parka jacket and trainers. He spoke to Emily subconsciously and discovered that it was Victor that had attacked her in the camp, as he suspected. He had hoisted her up by the neck and, strangely, he had told her, "It's not you," before dropping her.

Alone in Transmogoria, surrounded by dark souls that moved in and out of focus, Emily was terrified. She cried for her mother and begged Dylan to help her but all he could do was say sorry, over and over, until Emily almost screamed at him that it wasn't his fault. Although it was good to hear, he knew deep down that he was the cause and he almost shattered his mother's vase when he slammed his fist onto the dining room table in anger and frustration. Then it had dawned on him; what if Emily wasn't dead? What if she was simply unconscious?

Fifteen minutes later, Dylan was heading towards his camp and he stopped running when the willow trees came into view. He leant forward, hands on his knees, catching his breath. His mind racing, again.

What if I trample over evidence? Should I have told the police? What if Victor's burying her?

That last thought terrified him and it took all of his strength to keep going. Creeping towards the willows, he felt he was being watched.

Anxiety piqued, he flung his torchlight from side to side. The shadows shied away from the light but didn't move spontaneously and his shoulders sagged with relief. There was no-one there, although the camp entrance had clearly been disturbed.

Ignoring the damp seeping through the knees of his trousers, he crawled below the tree's canopy and filled its interior with torchlight.

Emily wasn't there.

He slumped, crest fallen, onto a plastic milk-bottle crate and whispered, 'Where are you, Em'?' before spotting blood on the side of a stone.

Emily's voice slid into his mind like a breeze through Autumn leaves, '*Did you find me?*'

Stupidly, he shook his head. 'There's blood. Victor must have hidden you.'

'Killed,' Emily corrected, sadly.

'Don't say that.'

'You can talk to the dead, Dylan, so I must be.'

Dylan resisted the urge to say sorry, again. Somehow, he had to fix this and bring her back. It wasn't her time and it *was* his fault; he wasn't there for her.

He knew that if he phoned the police station they wouldn't believe him, but Fiona might. Hopefully, she would still be at Emily's house and that's where he headed, as fast as his damp, cold legs could take him.

CHAPTER 31

IT'S MY PARTY

Dylan flung open Emily's new gate just as Dai was locking his front door.

'Well, if it isn't the local shit stirrer. Bit early for spreading stories, huh? The coppers told me what you said. How could you say she's dead?' he demanded, jabbing his car key into Dylan's chest.

Dylan reeled backwards, more in shock than pain. 'I *did* speak to her,' he pleaded. 'She was attacked and she ... she died. Although, she could just be unconscious. Her body's in the woods. Well, it should be, but it wasn't. At least, not where it should've been, anyway. There was blood, though, so her attacker must've moved—'

Dai raised a fist to Dylan's face. It hovered there, shaking.

'SHUT UP! You mumbling, lying, bastard. Emily's not dead. She's in the hospital. They found her on a train headed for London. A bang on the head. Confused, but very much alive.'

Dylan stared, opened mouth, until Dai's huge hand shoved him backwards onto the grass. He propped himself up on his elbows and asked without a hint of sarcasm, 'How can I talk to her, then?'

Dai towered over him, fist raised once more, forcing Dylan to crawl away.

'You're off your head, ya freak!'

Dylan knew he was coming across as a gibbering idiot, but he had to know Emily was okay, if it really was her. 'Wait, I'm sorry. I'm just confused, you know, from shock. I-I didn't know what I was saying. Can I come with you?'

'Ha! After what *you've* just said? Fat chance.'

Dai jumped in his car and sped off, leaving Dylan dazed and alone.

Kerry was waiting in the hospital reception when Dai came hurtling in, and directed him into a side room.

'Where's Zara and Emily?' he demanded, realising the room was empty.

'Please take a seat. The Doctor wants to speak to you, first. It's just procedure,' assured Kerry, before stepping back towards the door. 'I won't be a minute. I'll let him know you're here. Fiona will keep you company.'

Dai paced the room, irritated, until Kerry finally returned with Dr Dhata who quickly revealed the results of Emily's examination.

Emily had suffered minor cuts and bruises over her body with particularly severe bruising to her upper arms and neck. Their main cause of concern, however, was that she had sustained quite a severe blow to the left side of her head. Although the CT scan hadn't revealed any obvious brain lesions, it appeared that the trauma had affected her temporal lobe causing pure retrograde amnesia. Severe memory impairment and disorientation had also caused significant changes to her personality.

Dr Dhata went on to explain the global onset of psychogenic amnesia and its symptoms before Dai interrupted him, 'Whoa, whoa! Hang-a-banger, Doc. Too much jargon. Is Emily okay?'

'Mr Morris, your daughter's physical health is fine. She has simply lost her memory.'

Dai looked up at the ceiling, crossed himself and sighed. He grabbed the doctors hand and shook it vigorously. 'Aaw, thank God for that. You scared the life out of me, then. I thought it was something serious.'

Dr Dhata, wrenched his hand free, shaking his head. 'No, Mr Morris, you don't understand. It *is* serious.'

Dai slumped back against the desk. 'What? She'll get her memory back ... Won't she?'

'I can't say for sure. People who experience psychogenic amnesia can have impaired episodic memory. They can wander around not knowing where they are going or why—'

'Is that why Emily got on that train to London, then?'

'Yes, possibly. The other thing with this type of amnesia is that the patient has no accessible memories pertaining to their previous identity and this can result in the perceived acceptance of a new identity.'

All signs of relief and colour had drained from Dai's expression and he sat there dumbfounded, head cradled in his hands while Dr Dhata opened Emily's case notes, flicking from page to page, laying out the cause and effect of each symptom.

Kerry was acutely aware that Dai was in shock and grabbed the doctors sleeve. 'Dr Dhata, I don't think Mr Morris heard any of that.' She crouched in front of Dai and put her hands over his, pulling them gently away from his face.

'You okay, Dai?' she asked, smiling up at him. 'Would you like some water?'

'Yes please.' He sniffed, looking embarrassed.

Kerry handed him a plastic cup and his hands shook when he brought it towards his face, spilling water down his top.

'C-C-Can't take me anywhere, see,' he said, smiling half-heartedly. He downed the water and scrunched the cup into a ball. He blew out hard and jumped to his feet, throwing the cup into the waste bin. 'Okay! So, Emily has no idea who we are, *at the moment*, but she will remember. It's just gonna take time, right?'

Dr Dhata sighed. 'Mr Morris, at the moment your daughter is not here. She is locked away inside her head.' He pointed at the wall before explaining further. 'That girl in there has created a new identity. She doesn't recognise Zara and you must prepare yourself for the possibility that she won't recognise you, either.'

'She'll know who I am, mun. If she doesn't, then I'll—'

'Mr Morris, you must tread carefully. Her mind is fragile. As far as she is concerned, she is Parthena Love *not* Emily Morris.'

'Who?'

'She's referring to herself as Parthena Love.'

'That's crazy.'

'It might seem that way, but it's not. Her mind is paused. She must learn to trust you both, otherwise she may refuse to stay with you and … and she may have to be taken into care.'

Dai lunged toward the doctor, and Kerry and Fiona struggled to restrain him.

'Nobody's taking my daughter!' he screamed. His fist millimetres from the cowering doctor's eye.

'Shall I get security?' Dr Dhata asked, nervously.

'No, its fine,' assured Kerry. 'Dai, please calm down. Emily's not going anywhere.'

Fiona stepped forward saying, 'Look at me, Dai.' He ignored her, his face full of rage, so she raised a hand to his cheek, turning his head towards her. 'Look. At. Me.' His eyes slid sideways, but he wasn't focusing. 'No one's taking her away, okay?' she reiterated. 'The doctor's just explaining that you have to take things easy. Baby steps. Emily's disoriented and confused, as though she's seeing everything for the very first time. She needs to know she can trust you. That's when the healing process can start. She needs familiar surroundings and faces,' she explained, calmly.

Dai's body finally relaxed and Fiona released her grip.

'You can't see Emily like this. You'll scare her. You need to chill,' added Kerry.

Dai held up his hands. 'I'm sorry. You're right.'

'I will take you to see your daughter, but, as I said, please be prepared,' advised Dr Dhata.

Dai nodded.

Kerry stepped back. 'I've contacted the force psychologist, Dr Francis, and he's taking your daughter's case on. He's a good guy. He knows his stuff and he can really help Emily with your co-operation.'

'Thanks. Sorry about my outburst, Doc,' Dai said, shaking his hand once more.

'No problem. Let me take you to your daughter.'

~

When Dai entered the examination room, a tearful Zara dashed over, flinging her arms around him.

'Aaw, Dai, what're we gonna do?'

'Who the bleedin' 'ells this, then?' Emily asked, looking Dai up and down. 'Cor blimey guv', you're a looker 'ain't ya! That your fella then, missy?' she asked Zara, causing Dai's jaw to drop.

'Emily, it's me … your dad. Don't you recognise me?'

'Oh for gord's sake. What is it with you lot? My names Parthena, Parthena Love, but my friends and regulars call me Party, 'cause I'm the life an' soul, ain't I.' She laughed.

Dai looked horrified as his daughter strutted around with a swagger and arrogance that he had never seen before.

When Fiona entered the room her uniform unsettled the girl.

'Hey, you ain't sticking darbies on me, again. It gave me right old collywobbles when that copper nabbed me. Talkin' a load of codswallop an' all, he was. I can tell ya.'

Emily sauntered over to Dai and inspected him from top to bottom, walking around him as though she were deciding whether or not to buy him.

'Well, look at your blooming face. Swear you'd seen a ghost or summat, if you ask me.' She lifted a finger in the air and paused. 'Although, the question you should be asking is, how the 'ell did I get in this bleedin' body? Look at it.' She pulled her blouse forward and stared down at her chest. 'Ain't nuffink there, yet. How ma gonna work with this? I used to be proper eesome.'

CHAPTER 32

I HEAR YOU NOW

Friday 23rd October, 1981

Dylan's brain felt like it was being squeezed by an unseen force; he had slept through Thursday and had awoken in the early hours in tremendous pain. He decided to take something for his headache and crept out of his room.

The house was eerily quiet. No snoring, breathing, or the sound of his father's squeaky oxygen mask.

He grabbed the banister, turned to descend the stairs, and caught a glimpse of something back in his room.

Something in his bed.

Him.

He was shedding his body so often that his skin was becoming slacker than a wizard's sleeve.

Newt hopped onto the banister, his beak nudging his fingers, and cawed, knowingly.

'I know. I know. I shouldn't go. But I have to find her.'

Dylan reached for his body and felt it pulling him, like a

magnet. He fought against it, withdrew his hand, and trailed through the lobby.

He passed his family's incorporeal doors and instinctively stopped beside his own. Although he couldn't see anything within, he felt the pressure of something foreboding pressing against his door with innumerable, unseen hands. He leant in and was overwhelmed by a sudden, ear-popping, surge; a pressure so immense that he felt he was falling down a pit shaft.

He imagined thousands of long, black, spindly fingers pushing against the door's surface, expanding and stretching it like cellophane but never quite breaching its tensile strength. He raised his hands to his ears and the pressure waned. The fog changed intensity and his soul shifted. Dark figures formed before his eyes and slashed at his arms, before melting away in a swirl of nothingness, like his mother's cigarette smoke disappearing out of Uncle John's car window.

He peered wide-eyed into Transmogoria.

Emily was here, somewhere.

Walking through Transmogoria was like wading through a river of dark treacle. It smothered him, bound him, and Dylan quickly realised that fighting its hold only made it worse, steadfast. Mind relaxed, he imagined himself sinking into a dark hammock and the souls slid past him with ease.

He called out Emily's name, his voice carrying through the fog like an echo unwilling to fade.

The fog in front of him shifted, forming a figure. Its features slowly becoming discernible like a shaken Polaroid picture.

It was Emily.

Her body was juxtaposed against the cold, sombre fog by an iridescent shimmer, which slid away from her like a silver snake, before fading into the distance.

She looked like an angel.

'You're here,' she said.

'Yes, and you shouldn't be. I have to find a way to get you back.'

'It's okay, Dylan. Forget about me. I'm fading. Live your life.'

'What? No.' He shook his head, uncomprehending. 'Your soul shouldn't be here. You're not dead; some woman has stolen your body. '

'It's not your fault.'

'But you're all alone,' he protested.

'No. The nice man is helping me. I think it's my Grancha.'

'Tom? Are you sure?'

'Dylan.'

'What?'

'DYLAN!!!'

He felt a pull dragging him away from Emily. He blinked furiously. His eyes, overwhelmed with light and colour, slowly focused on his mother.

'Wha'?'

'Wakey wakey, Dilly Willy!' sung Chrissy. She pulled a face like she'd just sucked on a lemon. 'Oooh, that's weird. Déjà vu, again.'

'Really?'

'Yeah ... Anyway, c'mon. Move your arse.' She flung his curtains wide, blinding him. 'You've got your first appointment with Dr Francis at ten. WPC Brasking will be here, soon.'

'Do I have to go?'

'Yes.'

'Awww, Mam, please,' he begged.

'Don't be scared. This is your chance to prove you're not mad. I'll sort breakfast. What d'ya want?'

Dylan yawned and stretched his arms. 'Ready Brek and cornflakes, please.'

Chrissy pointed at him. 'You've been scratching in your sleep. Nightmare?'

Confused, Dylan looked down at his arms, which were covered in bloodied scratches.

~

WPC Brasking picked them up in her panda car promptly at nine-thirty and drove them to Dr Francis' private clinic in Caerphilly.

Being in a police car should have been awesome for a young boy like Dylan. Dreaming of chasing bad guys with flashing blue lights and sirens blaring. Showing off his truncheon skills before handcuffing the villains, telling them they'd be eating porridge in a dank cell for the rest of their lives, and throwing them in the back of his squad car.

But not Dylan.

He just bombarded Fiona with questions about Emily, then became annoyed when she was uncooperative, quoting patient confidentiality. The only thing Dylan gleaned from her answers was that Emily had sustained a bad head injury and had lost a chunk of memory. To compensate for this hole, her brain had conjured up a new identity for itself.

She was now calling herself, Parthena Love.

Dylan was desperate to prove they were all wrong, but his fear of being locked up in a padded cell prevented him from saying anything he'd later regret.

Parthena Love was a Coblyn.

Dylan had to find a way to get her out of Emily's body, and soon.

But first, he had to get through today, and the other five sessions with the psychologist, while sounding, and acting, like a sane person. He was positive Emily hadn't fully passed over but she said she was fading, whatever that meant, so he knew he didn't have long before Parthena would be here permanently.

Demonic possession?

The book had told him all about Coblynau and he hoped it knew how to get rid of one for good.

Exorcism?

When Fiona pulled up at a set of traffic lights Dylan saw Victor Gaunt down a side street.

'It's Victor!' he yelled, alerting Fiona.

Fiona turned in the direction Dylan was pointing and, sure enough, Victor was strolling along the road leading to Pontyfechan.

Unable to pursue him, Fiona unclipped the police radio from the dashboard and called it in.

CHAPTER 33

GAMES WITHOUT FRONTIERS

His sessions with Dr Francis were private. His responses might not be entirely truthful if a family member were present and, for once, Dylan was grateful for rules.

Dr Floyd Francis was only just into his thirties, but to Dylan he was old. He had thick, scruffy, dark-brown hair and half-frame, rimless, reading glasses that dangled off the tip of his nose. His shirt could have done with being a size larger, but Dylan assumed he preferred it tight to show off his athletic physique. Yet it wasn't his muscular body that stood out the most, it was his bright, impossibly white, teeth; he looked like a walking advertisement for Macleans toothpaste.

His office looked like it had been carved out of a solid block of wood. A beige coloured ceiling was met by wood paneling on the walls, which were covered in wooden picture frames of all shapes and sizes containing images designed to stimulate patient's thoughts. Although Dylan just assumed that they had been painted by Dr Francis' children.

On the room's left was a large bay window with dark, wooden frames, and on the right, opposite the window, were three huge wooden bookcases filled to the brim with vintage, brown books interleaved with African wood carvings. All the furniture in the room was made from dark wood, from the weirdly shaped leather chair that was behind his chunky desk to the long, half-settee below the window. The only item in the room that didn't look wooden was the oval, paisley rug in the centre of the room, and the typewriter and telephone on his desk.

It smelt like a museum minus the artefacts.

After brief introductions and an explanation of the format of the sessions, Dr Francis, or Floyd, as he preferred Dylan to call him, sat Dylan on a small chair. Floyd sat opposite him and slid a small, square table between them. The top of the table was covered with green cloth like a snooker table, on which he placed a stack of cards, notebook, and pen.

All Dylan had to do was look at the inkblot pictures on the cards and tell him the first thing that came into his head.

Simple.

The pictures were printed on white card and they reminded Dylan of the paintings he'd done in infant school. The teacher had gotten everyone to fold a piece of paper in half, creasing the centre of the page, and then re-open it. Then the class painted an image on one half of the page, whilst leaving the opposite side blank. Once their masterpieces were complete they folded their sheets once more and pressed down firmly, transferring a mirror image of their painting onto the blank side. When they gingerly peeled them open, there were gasps in the classroom when the children saw the amazing design that had miraculously formed on their page.

From what Dylan remembered, they were butterflies, always butterflies.

The first image Floyd showed him looked like a black animal's head with white eyes, fangs, and large ears.

Dylan wasn't sure what he had to do with the card.

Could he rotate it?

Flip it over?

Should he describe it with one word or a sentence?

He was so worried that saying the wrong thing would get him sent to a nuthouse that he began to cry. Not just a few tears creeping into the corner of his eyes and welling up until they edged over the top of his eyelids. No. These were full-on, holding his breath, quivering lip, and going blue, tears.

Floyd wasn't sure how to react, so he handed Dylan a tissue and sat in silence.

When Dylan finally caught his breath and calmed down, Floyd handed him a beaker of squash and slid a plate of custard creams in front of him.

Dylan looked him over, suspiciously.

'Your mother told me you like them. Help yourself,' he said, gesturing to the biscuits. 'I know that you're scared of what I'll think of you. But there really is no need to concern yourself, Dylan.' He smiled, but it didn't seem genuine. 'There are no correct answers. Just tell me what you think of when you see the images, okay?'

Dylan took a sip of squash, grabbed a biscuit, dunked it in the orange squash and took a bite. By the look on Floyd's face he had already decided he was mad, so he had nothing to lose.

'Is it a wild cat?' asked Dylan, as he studied the image once more.

'It's subjective, Dylan. Just say what you see.'

'A big, wild cat,' he said, proudly.

Floyd scribbled something in his book and revealed the next image. This process continued for nearly twenty minutes and there were only ten cards. Dylan deliberated over each card for far too long, even after Floyd reiterated several times that it should simply be the first thing that popped into his head.

But that was just it.

Every time he saw a new image something within it reminded him of the shadow man in the graveyard, or Mr Red Eyes, or a smoky soul wisping its way in and out of his vision. He daren't mention any of these things, so his images became butterflies, moths, snakes, birds, or fluffy rabbits.

Anything *but* what he was really thinking.

~

Floyd finished writing his notes and put the small table to one side. He pointed to the weird half-settee and asked Dylan to lie down while he sat behind his desk. Dylan didn't feel comfortable lying down, but he wasn't exactly sure where to sit.

Why did it only have one arm?

He had never seen a settee like this before. He chose the end with an arm, sat down next to it, and twiddled his thumbs. He stared across at the plate of biscuits and regretted not grabbing some before Floyd moved the table. All morning, he had felt ravenous and cold through to his bones; his Ready Brek glow having worn off ages ago.

'If you like to fidget, there are puzzles and toys in the wooden box beside the chaise longue,' suggested Floyd.

Dylan just stared, blankly.

'Oh, sorry, Dylan. It's French. It means long chair. It's what you're sat on,' he explained.

Dylan leant over the arm and found the box. He grabbed a Rubik's Cube and sat back.

Floyd retrieved a tape recorder from his desk drawer, inserted a tape, and clicked a few buttons. He grabbed his notebook and pen, leant back in his chair, and crossed his legs atop his desk.

'You look so uncomfortable sat like that, Dylan. There's

plenty of cushions. Please, lie down and relax,' suggested Floyd, firmly.

Yes, Dylan.

Relax.

Open your mind.

Tell Floyd about all these imaginary friends of yours.

What? Dead people, you say? I think we'll book you a padded cell, right away, young man.

Dylan shook the thoughts from his head and laid down facing the doctor.

'Relax, Dylan. Slow your breathing. Deep breath, pause, then slowly release. In ... and out. In ... and out.'

Dylan felt stupid, but he did what he was told; he didn't want to appear rebellious.

'From what I've seen so far, with the picture test, you seem reluctant to answer truthfully. You took your time over your responses, which suggests you're holding back or hiding something. These stimuli and tests are merely to help me understand your current state of mind. Let me in. I need to get to know you. Who is Dylan Wolfendale?'

He had seen enough television programs to know that simply saying 'no comment' would just infuriate his interrogators and result in more trouble. He had to give Floyd something. Something that steered him away from anything supernatural.

'He's a school boy,' he replied, timidly.

'Third person,' mumbled Floyd, scribbling something down.

'You said, who *is* Dylan Wolfendale? You didn't say, who *are* you?'

'Yes. Yes I did. Absolutely right. Very intuitive.'

His facial expression didn't look congratulatory and Dylan regretted his comment.

'What are your likes and dislikes?' continued Floyd.

'Custard creams and bullies,' was Dylan's curt reply.

Floyd smiled and scribbled in his book. 'Good. Let's deal with the dislikes. Do you know many bullies?'

'Yeah.'

'Have they bullied you?'

'All the time.'

'How does that make you feel?'

'Angry.'

'Do you want to hurt them back?'

Dylan rotated the Rubik's cube and completed his first side. The white side. It was always the white side, which was strange because blue was his favourite colour. He had never gotten further without destroying the completed side. Dylan stared at the white squares, his mind drifting.

He slipped out of his body into the fog of the lobby. Ignoring the feelings of guilt for cheating, he approached Floyd and tried to decipher his scribbled notes:

Illeism—Intellect not stunted. Personality disorder? Not egotistical. Rational fear/anxiety.

He sighed.

He was none the wiser.

Floyd's soul slithered eellike down his forearm and into the fingertips holding his pen. Dylan briefly contemplated touching it but his arms itched just thinking about it. He had promised himself that he would never defile another person's body and he aimed to keep it.

He wasn't like Crulus.

Closing his eyes, he relaxed and felt the tug of reality.

Dylan looked up from the cube and replied, 'Yes, but I don't have the guts to fight back.'

Floyd blinked and shook his head. 'Haven't you already said that?' He flipped through his notebook.

'That's déjà vu. It's a phenomenon,' Dylan pointed out.

Floyd sighed. 'A strange one, too. Right, where was I?'

'Bullies,' reminded Dylan, rotating the cube.

'Ah, yes. Would you fight back, if you could?'

Dylan nodded.

'Sorry, Dylan, can you verbalise your answers for the sake of the tape, please?'

'Yes.'

'Care to elaborate?'

Dylan shook his head without looking up.

'Is it lack of confidence or do you not like violence?' Floyd pushed.

'Both. I'm scared of being hurt but I'm also afraid that, if I did fight back, the teachers, or my dad, would tell me off.'

'Does your father smack you, if you're naughty?'

'Yes.'

'Does that make you angry, too?'

'No, it makes me sad.' He smiled: second side completed and the white side was still intact!

Floyd saw his smile and scribbled in his book.

Bad timing, Dylan.

'Why is that?' Floyd continued.

Dylan sat up and pulled his knees toward his chest. 'I'm sad because I did something wrong and made my dad hit me.'

'Is he sad when he punishes you?'

'Yes.'

'What about your mother, is she sad, too?'

'She's always sad,' he replied, a bit too abruptly.

'Why?' Floyd asked, twiddling with his pen in anticipation.

It suddenly dawned on Dylan how to divert Floyd's attention away from what was really happening to him.

'My Auntie, my mam's sister, was murdered.'

Floyd's ears pricked up. 'Oh, my. I'm so sorry. When did this happen?' he asked, sitting up.

'The day I was born. They kept it from me. My uncle only told me a few weeks ago. My mam don't know that I know.'

'I see ... This must have been very upsetting for you?'

Floyd was hooked. Dylan could see it in his eyes, but he still had to be careful; he couldn't risk mentioning the book. 'Yes, but now I know why she's sad. She misses her twin sister.'

'Twins you say? Yes, I can imagine she would be extremely sad.' Floyd scratched at his chin, paused for a few moments, and then asked, 'Did it make you angry that they kept this from you?'

Dylan had nearly completed his third side of the cube, but the white side was now totally messed up. He leant over the arm of the chair and dropped it back in the box.

'Not really,' he finally said. 'I'm just sad that I never met her. I wish I could speak to her and, you know, say hello.'

Floyd edged forward on his seat. 'So you'd *like* to talk to the dead in order to speak to her?' he asked, his pen poised.

Dylan nodded.

'For the tape, Dylan,' Floyd reminded.

'Sorry. Yes. Yes, I wanted to speak to the dead. I'd like to meet her ...' He shrugged. 'But I can't.'

Floyd glanced at his wrist watch and sighed. 'Unfortunately, we're out of time. My next client is due, so we'll continue next session. You've been absolutely brilliant, Dylan, and, I don't normally do this, but I can see you're worried, so let me reassure you. You've got nothing to worry about. We have to do all the sessions, though, to be certain, but *please*, don't worry, okay?' He held out his hand.

Dylan smiled with relief and walked over to Floyd's desk to shake his hand.

On the desk next to the phone was a Rolodex, which displayed his next appointment. Dylan glanced down at the handwritten name.

Miss Emily Morris.

CHAPTER 34

FUNKYTOWN

After Fiona had deposited Zara Morris and her daughter into Dr Francis's reception, she sat in her panda car and almost nodded off waiting for the Wolfendales to appear. Her mind was too foggy to remember when she had last slept for more than a few hours. It was like someone was in her head, waking her before REM kicked in. When Chrissy and Dylan finally approached, she quickly gulped the last of her coffee and stuffed the empty cup into the glove box.

Dylan seemed his usual distracted self, tapping repetitively on the vinyl door covering with his face within licking distance of the window, and when she swung the grumbling Ford Escort out onto the road Dylan slid past her rear view mirror causing her to chuckle.

'Sorry. No belts.'

Dylan slid back behind his mother and held onto the door handle. Although Floyd's session wasn't as scary as he had imagined, he was glad it was over. Despite being desperate to get Emily from Transmogoria, he couldn't read the book until tonight; Chrissy was adamant he went back to school. She had even prepared a packed lunch, which meant he couldn't read it dinnertime, either.

He opened his gaudy, green, Tupperware box and examined the contents: chicken spread sandwich, chunk of cheddar, Trio chocolate bar, and three custard creams. He nodded subconsciously.

Fiona was eager to speak to Dylan privately, so she took Chrissy home first and outside the school gates she turned to Dylan and said, 'Sorry about the sessions. You're not crazy, but we have to follow procedures. We both know there's some funky shit going on in this town. Have you seen Victor, recently?'

Dylan shook his head.

'Good. Whatever Howard Cobley had has passed to Victor.' She removed her hat and lifted her hair away from the side of her head. 'See this mark,' she said, pointing to her scar. 'It's the same as Howard's. Same place, too.'

'How'd you get it?'

'I was attacked as a kid. I woke with a sore head and this scar. The attacker had red eyes, too. It's the same virus. Although, I must have been immune, somehow.'

'It's not a virus,' he replied, flatly.

'What, so this *really* is a bodysnatcher?'

'Yes. The Cythraul is a demon, or the devil, which is why Fred knew about it.' Dylan kicked his heels against a wall, his head whirling with thoughts. If Crulus *had* attacked Fiona all those years ago, how did she survive? Why wasn't her soul kicked out, like Emily's? If it had been, how did she get back to her body? Finally, he asked, 'Can you remember anything about the attack?'

Fiona pursed her lips and shook her head.

'If Crulus attacked you, maybe others can survive, too. We just need to figure out how. Emily won't last long in Transmogoria.'

Fiona grabbed his arm and gently shook it. 'How do you know all this? No offence, but you're just a kid.'

Dylan dared not mention the book. 'The dead told me,' he admitted.

'You *really* can communicate with the dead?'

Dylan nodded and whispered, 'Nekrôspiél.' He took his lunchbox from his bag and offered her a custard cream.

'Thanks,' she said, taking one. 'How can Crulus go from one person to the next?'

'Dunno.' He shrugged and sat down. 'He forces your soul out and takes over. He attacked Emily, too.'

'But she didn't have red eyes.'

'Crulus' eyes aren't always red, either.'

'Oh, crap. Is he in her body, then?'

'No. He pushed her out and a Coblyn, that Parthena girl, jumped into her body.'

'Emily must have a scar, too. I'll try and look, later.'

Dylan pointed to Fiona's head. 'How come you didn't die when you got yours?'

'No idea. I was hoping you or your dead friends could answer that. What about these Coblynau?'

'What about them?'

'According to folklore, they're mine goblins. Miners fear them.'

Dylan had never heard of them before the book, so he shrugged without replying.

Fiona waved at nothing. 'Never mind. We need to find Victor before someone else dies. Can Crulus be stopped?'

Dylan stared into the distance. He just wanted Emily back before it was too late; he couldn't lose her forever. But Fiona was right, if they didn't stop Crulus, how many more were going to be killed, or replaced by Coblynau?

'I don't know,' he finally answered. 'But I hope so.'

'Me too,' agreed Fiona, crossing her fingers.

'How is Emily's body?'

'Emily's body?' Fiona shook her head and snorted. 'I still can't believe we're talking like this. It's crazy.' She plonked her arse onto the kerb next to Dylan. 'Dr Francis says its psychogenic amnesia, which is clever talk for memory loss, but your theory fits better. She's not just forgotten, she *really* believes she is Parthena Love from the eighteen hundreds. She sounds like a cockney, too.'

Dylan tilted his head like a puppy.

'Oh, sorry, it's a nickname for a Londoner.'

'Ah, okay.'

'Hopefully, these therapy sessions will give her the help she needs.'

'Emily doesn't need therapy; she needs her body.'

~

When Dylan finally got to his bedroom, it smelt fresh. Cleaned for the first time in ages, everything was out of place. Something crackled and hissed in his cupboard. He opened it and discovered all his stuff neatly stacked; he had no idea where anything was. He never understood why his mother couldn't lift things, dust, and put them back in the same place. He dug around until he found the source of the noise.

It was his walkie.

Mark was calling him. 'Dylan, do you copy? Over,' crackled the walkie.

He shut his bedroom door and put the radio on low to hide his conversation from Kaelum. 'Yeah. What's up? Over.'

'What's up? It's half-term next week and I haven't seen, or heard, from you in days *and* you ignored me in school. Over.'

'I wasn't ignoring you, well, not really. It's a long story. Over.'

'Emily's been off, too. Did you pair run off together?'

'She's dead.'

'WHAT? Piss off.'

'It's true. Crulus pushed her out of her body and someone took it. I have to figure out how to get her back. I need to ask the book.'

'Holy shit. I'll come over. I wanna help.'

'No, dad won't let you in. I'm grounded. I'll see what the book says. Over and out.'

'Okay, let me know. Over.'

Dylan tossed the walkie onto his bed and opened his wardrobe door. The pile of clothes in the bottom of his wardrobe were now arranged into neat stacks. He reached behind them but couldn't feel the book. He screamed, venting a mixture of anger and panic, while he hurled everything out of the wardrobe and rummaged through it. There was no bag or book. He flung shelf after shelf of neatly ironed clothes onto the floor until the wardrobe was empty.

The book was gone.

He began to hyperventilate, clenching and unclenching his fists as his rage bubbled over. Stepping over the mountain of clothes, he began emptying the cupboard.

'It can't be gone,' he muttered.

When he reached the back of the cupboard without finding it, he started ripping into his parents boxes.

'WHERE IS IT!'

His fingers began to tingle while his breathing and heart rate skyrocketed. He felt faint, but he continued to rip open boxes.

BANG! BANG! BANG!

Kaelum forced his door open against the stuff strewn across the floor. Chrissy was standing openmouthed behind him.

'Where is it, Mam?' spat Dylan.

'Where's what?' she asked, frowning. 'What've you done

to your room? I've just cleaned it. Wait till your father sees this.'

'Where's my book?'

'What book? I haven't taken any books. It's probably there, somewhere.'

Dylan shook his head. 'It's not. I've looked everywhere. It's gone. You must have taken it.'

Chrissy shoved her fists into her sides and bellowed, 'I. HAVE. NOT. TAKEN. YOUR. BOOK! You must have left it in school. Now, clean this mess up.'

'It was in a bag in my wardrobe,' he said, pointing at the wardrobe as if his mother didn't know where it stood. 'It was there before *you* cleaned,' he accused.

Kaelum stepped forward and jabbed Dylan in the chest, sending him backwards over a box. 'Listen freak. Mam hasn't got your stupid book!'

Chrissy grabbed Kaelum's arm and told him to leave, which he reluctantly did but not before lobbing something at Dylan's head causing him to yelp. Chrissy moved some stuff and slid her bum onto his bed. 'What book was it, love? School one or library?' she asked in a gentle voice.

Dylan sniffed and wiped his nose on his sleeve. How would he explain this without looking exactly like the nutter they were trying to disprove?

'Ummm ... No ... It's ... It's my friends book. I borrowed it. It's expensive, so I've gotta find it.'

'Okay, so what sort of book? What does it look like?'

'It's an old book with, like, metal things holding it together.'

'What's on the cover?'

'Ummm ... It's ... Er—'

'You must know what it looks like,' she insisted.

'It's a horror book. It's got this horrible looking, fake, fleshy cover and—'

'Oh, that disgusting thing. It looked like a dead animal, not a book.'

'Where is it? I need it, please,' he begged.

'I threw it away.'

Dylan flung his hands to his face and looked like he was going to pass out. 'You didn't?'

'Yeah, it was gopping.'

Dylan clambered over the boxes and pushed passed her.

'Where're you going?'

'To get it out of the bin.'

'Sorry, son, we'll just have to pay for it,' she advised, lowering her head. 'The bin-men have emptied it.'

Dylan bolted down the stairs without responding and, moments later, Chrissy heard the aluminium bin lids clanging to the concrete floor, followed by Dylan's screams.

Inconsolable, Dylan eventually sobbed back to his room and Chrissy didn't see him for the rest of the day.

When dusk descended, Dylan grabbed his walkie and told Mark what had happened. They needed to get to the local tip before the book was crushed, buried, or lost forever. The council tip was on the side of Machen mountain, nearly three miles away, and there was no way they could get there quick enough without his bike and he couldn't get that without alerting his parents to his elope. Luckily, Steven had a spare Raleigh Chopper that he was fixing up, so they agreed to meet outside Mr Garrett's shop.

~

It was five to five, when Dylan met the boys.

Machen mountain filled the horizon to their left, its ridgeline glistening from the low sun behind it. They had less than an hour of light to find the book, if it was still there.

They sped up the mountain as fast as they could go but

the uneven, steep incline was arduous. Their lungs were burning when their brakes eventually squeaked to a halt near the tip entrance just fifteen minutes later. They hunkered down behind some bushes and waited for the staff to close up at five-thirty.

When the last man locked up, Mark cut through the chain-link fence with Mostyn's bolt croppers and made a hole large enough for them to crawl through.

The tip had been flattened apart from two large truck loads of rubbish that were higher than Dylan's bedroom window. It was a mammoth task and Steven moaned that it was going to take them forever, but Dylan insisted they had to find it.

Emily's life depended on it.

Despite the handkerchiefs covering their mouths, all three boys vomited, and it took four hours to wade through the first stinky pile of household waste. With no sign of it, and his stomach constantly retching, Steven gave up and left, but Dylan refused to give up. Mark offered to stay until they found it; his mother had probably drunk herself to sleep, so she wouldn't miss him, anyway.

It was nearly two in the morning before they had rummaged through the second pile and found nothing. Dylan insisted they must have missed it and wanted to start again until Mark punched him in the arm.

The book was gone.

He had to live with it.

But could Emily live without it?

CHAPTER 35

TAINTED LOVE

Friday 13th November, 1981

For the past few weeks, Dylan was struggling not to breakdown. He rarely ate and couldn't sleep at night. Able to cross realms at will, the only thing that was keeping him going was his regular visits into Transmogoria to see Emily. He begged her not to give up, but her hopes were fading as fast as her spirit, which had reduced to a faint shimmer. If she fully crossed-over, she would be lost forever. Nekrôspiél gave him the ability to speak to her anytime, but the thought of never seeing her again was tearing his soul apart.

Dr Francis had declared him clinically sane, stating that the stress of discovering his aunt had been murdered meant his childhood imagination was trying to fill the void in his subconscious, or something along those lines. Dylan lost interest once Floyd said the sessions were finished; some things were worse than being a fruitcake.

Parthena Love and Dean Johnson were courting.

Apparently, she had been drawn to his boyish good looks

and his strong, manly personality. At least that's what Dean's cronies told everyone. Dean waltzed around the school with Parthena draped off his arm, like they were King and Queen of Draigwen.

Dylan couldn't bear to see him slobber all over Emily's body and, when he saw Dean's tongue lapping all over her face and wriggling inside her beautiful mouth, he was physically sick.

He had to do something.

Anything.

Emily deserved her body back.

'What does she see in that fat, bald slob?' asked Steven, stuffing his gob with chips.

'Maybe he's paying her,' offered Mostyn.

They both laughed until Dylan glared at them.

'Wha'?' asked Mostyn, raising his palms skyward. 'Emily reckons she used to be a prostitute.'

'Shut up, Mossy!' spat Dylan. 'It's not Emily.'

'Yeah, yeah, so you keep saying.'

Mark shoved his shoulder into Mostyn. 'You never believe him, do you?' he accused.

'Oh, come on, mun. It's crazy talk.'

'So's changing your name to Party. What difference does it make, anyway? Leave him alone,' snapped Mark.

'Jeez, I was only playing. Bunch of miserable wankers.' Mostyn jumped off the wall and retrieved his bag. 'I'm off to meet Franklyn.'

The boys sat open mouthed like a row of *Whac-A-Mole* holes, while Mostyn disappeared into the throng.

'Why's he bothering with Kevin?' asked Mark.

'You should know,' replied Steven, in an accusing tone. 'He's *your* friend.'

Mark punched him, giving him a dead leg.

'Owww! But he is, though,' whimpered Steven, rubbing and hobbling on his lanky limb.

'He's *our* friend, and I dunno why he's bothering with Kevin. Buying stolen goods?'

'Well, it is Friday the thirteenth. Bad shit's gonna happen,' warned Steven.

Dylan sat in silence, eyes transfixed on Party and Dean canoodling over the far side of the yard. His anger only visible via the veins bulging in his neck.

'Listen, Dylan, are you still grounded?' asked Mark. 'If you're not, do you fancy going to the chapel jumble sale on Sunday?'

'I've got no choice,' moaned Dylan.

'How come?'

'I'm still in their bad books. Mam's booked a table to sell stuff, so I've gotta help.'

'Oh, well, at least you're not grounded,' Mark pointed out.

'I know, but I missed Bonfire night,' moaned Dylan.

'You didn't miss much. I only made twenty pence doing penny-for-the-guy, and it took me three days to make him,' whined Steven. 'I didn't put him on the bonfire, though. I shoved him in the shed for next year.'

Mark shuffled his bum across the wall, filling in the gap left by Mostyn. 'There'll be someone at the jumble who can help you, you know, with Emily.'

Dylan's head snapped around as if it was spring loaded. 'Who?'

'Madame Zina.'

'Who the hell's she?'

'Fortune teller and spirit thingy. She might help. It's worth a try,' offered Mark.

'I suppose,' agreed Dylan, reluctantly. 'How much is it? I've had no pocket money for weeks,' he added with a sigh.

'It's okay, my mam knows her. I'll get you in for free.' He winked and ruffled Dylan's hair. 'She likes me.'

Dylan brushed his hand away as if he was swatting an angry wasp. 'Why does everyone mess with my hair?'

'Cause it's sooooo fluffy,' squealed Mark, diving on him.

'Geroff ya weirdo!'

'You're the weird one, Psychobum.'

Dylan sat up and checked his watch. Dinner time was nearly over and Dean still had his tongue buried in Emily's throat. Party was abusing her body and Dylan couldn't bear it. He felt sick. Tears welled in his eyes and he quickly wiped them in his sleeve.

'Oh, Wolfy, have you heard anything about Sian's killer?' asked Steven.

'Bloody hell, I forgot you were there, butt'. You were so quiet,' noted Mark.

'I didn't wanna disturb you two love birds. Oooh your hair is sooo fluffy, Dylan. I love you, I do,' he mocked.

Mark flicked his ear. 'Shut up, knob.'

'Well, Wolfy?' nagged Steven.

Dylan scrunched up his face. 'How would I know?'

'Mark said that sexy copper was around your house when they thought you were a schizo', so I thought she might've said something.'

'Fiona only found the scar on Howard and Emily; it wasn't on Sian. Either Crulus killed her differently or it was a boy that did it, like Sian said,' explained Dylan. 'She's okay, though; she's with her Nan,' he added, pre-empting Steven's next question.

'Good,' said Steven, although he didn't look convinced.

Mark jumped off the wall and brushed himself down.

'Where're you going?' asked Steven. 'The bell hasn't gone, yet.'

'Homework catchup. Not that it matters, though. They're

moving me to D block after Christmas. I'm officially a thicko.' He shrugged. 'Catch you later.'

Dylan's body sagged, and his head flopped into his waiting hands. Everything was turning to rat shit. Mark used to be good at all subjects. It was almost as if he *wanted* to get away from Harwood's form class. How would he cope without Mark? He wasn't much bigger than Dylan but, metaphorically speaking, his balls were humungous. Plus, with Mostyn fraternising with the enemy, Dylan might not be able to rely on him, either. Perhaps Mostyn was a double agent.

As if to confirm his suspicions, he spotted Mostyn leaning against the gym wall in deep conversation with Kevin. Kevin's spectral friend with the scruffy, out-dated, school uniform, hopped and danced around on his wooden leg, like a demented Pinocchio. When Kevin handed Mostyn money, he handed Kevin a small brown package in return.

It was all very Russian spy-esque.

Peg-leg hobbled forward, his head swivelling towards Dylan, face pulsing and morphing. Shadow replaced flesh while his mouth opened back to his ears, as if an invisible knife had slit his cheeks open. His jaw parted wide to reveal innumerous sharp teeth within a horrific smile, and his eyes, black and glistening, stared straight at Dylan.

Peg-leg could see him.

To see, is to be seen.

The bell sounded to announce the end of dinnertime, breaking Dylan's trance, and when he looked back towards the gym, Peg-leg was gone.

Dylan climbed the steps and followed Dean and Party through the corridors whilst maintaining a safe distance. Dean couldn't keep his hands off her and Dylan's nausea returned twofold. If Madame Zina didn't have any useful suggestions, Dylan would have to try something drastic. He turned the corner by the main hall and nearly walked straight into Gareth.

Dylan took a step back and looked him up and down. 'What're you doing here?'

'The book. It's gone.'

Dylan lowered his gaze and scratched at his face. 'What? No, it's just ... Umm, my mam moved it,' he mumbled.

Gareth shook his head. 'The book may already be in wrong hands. Get it back or Emily will be lost forever.'

'Wait, how did you—'

'That wasn't Emily that walked by. You know what she is.'

'Yes, but I don't know what to do,' he whined. 'The book has—'

'Gone,' finished Gareth. 'I know. Find it, Dylan, and fast!'

'Wait, where did you get the book, anyway? Can't you make another one or something?'

With a slight head-shake, Gareth sighed. 'It's centuries old and can only fulfil its purpose once. It *cannot* be replaced. Time is of the essence. You're the only one who can save my sister.'

Dylan felt a cold emptiness when Gareth walked past, and it left Dylan feeling even worse than he thought possible. How the hell was he going to find the book? Why was he chosen, anyway? He must be the worst Psychopomp ever.

CHAPTER 36

EVERY LITTLE THING SHE DOES IS MAGIC

Sunday 15th November, 1981
Larkmead Chapel

The chapel doors were closed whilst sellers setup their stalls and excited buyers jostled impatiently along the driveway, pushing and shoving against the chapel gates, eager for secondhand bargains. Attendances to Reverend Foster's Sunday service had risen dramatically since the recent deaths, especially as the killer was still at large. Also, with the threat of miner's strikes abundant, the locals needed comfort and reassurance during such worrying times. Business was booming and Fred was loving the attention.

Due to a forecast of light rain for later that morning, all the stalls had been setup inside the hall except for Madame Zina's; she had brought her own brightly coloured tent, which she and her assistant were setting up on the grass beside the graveyard.

Inside the hall, Kaelum and Dylan were helping Chrissy setup her stall. Two rickety wallpaper pasting tables were sagging from the weight of the clothes and toys that she had brought to sell; the latter chosen by Chrissy with very little input from the boys, and Dylan had reluctantly towed them over to the chapel on his go-kart. Most of them were multiplayer games like Buck-a-roo!, Dragster, Twister, Downfall and Frustration, which Chrissy said were no longer played. This irritated the hell out of Dylan. The only reason they weren't playing the games was because his father had been hospitalised, Kaelum was a dick, and his mother had been staring at the bottom of a bottle these past few months. But what upset Dylan the most was the huge box resting on top of his go-kart, which contained his entire Action Man collection.

When the bells rang at nine and the chapel flooded with hordes of buyers, Dylan couldn't bear to watch his toys getting sold for pennies. Mark and Steven were waiting for him by the ice cream van on the driveway and, as he approached, he spotted Fiona by the gates. He waved but she didn't reciprocate; she was engrossed in whatever she was dealing with.

When he reached the van, Steven was devouring a ninety-nine ice cream with two flakes, slurping away like a dog licking his balls.

'Are we going in before all the bargains go, or wha'?' asked Steven.

Mark shook his head. 'Nah, you go in. Me and Dylan are going in there,' he said, pointing at Madame Zina's tent.

'Why? Dylan probably knows more than her.'

'I have to try something. I need to get Emily back,' explained Dylan.

Steven stuffed the last of his cone in his mouth and wiped his mouth on his sleeve. 'You didn't save Sian,' came his hurtful, muffled reply. A lump of ice cream slid over his bottom lip and plopped onto the driveway. 'Did you?'

Dylan fought to stop his lip quivering. 'That was different; she was dead. Emily isn't, at least, not yet.'

'Whatever,' snapped Steven, before storming off.

Dylan would have done anything to get Sian back, but it was impossible. He could talk to the dead, but he couldn't resurrect them. 'What's up with him?'

Mark compressed his lips. 'No idea. Anyway, what's up with you?'

'What do you mean?'

'Something's wrong. I can tell.'

'Kevin's Bogie saw me.'

Mark's mouth gaped. 'Oh, shit. Peg-leg?'

'Yeah, and his face—'

'What about it?'

'Never mind. Come on.'

The inside of Madame Zina's tent was divided into two: a waiting area with several chairs, and a divination room. Her assistant ushered them inside with a swish of her robed arm. The tent had an African feel to it; brightly coloured material and beads adorned the walls, while wooden masks and statuettes were doted everywhere.

Madame Zina, a large African woman, sat across a small table. She wore a colourful, East African dress, which Dylan thought was beautiful.

'Please be seated,' she said, when they approached.

Dylan opted to get on her good side straight from the off. He couldn't afford to offend her or the spirits, *if* she could communicate with them. He needed answers, and flattery, *apparently,* gets you anywhere.

'Your dress is gorgeous, Madame. Is it African?' asked Dylan, much to her surprise.

'Thank you. Yes, it is a Kanga.'

'Tribal?'

'It is our traditional dress, but each has a unique message or *Jina* written in Swahili on the *Mji*, the central part of the dress. My dress says, *Sisi sote abiria dereva ni Mungu*, which means we are all passengers, God is the driver,' explained Zina.

Both Mark and Dylan struggled to understand her broad African accent, but they got the gist of what she was saying.

'Lovely message,' Dylan said, nervously. He was starting to get anxious and wished Mark hadn't offered to come in with him.

'Let us get the formalities out of the way and then we can proceed with the reading,' she said.

There was an awkward silence for several seconds before Mark nudged Dylan's arm and whispered, 'You have to cross her palm with silver.'

Dylan's eyes went so wide Mark was sure they were going to pop out into his hands.

'You said it was free,' whispered Dylan, through gritted teeth.

'Ah, yeah, about that. She still needs a coin, though.'

Embarrassed, Dylan rummaged around in his pocket, placed a fifty pence piece onto the table, and mumbled, 'Sorry.'

Zina's assistant appeared out of nowhere and whisked it away faster than lightning.

She must have smelt that money, thought Dylan, when Zina asked for his hands.

'Umm, actually, I haven't come for that. I need your help.'

Zina looked from boy to boy and Dylan could almost feel her eyes scratching at the back of his skull. Finally, she relaxed back into her chair and crossed her arms. 'Explain,' she said, curtly.

Dylan cleared his throat and sat up. He had practised this conversation over and over in his head, but now, with Madame

Zina waiting in anticipation, he couldn't think how to broach the subject.

'My friend's body has been taken over by an evil spirit. I need to get rid of it.'

'This is a joke, yes?'

'No!' pleaded Dylan. He jabbed Mark in the arm. 'Tell her.'

'He's telling the truth,' agreed Mark.

'If you are lying, I *will* tell your mother, Mark.'

'It's true. I promise. Dylan can talk to the dead.'

Dylan held his head in his hands like the Edvard Munch painting.

'Is that so? Well, maybe your friend is sat on the wrong side of the table, huh? Maybe *I* should be paying him.' Her level of sarcasm was off the scale and Dylan didn't know where to look. He expected to be evicted any second, but she simply uncrossed her arms and pointed at him. 'Okay, child. Continue.'

Dylan tripped over his words trying to explain and blurted out everything apart from the missing book. When he mentioned Emily becoming Parthena Love, Zina held up her hand to silence him.

'Did you bring something of hers, like I asked?'

Dylan's jaw sagged and he stuttered, 'I-I-I didn't know, I had t—'

'Here,' Mark cut in, pulling a tie from out of his pocket. 'I stole it from her locker,' he admitted.

Dylan was about to interrogate him when Mark held a finger to his lips.

Zina laid the tie on the table and placed her hands on top. She closed her eyes and began chanting Swahili in a baritone voice. The pitch of her voice fluctuated until it was just shy of a scream, then her eyelids opened for a brief moment to reveal nothing but white.

Dylan shivered and looked away in a mixture of disgust and fear. Her trance seemed endless. He grabbed Mark's sleeve and mouthed the words, 'what's she doing?' but Mark simply scrunched up his face.

After several minutes, Zina fell silent and her body relaxed. She opened her eyes and looked straight at Dylan. 'Emily has nearly traversed the threshold. She doesn't have long.'

Dylan slid to the edge of his seat. 'What can we do?'

'If you truly are capable of communicating with her, you must implore her to follow her life cord back to her body before it's too late.'

'What's a life cord?' asked Mark.

'When a spirit travels between realms there is a cord that tethers your soul to your body.'

'I think I saw it. She had this weird, silver light around her, which fell away from her in a thin line. But I didn't have one.'

'You must have,' Zina corrected. 'All souls have a cord. It only goes when they die.'

He couldn't remember seeing his, but Emily's was definitely there. It surrounded her whole being as though every molecule in her skin was sparkling.

'Okay, but how does Emily get Parthena out of her body,' asked Mark, jumping in.

'Kindoki has taken over her body. It will not be easy to remove it.'

'What's Kindoki?' asked Dylan.

'Evil possession. In the Congo many children are abandoned or beaten in brutal rituals if their family believe they are possessed by Kindoki.'

'How do we get rid of her?'

Zina rose to her feet and began pacing up and down swishing her Kanga back and forth as she deliberated. 'You need to bring her to me,' she said, finally. 'I will try to remove Kindoki and bring her back to you, but I make no promises. Time is fading. Go. Bring her to me,' she demanded.

As they got up to leave, Dylan thanked her and held out his hand. The instant their hands touched her smile vanished and she grimaced in pain. She snatched her hand away and reeled backwards into the tent.

'AKUJI!' she screamed.

Mark grabbed Dylan and shook him. 'What did you do?' he snapped.

'Nothing,' pleaded Dylan.

'Sorry, Madame Zina. What did he do?'

Her broad accent was almost incoherent when she became more and more distressed, repeating words and mumbling sentences over and over. She shook violently, eyes rolling back into her head once more, as though she was having a seizure. Her un-seeing eyes glared at them, sheer terror etched across her face.

'Akuji! Dead and Awake! Dead and awake! Not of this realm ... You are more powerful than ... I-I could offend them. Evil is here. You must go! You go, now. Pleeeeeease!' she wailed.

Her assistant dashed in, grabbed them by their scruffs, their feet hardly touching the ground, and threw them out.

A small crowd had gathered outside the tent and the two boys quickly dispersed through it. Mark dashed back inside the hall looking for Steven, while Dylan headed into the graveyard and sat behind a tall gravestone away from prying eyes.

Something moved in his peripheral vision causing him to turn that way.

Yr Angau was standing by a drain near the outer wall. He lifted his withered arm and pointed into the drain.

Hesitant, Dylan slowly wandered over but stopped a few metres short, scrutinising his features. He was emaciated. His tissue paper skin barely covering his skeletal structure, but it wasn't horrific.

It was sad.

Dylan's eyes followed his bony finger, unsure what he was trying to show him. The smell emanating from the drain was vile and he pulled his sleeve down over his hand to cover his mouth and nose. He edged forward until he could see into the drain.

A large, bloated body was blocking the pipe.

Dylan stumbled backwards. 'Who did this?'

Yr Angau didn't reply. He simply pointed in the direction of the chapel, but Dylan couldn't tell who he was pointing at; there were people everywhere.

'Which one?' Dylan asked, but the shadow man had evaporated.

CHAPTER 37
HIT ME WITH YOUR RHYTHM STICK

The smell was making Dylan ill, and Fiona recognised it before reaching the drain. The smell of death and decay was becoming all too familiar. Howard's smell had stayed with her for weeks; his decaying essence embedded in her skin and hair. Even food tasted off after that day.

Covering her mouth and nose, she leant forward and shone her torch into the drain. The body was so bloated it was impossible to identify the victim, but judging by the clothes that dug into the swollen corpse's skin, it was a man. That was about all she could confirm.

She re-joined Dylan and took a deep breath.

'I need to call this in,' she said, unclipping her radio.

'Yr Angau led me here,' mumbled Dylan.

Fiona winced and rubbed her head.

'What's wrong?'

'My scar's hurting,' she said, rubbing her head. 'Something's not right.'

A loud squeaking noise startled them and they spun around in unison.

Mostyn was tugging Dylan's go-kart behind him. The box of Action Man toys were still on the seat.

'What're you pair whispering a—' An involuntary retch forced his hand to his face. 'Ach-a-fi! What's that smell?'

'It's the drains,' replied Fiona, quickly. 'I was just about to get the builders to take a look.'

'What're you doing with them?' asked Dylan, pointing to his go-kart.

'Bought them off Kaelum for two quid,' replied Mostyn, with a cheesy grin. 'I'll make a tidy profit on these. How come you didn't want them?'

'I did! My mam made me sell them,' whined Dylan. 'But why have you got my go-kart?'

'It was all in, mun.'

'What? No!' shrieked Dylan, lunging for the go-kart's rope. 'The go-kart wasn't for sale. My dad made me that. Give it back!'

Mostyn swatted Dylan's hand away and turned on his heels. 'Tough! It's mine, now.'

Dylan made to chase him, but Fiona yanked him back.

Crashing sounds and screams were emanating from inside the chapel and buyers were spilling out of the doors, jostling and tripping over each other to get away from the melee.

Women dropped what they had bought, scooped up their children, and ran.

'What the hell's going on?'

'Dunno, but it doesn't look good,' she answered, before grabbing her radio. She quickly informed Tony about the body of an IC1 male and the sudden disturbance, requesting immediate backup. She re-attached her radio and grabbed Dylan by the shoulders. 'Stay here, and don't move, okay? You're safer here.'

'But my mam's in there,' he replied, shaking free. 'I need to get her.'

She withdrew her truncheon. 'Fine. But stay behind me.'

When they reached the chapel's wooden doors, a woman came hurtling out, shouting in a shrill voice that someone had gone doolally. Blood was streaming down her face from a large gash above her hairline, and she looked terrified. Fiona shoved Dylan against the wall to the left of the doors and peered inside. There were casualties everywhere.

A voice from the far end of the hall boomed out, 'Kordialis! I can feel you. Show yourself or innocents will die!'

It was Desperate Dan.

'The builder's gone nuts,' explained Fiona. 'I need to get people away from him until backup arrives. Stay here!'

'What about my mam?'

'Please, Dylan. Stay here.'

Fiona forced her way through the hysterical, fleeing crowd, and ducked just in time to avoid a large wooden table, which sliced through the air and splintered into pieces on the wall. A huge chunk of wood flew off and smashed its way through the beautiful stained glass window, sending shards of glass raining down on people's heads whilst they fled. Desperate Dan lifted another table full of jumble with one hand, as though it were papier-mâché, and hurled it at the fleeing public. Two old women, who had been cowering underneath that table, screamed as the builder towered over their exposed position.

'Where is he?' he yelled, spitting phlegm.

The nearest lady fainted into the other's arms when the builder's snot and saliva flew into her face. Her friend hugged her tightly and closed her eyes moments before her head was crushed.

Dan advanced through the chapel hurling furniture out of his way, as if it was balsa wood.

Fiona crept through the hall encouraging those cowering under tables and hiding behind stacked pews to leave immediately. There was already dead everywhere. She convinced a few of the terrified choir boys and old men into helping the injured to their feet and getting them out whilst the crazed builder continued his pursuit through the hall.

Dan suddenly halted his charge and sniffed the air. He swivelled his head sideways and glared at the people escaping through the doorway. His thick muscular arms flexed under his tight T-shirt and the veins in his neck pulsed and squirmed like slender snipe eels.

'YOU!' he bellowed, pointing toward the escaping injured.

His voice was so deep that Fiona felt it vibrate through her chest like a bass drum.

Dan stomped toward the door, his huge builder's boots thudding into the wooden floor with each step.

'RUN!' screamed Fiona. 'GET OUT!'

She ran for the entrance in a diagonal, hoping to get there before him. Her only option was to shut the doors, trapping those that were left inside, and try to hold him off with her truncheon until help came. As the last few walking wounded hobbled out the door, a figure stood silhouetted in the doorway.

It was Dylan.

'Get back!' she bellowed, but Dylan was frozen with fear. His whole body shook with each thudding footfall.

Fiona reached Dylan a split-second before Dan's massive hand reached for his throat. She yanked Dylan backwards and raised her truncheon above her head. With a high-pitched, war-cry scream, she swung at him with all her might, but before her truncheon made contact, a large table leg connected with Dan's huge jaw with an almighty crack, sending blood and teeth flying one way, and the builder the other.

Kaelum dropped the table leg and dashed over to Dylan.

'Are you all right?' he asked, brushing the hair out of Dylan's eyes and shaking him by the shoulders.

Dylan's shocked eyes took a second or two to focus before he stared at his brother and said, 'You sold my go-kart.'

Kaelum laughed. 'He's fine.'

'Where's mam?'

'She's okay. I hid her in a side room with some others when that knob started chucking shit about.'

Fiona grabbed Kaelum's arm. 'Thank you. That was very brave. Can you help me get his arms behind his back, so I can handcuff him before he wakes?'

'Yeah, sure,' agreed Kaelum, before following Fiona.

Dylan was gobsmacked; not because the builder nearly attacked him, but because Kaelum was being so nice. It was so out of character for him that Dylan wondered if he had taken a bang to the head, too.

'I think that's Crulus,' whispered Dylan, in Fiona's ear when she clicked the last cuff in place.

'*Really*, you don't say?' she said, her sarcasm lost on Dylan.

'Yeah, he was calling out for Kordialis from my dead book.'

'What book?' asked Fiona, a little too loudly.

'Erm, it's hard to explain,' Dylan said, gesturing to Kaelum.

'We'll talk later,' she replied, with a nod. 'Go find your mam. Your brother can help me watch this one until the cavalry arrive.'

Several police cars and ambulances screeched to a halt on the drive.

'Talk of the devil,' she said.

Simon and Jukesy came hurtling around the corner, truncheons in hand, and discovered a petite WPC Brasking with one foot on the builder and her hands on her hips, as though she had just shot a grisly bear.

'You took your time,' she said, smirking.

'Blimey, Doris, how'd you manage to nick him?' puffed Jukesy.

'My little helper knocked him out,' she explained, smiling at Kaelum. 'I think he deserves a medal. Best you boys get this beast behind bars before he wakes up. He's not a friendly giant.'

'Who is he?' asked Jukesy.

'Desperate Dan,' said Fiona, smiling.

'Desperate Dan?' asked Simon, incredulously.

'Yeah, look at that jaw.'

'Oh, yeah. How'd you flippin' knock that out?' asked Juksey, nudging Kaelum in the arm.

Kaelum rubbed the knuckles on his right fist and shrugged, which earned him a cheeky smile and wink from Fiona.

'He's a builder. Possibly the foreman,' Fiona explained. 'They've been onsite for weeks working on the drains. I've spoken to him, before.'

Simon Davies leant forward to lift him and struggled to even lift his torso off the floor. 'Shitting hell, he's a right lump,' he said, wheezing. 'C'mon Jukesy, grab his legs, mun.'

The pair groaned and stumbled their way through the doorway with Dan swaying inches off the ground, and almost knocked over Tony who had materialised in the entrance.

'You okay, Fi'?' he asked.

'Yes, all good, Sarge. Thanks to this young man,' she replied, rubbing Kaelum's shoulder.

Tony nodded in acknowledgement, before pointing a thumb over his shoulder. 'Is that the body?'

'No.' Fiona pulled him away from Kaelum, and whispered, 'The body's in the drain over there. It's bloated and rancid. I'd say he's been dead weeks 'cause the decomposition is *way* worse than Howard's was.'

'What time did you discover the body?'

'Umm, not sure. About twenty minutes ago,' she said, looking at her watch. 'So, around ten fifteen, give or take a few. There's multiple dead and injured inside.'

'Major incident, then. Forensics and MIT will be all over this, so expect a grilling from Grumpy soon, unless you're injured?'

'No, I'm fine, Sarge. Just a bit shaken up.'

'Shame, it would've given you an excuse to disappear. You know how Grumpy hates uniform.'

'Is that why you've escaped your desk?'

Tony guffawed. 'Sort of. He knows you've been sniffing around his murder case. Don't look so shocked; I'm not stupid, either.'

'But, Sarge, I was just—'

'Save it. Watch your back, Fi'. I don't want you suspended, or worse. Stick to your FLO duties. Now, go and get plenty of witness statements to corroborate your story. I'll get Jukesy to speak to the boy there and—'

'Actually, Sarge,' Fiona cut in. 'He's Dylan Wolfendale's brother, so I'd like to take their statements, you know, as their FLO.'

Tony sighed. 'Fine. I'll get Nansi to identify those that *actually* saw something and get the rest to disperse.' He smiled and nudged her shoulder. 'About time she did something.'

Fiona laughed. 'Too bloody right.'

'What set this guy off, then?'

Fiona hesitated. She really needed to get her story straight in her head before Grundle interrogated her. Painful stomach pangs had already started, and if Grundle didn't believe her story he might want to interview the boys himself. She doubted Dylan would keep it together this time.

'Not sure. Drink or drugs, perhaps?' she finally answered. 'His veins and muscles were pulsing, so more likely the latter.'

'Okay, I'll tell Bodie and Doyle to get him into a cell before he wakes.'

'I already have.'

'Tidy. We'll see what mood he's in when he comes to. Then we'll see if it's safe to get him checked by the doc. Good work, Fi'.'

'Thanks Sarge.'

The external entrance to the vestry creaked open and Fred stepped out onto the grass, closely followed by several people who had hidden during the disturbance. Fred appeared unfazed and Fiona wondered whether he'd totally missed the incident unfolding.

Distressed, Chrissy ran over to Kaelum and flung her arms around him, kissing his forehead and stroking his hair. She didn't even acknowledge Dylan's presence or ask how he was.

'You're amazing, Kaelum. What would we have done without you?' she cooed, smothering him with more kisses. 'I love you, so much.'

Having gained the power of invisibility, Dylan sighed, and walked down the driveway, alone.

CHAPTER 38
SAVE ME

Although both Dylan and Fiona could see Yr Angau, he only seemed to communicate with Dylan, and Fiona suspected Dylan knew more than he was letting on.

Despite the law's requirement for an adult to be present during interviews, Fiona convinced the Wolfendales to let her interview both boys privately in their respective bedrooms, so they wouldn't feel awkward speaking in front of their parents and, therefore, withhold vital information. Luckily for Fiona, Gwynfor wasn't feeling well, so they agreed to her plan without question.

She deliberately left Dylan's statement until last and, as she suspected, Kaelum left the house immediately after their chat, presumably to boast to his friends about his gallantry.

She quickly wrote a statement for Dylan to sign with no mention of their shadow friend.

'I'll get your parents to sign them, later, seeing as you're both minors,' she said, slipping the statements into a folder.

'Miners?' repeated Dylan.

'Minors, as in children, not the black faced guys down the pit,' she said, laughing.

'Oh.'

'What made you think the builder was Crulus?'

'Because he was shouting for Kordialis. Howard did, too.'

'Okay. Who's Kordialis?'

'The man in my book.'

Fiona put her head in her hands and sighed. 'Listen, Dylan, you're gonna have to explain things because nothing makes sense. I can't help you if you keep things from me.'

Dylan sat back on his bed, crossed his legs, and tucked his feet underneath.

To put him at ease, Fiona shuffled her bum backwards until her back rested against the wall beside Dylan's Iron Maiden poster. While Dylan tried to explain, she sat in relative silence, apart from the odd, *yes*, *okay*, or *hu-huh*.

He told her everything: the sightings, Gareth and the book, the Bogies, Coblynau, Cythraul, Transmogoria and his out-of-body trips, Madame Zina and most importantly, for Dylan at least, about Emily's fading life cord.

When he finished, a wry smile curled Fiona's lip and he was just about to ask what was so funny when she said, 'Did you say Bogies?'

Dylan guffawed, relieved that she found the name funny, rather than what he'd explained. 'Yeah. Apparently, they tempt you to do bad things. I saw one stuck to Kevin's back, so maybe that's why they're called Bogies. You know, 'cause they're sticky.'

Fiona laughed. 'Yeah, I get it. So, Kordialis is trapped in your book?'

Dylan pursed his lips and shrugged. 'I think so.'

'Well, that's the answer, then,' she said, slapping a hand on her thigh. 'If Crulus wants him, we'll just give him the book. I'll get it to him before he's released on bail. Job done.'

'You can't.'

'Why not?'

'The book's gone.'

'Gone where?'

'My mam found it, and threw it out. We searched the local tip, but couldn't find it.'

'We? Who else knows?' Fiona asked, sliding forward, head swivelling at Dylan.

Her hazel eyes bored into his skull and he shifted nervously, eyes dropping to the horrid seventies carpet. His stomach twisted like it always did when adults quizzed him, and his words tumbled out way too fast, 'Erm, not many. Only Mark and Slinky, honest ... Oh, and Emily. I would've told Benny, too, but Crulus killed him.'

'Crulus killed Benny Lewis?'

'Yeah,' mumbled Dylan, sadly.

Fiona held her head, once more, and closed her eyes. As Benny's death was deemed accidental, MIT weren't involved, and his family had already cremated him in a private ceremony, so there was no way to confirm if he had the scar. She snapped out of her trance saying, 'No more surprises. Is there anything or anyone else?'

'Oh, I told Mossy, too. He was the one who had my go-kart earlier. He doesn't believe me, though.'

Her fingers grazed her forehead as she breathed out hard. 'Well, I *really* don't think you should tell anyone else, okay? We have to be careful. I could lose my job and, well, we'd just come across as lunatics. Look what happened when you spoke up about Emily; they nearly sectioned you.'

'I had to tell someone,' croaked Dylan, his voice breaking. 'I needed help.'

'Aaw, don't cry. Come and have a cwtch,' she said, pulling him close and wrapping her arms tightly around him. 'We'll get Emily back, I'm sure of it. Is there another copy? Actually, forget that, stupid question. If there's a demon locked in that book then it's obviously unique, sorry.'

'That's okay,' replied Dylan, sniffing back tears.

Fiona glanced at her watch. 'I'd better go. Your parents will be wondering why it's taking so long.'

'All right.'

'I need a chin wag with Desperate Dan, a.k.a. Crulus, and see if he'll tell me what he wants with Kordialis.'

'Please be careful.'

She ruffled his hair. 'I'll be fine. I assume Crulus doesn't know Kordialis is trapped in that book, otherwise he wouldn't be roaming the streets looking for him. Best if I don't tell him, though, just in case.'

~

The boys met at their usual spot on the wall outside Garrett's newsagents. Dylan was becoming a dab hand at sneaking out of the house unseen and, when he rounded the corner, Steven and Mark were already waiting for him.

'I'm starting to like this bike,' said Dylan, grabbing hold of the handlebar of Steven's Chopper. 'It's better than my Strika.'

'That's 'cause it's not a baby's bike,' joked Steven.

'It's not my fault, Slinky. I can't have Kaelum's Grifter until he gets a new bike, although I'd prefer a BMX,' grumbled Dylan. He glanced around. 'Mossy not coming?'

'Doesn't look like it. So, what's the plan, then?' asked Mark. 'You sounded manic on the walkie, earlier.'

Dylan reminded him about the silver life cord that Madame Zina had mentioned. If there was a chance Emily could follow hers back to her body, then they must try. What he wasn't sure of was what, if anything, would happen to Party. Would she be forced into Transmogoria, or just disappear altogether? The book probably would have answered that for him, but without it they would just have to suck it and see. This was the only option to get Emily back; it *had* to work. Parthena and Dean had been seen out most evenings and Dylan hoped tonight wouldn't be an exception.

'So, when we find them, we just distract them while you get Emily to jump back into her body?' asked Steven.

'Yeah, sort of,' replied Dylan.

Steven's lips curled into a sneer. 'If it's that easy, you could've saved Sian.'

Dylan was aghast. 'Wha'? No ... I-I couldn't. Her body was dead.'

Steven simply shrugged, pulled a Sherbet Dip from his pocket, and began sucking the fizzy, sweet powder off the liquorice.

'What about Scrapper?' asked Mark, changing the subject.

'That's where you come in.'

'Me?' asked Mark, thumbing his chest.

'Yes. Did you bring your torches?'

'Yeah,' replied Mark, holding up his Ever Ready torch. 'I can't hit him with this. It's tiny.'

Dylan laughed, but it faded fast; this wasn't the time for frivolity. 'I don't want you to hit him. I want you to put on your best manly voice and make him think you're a copper or something.'

'Won't he see me?'

'Not at first. It'll be dark by then and you'll be shining your torches in his face. He won't know who it is. You're good with voices, so you'll definitely fool that moron.'

'Ah, okay, I get it,' nodded Mark.

Steven had no lights, sirens, or playing cards on his refurbished Tomahawk, so he sat back and watched while the other boys put their bikes into stealth mode, once again.

After a radio check, the boys cycled to the Broadmead housing estate with the cold air whipping its way up Dylan's loose sleeves, and he shivered uncontrollably despite the fast pace.

When they reached Bryngwyn Road they cut through a small path between the houses and out into the lane behind. They hid their bikes behind a row of garages and made their way up the grass bank. There was a small plateau about half way up, amongst the bushes, where a park bench overlooked the estate and the beautiful Sirhowy Valley beyond. The bench was a popular spot for courting couples and it was where Mostyn, heading home from army cadets, had seen Dean several times that week. The remains of a bonfire dominated the middle of the clearing, and Dylan watched with fascination as the wind whipped the ash into tiny dust-devils.

The boys crept behind a green, metal, electricity substation cabinet at the opposite side of the clearing, and waited for Dean and Parthena to arrive.

It was three-thirty, so they had roughly an hour to kill before dark.

Dylan pulled one of his Pocketeers from his pocket but the clicking sound from the ball bearings was too noisy, so he put it away, and sighed.

Mark brought his paperback copy of *The Lion, the Witch and the Wardrobe,* but gave up reading after ten minutes due to the fading light, the constant humming from the electrical switchgear, and Steven's boredom induced fumbling and twitching.

Steven rustled a packet of cheese and onion Fangs open and crunched away. He stopped chewing when he clocked the boy's open mouths. 'Wha'?' I'm hungry.'

Dylan shushed him. Footsteps crunched along the gravel path.

Once they'd passed the boy's hiding place, Dylan peaked around the corner.

It was Dean and Parthena.

Parthena looked amazing in her plaid skirt and peach blouse, but Dean looked like a right Bovver Boy. His hair was shaven to almost nothing and he wore skintight, bleached denim jeans with turnups that sat over the top of his twelve-hole Dr Marten's boots. Under his green Harrington jacket he wore a bright white T-shirt, which was juxtaposed by bright red braces adorned with Swastika and Union Jack badges.

Dusk was descending rapidly, but it was still too light to implement their plan. Despite the constant electrical hum, they could hear Dean and Parthena's faint voices.

'You're so pretty, Party. I still can't believe you're mine,' said Dean.

'Are you gonna honeyfuggle me all night?' asked Parthena in a soft voice.

'I haven't got a clue what you're saying half the time. You talk funny.'

'Really? So do you, ya Welsh carker.'

'See what I mean, mun?'

'Yeah, and what sort of codswallop is *mun*, anyway?' she asked. 'Ain't never bleedin' 'eard of it.'

'Mun, just means man, I suppose.'

'I ain't no geezer. Come 'ere, I'll show you.'

Dylan's curiosity piqued when their voices ceased and he peered out just as Dean was nuzzling her neck. He kissed her hard on the lips, with one hand snaked under her blouse and the other buried between her thighs.

It took all of Dylan's strength not to scream at him to get off her. Instead, he closed his eyes and called out to Emily in his mind. 'Emily, are you there?'

'Yes, I'm here.'

She sounded miserable and Dylan fought back tears. 'I need you to do something.'

'What?'

'There's a silver thread leading away from you. Can you see it?'

'Yes, but it's very faint.'

'Okay. I need you to follow it. It'll take you to the door to your body. It looks like a shimmering light.'

Emily's voice lit up in his mind. *'Really? Is that it? I can come back!'* she replied, excitedly.

'I hope so. Not sure if Party will just leave your body or not, but you *have* to try,' he begged.

'I will.'

'Let me know when you reach it 'cause we'll need to distract her.'

'Okay.'

When it was dark enough to implement their plan, Emily had already reached her door, so Dylan suggested she try putting her arm through to see what happened. At first she felt a hidden force pulling her whole essence toward the door but, when she edged her hand into the flickering light, she felt resistance. Dylan told her to hold off until they were ready and, when he gave her the signal, she was to push with all her might.

The crouched boys all groaned when they tried to stand.

'I've got pins and needles,' whined Steven, rubbing his legs.

'So have I. Keep your voice down,' whispered Mark.

'Yeah, but your legs aren't as long as mine.'

The boys crept quietly along the path, trying to keep a metre or two between them, but it was hard to see where they were going.

When Dylan emerged from the bushes, he ducked down and waited for the others to catch up, but Steven wasn't paying attention. He stumbled into Mark, who fell with a thud.

'Who's there?' bellowed Dean.

'Now!' shouted Dylan.

All three boys shone their torch beams into Dean's face, blinding him.

'Police. Stand still!' bellowed Mark, in the deepest manly voice he could muster.

Dylan diverted his torch beam into Parthena's eyes and, in his mind, he shouted, 'Now, Emily!'

Emily lunged at her door and shoved as hard as she could causing Parthena to yelp and clasp her hands to her head.

'Keep pushing,' said Dylan. 'It's working.'

Emily was desperate. *'I can't get through.'*

'Don't stop. Something's happening.'

Parthena fell onto her back and screamed, 'My head!'

Dean tried to lift her, but she kicked him away. He pointed in the direction of the torch lights. 'Hey, Copper, help her!' he begged.

Parthena's head violently rocked from side to side, and she thumped her fists against it. 'This is MY body, now!' she screamed. 'I ain't moribund, yet. GET. OUT. YOU. BITCH!'

'Shit! Party knows you're trying to get in. Hurry, Emily!'

'I'm trying. She's too strong. I can't do it, Dylan. Help me!'

'I don't know what else to do,' he whined.

Steven's torch went off, so he tilted it, and stared dumbfounded at the bulb. After several slaps, the torch flickered back into life, and lit up his face for all to see.

'Slinky!' yelled Dean, bounding towards them, fists clenched. 'You're dead.'

CHAPTER 39

KILLERS

The boys split up and ran full pelt through hedges and bushes, over fences, and through back gardens to evade capture. Dylan fell constantly but kept going, oblivious to his cuts and abrasions, and the garden pond he plunged into. Eventually, he doubled back and reached the garages a split-second before Mark, but Steven was nowhere to be seen.

Twenty minutes later, Dean and Parthena noisily stomped past the garages. Believing Steven had gotten away, Mark cocked a leg over his crossbar and cycled off, despite Dylan's protests.

Dylan wheeled Steven's Tomahawk down the side of the garage and, holding onto both handlebars, he mounted the Chopper and slumped his shoulder against the cold, garage wall, and waited. Devastated that the plan to get Emily back had failed miserably, he felt powerless with no idea how to save her. The book was the key; he hated his mother for throwing it out. Gareth said it could only fulfil its purpose once, and now it was lost forever.

So was Emily.

With silent wings, Newt flew onto his shoulder and nustled into his neck. It tickled, but Dylan was oblivious, his mind in turmoil.

Dylan called Steven on his walkie, but there was only static. Deflated, Dylan wheeled both of Steven's bikes down the road to Mark's house. There was no sign of him, so he wheeled both bikes into Mark's shed, and sauntered off down the path.

Despite Newt's comforting presence, Dylan cried all the way home, and whilst he slept.

He was still sobbing after the voice woke him.

Dylan dressed in a blur, slid out onto the cold ledge, and dropped down into the barren flower bed. Less than ten minutes later, he was creeping past the garages once more, searching the moonlit ground, his torch forgotten on the bedside table. His heart felt like a balloon being squeezed in a child's hands; the taut, bulging edges being forced between his ribs.

A small cracking sound stopped him dead, and he checked the middle-ground, his eyes rolling over the one thing he didn't want to see, but knew was there. Rodents were chewing and gnawing on something—tiny mouths, sloppy chewing, bones crunching.

Steven was on his back with a huge, furry, moving scarf around his neck.

Dylan blinked, trying to re-focus his eyes and stumbled. Gravel crunched under his feet, scattering the scarf. He shuffled his trembling legs forward, fighting the urge to flee.

Newt hopped onto a mound of grass and cawed knowingly.

Dylan refused to acknowledge Newt's presence and his reason for being there. He wiped his eyes, clearing his vision, then wished he hadn't. Steven's terrified gaze stared up at him through dark, soulless eyes from within his almost decapitated head; the vertebrae in his neck scored with deep, round, saw cuts.

Impossibly, Steven's chest rose.

Dylan yelled his name and dived forward.

He knelt next to his fallen friend, but no blood flowed from his wound. His chest fell, but not through exhaling; a rat, slick with blood and goo, like a newborn pup, slid out of the gaping hole in Steven's neck. Blood oozed from the wound, slow and sticky, reminding Dylan of his mother's hot jam tart.

An involuntary retch filled Dylan's mouth with bile and he vomited. He retched until his stomach was empty and the continued spasms simply caused pain. Stringy bile dripped from the corner of his mouth as he ran trembling hands over Steven's body—squeezing his hand, brushing the damp hair away from his eyes, placing a hand either side of his cheeks and gently pushing his head back into place.

Dylan had known even before he'd left his house that Steven was dead, as his loud, statically-charged, voice had been in his head, begging him to steal a body.

Monday 16th November, 1981
Draigwen Town Comprehensive School

Mostyn and Mark hid behind the bike sheds when the yard monitor and the last remaining teacher headed into the side door to the assembly hall. It was eight-forty and Mark was worried; Dylan was never this late. He felt a tinge of guilt for ditching him last night, which flared into a full-on panic when he saw Dylan bimbling, head down, through the gate, his feet dragging behind him as though he wore lead shoes. Electric shock hairstyle, droopy eyelids, and patches under his eyes that were punch dark made him look ghastly.

Had Dean caught him?

Mark tried to lighten the mood by saying that Dylan looked how his mother did every morning; it didn't help.

Dylan began to cry, and he shook so violently that Mostyn thought he was fitting. He slumped forward and the boys didn't know if he was going to collapse, puke, or both.

Mark grabbed him before he could fall and sat him down. 'What's the matter? You're scaring us.'

Dylan was hyperventilating, his voice garbled, and he grabbed Mostyn's trouser leg.

'Shall I get the nurse?' asked Mostyn, trying to be helpful.

'He ... He's ... Oh, God, I-I can't—' cried Dylan, his voice high. His head flopped into his hands.

'Deep breaths. No rush,' said Mark, calmly. He glanced at Mostyn who looked just as clueless as he was.

Every time Dylan settled his breathing and started to speak, he cried again, and it took until the bell rang at eight-fifty-five before he finally blurted out, 'Slinky's dead!'

Both boys sat down, slack jawed. It was ages before either of them spoke.

'When? How?' Mostyn asked, breaking the silence.

'Nah, that's not possible,' said Mark, dismissive. 'Not Slinky.'

'I ... S-Saw him,' sobbed Dylan.

'*Really?* How'd he die then?' asked Mostyn, crossing his arms over his chest.

'His head ... Saw marks—' An image flashed into Dylan's mind and he glared at Mostyn. 'Where were you last night?'

'Busy,' replied Mostyn, abruptly. 'Who did this?'

'Scrapper!' yelled Mark, into his face. 'He chased us last night. Slinky never got back to the bikes. That bastard must've caught him.'

'You told the cops?' asked Mostyn.

Dylan shook his already trembling head.

'Good.'

'Why's that good?' asked Mark.

'They'll chuck him in a padded cell, this time,' advised Mostyn.

Mark nodded, then added, 'But we should tell someone.'

'Mostyn's right,' agreed Dylan, his voice steadier. 'How would I explain knowing Slinky's dead? I'll either be a nutter or a murderer.'

'We need to do *something,* though,' said Mark, lifting Dylan up. 'Slinky's our friend.'

'I'll tell Fiona, she'll understand,' assured Dylan, before adding, 'although she wasn't at the station when I rang earlier.'

'Yeah, act like nothing's happened,' proposed Mark, before quickly wiping his face on his sleeve. 'We say nothing until Dylan's spoken to Fiona.'

'Act normal? Slinky's dead, mun!' snapped Mostyn, tugging on his long, greasy hair.

Mark glared at him. 'Get a grip, or we'll be in the shit.'

'We? I wasn't even there,' reminded Mostyn, before wandering off.

CHAPTER 40
DON'T STAND SO CLOSE TO ME

Draigwen Police Station

Fiona bribed the duty custody sergeant, Bill Parkes, with coffee, biscuits, and a smile to get five minutes alone with Desperate Dan, who had now been identified as twenty eight year old, Craig Bishop, a foreman for local building firm, DT Construction.

It was six-forty A.M. when Fiona slid open the catch on the front of cell number six, lowered the flap, and peered inside.

Craig was prone on the blue, plastic mattress.

No amount of shouting or banging made him move. She was debating opening the door, when his head slowly swivelled sideways. He stared at her with a wretched smile creasing his face and pain coursed through the side of Fiona's head, making her nauseous.

Her scar had never felt so painful.

'Are you Crulus?' she asked, regaining her composure.

There was no reaction or reply, but the pain in her head seemed to answer her question.

'Killing old biddies, huh? Wow, you must feel *so* powerful. Pathetic! Well, your killing spree is over, now.'

Craig was inanimate. She wasn't sure if he had even blinked. It was unnerving.

His contorted face appeared in the hatch so swiftly that she screamed. He grabbed her wrist before she could flee and his heinous smile melted away in an instant.

'What are you?' he asked, tossing her arm away.

Fiona's scar writhed and seared through her skull like a hot worm and she fell, slamming her head against the opposite wall.

Blood oozed and the room spun.

'I'm a woman,' she said, sarcastically.

Craig lifted his huge hand and wagged a finger at her. 'No, you're something more.'

'Well, you're never gonna find out. If I'm right, that's Victor Gaunt's body you've left in the drain, so that makes at least ten people you've murdered, if we include poor Benny and the body at Cardiff bus station. You won't smell freedom for a *very* long time.'

He doubled over with laughter and, for a second, she lost sight of him. Then his face filled the hatch and his voice echoed down the corridor, 'Pathetic soul. You have no idea what you're dealing with.'

Bill Parkes hurtled through the custody suite door, rushing to her side. 'What happened? Did he hit you? Oh, God, you're bleeding.'

'I'm okay, Sarge.'

'Can you stand?' he asked, helping her up.

'Yeah, I'm fine. I slipped, that's all,' she lied.

'Clumsy sod. You pair finished chin wagging?'

Fiona gently shook her head. 'No, just a few more minutes.'

'Fine. I'll get the first-aid kit,' he offered, before disappearing into the custody office.

Still woozy, Fiona leant against the wall as Craig's face edged through the hatch. The more he stared, the more her scar burned. She failed to notice the blood trickling down her spine.

'What do you want from us?' she asked.

Craig slid his lips away from his teeth and stringy saliva hung between them. The skin on his face morphed and, for a split second, Fiona saw spiky tendrils protruding from his cheeks and forehead. Fiona blinked and shook her head. Craig's face reappeared.

'Kordialisssssss,' he hissed, through gritted teeth.

'So, if you find him, you'll leave us in peace?'

'Yesssss.'

'Good, then I'll—'

'You'll do nothing,' he interrupted. '*I* will find him.'

Fiona pointed a finger at him. 'So you know where he is, then?'

'He is near.'

Fiona stepped a little closer. 'Maybe, but you don't know *where*, otherwise you would have found him.'

'Quibbling over semantics won't change the outcome.'

'And what would that be?'

'Kordialis will die.'

Bill strolled down the corridor waving a small, green box in his hand. The white cross on its side almost faded into non-existence. 'Sorry, Fi', the kit's nearly empty,' he advised. 'Someone's used it and not updated the accident book.' When he saw the back of Fiona's head he started to panic. 'Jesus! You're gonna need stitches, not plasters. We need to get you down—'

Fiona paused him with a single digit. She leant as close as

she dared to the hatch and felt Craig's warm breath on her face. Strangely, it smelt of rot.

'Who is Kordialis?'

Craig simply smiled and moved back into the cell.

'Tell me!' she demanded.

Bill took the silence as an opportune moment to end their chat. He slammed the hatch shut and locked it in place. 'Enough! C'mon, you're bleeding bad,' he said, leading her by the arm out of the cell block.

Just before nine A.M., DI Grundle officially opened the murder investigation for the chapel drain body and discussed the pathologist's report. Preliminary investigations confirmed Fiona's theory; the body belonged to local crackpot, Victor Gaunt, who was wanted for questioning over Howard Cobley's death. Once again, the pathologist's estimated time of death—between three and four weeks ago—was way off the mark considering when he was last seen.

Forensics were now under scrutiny.

Grundle attributed the extended decay of the cadaver to the moisture and water in the drain even though the pathologist stated that there was not enough water in the drain to speed up the decomposition and, if anything, the presence of the running water through the drain was more likely to preserve a body for longer rather than speed up its decomposition, as surface necrophagous insects would wash away. Understandably, Grundle refused to believe that Victor Gaunt was a dead man walking and he vowed that if any officers spoke of zombies they would be dismissed from the force.

Due to the decomposition and the lack of physical evidence, there was nothing to suggest that the detainee, Craig

Bishop, had anything to do with the death of Victor Gaunt. However, he refused to discount it completely because DT Construction had been working on the drainage system since the twenty-first of September. When Grundle announced that he would be seeking a court order to continue holding Mr Bishop without charge, Fiona sighed with relief.

'Oh, Doris!' shouted Grundle, waving a folder in the air. 'I've got your statements, but I'm not sure who this, erm—' He flicked through the file before jabbing a finger on a page and reading part of her statement aloud, "... *the aggressor shouted for Kordialis*." Who's he? Was he at the scene, 'cause I can't see any statement from him?' His face disappeared behind a cloud of pipe smoke and several officers at the front of the room began coughing. He merely glared at them, tossed a packet of Ready Rub on the table, and waited for Fiona's reply.

She stood and steadied herself with a hand on the table in front of her. Her head was pounding, but she didn't want to show weakness in front of Grundle. She cleared her throat and replied, 'No, he wasn't there, Sir.'

'Okay. So, that's another person of interest to add to the list, Edwards.'

'Yes, Sir,' acknowledged Kerry, who was sat at the front.

'Did *anyone* see this Kordialis fella at the chapel?'

'No,' replied Fiona.

'If he wasn't there, why the bloody hell was that wrongun in the cell smashing the place up? Also, why hide the guy you've just killed in a bloody drain if you're gonna start a ruckus and kill innocent bystanders in full view? It doesn't make sense.'

The officers looked at each other, but no one was willing to offer an explanation.

'Motive?'

'None, Sir,' replied Kerry, shifting in her seat. 'There were no physical injuries to the body, either,' she added.

'Does Bishop know Victor's family or acquaintances? It was public knowledge that we had a warrant out for Victor's arrest, so did someone seek revenge for Arwel's death, perhaps?'

'Reverend Foster said he didn't witness any altercations between the builders and members of the public. To his knowledge, the only people to enter the property whilst the work was going on was Fi' and a few parishioners visiting family graves, which he's vouched for,' advised Kerry.

'Good. It's possible Bishop was paid to kill him or, more than likely, they fought and Victor came off worse,' suggested Grundle.

Fiona watched him pace back and forth, puffing on his new pipe, and debating his next angle. He was looking older by the day: clusters of small, dark veins on each cheek, and crows feet that were getting so deep they looked drawn on with a HB pencil. Although unfit, overweight, and a heavy smoker, Grundle was energetic when it came to his work. Like most officers, Fiona hated him, but she respected his policing knowledge and experience, even if his methods were undesirable. Yet, it didn't matter how good he was, the evidence against Craig Bishop was thinner than the oxygen in this smoke filled room, and she had to ensure Crulus wasn't released, whatever it took.

'He was *extremely* aggressive when I first met him,' lied Fiona. 'He killed Victor.'

'What makes you so sure?' asked Kerry.

'Well, he, umm ... He was very annoyed that the caretaker, Arwel, had buggered off. He had to waste a resource guarding the gate, you know, er, for safety and that. He said it was delaying the works and costing him money that he couldn't afford to lose. He was violent, too; throwing tools around, like a right nutter.' She knew it was a pathetic reason, but it was all she could think of.

'Interesting,' said Grundle, stroking his beard. 'Perhaps he's unstable. Thanks, Doris, sit down before you fall down. Kerry and I will be interviewing Bishop, so let's see if we can crack his shell a bit. Kerry, over to you.'

'Thanks, Sir. We've got officers coming in from C and E divisions to assist with door-to-door. Uniform will need to re-visit the chapel witnesses to establish if they know, or saw, more than they've let on. Nansi, I want you on FLO duties for this one, so you can inform Mr Bishop's family that he's our guest. Don't mention the murder, though. Just see what they know.'

Grundle glanced at his watch. 'Right it's ten-twenty. Kerry, let Sergeant Parkes know we'll be interviewing our guest at eleven in interview room one.

PC Jukes lifted the metal cloche off the prisoner's food and stuffed a sausage in his mouth like a greasy cigar. He thought about spitting on the plate but changed his mind when Bill Parkes peered over his newspaper.

Jukesy pulled the sausage out of his mouth and grinned. 'He won't miss it.'

When Bill returned his attention to his newspaper, Jukesy replaced the cloche, and stuffed the sausage back into his mouth. He opened the key safe, grabbed the cell key, added a timed entry to the custody log book, initialled it, and unlocked the custody suite door.

His boots squeaked on the polished corridor floor and he glanced down at his sorry looking toecaps and shrugged. He was already on his second warning for poor presentation this month, but he couldn't understand why he had to polish them. It wasn't as if it mattered when he was stamping discipline into a local reprobate.

He slid open the catch on the front of cell number six, lowered the flap, and locked it horizontal, so it made a small shelf. He placed the food tray on the flap and peered inside. Craig Bishop was sat on the edge of his mattress, staring at the floor.

'Oh, butt', scran time,' announced Jukesy.

Craig didn't move or acknowledge his presence.

Jukesy impatiently tapped the tray. 'Oh! I'm not staying here all flipping day.'

Craig rose to his feet, cricked his neck, and walked slowly forward.

'Good. You'll need it, they'll be interviewing you, soon.' He slid the tray forward with one hand but before he could retract it, Craig lunged forward and grabbed hold of his wrist.

Craig's body instantly went rigid. His skin turned bluish-grey and fluid-filled blisters appeared on his hands and neck. The skin around his eyes and mouth went slack as the skin began to slip, and then his whole body bloated, as if inflated by some unseen pump. The skin on his neck and stomach bulged and stretched against his waistband, collar, and cuffs. Dark fluid and blood forced its way out of every orifice, while the skin turned a greenish, marbled colour before it ruptured. The decomposed body collapsed onto the floor emitting foul-smelling gases, while fluids puddled underneath.

Jukesy pushed the food tray through the opening, sending it crashing to the cell floor. The temperature in the cell had plummeted. When he slid the bolt and slammed the cell hatch shut, he left hand prints in the metal's frost.

He cricked his neck and left the custody suite, locking the door behind him. He placed the cell key back in the safe and nodded at Bill.

'See you, Jukesy,' murmured Bill, barely raising his head from his newspaper.

CHAPTER 41
NEVER SURRENDER

Draigwen Town Comprehensive School

When the boys gathered on the wall at dinnertime, only Mostyn seemed in the mood for food, as he stabbed his wooden fork into his tray of chips, cheese and gravy.

'How can you eat that?' asked Mark.

'It's lush,' replied Mostyn, smiling.

Mark shook his head. 'No, I meant, how can you eat *anything* after what's happened?'

'Your body's a machine. You have to eat, especially during stressful times. It's fuel. That's why they issue ration packs to soldiers when they go off to fight. They need it, see.'

'I'm not hungry,' said Dylan, absentmindedly, as he watched Dean and Parthena giggling in the food van's queue. His mind was whirling. He couldn't understand what would bring Dean to kill Steven. This was no accident; this was brutal. With Ian and Sian already buried and nobody locked up for their murders, Dean must be enjoying ending lives and getting away with it. Dylan knew he had to find proof of Dean's guilt before he killed again, but first he had to find a way to get Parthena out of Emily's body.

'Be a sweetheart and move along, won't ya?' urged Parthena, shoving a small boy out of her way.

The cockney accent rolling off Emily's tongue sounded so alien that Dylan just stared at her in disgust.

Mostyn jabbed his wooden fork at Dylan. 'You have to admit they do look good together.'

'Knob! He could've killed Slinky,' suggested Mark, his voice low but firm, but Mostyn wasn't phased.

Dylan dug around in his pockets, but they came out empty. 'Anyone got change?' he asked.

'Yeah, why?' replied Mark, reaching into his trousers.

'I'm gonna ring the police from the phone box down the road. I need to speak to Fiona.'

'Don't waste your money,' said Mostyn, pointing across the yard.

Two police officers were walking briskly through the yard, parting the swarm of kids like Moses and his staff.

'Fiona!' shouted Dylan, jumping off the wall and running at her.

'Hi, Dylan. Is that your friend, Mossy?' she asked, looking at Mostyn.

Dylan nodded then tugged on Fiona's sleeve whispering, 'I need to speak to you, urgently.'

'It'll have to wait,' she said, pushing him aside.

Fiona and Simon stepped closer to the wall and gestured for the boys to get down, which they did.

'Are you Mostyn Lloyd of number nine, Cefn Coed Road on the Cerrig Brig estate?' asked Fiona.

'Er, yeah,' mumbled Mostyn, still chewing.

Fiona stepped forward, grabbed his arm, and slid her handcuffs off her belt.

'Mostyn Lloyd, I am arresting you on suspicion of the murder of Steven Evans. You do not have to say anything, but it may harm your defence if you do not mention, when questioned, something which you later rely on in court. Anything you do say may be given in evidence,' recited Fiona, clicking a handcuff to his right wrist. 'Do you understand?'

Mostyn flung his chips across the floor and tried to pull away. 'Get off me!' He tried to prise his hand out of the cuff but it clicked tighter into place, causing him to cry out.

'Stop resisting and it won't hurt,' advised Fiona.

'NOOOOO!' screamed Mostyn, tears running down his face. 'I didn't kill Slinky!'

Dylan tried to grab Fiona's arm. 'It was Scrapper. Mossy wasn't there!'

'Arms behind your back, please,' demanded Fiona, before shoving Dylan aside and locking the second cuff in place.

'Tell them!' shouted Mostyn, as Simon led him away. 'You know it wasn't me.'

'Dylan's right,' agreed Mark. 'Scrapper chased us. We split up. I ran down to the street and double backed to the garages. Dylan went up the banking, or back the way we came ... Or maybe into Bryngwyn and then up to ... Umm ... We met up at the bikes, see, but we lost Slinky. We waited, but he didn't show. Scrapper *must've* done it. Arrest him, not Mossy!'

Fiona held up her hand to silence Mark's rambling. 'Boys, please. That's enough.'

'But it *was* Scrapper,' whined Dylan.

Fiona raised a finger to her lips and looked over her shoulder. When she saw Simon and Mostyn disappear through the gates, she yelled at the crowd of gawping kids, 'Right you lot, get back to class or you'll be under arrest, too!'

CLAP! CLAP!

'C'mon, I haven't got all day. Move it!'

When the crowd finally dispersed, Fiona lowered her voice and said, 'Were you there when Steven was killed?'

They shook their heads in unison.

Mark raised a hand and said, 'No, but—'

'Have you spoken to him?' Fiona interrupted, looking straight at Dylan.

'Yes,' replied Dylan. 'Scrapper chased him and he was crouched down in some bushes hiding from him when something looped over his head and dug into his neck. Slinky couldn't breathe and then he just—'

Dylan's words became incoherent as he sobbed and Fiona pulled him close.

'It's okay, we'll sort it. Who's Scrapper?'

'Dean Johnson.'

'Oh, him. Well, we'll need to interview both of you *and* Scrapper back at the station. Was there anyone else around last night?'

'Emily, Parthena, Party, or whatever she's calling herself,' said Mark, sarcastically.

'Okay, we'll pull her in, too. I might not be conducting the interviews, so you can't mention knowing Steven was dead before we arrested Mostyn, okay?'

They both nodded.

'Why did you arrest him?' whispered Dylan.

'I can't say.'

'I thought we were friends?'

'We are, but I can't disclose evidence. Just trust us to do our jobs.'

CHAPTER 42

KILLER'S EYES

Draigwen Police Station

Scenes of crime officers swarmed the rear entrance in their large, hooded, white overalls, like an army of Michelin men. The exit road was sealed off with police tape, and there were specialist support vehicles dotted over the adjacent pavements and grassed areas.

Seeing SOCO vehicles gathered at the station was not an unusual sight; they often based themselves at the nearest station to an incident, but Fiona couldn't fathom why they had sealed off the whole road. She swung the panda car up the one-way system and found a parking spot near the vehicle workshop.

She led the four kids into absolute chaos: the enquiry office was rammed with officers and Tony looked like he was about to explode. There were officers from other divisions milling about, along with MIT, forensics, and the standards department, which was never a good sign.

Dumping the kids in reception, Fiona entered the enquiry office; the fag smoke was horrendous. She dumped her hat and coat on her desk and opened a window, but even the fresh air struggled to find a way through the foggy office.

'Why are standards nosing around? What the hell's going on, Sarge?' she asked, when Tony finally stopped to catch breath.

'Chaos, that's what. What took you so long? Grumpy wants me to put you on a warning.'

Her jaw dropped. 'Really? That's not fair. I was rounding them up,' she replied, gesturing to the three nervous boys and one stroppy girl sat in reception.

'Friends of the killer, then?'

'Yeah, sort of. What's with SOCO? They don't normally cordon off the station?'

'They do when there's a decomposed body in the cells,' he replied, eyes wide.

She felt the blood drain from her limbs and sat down. 'Craig?'

'Yeah, how'd you know?'

She stared at the floor, her mind racing as fast her pulse, and she felt sick. Crulus was free to kill and there seemed no way to stop him. Whoever this Kordialis was, he had pissed off one seriously sick, murdering freak. Dylan's book was the key to ending all of this. They had to find it and give it to Crulus before he killed again. But where or, more importantly, *who* was Crulus, now?

'You've gone white. Coffee?' Tony asked, stirring Fiona from her thoughts. 'I'll make it. I could do with a break.'

'Yeah, thanks,' mumbled Fiona.

Tony squeezed his way to the door.

'Oh, Sarge, who was the last person to see Craig alive?'

Tony rolled his eyes. 'Who do you think? Bloody Jukesy. Nobody's seen the twat since. You wait till I get hold of him! Do you take sugar?'

Taking her silence for an answer, Tony walked off.

In the reception, Dean punched Dylan in the leg several times before Mark intervened. Dylan's anger had been held captive for so long that he felt his insides would melt any second. Steven was dead and all Dean could think about was saving his own skin; he was adamant that he had no idea why he had been brought in.

Dylan needed the truth. He knew exactly what he had to do and he no longer cared about the consequences. When Dean swung another punch at his leg, Dylan caught his wrist and held it tight. As the electrical sensation tingled its way up Dylan's arm, Dean's face distorted with pain. His soul fluttered below his skin's surface and Dylan contemplated ending him there and then; his whole soul was laid out for Dylan to examine.

In a split-second, he scanned every thought and deep seeded memory embedded in Dean's tiny little mind, looking for anything to condemn him.

He found nothing but pain.

Daily beatings were the norm. That's how Dean's father had been taught by his father before him, and so it became the family tradition.

"If you can't take it like a man, then you aren't a man, and you certainly aren't a Johnson!"

But Dean didn't want to be a Johnson.

He didn't want to beat his kids and make them feel like dogs tethered to a post and left out in all weather. He no longer wanted to feel pain instead of love, or be afraid to show love because it wasn't manly and not the Johnson way.

Dean just wanted to be normal.

The only thing grounding him at the moment and bringing him the normality he had craved since he was a small boy was Parthena Love.

Dean was infatuated.

Dylan suddenly realised that he was desperately trying to rid the world of the one and *only* thing that was giving Dean the glimmer of hope that, one day, he could actually be normal.

Dylan suddenly felt like *he* was about to be the abuser. If he succeeded in sending Parthena back to Transmogoria, and out of Dean's life for good, Dean would lose his chance to become normal and, instead, would be all consumed with darkness, anger, and hate, much like Anakin Skywalker. He felt sorry for his adversary after what he'd seen, but one thing was for certain, Dean was no killer. He was just a sad, pathetic, cornered animal who lashed out at weaker animals rather than his own abuser.

When Dean yelped like a dog, and clamped his hands to his head, pain etched across his face, Dylan released his grip.

'What's up with you?' asked a stern voice from behind them.

It was Mr Harwood.

'Headache, Sir,' whined Dean, rubbing his temples.

'Why're you here?' asked Mark, nervously. He looked petrified.

'Cretin! I'm your responsible adult. They can't interview you without one,' he explained, smirking.

The enquiry office door swung open and Fiona stumbled forward with both hands full of blank cassette tapes and interview pads. 'Edward Harwood?'

Harwood nodded and held out his hand. 'You must be WPC Brasking.'

Fiona stared at his hand, dumbfounded. 'Yes. Thanks for coming.'

Harwood took a step forward and, for a second, Fiona thought he was going to help. Instead, he pulled a fag from behind his ear, slid a gun-shaped lighter from his pocket, and proceeded to engulf her in smoke. 'That's all right, love. Anything to help the fuzz. There's some sick bastards about,' he said, staring at the boys.

Fiona sighed. 'Indeed.' She looked across at Dean who was rocking back and forth in his seat and rubbing his head like a genie lamp. 'What's he whining about?'

'Oi, don't be a grumble and grunt! He's hurt his loaf,' snarled Parthena, pulling Dean closer. 'Leave him be.'

'Well, Dean can't get out of it that easily. He's up first, and it looks like I will be doing the interviews after all,' advised Fiona.

Dean and Parthena both admitted seeing Steven after they caught the boys spying on their courtship. Dean admitted that it was definitely Steven he chased, but at no point did he catch up with him, and he emphatically denied murdering him. Parthena corroborated his story, which also fitted into what Mark had stated in his interview. Although, there was a sizeable time gap between the chase and the boys seeing Dean and Parthena walking past the garages—sufficient time to commit murder.

Fiona left Dylan's interview until last and managed to convince Harwood that it was a private discussion surrounding Dylan's psychologist's results. When she told Dylan that Crulus was on the loose once more and, worse still, that he was now in a copper's body, Dylan shrieked, so she was glad that the interview room was soundproofed.

Things were going from dreadful to diabolical and this was having a massive effect on Dylan's health. He looked terrible: gaunt, haggard and forlorn. Dylan put it down to lack of sleep, but Fiona sensed there was more to it than that. Most adults would struggle with grieving over one person, but

Dylan had lost two in less than a month. His plan to save Emily had failed and now one of his best friends was being dissected on a cold, steel gurney. She was unsure how much more he could take before he suffered a complete mental breakdown and ended up in a looney bin.

Police resources were stretched to the limit, so there was no way Tony would agree to assign any staff to search for a wrinkly old book regardless of what credible lie she spun. She promised to search for it in her spare time, although her heart was telling her it was lost for good. All Dylan could do now was try and be a normal kid and let the police try and catch Crulus, *again*. But this time it would be a herculean task, after all, who's going believe that PC Jukes is dead and a supernatural demon is walking around in his body? Crulus could have touched anyone and, although Jukesy was a complete twat most of the time, he didn't deserve to die so young.

Crulus' words echoed in her head: *'What are you?'*

Such a strange question. What did he mean by it? She slid her fingers through her hair, tracing the edge of her scar. She thought back to 1970 and their first encounter. What had stopped him from killing her back then? Crulus had grabbed her again, but she still hadn't succumbed to his power. How was she any different from Jukesy?

'... you're something more.'

Fiona shook the thoughts from her mind and stared helplessly at the whimpering, grim-faced Dylan sat across the table.

She had to help him.

Fred was the only person who could assist them, even if he was a bit blasé about everything. Perhaps he knew of some ancient, religious ritual, or exorcism, that might get rid of Crulus permanently. She would even endure his Sunday service, if it would help sway him.

Mr Harwood reluctantly agreed to drive the kids back to school, which Fiona was ecstatic about until Kerry caught her drinking coffee in the canteen. She tossed Fiona a bag of chocolates and said, 'They're for when you interview Mostyn Lloyd.'

'Me?'

'Yeah. Grumpy wants you to charm a confession out of him. C'mon.'

Mostyn had been interrogated for over three hours and his butch, military-wannabe exterior had completely disintegrated; he was now a blubbering mess. To Fiona's surprise, they had found a partial print on the murder weapon, but Grundle preferred a confession to ensure conviction.

Judging by the thick cloud of smoke Kerry and Fiona waded through as they entered the office, and the DI's furrowed, sweaty brow, Grumpy Grundle was, well, grumpy.

It was quite clear, even to a non-pathologist, that the body in cell number six was not that of a person who had been walking and talking less than six hours ago; the decomposition was weeks rather than hours. If Grundle hadn't seen it with his own eyes he would have brushed it off, once again, as incompetence by the pathology team. This was now the fourth body that appeared to decompose extraordinarily fast compared to the alleged time of death and he was rattled.

'Who authorised your visit to Custody? Actually, don't bother answering that, I *know* it wasn't authorised. Why were you there?'

'I, erm ... Just clearing things up, that's all,' mumbled Fiona, who was nervously rubbing her hands down her skirt pleats.

Grundle grabbed his leather Ready Rub pouch and

stuffed a clump of tobacco into the bowl of his pipe, tamping it down with a small metal tool. He slid the stem between his lips and held a lighter flame over the bowl.

Fiona was mesmerised by the flame, which was drawn down into the bowl with each inward breath, as though the flame was being charmed.

'What?' asked Grundle, blowing a lungful of sweet cherry smoke in her face.

To Fiona, it wasn't a beautiful, crisp, aromatic smell that filled her throat, it was a vile, choking taste caused by the devil crapping in her mouth. She couldn't help but cough and splutter before she replied, 'I asked him about Kordialis.'

'And?'

Fiona shrugged. 'He refused to say who, or where, he was.'

'Did he seem unwell?'

'No.'

Grundle took a few more puffs and waved his hand through the smoke, creating swirls that looked like nicotine flavoured ice-cream in the air above his desk. He slumped back in his chair, sighed and said, 'Standards are all over us like a bad case of VD. They're even testing the prisoner's food for poison. I've had to suspend Bill Parkes pending an internal enquiry. It's a total shit storm and you—' He stood and jabbed a finger at Fiona. 'You are lucky you're not dismissed from the force! Now, go and get me a sodding confession!'

~

Fiona's chocolate bribe only succeeded in ridding Mostyn of more stomach lining and, four toilet breaks later, his innocence remained resolute. When they had given up any hope of a confession, Simon entered the room causing Fiona to suspend the interview and stop the recording. He handed Kerry a small plastic bag and whispered something in her ear.

Once he had left the room, Kerry restarted the tape and slid the clear plastic bag toward Mostyn and his court appointed public defender.

'Do you recognise this necklace? For the benefit of the tape, I'm showing the defendant a ladies nine-carat gold necklace with a small locket attached,' said Kerry.

Mostyn leant forward and studied the necklace before shaking his head. 'No. Never seen it.'

'Are you sure? Look closely.'

He picked the bag up and studied it before simply saying, 'Nope.'

'Mostyn, this necklace is engraved with the words, "To SH with love." Do you know who SH is?'

Mostyn shook his head.

'For the benefit of the tape, the defendant has just shaken his head. Well, I can confirm that the parents of murdered schoolgirl, Sian Hawkins, have just identified this necklace as belonging to their daughter, but it was not on her body when it was discovered. Do you know where we found this necklace?'

'Don't know,' mumbled Mostyn.

Kerry leant forward like an eager fisherman about to reel in his biggest ever catch and snatched up the bag, waving it in front of Mostyn's face. 'This was found in *your* bedroom, earlier today.'

'Someone must've planted it.'

'And this, too,' continued Kerry, holding another evidence bag containing a bloodied wire saw.

Mostyn's reply caught in his throat. His stomach wretched until his bloodshot eyes nearly popped from their sockets, but there was nothing left.

Finally, after catching his breath, he screamed.

'Mostyn Lloyd, I am now charging you with the murders of both Steven Evans *and* Sian Hawkins. You shall appear at

Draigwen Magistrates Court later today where you will be formally charged. The magistrate will then decide whether to bail you or detain you until your court hearing. Do you have anything to say?'

Mostyn begged for his mother, and the public defender simply shook his head.

Fiona sighed. 'Interview ended at sixteen-forty-six.'

CHAPTER 43

VIDEO KILLED THE RADIO STAR

Wednesday 18th November, 1981
Larkmead Chapel

Fred cradled his cup of tea and listened intently while Fiona and Dylan brought him up to speed. The flames from the coal fire flickered in his half-moon glasses and several logs cracked loudly, shifted, and sent sparks flying up the chimney, but the reverend didn't flinch.

His demeanour didn't alter even when Fiona described how Craig's body had decomposed at an accelerated pace—like Arwel's—after Crulus jumped from one body to the other. Fred remained unfazed, like it was an everyday occurrence rather than a supernatural wanton disregard for life.

The only time Fred flinched, albeit subtle, was when Dylan described Emily's life cord and mentioned that his own body didn't have one, yet he could still find his way out of Transmogoria. Fiona knew Fred's reaction wasn't a good sign. Dylan's absent life cord was obviously a concern, but she didn't want to worry him unnecessarily, especially after he broke down describing Steven's death.

Mostyn's murder charge was a huge shock to both boys; they refused to believe their friend had committed such an atrocity, despite the overwhelming evidence. At only eleven years old, Dylan had endured more in a few months than most people experience in their lifetime and she sincerely hoped that Fred could help him.

'So, you've been having Ooo Bees?' asked Fred.

Dylan stared at Fiona, unsure how to answer.

'Ooo Bees,' repeated Fred, smiling. 'Out of body experiences. O. O. B. E. or Ooo Bees, as I like to call them. They sound less scary that way.'

'They're not scary at all,' announced Dylan, proudly.

'Well, that's good to hear,' said Fred, sitting forward. 'Ooo Bees occur in the veil—the threshold between the living and the dead. Think of it like an endless corridor between our world and that of the dead. In fact, it has been documented as being boundless.'

'Why?' asked Dylan, reaching for a custard cream.

'I'm glad you asked that, young man, because it's very interesting. But I will need some help explaining it.' He lifted his walking stick and pointed to the book shelf. 'Could you fetch that rather large book for me?'

Dylan gawped at the thick tome lying across the shelf. The book had huge metal hinges and a clasp made from nails, almost identical to his lost book. He jumped up, raced across the anteroom and reached on tip-toe to the books, which were layered in thick, undisturbed dust. He snatched the book from the shelf, and swiped a carpet of dust off the cover, but there was no rotten flesh; just a plain, weathered, leather cover.

'Oh,' said Dylan, excitement waning. 'That's not a dead book,' he mumbled, handing it over.

'Dead book?'

'It's what I called mine. It had clasps made of nails, too,' explained Dylan, before sitting down.

'I see. Well, I don't know about yours, but this *is* a special book and there's a very good reason for the nails, which I'll explain in a minute. This book has been passed down through the centuries from Reverend to Reverend. It contains the recorded sightings of the Devil, his demons, and any supernatural occurrences that affected their flock.' Much like Dylan did, Fred slowly worked a nail back and forth, squeak after squeak, until the metal catch swung open. He laid the nail out in front of him. 'These are coffin nails; they prevent spirits from passing through.'

'But why would a spirit want to open the book?' asked Fiona, bemused.

Fred stifled a yawn and peered into his teacup. 'Could you put the kettle on, dear? You get rather weary at my age without something to perk you up. I'd offer you a sherry, but I know you'd refuse, what with you being on duty.'

'Actually, I'm off duty,' replied Fiona, gesturing to her civilian attire.

'Sorry, how silly of me. Sherry it is, then,' he said, pointing to a bottle on his sideboard.

Fiona smiled and picked the tray off the table. 'No, tea will be fine, thanks.'

'As you wish,' replied Fred, sadly. 'In answer to your question, they blocked spirits from ascertaining the book's contents. You see, there could be discoveries in the book that might banish such evil.' He opened the book and flicked through the pages for several minutes until he found what he was looking for. 'Ah, here it is. An entry from Reverend Tomos Llewellyn, curate-in-charge, dated the fourth day of March, in the year of our lord, 1831.' Fred ran his finger over the text and mumbled some of the words before tapping his finger on the page. 'This is it!' he said, before reading the text aloud, 'Should thy threshold be breached, time standeth still. The deceased speak with thee, unbound by hours as they are reckon'd in thy living world. This was proven to me by master Samuel Herbert Hopkins, fourteen years since born, of Maesycymmwr.' Fred peered over the top of his spectacles and studied Dylan's reaction. 'This boy was like you. He could speak with the dead and help them to passover. He was a soul guardian and—'

'A what?' interrupted Dylan.

'It's what you are.'

'My book said I was a psychopomp.'

'You guide souls to the afterlife. Such guides are observed by different cultures and religions resulting in many different names: soul guardian, spirit-walker, death-walker, psychopomp and shaman, to name but a few. Does the mention of a time barrier suggest otherworldly powers, perhaps?'

'Time travel?' asked Fiona.

'Possibly.'

Dylan's eyes went wide. 'Be kind, rewind,' he muttered, under his breath.

'What's that?' asked Fred, tapping his hearing aid.

Dylan jumped to his feet. 'I can go back and save Emily!' he bragged, but Fred waved him back down.

'Not necessarily,' Fred said calmly, not wanting to sound too negative. 'I just wanted to let you know that you may have undiscovered abilities. How you discover and utilise your powers is not for me to say; I don't possess them. All I can do is tell you what previous reverends have recorded.'

Dylan grabbed the brass handle of Fred's poker and began whacking the lit coals in the fire, sending bright red embers into the air above the fireplace. 'Stupid powers!' he scoffed. 'I can't even bring the dead back.'

'You are not God,' cautioned Fred, flicking through the book in his lap.

'Fine. Why do I have to guard souls, then? Can't *he* do it himself?' whined Dylan, pointing to a bronze effigy of the crucifixion on the mantelpiece.

Fred sighed and looked over at Fiona.

'There must be others like me and Newt,' continued Dylan, 'I didn't help Sian passover and—'

'Who's Newt?' asked Fiona and Fred in unison.

'He's a psychopomp, too.'

'Really?' asked Fiona, wondering if this new kid had anything to do with the murders. 'Is he at your school?'

Dylan laughed. 'No. He's a crow.'

Fiona glanced at Fred and, as if reading her mind, he said, 'Corvids are often portrayed as psychopomps, so it's possible. I presume there are many others like you, Dylan. We just don't know who.'

'Well, if you're such an expert, do I have to help bad people, too?'

Fred shifted uncomfortably in his chair. 'I don't profess to be an expert. We are simply trying to help you to understand and cope during these terrible times. Anyway, bad souls shouldn't be judged; that is the Lord's work.'

Fiona's thoughts drifted back to the last time she sat having tea with the reverend and she remembered something he had said about the bodysnatchers, like Parthena.

'Fred, do you remember when we talked about misplaced souls and bodysnatchers?'

'Yes, I remember. Not the aliens, though,' he chuckled.

'You mentioned people's personalities changing. What exactly did you mean by that?'

'They're weakened,' said Dylan, cutting in. 'My dead book said that people having heart attacks or in comas can be taken over by Coblynau.'

'That's correct, Dylan. It's widely believed that someone resuscitated or recovering from a coma could wake with a different soul. For instance, a straight man waking up gay; a person acquiring skills that they never previously had, such as playing a musical instrument; a married man suddenly forgetting his family which, I suppose, is similar to Emily's predicament.'

Dylan stopped poking the fire and looked over his shoulder. 'Party knew Emily was trying to get back into her body,' he explained. He began pacing up and down the room, clicking his fingers and twirling his hands, while he rewound his thoughts. 'She shouted something ... Umm ... Get out of my head. That was it. She knew what we were doing.'

Fiona clicked her fingers. 'I think I've got it!' she beamed. 'If we could put Parthena to sleep, somehow, then we—'

'Can get Emily back,' finished Dylan. He grabbed his coat and headed for the door.

'Wait, where're you going?' asked Fiona. 'We can't rush into this, it needs to be planned.' Despite the authority her police status brought, school absences would complicate things and draw unnecessary attention. Not only did she have to kidnap a child, she had to *somehow* render her unconscious without killing her. 'I can't just go whacking innocent people over the head with my truncheon.'

Dylan pointed to the door. 'I know. I was going to get Mark.'

'He's here?' asked Fiona, incredulously.

'Yeah. I left him in the graveyard.'

Fred lifted the pot of tea. 'Well, go get him. Poor boy must be freezing. I'll pour him a cuppa.'

CHAPTER 44
BACK IN BLACK

While Fiona ran through some ideas, Mark stumbled through the room, unable to look left or right without turning his whole head sideways due to the hood on his snorkel parka being zipped to the end, tunnelling his vision. He unzipped it and shoved his arse into the fireplace until he was nearly sat on it.

When Fred disappeared into his pantry, Mark slid forward and filled one of his parka pockets with biscuits, emptying the plate. When he saw everyone staring he mumbled, 'Wha'?'

'You're not invisible,' advised Dylan, shaking his head.

Fred reappeared with two long, metal forks and a packet of crumpets, which he handed to Dylan.

Giddy with happiness, the boys stabbed a crumpet onto their forks and held them a few inches from the fire's glowing coals.

'You warming up, okay, Mark?' asked Fred, sitting back down.

'Yes, thanks,' replied Mark, before turning his attention to Fiona. 'How come you're not in uniform, like your partner?'

'Sorry?'

‘That copper outside. Isn’t he with you?’

‘Oh, shit!’ she croaked, almost choking on her words. ‘Jukesy.’

‘Who?’ asked Fred, ignoring her blasphemy.

‘He’s Crulus!’ she yelled.

‘Oh, don’t panic, dear,’ said Fred, opening his arms wide. ‘Look around you. This is a house of God. The Devil cannot enter,’ he assured, but his eyes didn’t look convinced.

Through the stained-glass windows they could see Crulus was hovering around by the gate, the glow from his rufescent eyes curving around his eye sockets. They watched as he jammed Jukesy’s truncheon into the rusty chain wrapped around the gate and twisted it. After a few rotations, one of the chain links snapped, sending the lock and chain crashing to the floor. Crulus lifted the latch, swung the gate open and stepped through.

‘What do we do? He’s coming!’ squealed Mark, waving his forked crumpet around like some mad wizard.

Fiona grabbed Fred’s huge key-bunch off his desk and ran through the chapel. She jangled the large metal ring and fumbled each key, one at a time, into the ornate lock on the chapel doors, and twisted. Some failed to turn altogether, while others appeared to work initially but, after only a quarter rotation, they failed to fully engage the lock’s mechanism.

‘Shit! Which key is it?’ she screamed, but Fred was out of earshot.

Dylan watched in awe as a dark blur glided up the driveway toward the chapel and stopped just short of the chapel doors. ‘He’s by the doors. HURRY!’ he screamed, his voice rising several octaves.

‘Bollocks,’ mumbled Fiona, having dropped the key bunch for the third time. ‘I’m trying!’

The flickering fire’s reflection was obscuring their view, so

Mark cupped his hands up against the glass. He couldn't see anyone near the doors and the policeman was still walking up the driveway. 'He's not by the doors,' corrected Mark. 'The copper's still walking up the drive.'

Dylan wiped his condensed breath off the glass with his sleeve, cupped his hands, and looked again. The dark figure was still standing near the doors, but Mark was right, Crulus was only halfway up the driveway. Dylan squinted, trying to focus on the dark figure, when it suddenly dawned on him who it was.

Yr Angau, the graveyard watcher, was guarding the chapel.

The two figures stared each other out like gunfighters with itchy trigger fingers.

Crulus moved first. He hurtled towards Yr Angau with such speed that Dylan's eyes struggled to follow. Just before he reached him, Crulus dashed sidewards, first to the left and then almost instantly back to the right, but Yr Angau matched his speed and agility, despite his frail physique. When it looked like Crulus had outrun the watcher, the watcher's dog, Brass, materialised and forced him back once more.

'Why's he running back and forth?' asked Mark, confused.

'He's trying to dodge Yr Angau.'

Fiona burst back into the room jangling the keys in front of her. Her hair was wild and she was red-faced. She looked petrified. 'I can't find the right key,' she cried, waving the bunch at Fred. 'Which is it?'

'I don't think it matters. Come and see,' said Dylan, waving her over.

Fiona peered out of the window just as the graveyard watcher jammed a bony hand out in front of him. Crulus was thrown backwards by some unseen force and landed with a bone cracking thud several metres away, his skull slamming into the cobbled sidings that lined the gravel driveway.

'He's like Yoda,' announced Dylan.

All Mark saw was the policeman running at the chapel and then flying, unceremoniously, back down the drive. Mark leant close to Dylan and whispered, 'This supernatural shit is awesome.'

'The wrinkly old git threw him away, like he was nothing. He didn't even touch him,' explained Dylan.

Fiona chortled at that, giving him a sideways glance. 'Bet you wouldn't say that to his face, though.'

Dylan blinked. 'I was only joking,' he said, a little defensive.

'He's not just folklore,' noted Fiona, turning toward Fred, who nodded.

'Apparently not,' admitted Fred. 'He's fulfilling his destiny; protecting the peace of the dead.'

Crulus made several more failed attempts before he bent forward, hands clasped to his knees, gasping for air. The strength of Crulus' soul was limited by the human vessel he possessed and Jukesy was quite clearly unfit. He slowly raised one arm, pointing a finger at the huddled figures in the anteroom window.

'You can't hide forever, Kordialis!' he roared, before turning on his heels. Jukesy's boots thudded and crunched down the gravel driveway, before finally disappearing into the darkness beyond the gate.

'That's twice he's been here looking for Kordialis,' noted Fiona, as the graveyard watcher's head swivelled towards the chapel.

Glowing with intensity below their shrivelled eyelids, his eyes found Dylan. The sinews in his hands twitched like piano strings as he pulled his suit collar down and brushed it back into place.

He nodded.

Just once.

Then melted into shadow.

CHAPTER 45

PLEASE DON'T GO

Thursday 19th November, 1981
Draigwen Town Comprehensive School

News of Mostyn's imminent Crown Court murder trial was headline news on HTV, which meant there were permanent TV crews pitched up outside the school gates. As police officers were patrolling in and around the school to maintain order, Fiona was able to implement her daylight mission under the guise of FLO duties. To prevent the cameras filming her vehicle's occupants, Fiona drove straight through the school gates and parked out of sight near the canteen's loading bay, before escorting two women to the school secretary's office.

Mrs Rogers was expecting her and directed them to an unused classroom in block B. She advised Fiona that she had just confirmed with Mr Harwood that Miss Morris and Masters Wolfendale and Jones would be with her shortly. Being nosey, Mrs Rogers asked Fiona if she required any assistance but when Fiona politely declined stating 'police business,' she begrudgingly left them to it.

'Thank you for agreeing to this, Zara,' Fiona said, once Mrs Rogers had left. 'If you hadn't told me about Madame Zina, I would never have thought of it.'

Zara looked across at Zina and smiled. 'I just hope you can get the old Emily back. It's just not the same without her being, you know, her old self.'

Zina held her hand, looked deep into her eyes and said, 'I'll do my best. It's up to your daughter to remember and help me fight Kindoki.'

'I know,' agreed Zara, wiping her eyes.

Zina looked over Zara's shoulder at Fiona who was gesturing to the door. 'Thanks, Zara. Please wait in the corridor while I hypnotise Parthena and Dyl—'

'Don't call her that,' Zara cut in. 'Her name's Emily.'

'Apologies. Remember, no matter what you hear, you are to remain outside. I cannot afford distractions.'

'I understand.' Zara stopped short of the door and stared at the floor, motionless. 'But why is the other boy coming in?' she finally asked.

'He won't. Mark will be keeping you company,' explained Fiona.

Dylan and Mark arrived before Parthena, so Fiona whisked Dylan into the classroom and asked Mark to escort Zara to a small row of plastic chairs half way down the corridor.

'I'm not touching him,' snapped Zina, backing away from Dylan.

'We don't have much time. Parthena will be here any second,' reminded Fiona.

'What's the plan?' asked Dylan.

'Madame Zina will hypnotise her, which will hopefully weaken her enough so you can get Emily to recover her body, however that works.'

'Great,' beamed Dylan.

'I know. I surprise myself sometimes,' smiled Fiona. '*Sssh*, here she comes.'

Zara had told her daughter what was going to happen before she left for school and, surprisingly, she agreed to it. Once they were both seated, Zina explained the procedure.

First, she performed a fake hypnotism on Dylan, so as to allay any of Parthena's fears about what she might experience.

After several minutes, Dylan pretended to be under, so Zina began hypnotising Parthena.

With a metronome on the desk between the children, Zina began to relax her state of mind, slowly drawing her under. When she was certain that she was fully hypnotised, she tapped the desk in front of Dylan. He acknowledged her and slowly closed his eyes, once more, crossing the threshold into Transmogoria.

He called Emily's name.

A candy-floss figure appeared out of the moving shadows, which slowly materialised into the image of Emily, but her shimmering glow was all but gone.

Her life cord had nearly extinguished.

It was now or never.

'Emily, I need you to follow your cord, again.'

He reached for her hand and gently took hold of her entire soul. A warmth flew through him like nothing he had experienced before.

Blissful.

Her life-force twinkled across her face as if her entire soul had been sprayed by millions of tiny ice crystals that lit up the contours and gave her soul substance.

She was beautiful.

'I'm ready,' she replied.

The ice crystals shifted and Dylan felt her smile radiating towards him. 'I'll guide you this time,' he explained.

Squeezing her tightly, they drifted through Transmogoria following her faint thread of life back to her door and its reluctant squatter. Gliding through this supernatural realm, without making any footsteps or feeling any ground beneath them, was tranquil, and Dylan had to resist the urge not to stay there with Emily for all eternity.

They stopped at the flickering lights of Emily's door.

'As soon as you feel resistance, don't stop. Keep pushing forward. I will help you, okay?'

Dylan's voice seemed to echo, as though he could hear himself sat at the desk through Emily's door.

'Do it now.'

'Okay,' replied Emily, reaching a hand through the shifting iridescence before her.

Dylan watched as the initial surge sucked her hand deeper into the lights then it stopped abruptly and an unseen force pushed back.

Parthena.

~

Fiona and Zina sat quietly in the classroom watching the two children intently, not that there was much to see. Occasionally, Dylan's eyes flickered and his body twitched, but Parthena was limp like a rag doll, arms in her lap, waiting for Zina's next command.

Parthena's chest suddenly heaved, sucking in erratic breaths while her body jerked and shook. 'No. Stop. Nooooo. Get out!' she cried.

'I thought she was unconscious?' asked Fiona, reaching for her.

Zina stood up and held Fiona back with one hand. 'I *never*

said that,' she replied, shaking her head. 'They are always fully conscious through the hypnosis. I needed to subdue Kindoki.'

Fiona flung her hands in the air and fumed, 'It's not going to work, then. What a waste of bloody time!'

In Transmogoria, Dylan sensed Parthena's fiery reluctance to leave, so he leant on Emily's soul, willing her through her door.

It seemed to work.

When Emily began edging forward, Dylan saw something breaking through the iridescent surface, and he urged her to push harder. Their concerted efforts were yielding results.

But then, without warning, Dylan felt a force pulling him elsewhere.

Another soul was calling out to him.

It was so strong that he couldn't ignore it, and his hand slipped off Emily's soul.

'Sorry, Emily, I have to go. Keep pushing through. It's working!' he assured her, as he was pulled backwards through Transmogoria and into the sepia lobby.

Wispy images came and went until a new image formed before his eyes. He recognised it straight away; it was his living room.

A figure appeared before him, faint at first, but then the image focused.

It was his father, Gwynfor, lost and confused.

'I don't understand,' mumbled Dylan.

He did, but he refused to believe it.

Gwynfor's head tilted to the side and he squinted, trying to focus on what he was seeing. 'Dylan, is that you? What's wrong with Mam? She's not listening to me!' he shrieked.

The panic in his voice stopped Dylan's advance and he browsed the room.

His mother was leaning over his father's chair, smothering something.

No, not a something.

A someone.

His father.

'Oh, God,' croaked Dylan. 'Not you. Not now ... Please, Dad.'

Gwynfor followed Dylan's stare and dropped to his knees when he saw himself slumped in his own armchair, his oxygen mask discarded on the floor.

Instinctively, Dylan swiped his hand in front of him and the sepia toned world sped up, became realtime. The vision played out like a scene from a black and white movie. Chrissy grabbed at Gwynfor's wrist and then his neck, searching for a pulse. She laid her head on his chest, then frantically checked his wrist and neck several more times.

She began to scream.

For Kaelum.

For Dylan.

For anyone.

Her shaking hands yanked his shirt open and she rested her head on his chest, desperately willing a heart beat to vibrate her eardrum. The silence contorted her face into another scream. She started thumping his chest with her fists, then blowing into his mouth, struggling to catch her own breath between breathing for Gwynfor and her own fitful sobs.

Finally, she slumped back onto her knees and screamed.

'I'm here, Chrissy. I'm here!' shouted Gwynfor, his voice clear and vibrant; no more rasping or chesty sounds.

'She can't hear you,' sighed Dylan, stroking his arm.

Chrissy's shaky fingers spun the dial on their house phone, but her finger kept getting caught in the dial causing her to constantly re-dial.

An age passed before Gwynfor heard her panicked voice bellowing down the handset at the emergency operator.

'I can't be dead. I can't be,' pleaded Gwynfor. 'You're here.'

Dylan slumped to his knees next to his father. 'Sorry.'

'For what?'

'This is what I do when I daydream. I help people passover.'

Gwynfor's jaw fell open.

Lights materialised in the corner of the room, twinkling and flickering with more and more urgency.

'Will I see you, again?' asked Gwynfor.

Dylan had never seen him so forlorn. 'No,' he replied, lowering his head. If tears existed there, they would have overwhelmed him. 'We can talk whenever you want to, though.' He smiled through quivering lips. 'I'll always be here. I love you to bits.'

'Love you, too, Son.'

Gwynfor took a final look at his grieving wife. 'Can she see me?'

Dylan's head shook.

'Oh.'

The sadness in his voice tore Dylan's heart right out of his chest and he grabbed hold of his father's shoulder, more to steady himself than to comfort him.

Gwynfor leant forward and lightly brushed his hand across his wife's face, trying to wipe away her tears.

Chrissy lifted her hand to her cheek, as if sensing him.

'Look after her, won't you.'

'I do. I mean, I *will*,' replied Dylan, flinging his arms around his father's soul, which slipped through his fingers like grains of sand.

Something red glinted behind his father's soul.

Then another.

Centred in a dark shape, the red dots brightened until the shape enveloped his father and dragged him backwards.

Dylan knew that it was Crulus before he had even spoken a word.

'Now, I see you, Kordialissssss,' he hissed.

Then they were gone.

The sepia fog swirled and his living room became the classroom once more.

Fiona was struggling to hold Parthena, who was screaming and flinging her arms and legs around as though she were fitting, while Zina was singing some ridiculous African chant about Kindoki and prancing around like she was the possessed one.

Emily's voice made Dylan jump to his feet because the words weren't in his head; they were coming from Emily's lips.

'Help me, Dylan,' she said, but in the same breath, Parthena screamed, 'Get. Out. You. Grumble. And. Grunt!'

Both souls were fighting over ownership and he grabbed her hands tightly.

'I'm here, Emily! Push her out. You can do it. Just follow my voice,' he pleaded.

They watched as Emily's face switched constantly from desperation to anger, and her accent from Welsh to Cockney, as the inner struggle waged on.

'Give it up. You're already brown bread!' sneered Parthena.

'No, it's my body! Get out!' cried Emily.

'You're getting right on my thruppennies!'

'Then leave!'

'No, this body's mine, now. Hit the frog and toad, missy. You can't beat me!'

AARRGH!!!

The scream was so loud that Fiona dashed over to cover her mouth, fearing it would alert nearby teachers, but it stopped as suddenly as it had come, and Emily's body sagged into silence before she had even reached her.

Now, the only sounds were the girl's faint breaths, and distant footsteps running along the corridor.

Dylan felt her fingers twitch, and her eyes slowly flickered open.

'Dylan?' she whispered.

Dylan's eyes lit up, and he stroked her hair.

'Emily?' he asked, as a smile spread across his face.

She sat up, looked deep into his eyes and smiled back, but the smile slowly melted into a smirk.

'Gotcha,' sneered Parthena.

Dylan released her hands and fell in a heap at her feet, sobbing uncontrollably.

'Look at that boat race!' hissed Parthena, before flinging her head back and howling with laughter, causing loud commotion and raised voices in the corridor.

Zara burst into the classroom, quickly followed by Mark, who was desperately trying to stop her.

'Is she back?' asked Zara, her eyes flitting between Zina and Fiona.

'Oh, yeah, she's gone,' said Parthena, softly.

Zara placed her hands either side of her daughter's head. 'Really?'

Parthena leant forward, inches from her face and nodded. 'Yeah, you wouldn't Adam and Eve it. She just upped and went!' She grinned, viciously.

Zara began to cry.

'Don't ya love me anymore, Mama?' sneered Parthena.

Zina gathered her things and led the distraught Zara out of the classroom while Parthena sung *Knees Up Mother Brown* and skipped along behind them.

Once they had left, Fiona and Mark hoisted Dylan onto a nearby chair.

He was a mess.

Sweat matted his hair to his forehead and every nerve in his body was twitching. When Fiona asked him what had happened, he just stared blankly, while his pupils rolled back into his head like a fruit machine on nudge.

Mark curled his lip in disgust when he saw his friend's white eyes. 'Urgh! Gross.'

'He's in shock,' advised Fiona. 'He needs to go home.'

They each wrapped one of his arms over their shoulders, but he sagged like a dead weight.

'Dylan, you have to snap out of it. We need to get you home,' urged Fiona.

Dylan's pupils rolled forward and quivered back into place. 'Gotta go,' he muttered.

'Yes, home. C'mon, I'll take you.'

Dylan stared up at her through bloodshot eyes and mumbled, 'I was distracted.'

'Emily wasn't unconscious. I'll have to think of something else. It's not your fault.'

'It is!' spat Dylan. 'I wasn't with her. I was with another.'

'Who?' asked Mark.

'My dad ... He's dead. Crulus took him.'

Both Fiona and Mark stared at each other in disbelief. Why was this kid dealing with so much suffering? If this was simply a case of good against evil, then evil seemed destined to win, and poor Dylan was taking every single one of the demon's blows.

This wasn't a gift; this was a curse.

Fiona felt tears building, so she wrapped her arms around Dylan and tried to squeeze them away. When she saw Mark crying, they huddled in the centre of the classroom and wept.

After a few minutes, Dylan tried to wriggle free. 'I need to find Kaelum,' he said, sniffing. 'My mam needs us.'

'Of course,' replied Fiona, wiping her eyes. 'Your brother won't know, will he? I'll let Mrs Rogers know I'm taking you both home.'

'Erm, I-I better go back to class,' mumbled Mark, shuffling nervously. 'Sorry about your dad,' he added, as Dylan left the classroom.

Fiona nudged Mark's chin up with a finger. 'We did everything we could.'

'I know. I just wish he'd got Emily back. What went wrong?'

'Parthena wasn't unconscious. She knew something was happening, like last time. Anyway, it doesn't matter, not with his dad gone. Poor dab.'

'So, that's it. Emily's gone?'

'Looks that way,' Fiona admitted with a shrug. 'But we have to be hopeful for Dylan's sake.'

Mark felt useless. There was nothing he could do to help his friend. He wished they could go back to when they were in junior school, to a time before Dylan's imaginary friends became real. A time when all they had to worry about was which Action Man each of them would play with, German or British. A time when the nearest they came to worrying about death was when one of them sunk all of the other's ships whilst playing Battleship.

'I probably won't see him until next week, now. I've got to have a tooth out, tomorrow,' he sighed. 'I hate dentists, but I'll be knocked out this time.'

'Sorry?'

'Oh, I screamed the place down last time they tried to take it out *and* I was sick in the chair, so they're going to gas me, this time.'

Fiona grabbed Mark and kissed him on the forehead. 'You're a genius!' she said, pinching his cheeks.

CHAPTER 46

NO REPLY AT ALL

Tuesday 1st December, 1981
Larkmead Chapel

Reverend Foster had never been so busy. This was his fourth burial in less than four months, with more to come once the police released the bodies, and his Sunday service was once again packed to the vault.

A terror was gripping Draigwen with many professing that it was the Second Coming. Even the weather had been at apocalyptic levels last week with over one hundred tornadoes touching down across the UK. He tried to allay his parishioners fears during his sermons by withholding the supernatural truth, yet he hated doing so. The only place he didn't lie was in the ancient manuscripts, and this was the first time he had ever felt the need to write his own entry since being ordained thirty-three years ago. He had learnt the art of calligraphy for just such a purpose, but his lack of practice showed in his first few scrapbook drafts. He also found it hard to describe these supernatural events when he was being drip-fed them, secondhand, by an eleven year old boy whose father was now laid out in a coffin below his pulpit.

~

After Gwynfor had been laid to rest, Chrissy had collapsed and was taken to the vestry, where she was being comforted by Kaelum and Uncle John. The rest of the mourners had already left for the wake, which was being held at Draigwen Rugby Club, and they were probably already downing their second pints of beer by now.

Fiona gathered Fred and the boys on a chapel pew and told them of her plan to knock Parthena out with dental anaesthetic. Her old school friend, Heather, was a dental assistant, and she was perfectly placed to help them, seeing as Fiona had let her off with several unofficial cautions for drink-driving.

After the hypnosis debacle, Zara would be reluctant to try anything else, which meant they would have to kidnap Parthena to get her to the anaesthetist.

Simple.

'But what's the point?' whined Dylan, his eyes red and puffy. 'Even if we get Emily back, Crulus will still be around to destroy our lives.'

'I can't find anything in the manuscripts that would help, either,' added Fred, 'But I shall keep looking. I won't give up on you.'

'Without my dead book he'll kill us all,' moaned Dylan, who continually tugged at his shirt collar. He hated his throat being restricted, but his mother insisted he dress properly because his father would be watching from above.

He wasn't watching.

He wasn't talking, either.

No matter how hard Dylan tried, he just couldn't reach

him. Neither could his Nan, and you could usually hear her yacking in the next valley. It was as though his father's soul had been cased in lead or, worse still, snuffed from existence altogether.

'I can't hear my dad,' announced Dylan.

'How come?' asked Mark, flicking through a copy of the bible trying to look interested.

'Dunno, I can hear all the others, just not him.'

'Others?' asked Fred.

'The dead. They babble away in my head all the time, like radio static. Sometimes they get too loud, so I just tune them out.'

'Did your book give any hints on how to stop Crulus?' asked Fred.

Prevent him from taking more lives.

Dylan finally prised his top button open, slackened his Windsor knot, and sighed with relief. 'No, it just said I'd know when the time came, but how will I know without the book?'

'What book?' asked John, who had stepped into the chapel, quickly followed by Kaelum and his mother.

'Doesn't matter,' mumbled Dylan, sliding his tie upwards to hide his open collar.

'Your mam wants to go home, so I'll drop you off, then head over to the wake to let everyone know she won't be attending,' he explained, but nobody moved. 'C'mon, boys. Lets go,' he urged, jangling his car keys.

Fiona and Fred stood up to say their goodbyes.

'Thank you for a superb service, Reverend,' said John, shaking Fred's hand. 'Gwynfor would have loved it, especially the male-voice choir. Their rendition of *Cwm Rhondda* was heart wrenching.'

Fred nodded and replied, 'Yes, yes it was. They're wonderful, aren't they. So talented. Such a lovely turn out, too. Gwynfor was a lovely man and so helpful, he'll be greatly missed by this community.'

Chrissy walked past without uttering a word and began to walk down the driveway.

Fred waved his arms like he was herding sheep. 'Off you go, boys. Safe travels, Mr Hawker. God be with you.'

Fiona, Mark and Fred watched the family head down to John's beetle.

Dylan paused to look back and wave at them before getting in the back of the car with Kaelum, who seemed very concerned about his little brother.

'Do you think they heard us talking?' asked Fiona.

'I wouldn't have thought so, dear. They would have said something if they'd heard such fantastical drivel. Tea?' offered Fred.

'No, thanks. I need to get back to the station, I'm already stretching these FLO duties to the limit. My sergeant will cotton on, soon. How are you getting home, Mark?'

'I'm not. I gotta go back to school. I'll walk, it won't take long.'

'Don't be silly. I'll drive you. We can have a chat on the way. Take care, Fred. I'll keep you updated.'

'Me too. As soon as that kettle's boiled, my head will be buried in the manuscripts looking for answers.'

~

No sooner had they stepped into the house, Chrissy delved into the drinks cabinet and scurried off to bed with a bottle of Malibu leaving Dylan and Kaelum alone, but there was no slanging match, today.

Kaelum had never been this quiet.

The awkward silence was deafening, so Dylan bounded up to his bedroom.

He discarded his jacket and tie, fell back onto the bed, and closed his moist eyes. He felt his soul slip out, then he yanked it back, sharpish; the thought of meeting Crulus in Transmogoria terrified him.

Ta-tap Ta-tap

Before Dylan could react, Kaelum edged into his room, sat down, and handed him a scruffy, vinyl bag.

'Open it,' he said, curtly.

Dylan unzipped it. Inside was a tatty, plastic bag wrapped in a thick elastic band. He unravelled it and slid the contents onto his lap.

It was his dead book.

Dylan's head swivelled around so fast his eyes couldn't keep up. 'How?'

Kaelum lowered his head and twiddled his thumbs.

'We looked everywhere for this,' continued Dylan. 'I can't believe you've found it!'

'I didn't,' replied Kaelum, shaking his head. 'I took it.'

'What? Why?'

'I fetched it out of the bin after mam dumped it, just to piss you off. When you went crazy, I thought it might be worth something, so I tried to sell it, but nobody wanted it.'

'*I* needed it!' snapped Dylan, jabbing a finger into his chest.

'I know, I'm sorry. I heard you talking about it in the chapel.'

Dylan's jaw went slack and he quickly averted his eyes.

'Can you really talk to the dead?'

For a second Dylan debated lying but, for once, he had to trust his brother, after all, if it wasn't for him they wouldn't have caught Crulus the first time.

'Yeah,' he finally answered.

'And dad?'

Dylan's shoulders sagged and he shook his head. He put

the book to one side and stared into Kaelum's eyes, which seemed to have aged overnight. He loved the idea of *actually* getting to know his big brother; they needed to do more bonding than fighting, and he suddenly realised that he now had to tell him everything, which he did.

Kaelum seemed chuffed that he had rendered a demon unconscious, even if his capture was short livid, and he offered to help in any way he could, which came as a total shock.

'Look after mam while I figure out a way to stop Crulus.'

'Is that it?' sighed Kaelum, 'Can't I come with you?'

Sibling rivalry aside, he loved his brother, so he really didn't want him involved in this, but how could he say no?

'I suppose so,' Dylan said, reluctantly, 'What about Mam?'

'She'll be out like a light once the drink kicks in.'

'Yeah, but what if she's sick? She could choke. We can't lose her, too.'

'Fine, I'll ask Uncle John, even though she hates his guts. I like him, though.'

'So do I.'

While the grave diggers were patting the soil down on top of their father's body, Dylan explained to his brother that the evil demon that had dragged their father's soul into some dense, otherworldly prison, was also the same one that had deprived them of Auntie Louisa.

'What a prick,' spat Kaelum. 'I wish I'd killed him, now.'

'Yeah,' sighed Dylan, 'Me too.'

'I wonder what she looked like?'

'Who?'

'Louisa.'

'Umm, they were identical,' answered Dylan.

'Oh, yeah.'

A smirk grew into a smile, which crept into a grin, and they both exploded with laughter. The brothers, together in grief, chuckled until their sides hurt, then gradually fell silent.

'The living room photos are all of Louisa, not mam,' said Dylan, finally.

'All this time. Why didn't Mam say anything?'

'Probably embarrassed 'cause she thought there was a murderer in the family. I can't even tell her the truth.'

Kaelum scratched his forehead and mumbled, 'If Crulus took dad, is he in hell?'

'I dunno. Somehow, I've gotta stop Crulus.'

Kaelum nudged him and pointed at the book. 'Well, find out what we need to do.'

'I will, but I'm not doing it with you watching me.'

'Fine,' snorted Kaelum, disappointed. 'Give me a shout when you know. I'll ring Uncle John.'

~

Dylan gathered some tissue paper in readiness for the upcoming nose bleed and placed his hand inside the book. The now familiar tingling shot up his arm and buzzed into his head like static from a million birthday balloons. His brain felt like it was being squeezed in a school woodwork vice as new memories scurried into every lobe and blood gushed from his nostrils.

Don't fight it.

Breathe, Dylan.

Breathe.

He tried to tilt his head back, while pinching his nose, but the blood ran down the back of his throat and trickled into his lungs when he took a breath. He coughed, spraying his wall in crimson droplets as silver fish danced across his eyeballs, and he gripped the side of his cupboard to stop himself from collapsing.

When the dizziness receded, the new memory popped up like an ejected Betamax tape. Dylan pressed 'play' in his mind and watched the new memory unfold through the eyes of the man in his head, once more.

The man was having an 'Ooo Bee' as Fred had so eloquently put it. Looking back out of Transmogoria, Dylan could see the blurred image of the man's location: the front porch of an idyllic Welsh mining cottage perched high on the hillside. A low, dry stone wall surrounded it, which led to a cobbled path that weaved and sloped its way down into the valley.

On the porch were two coal miners covered with coal dust that had coated not only their faces and clothes but also the inside of their noses, mouths and lungs. They were young, but life down the coal mines had scarred them inside and out, wearing their bodies thin before their time.

The man in Dylan's head was sat on a small wooden stool with his back to the cottage and his eyes closed to the real world. A half-full pint of beer balanced precariously between his thighs.

The other miner was leaning over the low wall and kissing a beautiful young woman, leaving black smudges on her cheek. He tried to grab hold of her, but she held his grubby hands away from her white pinafore and giggled, *'watch my pinny, Crwys.'*

He pulled a sad face and begged, *'Aaw, c'mon, don't be like that, Bronwen. Kiss me!'*

She pursed her lips and kissed him softly.

They were in love.

Inside Transmogoria, the other miner approached the woman's door and paused. He called out the name Orphenia and a figure took shape in the off-white fog before him; the woman from the porch, or at least her soul. Then another figure materialised out of the fog behind her. Dylan recognised his gaunt face and wizened arms straight away.

It was the graveyard watcher, Yr Angau.

The watcher glided forward, past the young woman's soul, and shoved his bony hand through the woman's door. His face contorted and his arm shook, then Dylan heard Bronwen scream out, *'No!'* before collapsing into Crwys' arms. The watcher yanked his arm backwards and pulled out what looked like a wriggling, sparkling, mannequin, causing Orphenia's soul to be sucked through the door in an instant.

The fog of Transmogoria fizzled away when the man stepped through his own door, opened his eyes and looked out across the porch.

The woman's eyes flickered open.

Realising who she was with, she wriggled free of Crwys' grip and shoved him away. She ran over to the man on the stool and passionately kissed his blackened face and neck before wrapping her arms tightly around him. 'I've missed you so much, Kordy. I was so scared in there.'

Crwys glared at the other man with eyes burning with jealousy and anger. 'Bronwen, what're you doing?'

The woman glared at him, a cruel smile creeping across her face. 'I'm Orphenia.'

'What? How? Where's Bronwen?' he bellowed.

'I tricked the old man into taking her,' announced the man on the stool.

Crwys screamed, knuckles white. Through gritted teeth, he said, 'She's all I had and *you* took her from me!'

'Orphenia deserved to live.'

'It's not her body. Damn you to hell, Kordialis!'

Dylan sucked in a deep breath as the memory came to an abrupt stop and his eyes flew open. He stared at the book in his lap and wondered what it had all meant.

What was Kordialis showing him?

Was Yr Angau the answer to Emily's problem?

Who was Crwys and where did he fit into this? Was he Crulus?

But there was one question niggling at the base of his skull, buzzing like an annoying fly. Could he trust these memories?

Good and bad are two sides of the same coin.

He began to wonder which side of the coin Kordialis was showing him.

He called Mark on the walkie and arranged to meet him outside Garrett's newsagents, then he shoved the book in his rucksack. He then rang Fiona at Draigwen police station and she agreed to meet them there as soon as she finished her shift.

But first, Dylan needed to get to the chapel.

He had to communicate with the watcher.

He said goodbye to John and stepped out into the garden. Kaelum was sat on his Grifter and holding Dylan's Strika with his spare hand. The wind blew his long fringe into his eyes and he ran his hands through his hair, pushing it back.

'What did the book say?' asked Kaelum.

'Not a lot, but I think I know what I have to do.'

This was already becoming the weirdest day Dylan had ever experienced. He had never interacted with his brother for so long. Strangely, he felt happy in his brother's presence; something he hadn't experienced for a very long time.

'Where to?' asked Kaelum.

'I need you to wait for Fiona and the others at Garrett's,' said Dylan, grabbing the Strika's handlebars.

'Why?' whinged Kaelum. 'Where're you going?'

'I need to speak to the watcher at the graveyard.'

'Lush, I'll come with you. I wanna see him, too,' he said, excited.

'Only Fiona and I can see him and, anyway, he may not show if you're there,' explained Dylan.

'You better not be ditching me,' snapped Kaelum, jabbing a finger at him.

Dylan shook his head and promised, 'I'll meet you when

I'm done. This is our last chance to get Emily back, and maybe dad, too.'

'Really?'

'Yeah, but only his soul. Dad's already gone.'

Kaelum's head drooped and he began flicking the playing cards clipped to his spokes.

Dylan nudged him out of his reverie and smiled. 'Go, there isn't much time.'

CHAPTER 47

RENEGADE

A Bedford police van and two panda cars screeched out onto the main road from Draigwen to Pontyfechan, flashing blue lights and sirens blaring.

They arrived at the school just as two plain-clothed firearms officers were circling a uniformed police officer, the butts of their rifles jammed into their shoulders, and their iron-sights aimed at his chest.

It was Jukesy.

The teacher, Dafydd Williams, was knelt in front of him, shaking with terror.

Although Jukesy only had his truncheon, Fiona, Simon, and Nansi quickly exited the van and shielded themselves behind their vehicle's front doors, while Kerry instructed firearms officers over the radio.

Staring down the barrels, Juksey's face contorted into the most heinous smile that Kerry had ever seen, then he offered a hand to Dafydd.

Dafydd's shaky hand slowly rose to meet Jukesy's.

'NOOOOO!' screamed Fiona, too late.

Juksey's body instantly went rigid, his skin changing colour before their eyes. His body inflated, stretching against his uniform until he looked like he had gained five stone in weight. A sudden, sickening, pop sounded as his skin ruptured, and he collapsed in a heap onto the school yard. Dark blood and fluids began to spread out from underneath his body, trickling across the tarmac.

Dafydd Williams flung a hand to his face when the stench hit him and he rolled away from Jukesy, his stomach convulsing and retching.

Jukesy's body had taken less than twenty seconds to decompose.

A firearms officer ran to Dafydd's side, grabbed a handful of his suit jacket, and dragged him away from the body.

'Stay away from him!' screamed Fiona, pushing past Kerry.

Kerry grabbed her arm and jerked her backwards. 'What the hell's wrong with you?' she snapped. 'He's the victim, here.'

Fiona knew Crulus was occupying Dafydd's body. How could she tell them without sounding crazy? Her mind was doing cart wheels.

'Fi', snap out of it! If you can't handle this, get back in the van. You're embarrassing yourself.'

'Infection,' blurted Fiona.

'What?'

'Hear me out. Howard, Arwel, Victor, and Craig all decomposed like that. What if it's some kind of new virus? Dafydd might be infected, too. He needs to be put into quarantine for his, and our, protection and ... and he could pass it onto those kids,' advised Fiona, pointing at the screaming kids in the yard.

Kerry knew Fiona was right. What she had just witnessed wasn't normal in the slightest and she couldn't risk the children's lives because she failed to prevent an outbreak.

'Fine,' she finally answered. 'We'll get the school cordoned off and the teacher quarantined. Nansi get on the radio and get this reported to the hospital as a possible viral outbreak.'

'Yes, Ma'am,' replied Nansi, unclipping her radio and walking off.

'Simon, get the kids into the main hall, A.S.A.P. I'll inform Public Health. Fi' get firearms to detain Mr Williams, but make sure nobody bloody touches him, we don't want this spreading.'

When Kerry turned back, Dafydd Williams was nowhere to be seen.

While the rest of his class were screaming or staring in shock at the rotting policeman on the yard, Mark slipped through the crowd and dipped behind a low wall, just as Dafydd ran through the school towards the main hall, puffing and sweating like he'd run a marathon rather than a fifty yard sprint.

When Dafydd slipped through a fire door into the canteen corridor, Mark dashed between two huge waste-food bins and, when he was sure that nobody had seen him, he followed Dafydd.

Dafydd was stood at the top of a small flight of stairs adjacent to the canteen. He spun around, pointing a finger at Mark, then he clutched at his chest, croaked, and fell back down the stairs. His head slammed into the last step with a sickening crack, spraying the nearby wall with blood.

Mark slowly inched toward him, kicked his foot, then jumped out of range.

Dafydd's body jerked and twitched for a few seconds, then went still.

Mark felt a surge of relief run through him.

Crulus was dead.

Excited to let Fiona know, he ran back to the fire door, which swung outwards away from his hands as a figure stepped through.

It was the Art teacher, Sarah Lewis. She took one look at Dafydd's crumpled body and screamed.

Mark grabbed her arm and tried to pull her back. 'Don't touch him, Miss.'

She prised his hand free and shook him gently by his shoulders. 'Don't be scared. It's his heart. Go to the Head's office and tell them to phone for an ambulance.'

'But Miss, please don't touch him. It's not him. He'll hurt you.'

'Don't be so silly. Go and get help.'

'But Misssssss,' begged Mark.

'NOW!' she snapped, pointing at the door.

~

Several minutes later, Mark ran through the school yard and hollered for Fiona. Then he directed her, Kerry, and two armed officers to where he had left Sarah tending to Dafydd. The two armed officers raced ahead, barrels raised. Dafydd was pronounced dead and Sarah was nowhere to be seen.

'The virus is spreading,' suggested Fiona, adding to the subterfuge.

'Does this look the same?' quizzed Kerry. 'He's not decayed. He's just fallen down the bloody stairs. Get a grip, Fi'.'

'But what about the teacher that was tending to him? We need to find her. She could be infected.'

'Check the school office. Take the boy with you and get him cleaned up; that blood on him could be infected. I'll get the station to ask the funeral directors to send a doom buggy to pick this guy up, and the other stinker, before there's a media circus out front. The coroner's officers can deal with them *and* this bloody virus. I'd rather chase after things I can actually see.'

The canteen door burst open and one of the armed officers gesticulated towards the canteen. 'DC Edwards.'

'What is it?' asked Kerry.

'Body of an IC1 male and female.'

'Oh, God, what now?' sighed Kerry. 'Okay, I'll be right there. Fi', get that boy out of here.'

Worry streaked across Fiona's face. Who the hell was Crulus, now? 'C'mon, Mark, let's get some fresh air. You're looking peeky,' she said, leading Mark outside.

Mark's bottom lip began to quiver and tears filled his eyes. 'It's my fault. I shouldn't have left her.'

'You wouldn't have been able to stop him, anyway, so don't blame yourself.'

'Dafydd was having a heart attack. If he'd died, then Crulus would be dead, too. But he's not, because I left Miss Lewis with him. It *is* my fault!'

'We don't know that. Nobody does.'

'She's dead, though, isn't she? He's got away, again.'

Fiona pulled him close and squeezed her arms around him. He was absolutely right, but they had to have hope. They had to believe that there was a way to rid the town of this evil before they all died. But what face was this evil now wearing?

'W-W-We're *huh* n-never *huh* gonna s-s-stop him, are we?' blubbered Mark.

'*Ssssh*. Don't cry. I'm sure Dylan or Fred will think of something.'

Fiona wiped his eyes. 'Listen, Mark, I need you to slip out of school and make yourself scarce. If Public Health quarantine the school you'll be stuck here and we'll need you tonight.'

'Why?'

'We're gonna get Emily back.'

'Will it work this time?'

'Yes,' she said, with confidence. 'Now, let's get you out of here.'

CHAPTER 48
VETERAN OF THE PSYCHIC WARS

Larkmead Chapel

The usual glow from oxeye daisies had died away weeks ago and the graveyard looked eerily dark under the waxing crescent moonlight when Dylan crept through it. When he reached his grandparents' grave, he dumped his bag and sat down.

He had no idea how to summon the watcher.

While his eyes scanned the graveyard, he caught glimpse of something glistening in the moonlight by the King crypt. The moonlight clung like dew to the outline of a dark figure rising slowly upwards from the crypt.

It was Yr Angau.

He glided towards Dylan—like he had done through Transmogoria—until he was just a few metres away. Stringy saliva stretched between his long, blackened teeth when his mouth gaped open, and Dylan instinctively covered his ears. Large blobs of spittle ejected from his mouth when the high-pitched wail screeched through the graveyard causing the owls and bats to abandon their perches.

When he stopped, Dylan peeled his hands from his head and stared into his rufescent eyes, which seemed to glisten, like the watcher was staring at a raging fire, rather than a small, shivering schoolboy. On closer inspection, the scars on his face didn't just look like the result of a fire. The gouges in his cheeks reminded Dylan of the scratches on the back of the crypt door.

Mr King had gone crazy in that crypt, tearing at his own scorched flesh until his final breath had ended his torment.

Dylan held out a shaky hand and said, 'Hi, I'm Dylan.'

The watcher's head twisted inquisitively, one way and then the next, but he didn't take Dylan's hand.

'Umm, can you help me?' mumbled Dylan. 'My friend's dead, well, she's not dead, exactly, she's ... er ... a Coblyn's snatched her body. Do you understand?'

The watcher silently edged forward.

Dylan took a half-step backwards, brought his hands up to his chest, and nervously twiddled his fingers. 'I saw this vision; a memory of you. You helped someone get their body back. So, can you help my friend, too?'

The watcher glided forward, his sinuous movements so fast that Dylan didn't have time to react. The watcher's bony fingers stretched around his forearm and the graveyard disappeared.

They were in Transmogoria.

The watcher raised a withered arm and pointed at a door just ahead of them.

Dylan approached the door and peered into the glistening lights.

It was Emily's door.

Dylan spun around. 'That's her! But we can't do it, yet. Party will fight it. We need to put her to sleep, then we can come back here. Is that okay?'

The watcher nodded slowly, reminding Dylan of Lady

Penelope's butler in *Thunderbirds,* then he melted away leaving Dylan alone with his thoughts.

He was so excited; they now had a foolproof way to get Emily back for good.

Before he reached his door, something sprung from the swirling darkness and clamped onto his leg, pulling him down. He desperately kicked and flayed his arms about, but the painful grip on his leg was too strong.

He couldn't shake it free.

He bent forward and reached down with his hand, feeling for whatever was holding him. Two red spots hovered within shadow.

Crulus was pinning him down.

Dylan screamed and swung his fists, but his hands just flew through Crulus like he wasn't there.

But he was; he was *right there!*

Dylan felt the pain through his entire body because it wasn't just his leg that Crulus held, it was his entire soul. Dylan didn't understand; his body wasn't here, so how could Crulus be holding onto his leg?

Dylan began to cry out for his mother, his father.

Father.

'Dad! Help me!' he screamed, but Crulus just screeched with laughter.

'He can't hear you!' hissed Crulus, and Dylan was sure he felt his rancid breath condense on his face despite the lack of atmosphere.

Crulus was breaking all of the rules of Transmogoria.

He was a ghost void of Dylan's touch.

Dylan wriggled, kicked, and punched with all his might, but there was nothing there to attack. He stared up into the piercing red eyes until his soul finally sagged and awaited termination. His only viable thought, to cling onto some kind of perverse positivity, was that he would soon join his father in whatever terrible fate had befallen him.

He felt Crulus looming over him, his breath burning through his sinuses like an overflowing sewer. Crulus' slimy tongue slid up the side of Dylan's face like a dog lapping at his owner.

'I told you I would get you, Kordialisssss.'

'I'm not Kordialis!' snapped Dylan.

He felt Crulus' hand under his chin and long fingers slide around his neck, squeezing tight; huge fingernails digging deep into flesh that wasn't there.

Dylan croaked, eyes scrunched shut.

Aarrrggghhh!

The scream was so loud that Dylan felt the pressure on his eardrum, then the tightness on his throat suddenly waned and he gasped for non-existent air.

When he opened his eyes, his brain couldn't comprehend the image it was receiving. Crulus was being hoisted into the air by innumerable dark, wispy figures causing him to squirm and writhe in pain while the swarm attacked him.

The myriad dead were tearing his soul apart.

Within seconds, Crulus faded to a distant, blackened dot as the swarm dragged him away.

~

Before leaving the Chapel grounds Dylan radioed ahead and told them he was on his way. When he free-wheeled down the road toward Garrett's shop he saw everyone huddled on the corner. The roar from the Ace of Spades card jammed in his spokes turned their heads his way, and Fiona stuck her fingers in her ears when his brake pads screeched.

The boy's bikes were already stowed in Garrett's yard, and Mark offered to hide Dylan's for him. Dylan bent over, hands clasped on his knees, gasping for air. He wasn't sure if it was worry or fear etched on their expectant faces when he limped over to Fiona.

'What's the plan? Did you get it?' he enquired.

'No, she's meeting us there.'

'What about Parthena?'

Fiona gestured to her car and Dylan peered through the rear window. Parthena was handcuffed to the door handle with a surgical mask over her mouth.

'What's the mask for?'

'It's to hide the gag. Why're you limping?'

'Crulus attacked me.' He pulled his corduroy trouser leg up to his knee. Several lines of blood had trickled down from deep, curved, nail shaped holes in his calf, which were already badly swollen. 'I'm okay; it's just cuts and bruises.'

Fiona winced at his injuries. 'Aaw, that looks awful. Crulus was at the school earlier.'

'Really?' asked Dylan, sitting down on the kerb. 'What happened?'

'There's been more deaths.'

'Oh shit! Who?'

'Sadly, two teachers, Dafydd Williams and Sarah Lewis. Edward Harwood was attacked, too. He's alive, but critical,' advised Fiona. 'But it was a bit of a strange one.'

'How come?'

'Dafydd and Sarah's bodies have the mark behind their ear, but Edward hasn't. He was violently attacked, but alive, just.'

'Harwood looked dead,' Mark pointed out, his hair sticking up in clumps. He had been crying.

Fiona looked puzzled. 'When did you see—'

'What made Crulus switch bodies so quickly?' asked Dylan, cutting her off.

'Dafydd had a heart attack,' advised Mark. 'Crulus would

have died right then, if I had stopped Sarah. It's my fault she's dead.'

'No, it wasn't,' reminded Fiona.

Dylan scratched at his chin while his eyes spun like clothes in a washer. 'The body is his weakness,' noted Dylan.

Prevent him from taking more lives.

'I've got an idea,' he said, clicking his fingers. 'Do we know who Crulus is, now?' he asked.

Fiona shook her head and lowered her gaze, while Mark and Kaelum sat in silence with nothing to add.

'Actually, it doesn't matter,' declared Dylan.

Fiona placed her hand on his shoulder. 'You should get your leg looked at.'

Dylan shook his head. 'I'm okay, it's not too bad.'

'If Crulus attacked you in Transmogoria, is it safe for you to do this?' she asked, glancing at her watch.

Dylan simply shrugged.

'Fine,' she said, with a sigh. She opened the police car and gestured to the back seat. 'C'mon, jump in.'

Mark and Dylan climbed in next to Parthena, while Kaelum sat in the front.

Parthena glared at Dylan with bloodshot eyes. Her wrists were red and swollen from tugging at her cuffs and Dylan wished he could make it better.

Surely, by getting rid of Parthena and bringing Emily back, he *was* making it better.

Wasn't he?

He thought back to the memory the book had shared. The miner, Crwys, had been so angry when Orphenia was brought back and he wondered how Dean would react with Parthena gone. He loved Parthena and Dylan was about to destroy all of that.

A split-second after pulling away from the kerb, a boy slammed onto the bonnet causing Fiona to slam on the brakes.

It was Dean.

His fists thudded on the window next to Parthena.

'Let her go! She hasn't done anything. Where're you taking her? Why's she wearing a mask?' He slammed his fists repeatedly on the roof until Fiona finally wound the driver's window down.

'She's been infected. We're taking her to hospital. Now, step away before I have you arrested.'

'What about them?' he asked, pointing to the boys in the back.

'They're infected, too. Now, go home, Dean.'

'Infected with what? Hey!' shouted Dean, but all he could do was fling his hands in the air while Fiona drove off at speed.

CHAPTER 49
DON'T YOU WANT ME

Trugaredd Hospital, Newport, South Wales

D*ing!*

The lift doors slid open to reveal a red-faced, out-of-breath, dental nurse. Her eyes flitted back and forth in their sockets like a spectator at Wimbledon. She nervously greeted Fiona and then led them quickly through a side door into the ward. As they had hoped, no one batted an eyelid at the police officer escorting a handcuffed patient through the hospital.

'The patient is asleep, and the nurse has just checked on him. She won't be back around for at least thirty minutes. Is that going to be long enough?' asked Heather.

'I'll only need a few minutes,' answered Dylan.

Fiona tugged Parthena into the private room and sat her down on a plastic chair. She unlocked the handcuff from her right wrist and clicked it onto the chair leg. Parthena lashed out at her face, but Fiona caught her hand before it landed.

'Whoa, calm down, Missy!'

Fiona pulled another set of handcuffs from her belt, and handcuffed her other arm to the chair. She pulled the surgical mask down, so it hung around her neck, and picked at the gaffer tape covering her mouth until a corner was sticking up.

'Ready?' she asked Heather.

Heather wheeled a cylinder behind Parthena's chair and opened the valve. Gas began to hiss through the mask in her hand.

'Ready.'

Fiona yanked the tape off Parthena's mouth and, when Parthena opened her mouth to scream, Heather swiftly pulled the mask over her face. Seconds later, Parthena was out cold. Heather checked her vitals and raised a thumb in the air.

'You've got at least ten minutes,' she advised.

'What about him?' asked Dylan, pointing to the sleeping patient.

'He's asleep. Just be quiet,' advised Heather.

'He could wake up. Gas him, too,' suggested Dylan.

Heather looked at Fiona with wide eyes. 'I'm only a dental nurse. I don't know his medical history, or how he'll react.'

'Just do it,' ordered Fiona. 'I'll take full responsibility.'

'You better,' demanded Heather, rolling the cylinder over to the sleeping patient and hovering the hissing mask over his face.

Dylan pulled a plastic chair into the centre of the room and sat down. Kaelum grabbed his arm, worry etched on his face.

Dylan smiled. 'I'll be fine.'

Fiona knelt in front of him and placed his hands in hers. 'Are you sure about this? I mean, he could be waiting for you.'

Dylan tried his damnedest to be brave, but his body had other ideas, and Fiona could feel him shaking.

'I'll be okay,' he said, unconvincingly. He took a deep

breath, held it for a moment, then slowly exhaled, taking a sly glance at his brother. He seemed quite nice, when he wasn't being a dick. 'But if I'm not,' he continued, 'look after Mam for me.'

Dylan's bottom lip began to quiver and Fiona wiped a tear from under his eye. 'Please be careful,' she said softly, kissing his forehead.

Dylan closed his eyes and drifted into Transmogoria before he could talk himself out of it.

When the hospital room vanished in a swirl of black, Dylan envisaged Emily's door in his mind and quickly glided to it. There was no sign of Emily or Yr Angau. He shouted for them several times but, despite numerous figures swirling in and out of the fog, they failed to materialise.

He started to panic.

He knew that several minutes in Transmogoria was only equal to a few seconds for the living, but how long would it take before the gas wore off? How much time would that equate to here, amongst the dead?

Something was wrong.

Not only could he feel it, he could hear it.

The myriad dead were whispering it in his ear.

Leave.

Danger.

Beware.

Too late.

'Too late for what?' shouted Dylan.

But the words just kept repeating, over and over, like Kaelum rewinding and playing the same song repeatedly.

Dylan felt something touch his neck and he spun around. There was nothing there, yet he couldn't shake off the feeling that he was being scrutinised.

'Who's there?' he yelled. 'Emily! ... Yr Angau! ... Is that you?'

Dark figures began to materialise all around him turning the off-white fog into dense anthracite that glistened and shifted as the figures taunted him. Faces and figures hurtled at him and passed through him like he wasn't there. He screamed and fell downwards when an horrific, disfigured face, with elongated ears and teeth flew at him, followed by an ear-piercing scream.

Die!

Weak.

Dead.

Child.

The voices taunted Dylan and he curled up in a foetal position and, for the first time ever, he well and truly prayed with all his heart for strength. He had always been a quitter, but not today, he *had* to keep going. He jumped up and scanned the area. Emily's door was almost indistinguishable under the volley of evil spirits flying around. He bellowed her name as loud as he could manage, both in his head and with his vocal cords.

Something shifted up ahead.

Glinted.

Barely visible.

It was Emily.

'Emily! Thank God. Quick, we need to get you back. Where's the watcher?'

Emily's figure shifted slowly to the side and Dylan could make out faint rufescent eyes in the figure to her right.

'We don't have much time. Pull Party out.'

The figures scarred face morphed into a huge grin and, when his features became more defined, Dylan realised that it wasn't the watcher.

It was Crulus.

This was his true face and it looked strangely familiar to Dylan as he glided closer, dragging Emily with him.

It was horrifically scarred, with thick, spiky tendrils that sprouted from its cheeks, and horns atop its forehead. His skin was cracked and peeling, and his lips were stretched into a snarl. Slimy spittle hung between long, sharp teeth but, despite the monstrous look, it was unmistakably Crwys' distorted face; the miner from the memory that Kordialis showed him.

Dylan's jaw hung open, but before he could react, he glimpsed something in Crulus' other hand; a glowing red-hot chain.

When the figures moved closer, Dylan finally recognised the soul being dragged along on the end of that chain.

'Dad!'

Instinctively, he shot forward but quickly stopped himself before Crulus could grab him.

'Let him go,' he begged. 'Take me instead.'

'Oh, I intend to, but I will destroy your body first.'

Dylan glanced over at Emily. Her sparkling life-force was merely a light breeze away from non-existence.

'Let them go and I'll go with you.'

Crulus' mouth opened impossibly wide and his long slimy tongue flopped out between crooked teeth. He laughed. The most grotesque noise that Dylan had ever heard.

'SSSStupid boy!' he hissed, his tongue swishing around his torn lips. 'You cannot bargain with me.'

'Pleeeease!' begged Dylan. 'Let Emily go.'

'Why?'

'Because I want you to *prove* you're more powerful than me.'

Crulus shifted closer and tugged on the chain causing his father to scream.

It was unbearable and it took all of Dylan's strength and composure not to run to his father's aid. He couldn't bear to see such a strong man resembling a stray dog, chained and beaten in Crulus' back garden.

'Explain,' demanded Crulus.

Dylan pointed at Emily's door. 'I've tried many times to drag that Coblyn out of there, but it is impossible. She is too powerful, even for *you*,' taunted Dylan.

'NEVER!' howled Crulus. He let go of Emily and the chain, launched himself forward, and plunged his arm deep into Emily's door. His arm wriggled for a few moments before going stiff. Then he yanked his arm backwards and dragged out a squirming, sparkling figure and held it, dangling, in front of his face. He stood there and smiled like a fisherman posing with a huge catch.

'You really *are* powerful,' admitted Dylan, taking a knee and lowering his head in mock worship.

'Yes, I am!' snapped Crulus.

Keeping his head bowed, Dylan watched Crulus tightening his hand around Parthena's soul. Her screams hurtled into Dylan's head like needles to his brain when Crulus' long fingernails sunk deep into her.

FLUP!

Dylan flinched as Parthena's soul was extinguished like Christmas lights popping on a tree.

She was gone.

When her soul shattered into a million tiny sparkles, Dylan jumped up, grabbed Emily, and threw her at her door but a tall, dark figure rose up in front of her, blocking the way.

'Hiya, Wolfy.'

He recognised the voice instantly.

'Slinky?'

Steven's spirit moved closer to Emily's door and Dylan could see the edges of his soul being drawn toward it, like grains of sand slipping through an hourglass.

'No!' bellowed Dylan. 'That's Emily's door!'

Steven edged closer and his face contorted with rage. 'I want to live, too!' he snapped.

'What? As a girl?' reminded Dylan.

'So? It'll still be me. I'll still like girls, and ... Don't you want me to live? ... Or have you forgotten about me, already?' he sneered.

'No, I ... You're dead, like, *really* dead. Your body's gone.'

'But why should she live? She's not your *real* friend, I am.'

'I know that, but—'

'But what? You have no idea what it's like to die. What it's like to be stuck here. I shouldn't be here. It wasn't my time!'

'I'm sorry. I really am, but that's Emily's body through there, and she deserves to live.'

'And *I* don't?'

Steven glided backwards, closer to Emily's door.

Dylan edged forward, he needed time. 'Wait! Yes. Yes, of course you do. You shouldn't have been killed, but you can't change that, it's not right.'

'You have no idea what it's like to crave living. To see, and touch, your family, again. I want to be a kid. I miss my mam!' cried Steven.

Dylan felt Emily slowly pull away from him, so he moved slowly to his left and stepped closer to Steven, hands in the air. 'Fine, I get it. I do. But, this isn't you, Slinky. You're not a bad person, like him,' he insisted, pointing at Crulus.

When Steven turned to look at Crulus, Emily hurtled forward, shoving Steven aside. As their souls collided tiny specs of light shot outwards, like a firework exploding, and then Emily disappeared through her door.

Steven's screams echoed through Transmogoria.

Dylan slumped to the floor. Emily was safe, at last. But when Crulus moved closer to Steven, Dylan suddenly remembered how easily he had taken Parthena's soul, and panic overwhelmed him.

Crulus' face contorted into a sneer. 'He doesn't care about you, boy. Come, join me. We will destroy him together. Then

I will help you return to the living,' offered Crulus, holding out a hand to Steven.

When Steven took his hand, Dylan placed his hands down, lifted his bottom in the air like an Olympic sprinter and propelled himself forward as fast as he could.

Crulus howled like a caged, demented creature and began pursuing.

Dylan hurtled through Transmogoria, certain he could already feel Crulus' breath on the back of his neck. He imagined a door in his mind and sped past door after door, time after time, until he neared his target.

The fog shifted up ahead and he caught glimpse of two dark figures moving quickly away from a door off to his right. He lowered his head for the final sprint, but Crulus was gaining on him. When the door shifted into view he reached out his arm and stretched for it, inveigling Crulus to follow.

'You. Cannot. Beat. Me.'

The fingers of Dylan's outstretched arm slid into the door and he felt the initial, opposing resistance pushing him back, then he felt the now familiar tug as it started to suck him through. He glanced over his shoulder just as Crulus slammed into him, knocking him flying into Transmogoria's dark void.

'Nooooo!' screamed Dylan, scrambling to his feet, but Crulus was already half-way through the door.

'Your body is mine, now!' declared a fading Crulus.

Sensing something was wrong, Crulus' hand burst into view, again.

Before Crulus could gain firm purchase and pull himself out, Newt swooped out of nowhere and attacked him; pecking and clawing at his hand until it slipped out of sight.

Crulus was gone.

Exhausted, Dylan slumped to the floor.

He raised his head just as the two figures re-emerged from the fog in front of him.

'Thank you,' wheezed Dylan, while Newt pecked his jumper.

Yr Angau nodded gracefully and stepped aside, allowing the other figure to glide forward.

'No more counting tiles,' said Andrew, smiling.

CHAPTER 50
ON WITH THE SHOW

Dylan opened his eyes and pointed at the handcuffed girl slumped on the opposite chair. 'Take them off,' he croaked.

Everyone stared at Dylan, dumbfounded.

Fiona walked over to his side. 'Are you okay,' she asked. 'It's not even been a minute. Surely, it's not done, is it?'

Dylan nodded. 'Let her go. That's Emily.'

More furtive glances bounced around the room until Emily coughed and shifted in her seat. She lifted her head, eyes flickering open, but the glare from the fluorescent ceiling lights snapped them shut, again. She shook her head, trying to focus on the people in the room.

When the blurriness dissipated, she tugged against her restraints. Sweat had matted her fringe to her forehead and tears streamed down her face.

She smiled through the tears and said, 'Hi, Wolfy.'

Fiona unlocked both handcuffs and Emily ran to Dylan, flinging her arms around him.

They embraced for several minutes before her body collapsed; weeks of pent up fear and terror oozing out of her.

'Well, that was easy,' said Kaelum, breaking the silence. 'I've not even completed two sides, yet.' He laughed, holding Dylan's Rubik's Cube in the air.

'I doubt it was easy,' argued Fiona, resting a hand on Dylan's shoulder. 'Sorry to break you guys up, but he'll be awake soon, so we'd better leave. Thanks for your help, Heather. We're quits, now,' she said, with a grin.

'Bloody right we are!' agreed Heather, wheeling the gas trolley from the room as fast as she could.

'No more drink-driving,' added Fiona, when Heather slipped out into the corridor.

A groan from the patient caused them all to look his way; he was beginning to wake.

'Hurry, we need to leave,' reminded Fiona.

'No, not yet. I want to hear what he has to say,' insisted Dylan, moving closer to the bed.

'Why? Who is he?' asked Fiona.

The patient opened his eyes and looked around the room, his head jerking back and forth.

Aaarrrrggghhhh!

'Kaelum. Fiona. Meet Crulus,' announced Dylan.

'What kind of magic is this?' snapped Crulus, confused.

'Quadriplegia,' advised Dylan. 'You won't be touching anyone for a very long time.'

'Death is merely a heartbeat away,' sneered Crulus.

Fiona ruffled Dylan's fluffy hair. 'Oooh, you're a clever boy.'

'He's not that clever,' sniped Crulus. 'He doesn't even know who he is.'

'What do you mean?' asked Dylan, edging closer. Although Andrew's body was paralysed from the neck down, he was still wary about venturing too close to Crulus.

'You and I are two halves of the same sin. I suspect you've hidden your memories somewhere I can't sense, which is why you, Kordialis, don't know who you *really* are. Who helped you to hide?'

Dylan's mouth hung open. It must've been Gareth; he gave him the book.

Crulus scoffed. 'In the last few months, however, I could feel you rebuilding; shedding your childish innocence bit by bit.'

I've been absorbing Kordialis' memories. That's why they're so vivid. He's inside my head.

'You admonished your friend for contemplating taking that girl's body, yet, here you stand, living and breathing a lie. Hypocrite!'

'Huh?'

'Do you think that's your *real* body? I thought I'd terminated your existence when I killed that woman but, my, you were quick to jump ship. When the twin sister's unborn child died in her womb, you stole the body.'

'You're lying!' countered Dylan, not wanting to admit what he already suspected since he discovered that his own life cord was missing.

'Hell, even your mother's body was snatched by a Coblyn,' added Crulus, smirking.

'Even if that's true, I don't care; she's my mam and I love her. You're only saying all this because you've been outsmarted by a kid.'

'Ha! You think you've won? You've just delayed the inevitable. I've always been in control. I've been manipulating your pathetic life for ages.'

'No, you haven't,' assured Dylan, pulling at his collar.

'Oh, yes, I have. Do you really think your friend, Mostyn, killed those kids?'

Dylan shook his head and glanced at Fiona. 'No, but—'

'He didn't,' announced Crulus, smirking. 'The fledgling death-dealer I've been moulding did it. Such an easily manipulated, abused and tortured soul. He sought an outlet for his pent-up anger. He was my puppet, and I, his master. He killed them and framed your friend, as I commanded.'

'Who is it?' asked Fiona, stepping in. She didn't want to admit that the police had failed, but it was quite obvious that someone other than Crulus had killed Ian, Sian and Slinky, and attempted to kill Mr Harwood. Plus, poor Ian had been raped, and she was pretty sure that Crulus wasn't that way inclined, and wouldn't have bothered using a prophylactic even if he was.

'If he's so smart, let *him* work it out,' sneered Crulus.

'Think, Dylan. Who could it be?' asked Fiona, when Dylan sat back down in his chair.

The dead's chatter filled his head with celebratory static and he struggled to tune the voices out. He breathed out hard, trying to focus his mind. He was pretty sure Dean hadn't done it even though, on the surface, he was the obvious choice. Sure, he was a bully, but he didn't have it in him to kill. Dylan was positive it was someone else, but who? Kevin? David?

'I'm not sure. I can't think clearly,' mumbled Dylan.

'Pathetic!' taunted Crulus. 'Your mind is as feeble as the child you stole. Once I'm free of this body, I will destroy you and every other pathetic soul in this realm.'

'Why?'

'To create Hell on Earth, of course. I shall flood this realm with Coblynau, and anyone who opposes me will be destroyed.'

Fiona pulled Dylan close and whispered, 'Can't he just slip back into Transmogoria, like you do?'

'Don't think so. Yr Angau has cursed Andrew's door.'

Dylan grabbed the patient chart that was hanging over the bottom of the bed and held it in front of Crulus' face. 'See this?' he said, tapping the last entry. 'Patient transfer booked for Wednesday, second of December, which is tomorrow.'

'So?'

'Sooooo, tomorrow you're off to a cosy, private clinic courtesy of Andrew's family and friends. They've raised a small fortune for the best private care home in Gwent. That head you're in is going to be wobbling around like a Weeble for years to come. Enjoy your living prison!'

CHAPTER 51
GHOST TOWN

Christmas Day, December, 1981
Larkmead Chapel

An icy wind blew through the valley and into the side of the police Land Rover causing it to lurch to one side when Fiona turned the corner. Gravel and salt crunched and popped under its snow-chained tyres, when she manoeuvred it up the driveway. She slid to a stop next to a snowdrift that was dwarfing a group of people that were huddled together near the chapel doors wearing colourful bobble hats and scarves.

Dylan ran up to the police car, cupping his hands against the side windows, exploring its darkened rear.

'Where's Mossy?' he mumbled, his face squidged against the frosty window.

Visions of frozen tongues slid into Fiona's mind and she giggled before slamming her shoulder into the door. It took several whacks before the ice on the rubber seal finally gave way and the door squeaked open.

'Where's Mossy?' repeated Dylan, rubbing clumps of snow off his woollen gloves.

Fiona brushed ice from around her door lock and said calmly, 'Let's just see what the judge says, shall we? He might be out, later.'

'Could he be stuck in a cell over Christmas?' asked a shocked Emily, who was trudging through the deep snow. Fiona didn't reply and Emily could have sworn she saw a smile pulling at the corner of her mouth.

'Why isn't he out?' asked Dylan. 'Crulus admitted that his fledgling death-dealer did it. Plus, he said he was abused, so he must've meant Kevin.'

Fiona locked her car and swivelled round to face them. The cold air bit into her cheeks and she whipped her hood up and hugged herself. 'Without hard evidence we can't prove that.'

'But I told them I saw Kevin buying something off Mossy by the gym. He was wearing gloves, too, so ... so, it must have been the murder weapon,' protested Dylan, angrily kicking snow. 'That's probably how Mossy's fingerprints were on it. Didn't they believe me?'

Fiona placed a hand on Dylan's forehead and gently brushed his fringe from this eyes causing his bobble to wobble when he pulled away, embarrassed.

'I'm just as upset as you, and I totally agree, but it's all circumstantial.' She took a beat before continuing, 'Every corpse without Crulus' mark was killed by someone else—different M.O.'s—but we need solid evidence for CPS to commit to a trial.' She hated not being able to tell them that MIT were close to arresting Kevin for the murders of both Sian and Steven, although Ian Pritchard's murderer was proving somewhat elusive.

Kevin vehemently denied being raped by his step-father, but they suspected he was lying. Kevin feared his stepdad's retaliation, not to mention the devastation and shame it would bring his mother. Despite the mounting evidence against him, Kevin's welfare was paramount, and Child Services had been informed. Mr Harwood would be questioned further, if he ever recovers from the coma.

'Find me the evidence to prove it was Kevin and I'll arrest him myself,' added Fiona, continuing the charade.

'He always was a nasty twat,' added Dean, causing heads to turn his way. 'Sorry, Reverend. I, er, I just mean he was a bad egg, you know ... worse than I was.'

Dylan glanced at Mark. He wasn't sure he could trust this new, reformed, Scrapper. Can a leopard really change its spots?

As if reading his mind, Mark rubbed his shoulder and said, 'Don't worry.'

Fred forced his way through to the front of the group, clapping his gloved hands together. 'C'mon, chop chop. Let's get the unveiling done before we all freeze to death, then we can debate things back in the warm with food in our bellies and love for Jesus in our hearts. After all, it's his birthday, too,' he said, smiling.

~

Fred finished reading the short eulogy in front of the shivering group and gestured for Dylan to step forward, but he had other ideas. He moved through the small group of people gathered in the graveyard and placed his hand on Dean's shoulder, a gesture which, a few days earlier, would have resulted in a fist in his face.

'I think you should do it,' Dylan suggested.

The group returned Dean's scrutinising gaze with accepting nods and smiles.

Dean nodded. 'Oh, okay. Thanks.'

He stepped forward to where a silk sheet had been crudely

hung over the graveyard wall and slowly pulled it down to reveal a small, brass plate mounted on a piece of wood.

The inscription on the plaque read:

IN MEMORY OF
Parthena Francis Love
25th DECEMBER 1870 ~ 18th NOVEMBER 1891
'Proper Eesome'
LOVE LOST BUT NOT FORGOTTEN

'Happy birthday, Party,' sniffed Dean.

'It's lovely,' said Fiona, patting Dean's arm. 'You gave her life some meaning during very strange circumstances, and she loved you for that, so don't forget it. In 1891 she was buried in a pauper's grave in London with no headstone or ceremony, but now she will always be remembered.'

'Yeah, she will. Thanks.'

'Don't thank me, it was all Dylan and Fred's doing, but we all chipped in for the plaque.'

Fred nodded. 'I agree, although I only had a small part in the matter. It was mainly Dylan's idea,' he explained.

Dean brushed his comments aside with a swipe of his arm. 'It doesn't matter. You all helped and that means a lot,' admitted Dean, running a finger across the letters that formed Parthena's name.

Emily placed a spray of blue flowers with tiny yellow centres onto the ground below the plaque.

'I can still feel her,' she said, tapping a finger to her temple. 'She was certainly a strong woman. I can vouch for that.'

'Yes, she was,' agreed Dean. 'Lovely flowers. What are they?'

'Forget-me-nots. They're beautiful aren't they? They mean love.'

'Really?'

'Yeah.' Emily wrung her gloved hands together, her eyes moving from Dylan to Dean, and back again. 'Listen,' she said, softly, 'I wanna thank you for being so understanding. This must be really hard for you.'

'It is. Every time I see you, I see her. I know you're not Party, it's just ... You know.'

Emily leant forward and kissed him on the cheek. 'She's made a man of you.'

'Right, into the warmth of the Lord!' shouted Fred, before herding everyone into the chapel.

~

Back in the vestry, Fred had stoked the coal fire and laid out an impressive Christmas buffet despite the damage to the chapel, which still hadn't been repaired. There were various sandwiches, pickled onions, pineapple and cheese *and* sausages on sticks, crisps, sausage rolls, fairy cakes, chocolate Christmas log, Battenberg, fruit cake and Chrissy's fruit trifle containing way too much brandy, which Dylan had 'borrowed' when her back was turned. She wouldn't miss it, though; her mind was hazy, to say the least.

Dylan's wasn't much better, although with Crulus trapped in Andrew's body, Dylan was now able to speak to his father, which was a gift in itself.

While thousands of kids in the valley had been opening their presents under twinkling tinsel and flickering Christmas lights, Mark had been collecting empty Skol lager cans off his mother's threadbare bedroom carpet. Phlegm had rattled in her throat when he'd planted a kiss beside her parted, dry, and lifeless lips. A spiderweb of stark, blue veins crawled across both cheeks and disappeared into the mountainous creases around her eyes. Nicotine and alcohol was not a good look; she looked ten years past her thirty-six years.

Mark had paused to rest his forehead against the nicotine stained net curtain and gazed at the Christmas tree lights in every front window and had wondered what his neighbours were eating. The silence had been dissected by sounds of laughter; new bike sirens and bells being rung; the low roar of new skateboard wheels on tarmacadam, and the clatter of metal rubbish bins overflowing with wrapping paper and boxes.

Before he could close the window to shut out Christmas forever, a breeze had brought with it the smell of turkey, vegetables and brandy sauce, which lingered and teased his sinuses until tears washed them clean, again.

When the others, with excited stomachs already full from Christmas dinners, simply nibbled at Fred's spread, Mark barged to the front and stuffed handfuls of food into his mouth and pockets simultaneously.

Dylan slunk to Mark's side while Emily was giggling with Dean, and he fought the urge to cry.

'I had a cap bomb and a spud gun. My dad chose them before he died,' he said, without taking his eyes of Dean. 'I wish it was a real gun, though,' he mumbled.

'What?'

'Never mind. What did you get for Christmas?'

'Loads,' lied Mark, his teeth smothered in mashed up food.

'Yeah, but what?'

'You know ...' He scratched his head with a handful of cocktail sticks, leaving crumbs matted in his hair. 'Just stuff.'

While everyone munched and gossiped, Fred sidled over to Fiona and handed her a pile of musty old letters.

'What're these?' she asked, confused.

'Reverend Tomos Llewellyn's letters, or what's left of them.'

'Oh, wow. You found them.'

'Yes, dear, and they turned out to be quite the interesting read. No rush to return them, though.'

'Thanks, I look forward to it. Do they reveal Yr Angau's identity?'

'Well, yes,' he replied, lowering himself into a chair by the fire. 'The gentleman's name was Albert, but his surname wasn't King.'

'So, why has it got 'P King' above the entrance to the crypt?'

'Duck man,' mumbled Mark, his cheeks bulging with food.

'Ah, now, that is misleading. You see, that wood has rotted and worn over the years, so it isn't quite all there. The name isn't 'P King,' dear, it's Brasking. The watcher is Albert Brasking, your Great, Great, Great, Great Grandfather.'

Fiona coughed violently due to the sausage roll that was trying to enter her lung, and she grabbed a napkin, spitting it out. 'Really?' she sputtered.

'I've checked the parish records,' he confirmed. 'There's no mistaking it. You are Yr Angau's descendant.'

'That's why Crulus couldn't kill you,' interrupted Dylan, clicking his fingers.

'That's right. His descendants are protected for eternity,' agreed Fred. 'If it wasn't for his sacrifice, Crulus would have killed you when you were a child.'

'And you wouldn't have trapped Crulus without his help, either,' reminded Mark, nudging Dylan in the arm.

'True. But I wouldn't have done *any* of it, if it wasn't for Emily's brother,' admitted Dylan.

'*My* brother?' asked Emily, wiping chocolate from her lips.

Dylan nodded. 'Yeah, he gave me the dead book.'

'That's not possible,' she replied, shaking her head. 'Gareth died before I was born.'

CHAPTER 52
THAT'S ENTERTAINMENT

Once the laughter and ghost jokes had diminished, conversations reverted back to festive discussions allowing a red-faced Dylan to slip outside, unseen. Pulling his scarf tightly around his neck, he sauntered through the graveyard and stopped by his grandparents' grave.

Leaning back against the cold stone, he told them how Crulus had killed Louisa whilst in Daniel's body but, even before he could finish speaking, he heard his grandfather, Lazarus, apologising to Daniel. When they started reminiscing, Dylan felt he was eavesdropping, so he wandered on through the graveyard and paused by Benny's grave.

After several minutes, he rummaged in his pocket and placed Benny's Space Invader game at the stone's base.

'I repainted the buttons,' he said, his breath condensing on the glittery black stone.

He rose and took a step back, glancing down the line of stones to the next fresh grave, hesitant. Slowly, very slowly, his boots crunched a few metres through the snow to Steven's shiny, black stone.

Whilst he read the inscription, a wave of guilt crept up his spine, even though, deep down, he knew that he had done all he could.

'Sorry, Slinky,' he mumbled.

'You will be.'

Dylan spun around, then lurched back against the graveyard wall when a hand tightened around his throat. He couldn't scream; he could barely breathe.

'Do you think you've won?' snarled Dean. 'Emily doesn't want a gormless troglodyte like you. Party might be gone, but that girl in there is still going to be mine. Watch this space.'

Starved of oxygen, Dylan's legs buckled, and he slumped into a heap at the foot of the wall, but Dean's grip was relentless. The anger in Dean's eyes made Dylan doubt that Kevin was the killer; Dean seemed intent on ending him right there.

He blacked out.

When his eyes finally flickered open, Dean was nowhere to be seen and Mostyn Lloyd was hoisting him up onto unsteady legs.

Thinking he was dreaming, Dylan slapped a hand across Mostyn's cheek.

'Charming! Nice to see you, too,' said Mostyn. 'And there was me thinking you'd missed me.'

Despite his fuzzy brain, Dylan was mortified and he quickly croaked an apology, blaming the disorientation.

'It's fine. Fiona dropped me home. I had to see my parents, first,' explained Mostyn.

Dylan nodded, but he wasn't fully listening. He glanced around once more, certain Dean would pounce again, and stared nervously at Mostyn.

'I sent that knob, Scrapper, packing.' Mostyn studied Dylan for a moment before whispering, 'You know I'm innocent, don't you?' He bit his lip and rubbed at his face but it wasn't from Dylan's slap; he was genuinely concerned what people thought.

Dylan had never seen him so worried. He rubbed Mostyn's arm, comforting. 'Yes, I know you're innocent and so do they,' he said, nodding to Fiona and the others who were trudging through the snow.

Emily pointed a finger at Fiona and smiled. 'I knew you were hiding something!'

'How did you get out?' shouted Mark, who was hovering at the back of the group, transferring sausage rolls from his pocket to his mouth.

Mostyn brushed snow off Dylan's coat and pulled a face. 'Because I'm innocent.'

'Didn't they have evidence against you?' Mark shot back immediately.

Everyone looked at Fiona for an answer, but her gaze was fixed on Mark. She could see despair in his eyes and something else, too. Loneliness?

'What does it matter?' insisted Dylan, groggily. 'Mossy's innocent!'

Mark laughed without smiling. 'I know,' he said, a little too defensive. 'Kevin did it, and he probably stabbed his paedo' step-dad, too.' He shoved his hands in his armpits and began walking towards the chapel. 'Are we going back in? I'm cold.'

Fiona stepped forward, blocking his way. 'In some ways, I really wanted it to be Kevin. It would've been easier than this,' she said, sighing.

Mark crunched his wellington boots back and forth as though he needed to pee. 'What're you talking about?' he mumbled. The despair in his eyes turning to fear.

'We needed the attacker to slip up, which is why I didn't tell you guys everything.'

Mark pointed a mittened hand at Mostyn and turned to

Fiona, eyes pleading. 'Whatever he said, he's lying. Kevin did it.' He started crying.

Both Dylan and Emily began defending Mark, but Fiona silenced them with the palm of her hand. 'Save your pity pleas.' They instantly stopped talking and she felt guilty for snapping at them, but she had to maintain control. She turned her attention back to Mark saying, 'Mostyn didn't say *anything* about you. Kevin had plenty to tell us, though.'

'Kevin's a liar, too!'

'Is he, Mark?'

Mark was becoming more agitated; his wellies had dissipated the snow and were now creating sludgy holes in the graveyard grass. 'Y-Yeah,' he stuttered.

'Well, Kevin told us that you gave him the wire saw, and the rifle he sold to Mostyn was actually yours, and it was you who asked him to dispose of a bag of animal remains in this very graveyard. All because—'

'No, I didn't!' Mark interrupted, but Fiona just raised her voice and continued.

'All because *you* found out his step-dad was abusing him. You threatened to tell everyone unless he did your bidding. Isn't that right?'

Mark guffawed. 'No, he's lying!' he snorted, his eyes moving from friend to friend seeking corroboration.

Dylan couldn't believe what he was hearing; his mind was in turmoil. But then a memory surged forward; the night they saw Harwood and Kevin in the shed, Kevin had nodded to Mark rather than retaliate after he'd struck him with a peg bullet, as though Kevin was acknowledging some private agreement.

Glancing at Mostyn, Mark lowered his head, mumbling, 'I did take your saw. I just liked the look of it. Sorry.'

'Friends don't kill friends!' blurted Dylan, the words tumbling out before his brain was engaged.

'What? I didn't kill Slinky. Trust me!' begged Mark, but Dylan avoided his gaze. 'I felt bad about taking it. I was gonna give it back, but Kevin said he'd buy it, and I needed the money. He said he was gonna sort someone out and I thought he meant Harwood but—'

Fiona spun Mark around. 'Now, we're getting somewhere. Kevin's already admitted planting evidence at Mostyn's, so we know he killed Sian and Steven, although, he cannot remember doing it.'

'See,' said Mark, glaring at the others. 'Told you!' He turned back to Fiona. '*So*, what do you want from me, then?'

'There was something odd about when Dafydd died and Crulus changed bodies, but I could never put my finger on it,' advised Fiona. 'Then it dawned on me. Dafydd's head hit the step, leaving blood there and on the adjacent wall, so how come you were covered in so much blood spatter? Who's blood was it?'

Mark's eyes flitted between her and Dylan, and his reply stuck in the back of his gaping mouth, unspoken.

'Earlier,' pressed Fiona, 'you said that Kevin probably stabbed his step-dad.'

'So?' spat Mark, giving her a cold look.

'Sooo, how did you know Harwood had been stabbed when we hadn't released that information to the public?'

Mark's head lowered and remained there for several seconds. When his head rose, his tears had stopped and anger scrunched his face into a hideous snarl.

'Harwood deserves to die!' he enunciated, spraying spittle in Fiona's startled face.

Fiona grabbed for Mark's arm. He jerked free and ran, but his boots slipped on the mud and he face planted the ground.

Fiona pounced on him, pinning him down.

'What possessed you to stab Harwood?' she asked, whilst

he struggled beneath her. 'I know it wasn't a Bogie or Coblynau; Dylan hadn't seen any near his friends. So *why*?'

His right hand slipped free of her grasp and he slapped her hard across the face. 'Get off me!'

'Answer me!' she shouted, her head recoiling. She twisted his arm behind his back and yanked it upwards until he screamed.

'He tried to abuse me!'

His words echoed through the valley and, when they faded, everyone fell silent.

Fiona released her hold on him and sat on the snow, appalled. Words failed her.

Mark sat up, rubbed his sore shoulder and cried, 'Do you know what it's like to be afraid everyday?'

Fiona shook her head. 'No, I—'

'I knew that sick wanker was a kiddie fiddler. I told the Headmistress, but she didn't believe me,' he croaked, tears and snot dripping from his nose. 'We'd seen him with Kevin, didn't we?' He glanced at Dylan, who nodded in agreement. 'I tried to help Kev', but he denied it and—' Mark stopped when he saw Mostyn and Dylan share a bemused look. 'Don't look like that. I'd have helped you, if Harwood had got to you, too.

'When Crulus killed those teachers, I ran through the corridor to get help. Harwood grabbed me with his vile, hairy hands, trying to usher me into a store room with some bullshit excuse. When that door clicked behind him, I knew I had no choice; I stabbed him, and ran.

'He did it to loads of kids, but they were too afraid. Even Pritch couldn't—'

Mark fell silent and gazed off into the distance, allowing Fiona and the others to exchange glances.

Nobody knew what to say.

Fiona now knew that Harwood was the main suspect for

Ian's murder and she felt guilty for pushing Mark so hard. She edged forward to comfort him, but he shoved her away.

'Leave me alone,' he snapped.

Dylan's emotions were erratic. He wanted to cuddle his friend and strangle him simultaneously. Why didn't Mark tell him? He could've helped. He'd rather face a hundred supernatural demons than deal with this. That's why Mark was flunking his tests; he wanted to get out of Harwood's form class. Feeling queasy, Dylan sat on Benny's gravestone while Emily held his hand. 'I'm so sorry. You should've told me.'

'And what would you have done? Ripped his soul out?'

'Yes!' replied Dylan, emphatically. 'It's not too late, either.'

Dylan knew that if he did, he'd be no better than Crulus, but he didn't know how to help his friend. He couldn't face losing him. 'Are you going to arrest him?'

Fiona was staring into the distance, scratching her chin. She looked at each child in turn; they had all endured so much in the past few months, but now, finally, they were united.

'Fiona?' urged Dylan.

She held up her hand, silencing him, and turned to Mark. 'Did anyone see you with Harwood?' she asked, even though she already knew the answer.

Mark shook his head.

'Good. Then you weren't there. Where's the knife?'

'At the bottom of Mynyddislwyn quarry lake.'

She nodded. 'It was self-defence. The man is a predator and what you did was very brave. Sadly, CPS and a judge might not agree, though, so we keep this between us, okay?' Fiona stood and stretched her hand out in front of her. 'C'mon, my little Demon Squad, does everyone agree?'

One by one, the kids placed a hand on top of Fiona's, and Newt landed unseen on Dylan's shoulder.

'Agreed,' they said in unison.

When they separated, Mark hugged Fiona, tears streaming down his face. 'Thank you.'

She placed a hand under his chin, gently lifted it up, and brushed his cheeks dry. 'Don't worry,' she assured, smiling.

'But what if he survives? He'll tell the police.'

'I seriously doubt that. Not after what he's done.'

Mark turned to face Dylan. 'Harwood's in a coma. What if someone else comes back?'

Dylan shrugged. 'Let's hope it's someone nice, then.'

CRULUS PLAYLIST

The eagle-eyed among you may have realised that the chapter headings are all titles of songs that were released, still in the charts, or still playing on the radio throughout 1981.

I, like Dylan, also started my first year of Comprehensive School in Wales, UK in the September of 1981, so I grew up on eighties music, and that decade still resonates with me. For that reason, I wanted my readers to immerse themselves in the atmosphere of Dylan's life, not just his story.

So, please, search for these songs on whatever music platform you subscribe to, or scan the QR Code below to get the Crulus Playlist on Spotify™.

Then sit back, relax, and soak up the early 80s atmosphere!

Acknowledgments

Firstly, I'd like to thank my best friend and wife, Jo, for keeping everything going—including me—whilst I spent hours, day after day, year after year, tapping away at my keyboard. Thank you from the bottom of my heart. I finally did it!

Secondly, I would like to thank my daughter, Shannon, for believing in her Papa even when the voices in his head told him he was useless and would never complete this novel. Your constant words of encouragement, day after day, kept me going.

To Wendy at SaberCoreArt23: thank you so much for the amazing cover art, and for your help and patience when I wanted it tweaked, numerous times. I sincerely hope my story is worthy of your amazing artwork.

I also want to give a huge thanks to the Indie Horror author community, especially author Patrick McNulty, who gave me confidence in my writing, and Elizabeth J. Brown; an amazing author and mentor who has inspired me and responded to my constant nagging with brilliant advice and guidance.

Plus, everyone from the Indie Horror community who took time to help me publish my debut novel, whether it was a full-blown conversation or a helpful one-liner, or simply just welcoming me into the horror community. You guys rock!

Thanks to Jim Ody, ML Rayner, Leigh Kenny, Sarah Jules, CS Jones, Stephen Barnard, MJ Mars, Ashley R Lister,

DE McCluskey, Phil Baker, Ben Young, Brad Thomas, Cat Mowat, Sharron Joy Reads, Trish Wilson and Corrina Morse.

If you haven't already done so, go check out these authors and book reviewers, and the groups 'Books Of Horror' and 'Indie Horror Chapter' on social media. They are awesome.

I would like to highlight my awesome beta readers, namely my wife, Jo, Maêgan Smith, and Elizabeth J. Brown, and also my awesome proofreader, Leah Fox. Your advice, time, and willingness to help has been incredible!

Also, a huge thank you to all of the wonderful ARC readers that read and reviewed this book. If you were an ARC reader and haven't reviewed it, yet, don't worry, there's still time to leave a review on whatever platform you choose.

An acknowledgment wouldn't be complete without thanking you, the reader. By purchasing this novel, in whatever format, you have made an old, socially awkward, introverted author extremely happy. I really hope you enjoyed Dylan and Fiona's story.

If you did enjoy it, please, please, let others know by sharing it on social media or reviewing it on whichever platform you prefer. Good reviews keep Indie Authors going!

If you didn't enjoy this book, then all is not lost, as everyone has different tastes. Please pass this book onto someone else (physical copies only). Who knows, maybe they will enjoy it.

If I've missed anyone, I'll get you next time.
Until then ...
Thank you, all.
Love Lark

AUTHOR NOTE

Please note that, as a British author, I use UK English spelling and grammar throughout my writing. Therefore, US readers may notice less Z's than they are used to. These are not typos, it is just UK English.

Also, as my novel is set in Wales, there are a few Welsh words and colloquialisms contained within this novel. Some of these are explained within the story, but some are listed below for clarity. Again, these are not typos.

Many of these words are not actual Welsh language words; they are derived from a blend of Welsh and English words, or 'Wenglish,' as the term was coined by John Edwards in his book, '*Talk Tidy' The Art of Speaking Wenglish* published by D. Brown & Sons Ltd in 1985.

If you are interested to know more, I suggest you search for "History of the Welsh Not" on the Internet, as that will give you some idea why the two languages blended in the South Wales Valleys and, sadly, the history of it and what the Welsh school children went through, is quite horrific.

Ach-a-fi: A general expression of distaste/disgust.

Butt: Short for 'Butty' - meaning a friend or colleague. Often used in a greeting; "Morning, butt'. How's things?"

Cannwyll Gorff: A Welsh folklore death omen - a corpse candle. A sinister light, which illuminates a person soon to be deceased or the pathway taken by a corpse to the church or burial place. Size and colour of the manifested light would differ depending upon the poor soul marked for death. Often seen by miners down the pit (coal mine) prior to major disasters.

Coblynau: (Plural) The Coblyn are Welsh fairies or goblins, usually associated with, or found in, the coal mines of Wales.

Cwtch: To fondle, snuggle or cuddle someone you like/love. Plural: Cwtches.

Cythraul: Welsh word meaning 'Satan,' 'Devil,' or other incantations of evil spirits.

Hang-a-banger: A Welsh slang term meaning 'wait a minute' or simply just 'wait.'

Mun: A derivative of 'man' or 'mate,' which is often used in greetings or to emphasise a point; 'Alright, mun?" or "Come on, mun!'

Tidy: An overused Wenglish term, which refers to something awesome, impressive or generally good; "Tidy necklace you've got there!"

Twp: Short for 'twpsyn' meaning 'stupid,' 'idiot,' or a person of low intelligence.

Yr Angau: Celtic legend similar to the Breton 'Ankou,' which refers to a graveyard guardian, but it can also refer to the Grim Reaper—the personification of Death.

ABOUT THE AUTHOR

Llrâc Nôdbé (pronounced 'Lark Nod-Bee'), or simply Lark for short, was born in the Sirhowy Valley, South Wales in 1970 and has spent most of his life arguing with the voices in his head, although, he usually loses. Therefore, he writes whatever the voices tell him to write, and they don't always have something nice to say.

Lark is an introvert with no confidence and zero attentiveness, so he's actually amazed that he's finished something he's started, even if it's taken him over thirteen years to complete!

Because he's spent most of his life there, Lark tends to live in the past, and you can find him lurking around the 80's.

For more information about Lark and his books, please follow 'The Voices Made Me Do It' on social media or scan the LinkTree™ QR code below.

Printed in Dunstable, United Kingdom

66735025R00234